The sense that she was being followed did not dissipate as she hurried along the edge of the cliff, though she could hear nothing but the wail of the river and the occasional lonely cry of an eagle hovering far above. She turned often to scan the path behind her, but it was narrow and twisting here, following the bulges of the rock so she could not see for any great distance. It began to angle downward sharply so she had to jump down the rocks in several places, once slipping on a patch of ice in her haste. She heard stones rattle behind her and she quickened her pace . . . some irrational fear drove her on. Then she saw the movement on the path several bluffs behind her. She stared intently and recognized the squat figures of the goblins, running swiftly. There were twenty or more of them now and terror seized her. . . .

More praise for the *Witches of Eileanan* series

"More depth and imagination than others in this field."   —Australian SF Online

"Kate Forsyth spices up a suitably complex power struggle with vividly depicted imagery and a worthy heroine."   —*Romantic Times*

"A wonderful and surprising story . . . a fantastic adventure."   —The TeenZone

Also by Kate Forsyth

The Witches of Eileanan
The Pool of Two Moons
The Cursed Towers
The Forbidden Land

The Skull of the World

Book Five of the *Witches of Eileanan*

KATE FORSYTH

A ROC BOOK

ROC
Published by New American Library, a division of
Penguin Group (USA) Inc., 375 Hudson Street,
New York, New York 10014, USA
Penguin Group (Canada), 10 Alcorn Avenue, Toronto,
Ontario M4V 3B2, Canada (a division of Pearson Penguin Canada Inc.)
Penguin Books Ltd., 80 Strand, London WC2R 0RL, England
Penguin Ireland, 25 St. Stephen's Green, Dublin 2,
Ireland (a division of Penguin Books Ltd.)
Penguin Group (Australia), 250 Camberwell Road, Camberwell, Victoria 3124,
Australia (a division of Pearson Australia Group Pty. Ltd.)
Penguin Books India Pvt. Ltd., 11 Community Centre, Panchsheel Park,
New Delhi - 110 017, India
Penguin Group (NZ), cnr Airborne and Rosedale Roads, Albany,
Auckland 1310, New Zealand (a division of Pearson New Zealand Ltd.)
Penguin Books (South Africa) (Pty.) Ltd., 24 Sturdee Avenue,
Rosebank, Johannesburg 2196, South Africa

Penguin Books Ltd., Registered Offices:
80 Strand, London WC2R 0RL, England

Published by Roc, an imprint of New American Library, a division of Penguin
Group (USA) Inc. Previously published in an Arrow Book edition by Random House Australia Pty. Ltd.

First Roc Printing, February 2002
10 9 8 7 6 5

Cover art by Judy York
Cover design by Ray Lundgren

REGISTERED TRADEMARK—MARCA REGISTRADA

Printed in the United States of America

PUBLISHER'S NOTE
This is a work of fiction. Names, characters, places, and incidents either are
the product of the author's imagination or are used fictitiously, and any resemblance to actual persons, living or dead, business establishments, events, or
locales is entirely coincidental.

for Dani, Michelle and Sarah,
soul sisters and kindred spirits,
in memory of the many wondrous adventures we've shared
growing up together

*Natural magic . . . is nothing more than the deepest
knowledge of the secrets of nature.*
Del Rio, Disquisitiones Magicae, 1606

*Nature performs in a natural way the things that the
magician achieves by his art.*
Pico della Mirandola, Conclusiones philosophicae,
cabbalisticae et theologicae, 1486

CONTENTS

A New Thread Is Strung

THE BLACK PEARL

Nila dived deep into the ocean, his eyes wide open, his arms curved before him. The aquamarine water fell into violet shadows and the young Fairge prince plunged into the dusky depths, his powerful tail twisting behind him. His nostrils were clamped shut, the gills on either side of his neck flowing open and shut as he breathed. Little phosphorescent fish darted all around him, and he saw the serrated shadow of a giant swordtail pass below him. He glanced up and saw the surface of the water, gleaming and shifting more than a hundred feet above him. The dark shapes of fish soared overhead like birds in the wind, and all about him the flowers of the sea bloomed in the delicate shades of rose and cinnamon and blue.

Nila hung in the water, his hands moving deftly among the clusters of ugly gray shells that clung beneath the rock shelves. He took a sharp-edged coral knife from between his teeth and used it to pry open the shells, swallowing whole the live tissue within. Every now and again he grinned as he tucked a little shining orb inside a bag woven of seaweed that hung around his naked waist.

3

Something made him turn. A tiger shark swam toward him, the jagged rows of teeth bared. The tiny eyes were fixed with terrible intent upon the Fairge.

Nila turned and dived, his tail undulating gracefully behind him as he plunged through a curtain of seaweed and sea anemones into a deep grotto. The tiger shark had to turn abruptly, almost ramming its nose into the reef. Nila watched its shadow pass back and forth, back and forth, until at last it slunk away and there was only the blue glimmer of water.

The Fairge prince waited, his heart hammering uncomfortably. He had been too long underwater, but he dared not swim to the surface to breathe until he was sure the tiger shark had gone. He looked about the grotto, searching for another way out, and saw a great corrugated shell, all encrusted with weed and barnacles. He pried it open with his coral knife and found nestled within a large opaque sphere. He grasped it and then, with a twist of his silvery tail, swam for the surface.

The light filtered down all about him. He glanced at the pearl in his hand and suddenly stilled, even though his lungs were burning for air. Unlike the other pearls he had found, this one was a dark, smoky color, unusually large and perfectly formed. He rolled it in his fingers, frowning, then tucked it carefully inside the pouch.

Through the light-dappled water he saw the wavering face of a girl, her brown hair hanging down as she peered anxiously into the sea. He beat his tail more vigorously, leaping up out of the water to seize her in his arms and drag her in. Her anxiety melted into relieved laughter, and he kissed her smiling mouth, sliding his hands down her brown naked flesh, transforming into his land-shape so he could tangle his legs with hers.

She clung to him, saying rather tremulously, "You were so long, Nila. What were you doing? I was worried . . ."

He mocked her gently. "Afraid I had drowned? Fand! You know I am the best deep-diver in my family. As if I could have drowned in these shallow waters!"

"Even those of the Fairgean royal family can drown," she replied. "You could have hit your head, or been taken by a giant octopus. I wish you would not swim where you know I cannot follow."

Fand was a slim girl with the full-lipped mouth and brightly colored eyes of a human, though her fingers and toes were as webbed as any young Fairgean. Her straggles of wet hair hung down to her knees, and she wore only a belt of seaweed and shells hung with a little curved dagger. The daughter of a Fairgean warrior and a human concubine, she was a slave to the royal family and had accompanied the Fairgean queens down to the southern waters to assist in the birthing. Nila was there with the other young warriors to protect the women and newborn babies until they were strong enough to brave the long journey back to the icy seas of the north.

Nila kissed away her fears, turning so they could drift together into the shore, the gentle waves lapping against their bodies, the sand warm beneath them. The little cove was protected from spying eyes by high bluffs of rock, so for once they felt free to take their time exploring each other's bodies, whispering and smiling, teasing and pleasuring. Usually they had only a hurried coupling among the sharp

rocks of the shore or in the cold, ghost-haunted ruin
of the witches' tower where no one else dared go.
This past month had been blissful for both of them.

Free for once of the idle cruelty of his many brothers, Nila had enjoyed sporting in the mild waters,
diving for pearls and making love to Fand in the soft
sand without fear of being discovered. Not that his
father and brothers would disapprove of his relationship with the young half-human slave. That, after all,
was what females were for. It had just never occurred
to any of his brothers to look twice at Fand, who
was considered rather useless, since she had not inherited the ability to transform into the Fairgean sea-
shape. Her delicately formed features and sea-green
eyes were too human to be beautiful, and there were
plenty of full-blooded Fairgean women to keep his
brothers occupied.

If just one of his brothers had suspected Nila was
emotionally drawn to the halfbreed, however, they
would have taken pleasure in taking her from him.
They would have used her for their sadistic games,
and then killed her when they had grown tired of
the amusement of Nila's pain. The Fairgean princes
had been raised to be brutal and ambitious, and there
was much hatred and rivalry between them. It did
not matter that Nila was the youngest of seventeen
sons and a long way away from inheriting the black
pearl crown. Life was hard for the Fairgean. Strength
and ruthlessness were admired, and mercy mocked
as weak.

Nila's mother had been a gentle woman, though,
and she had tried to shield her son from the vicious
contests of his older brothers. Since she was the least

of all the queens and the Fairgean king had so many other sons to distract his attention, she had to some extent succeeded. Nila had grown up knowing something of love and tenderness, and when his father the King had gambled his mother away with the toss of a sea-stirk knuckle, Nila had been filled with inarticulate rage and anguish. Away from the protection of the Fairgean king's cave and worn out by the brutality of her new husband, his fragile mother had soon died, leaving Nila with a profound hatred of his father and his kind.

He had known Fand all his life, for she had served in the King's court since she was a child. This was probably how she had managed to survive without the ability to transform, for the King and his immense retinue lived within the shelter of the caves, where hot water bubbled and hissed even when icebergs drifted in the ocean outside. Although she still had to fight for scraps of food, Fand had a stone ledge on which to lie and so did not have to struggle to stay afloat in the rough, icy waters or battle for a place on the rafts. Nila's mother had been kind to her and given her the occasional fragment of fish to eat and rags of fur in which to wrap herself, and so Fand had not died of starvation or exposure as so many of her kind did.

They had grown up together, King's son and slave, and the callous gambling away of the gentle woman they both loved had united them even closer. Nila did not share his brothers' contempt for halfbreeds. He remembered well his half-sister Maya who had been kind to him before she had been taken away by the Priestess of Jor. He loved Fand more than anything else in his cold, barren life. She returned his passion with equal ardor, and so they kept their love secret with obsessive care.

Nila stirred and stretched, filled with contentment. He rolled over so he could look down at Fand, whose eyes were closed, a half-smile on her full-lipped mouth. "I have something for you," he whispered. As he drew the black pearl out of his pouch, she opened her eyes, the curve of her lips deepening. The smile faltered when she saw what he was holding. She knew as well as Nila that black pearls were worn only by royalty.

"We can hide somewhere along the shore until the pod returns north," he said urgently. "They will think we have drowned . . ."

She rolled over and hid her face in her arms. "In these mild waters? You said yourself it would be hard to drown here."

"There are always dangers, as you yourself said. We could make them think we had been eaten by carnivorous coral . . ."

"You know your father would never be satisfied unless he saw your body himself," Fand replied wearily. "You know he needs as many fully trained warriors as possible for the assault against the tailless humans. Besides, you are still his son. He would tell the priestesses to find us and they would look through their far-seeing mirrors and then indeed all would be lost. *You* would only be beaten and humiliated. They would kill me."

Nila's hand dropped, defeated. "I wish . . ." he began but Fand sat up, shaking back her long hair. "It is no use, Nila," she said flatly. "You are a royal prince and I am nothing. Soon the King will remember my existence and think to give me away to one of his cronies who does not care that I am a mere halfbreed. He may even take me for himself. He has always had a taste for human flesh, you know that, and the younger the better. And when that happens, I shall no longer kick and kick to keep my head above water but just let myself drift down into Jor's cold embrace. And you will fight at your father's side and be given other women as prizes and in time you will forget your old playmate and lover. Do you think I do not know that is how it must be?"

Nila protested, catching her hands and trying to kiss her, but Fand held him off, her eyes wet with defiant tears. "I do not want you to pretend we can ever be together forever and happy," she said. "I want what is between us to be always true and real. No pretense. No lies. Did we not promise each other that, right at the very beginning?"

"But I want you forever and happy," Nila said. "I'm only the seventeenth son, my father does not care—"

"Do not be so naïve," she interrupted coldly, scrambling to her feet and brushing the sand from her arms. "He may not care for you but he is proud of his virility and of his sons' strength and skill. And remember what happened to your grandfather. Your father was the thirteenth son and yet he inherited after all your uncles were killed in the last disastrous attack on the land-hugging humans. Whole families were wiped out then and the Fairgean spent decades fighting to survive at all. His memories of that are as fresh as if the battle happened yesterday."

Nila was silent. He knew what Fand said was true. His fingers closed upon the black pearl and he said passionately, "I wish they all would die! Then I would be king and I could make you my queen and then we could be together forever and happy. I hate my father!"

"Be careful what you say," Fand said quietly. "You know the priestesses watch. Often I feel their eyes upon me. Come, we have been here too long. I must get back to the pod."

Kneeling by her side, he seized her hand, pressing the black pearl into her palm. "Can you not wear it secretly and know that I wish things could be different?"

Fand smiled down at him wistfully and swept her other hand along her naked body. "How could I hide it? What would I say when they found it? It is death to me to wear the black pearl, you know that." She lifted it so she could examine it, a perfect sphere the size of a storm petrel's egg and glimmering with smoky color. It was as large as the black pearl the King wore in his crown.

"It is beautiful. I wish that I could wear it proudly, saying to the world that I was your woman. But I cannot." She pressed it back into his palm, smoothing back the silky black hair that hung down his shoulders.

"Then I shall wear it!" Nila said. "So you shall know I am true."

"They will try and take it from you," Fand said in alarm. "It is provocative, wearing a black pearl like that! They will think you have ambitions for the throne. Remember how your brother Haji was murdered. If they do not challenge you in court, they will give you loreli fish to eat and you will die in agony like Haji did. Or you will find sea-urchins in your bed like they say your father's elder brother did, or a sand scorpion. Far better that you should offer the pearl to your father as a gift, though even that will be seen as seeking favor. You should throw the pearl back into the sea, give it as an offering to Jor that we may have fair weather for the swim back to the winter seas." She gave a little shudder, and Nila knew she dreaded that long, exhausting swim when everyone else plunged and dived through the waves as powerfully as the sea-stirks.

The prince looked down at the black pearl, weighing it in his hand. For a moment he was tempted to do as she said and throw it back into the sleepy blue sea, but then he shook his head. "No," he said with determination. "Jor himself led me to the pearl. I would never have found it had a tiger shark not tried to have me for its supper. I was driven into that grotto, I was meant to find the black pearl. If you will not wear it as a symbol of our love, I shall—and you shall know you are the queen of my heart."

She disregarded his sweeping declaration, clinging to his arm and begging him not to be a fool. All her arguments only made him more determined. "I shall have a care, Fand, I swear to you. Besides, can you not see into their hearts? You will warn me if they have evil designs."

Fand looked about her swiftly, and made a shushing noise. "Do you want the Priestesses of Jor to know what I can do?" she hissed. "Nila, the summer seas have gone to your head like sea-squill wine! I would rather be a slave than an acolyte of the priestesses. You must be more careful!"

Nila's expression sobered and he caught her to

him. "I'm sorry," he whispered into her messy brown hair. "You are right. I should be more careful. Come, let us get back to the pod before they start looking for us and notice we are gone together."

Fand straightened her belt of seaweed and shells, and combed back her hair with her fingers. "I shall walk back and you can swim in from the other direction," she said. "Nila, please, will you not give the sea back the pearl? I can see only troubled waters ahead for us."

His lipless mouth set in a straight, hard line and he shook his head determinedly. "No, Jor himself led me to the pearl. I shall not scorn his gift."

"Nila, you know I sometimes have the curse of future-seeing. I say again I see only storms and tidal waves ahead for us."

He laughed and swept his webbed hand out toward the sea, lying blue and still under a cloudless sun. "Well, I see only calm waters, my love. You know I was born with the caul over my head and they say that means I can never drown. Bring on the storms, I say!"

THE SPINNING WHEEL TURNS

THE FIRST BLOW

On the Spine of the World winter comes snapping and snarling like a wolf. The wind shrieks white for days, until snow shrouds the landscape and icicles hang like fangs from the mouth of the cave. In winter the world is reduced to absolutes of black or white, death or life, bitter cold or burning hot.

Inside the cave the bonfire leaped high, casting grotesque shadows over the intent faces and still bodies of the Khan'cohbans. They sat cross-legged in a wide circle, watching two figures who circled each other warily. There was no sound save the wail of the storm and the soft slap of the combatants' feet on the stone.

Isabeau crouched low, her eyes flickering over the face and stance of the warrior opposite her. He was much taller than she was, with two heavy curling horns on either side of his massive brow. He carried a long wooden stave, its metal ends flashing red as they spun in the firelight.

Faster than thought, the staff drove for Isabeau's shoulder but she threw herself to the right in a low dive, rolled and was on her feet again, just as the

wooden stave cracked against the rock mere inches
from where she had landed. Her staff was already
swinging upward in response. The warrior swayed
away as fluidly as water. Isabeau almost overbal-
anced as the wood connected with nothing but air.
As she recovered he spun on the ball of one foot and
struck her hard with the other, just below the junction of her ribs. She fell heavily, the breath knocked
out of her. More painful than the impact was the
disappointment. Only a few seconds into the contest
and already she had received her first blow. Two
more and the competition would end, with Isabeau
humiliated before her pride.

She rolled and sprang to her feet, her staff flying
up. The warrior's staff hammered into it, almost
knocking her down again. Her fingers stung, but she
only gripped her staff tighter, turning and thrusting
it up to try and slide under his guard. It was like
ramming the wind. He simply twisted away, turning
a cartwheel that took him well out of her reach.

He was striking at her again before she had a
chance to recover her breath, swift as a snake. She
swayed first one way, then another, evading his
blows, every sense in her body straining to anticipate
his next move. Her teacher had told her, "Become
one with your enemy. When your heart beats with
his and your minds move together, only then can
you know what his next move will be."

Isabeau breathed deeply in through her nose and out
through her mouth, endeavoring to control her breath
and with it that intangible essence the Khan'cohbans
called *coh*. Like many words in the Khan'cohban language, *coh* had many subtleties of meaning. God, life-

death energy, spirit. What the witches called the One Power, the source of all life, all magic. Eà.

She felt her heart and her veins fill with power as her lungs filled with air. For minutes they fought as if they were partners in an elaborate dance, wooden staves whistling as they spun through the air. Isabeau's Scarred Warrior teacher smiled in satisfaction. Then Isabeau was knocked flying again, and his mouth compressed grimly.

But then Isabeau brought her staff around in a low sweeping movement that knocked the Scarred Warrior's feet from under him. Her teacher punched his left hand into his right palm, the gesture of victory.

Isabeau was on her feet in an instant, triumph filling her. The Scarred Warrior attacked again, more fiercely than ever. Isabeau had to twist and sway and feint more nimbly than ever, panting harshly as she tried to control her breath. With an unexpected move, the Scarred Warrior spun and kicked high, and Isabeau fell as if she had been knocked down with a hammer.

For a moment all her senses reeled. She got to her feet slowly, disappointment clear on her face. That was the third blow. The contest was over.

Isabeau bowed to her opponent, lifting one hand to cover her eyes, the other hand bent outward in supplication. That was the proper way to greet a Scarred Warrior who had proved his mastery over her. Her opponent brought two fingers sweeping to his brow, then to his heart, then out to the snowy darkness. Then they both turned, heads lowered, and knelt before the old woman in the snow-lion's cloak. There was a long silence.

"This is the fourth long darkness that Khan has lived with us on the Spine of the World and so in our eyes she is like a child of only four, as blind and mute as a newborn kitten," the Firemaker said, her long-fingered hands sweeping through the air. Beneath the snarling muzzle of the snow-lion cloak, her old face was set in deep lines of pride and determination, the eyes between their hooded lids as blue as Isabeau's own. Isabeau bent her head lower, unable to help feeling a little prick of humiliation at her great-grandmother's words.

"She has lived through twenty-one winters, however, and so in truth is no child. She has been silent and learned as no child of four can. She has pleased her teachers and now, in the contest of the wooden stave, has struck a blow against one vastly her superior. In the eyes of the Firemaker and the Scarred Warriors, this is proof. Khan is ready to seek out her name and her totem."

Despite herself, Isabeau's eyes flew up in excitement. Her great-grandmother made the gesture of assent, and a little shift and murmur ran over the crowd. Isabeau lowered her face again, though her fingers gripped her stave tighter than ever. The naming-quest was one of the most significant events in the life of the Khan'cohbans. Isabeau would never be truly accepted as one of their own until she had undertaken the dark and dangerous journey to the Skull of the World, and returned safely with the knowledge of the White Gods' intentions for her.

Although Isabeau knew her destiny lay outside the Spine of the World, she still longed to undertake her quest and attain real status within the pride. The storytellers often told the tale of how her famous father Khan'gharad, Dragon-Lord, had won his name. Until Isabeau had survived the journey to the Skull of the World too, she would never truly understand her father and her great-grandmother, or her twin sister, Iseult, whose characters and philosophy had been so molded by the Khan'cohban way of life.

The queen-dragon had once told her that she would never find her true calling until Isabeau had embraced both her human and fairy heritages. *Thee must know thyself before thee can know the universe,* the queen-dragon had said. *Thee must always be searching and asking and answering, thee must listen to the heart of the world, thee must listen to thine own heart. Thee must search out thy ancestors and listen to what they may teach thee, thee must know thy history before thee can know of the future.*

So Isabeau had sworn to do as the queen-dragon had commanded, thus accepting a *geas* that had taken her far away from those that she loved best in the world. She had traveled up to the Spine of the World, spending six months of the year with her newly discovered parents at the Towers of Roses and Thorns, and six months with the Pride of the Fire Dragon in their snowy mountain home. In the summer she studied the lore of the witches in the great library at the Towers, and in winter she studied the art of the Scarred Warrior and the wisdom of the Soul-Sage with her Khan'cohban teachers. Although she was often lonely and unhappy, Isabeau had worked hard, eager to grasp the secrets of both cultures and philosophies, and now she had her reward in the words of the Firemaker.

Before Isabeau had a chance to feel more than a flush of pride and self-satisfaction, her Scarred War-

rior teacher came to her and dissected her perfor-
mance critically. She had been too quick to attack, he
said. "The art of the Scarred Warrior is not to fight,
but to be still. Not to act, but to react. When the
wind blows, the tree bends. When an enemy strikes,
the warrior responds. The warrior is not the wind
but the tree. You try too hard to be the wind."

She bowed her head, accepting his words. She
knew them to be true.

"You shall set out on your naming-quest in the
morning," her teacher said. "You must reach the Skull
of the World. Listen to the words of the White Gods
and return to the haven before the end of the long
darkness, or die."

Isabeau nodded. Fear touched her like an icy finger, but she repressed it sternly. He said then, in an
unusually gentle voice, "You fought well, Khan. I
thank you, for now I am released from my *geas* and
can once more hunt with my comrades. I had
thought it would be many years before I could once
again skim in the chase."

"I thank you," Isabeau replied. "It is not the art of
the student but that of the teacher which struck that
blow today."

Although his fierce dark face did not relax, she
knew she had pleased him. He said gruffly, "Make
your preparations. I shall see you in the morning,"
then dismissed her with a gesture.

Isabeau went then to the fire of the Soul-Sage. The
shaman of the pride was sitting in meditation, her
legs crossed, her eyes closed. In one hand she held
a stone of iridescent blue, flecked with gold. A falcon's talon hung on her breast from a long leather

cord around her neck. It rose and fell gently with her breathing.

Isabeau sat opposite her, closing her own eyes. She felt the soft brush of feathers on her hand as the little elf-owl Buba crept out of the blankets and into her palm. She cupped her fingers around the fluffy white bird, not much bigger than a sparrow, and let herself sink into nothingness. Against her sensitive palm she felt the flutter of the owl's heart and it was like a drumbeat leading her down into a profound meditation. For a long time she floated in this exquisite nonbeing, her heart and the owl's heart and the pulse of the universe in perfect rhythm.

So you go in search of your name and your totem, the Soul-Sage said without words.

Isabeau felt another little stir of fear and excitement. *Yes,* she responded. *The Firemaker thinks I am ready.*

I shall cast the bones for you, the shaman said after a long silence.

Thank you, teacher, Isabeau responded, her excitement quickening. She opened her eyes. Across the dancing flames the Khan'cohban's face was inscrutable. She passed the skystone in her hand through the smoke and dropped it back into the little pouch of skin she carried always at her waist. Taking a smoldering stick from the fire, she drew a large circle and quartered it with two swift motions. Then she poured the contents of the pouch out into her hand and brooded over them. Suddenly she threw the bones and stones into the circle without opening her eyes.

Isabeau gazed anxiously at the pattern the thirteen bones had made in the circle. She then looked at the

Soul-Sage, who was regarding the pattern intently.
After a while the shaman pointed one long, four-
jointed finger at the bird's claw.

"Sign of the Soul-Sage, a good omen for your
quest, so high to the roof of heaven," she said. "A
sign of death as well as wisdom, though, and shadowed by the closeness of the nightstone and the skystone. Change ahead for you, like the change
wrought on a landscape by an avalanche. Much danger and struggle." Her hand swept down to the fang
and the knucklebone and the fiery garnet, and then
across to the fish fossil. "Dangerous pattern indeed.
There are things in your past and in your unknown
which shall seize you in their jaws and seek to drag
you under."

The Soul-Sage had said "unza," another word with
many different meanings. With a gesture out into the
distance it meant "the unknown place," anywhere
beyond the pride's boundaries. With a circling gesture over the head it meant "the place of nightmares,"
the dreaming unconscious mind. With a sweep of the
hand toward the heart and then between the brows, it
meant secret thoughts, secret desires. The Soul-Sage
had used all of these gestures, and Isabeau struggled
to understand her meaning. "My unknown," she repeated with the same gestures and the Soul-Sage
nodded impatiently.

The shaman's hand then darted to touch the finger
bone. "Forces in balance, past, future, known, unknown. Puzzling. Quest could fail, quest could triumph." She touched the purple and white lumps of
quartz, and then the skystone again. "I think triumph,
though many pitfalls in your path. Beware too much
pride, too much impetuosity." Her finger circled the

fool's gold. "Deception, or perhaps a disguise. Hard to tell. A strange conjunction. Troubling."

She was silent for a long time, her hands folded again in her lap, then slowly she reached out and stroked the smooth green of the moss agate, tracing the shape of the fossilized leaf at its center. "Harmony, contentment, healing. Calm after the storm. You must be at peace with yourself, whatever you discover yourself to be. A good place for this stone. I think all will be well."

She looked up at Isabeau and her fierce face with its seven arrow-shaped scars was even grimmer than usual. "Not a good casting. Much remains dark to me. I do not know if you will return from your quest at all, let alone with a good name and totem. I am surprised to find your pattern so incoherent." Her finger reached out and touched the triangular scar between Isabeau's brows. "I had thought you already chosen by the White Gods."

Her hand dropped and she brooded over the pattern of the bones for a while longer before sweeping them up and purifying them one by one in the smoke of her fire. Isabeau longed to question her, but knew the Soul-Sage had said all she would say. The little frisson of fear passed through her again, raising the hairs on her arms and causing her stomach muscles to clench. Buba gave a little hoot of reassurance and Isabeau hooted back.

The Soul-Sage looked up from her task and gave an odd little smile. "But I forget," she said. "The owl chooses to fly with you. The owl is the messenger of the White Gods, the queen of the night and death and darkness, the Soul-Sage of birds. That is an omen that should not be forgotten."

Wondering if the shaman meant her words to be a comfort, Isabeau gathered together her shaggy furs and followed the Soul-Sage to the Rock of Contemplation, a small rock ledge that faced east toward the rising sun. She had to meditate here from sunset to sunrise, without food or water or fire, a harsh tribulation in the bitter cold.

The snowstorm passed some time during the evening and the clouds cleared away so she could see the stars, huge and luminous in the overarching sky. Although she sat still, she moved her fingers and toes constantly in their fur-lined gloves and boots, and concentrated on her breathing so that the blood in her veins ran hot and strong.

A while before dawn Isabeau saw, far away, a strange greenish glow that hung across the horizon like a slowly rippling curtain, edged with crimson and occasionally crackling with gold fire. Her own people called that fiery curtain the Merry-Dancers. She stared at it in awe and wonder until at last it sank away into embers. It too was an omen of some kind, though what it foreordained she did not know.

Then dawn came, the stars fading. Color slowly swept over the vast panorama of billowing cloud and peaked mountains. The clefts of shadowed valleys darkened to indigo, and the little owl blinked her round eyes and crawled within Isabeau's sleeve to sleep. Isabeau stood and stretched, chilly and stiff but filled with serenity.

The Soul-Sage came up the uneven steps and crouched at the back of the cave, not speaking but scanning Isabeau's face with eyes so heavily hooded that the color could not be seen. What she saw seemed to satisfy her, for she nodded curtly and indicated her pupil follow her back down into the cave.

The central bonfire had been built high and the members of the pride crowded about it. The first meal of the day was always communal, and as usual Isabeau was one of the last to receive her portion of gruel and dried fruit, being still nameless and without status. She waited till everyone else had finished, then clustered close with the other children, most not even reaching her waist, holding up her wooden bowl for the scrapings of the large pot. No one spoke to her or even glanced her way, but Isabeau was not upset by their disregard, being used to it.

Isabeau then knelt before the Firemaker and received her wordless blessing. The old woman drew her great-granddaughter to her and kissed her brow, a gesture of affection most unusual among the Khan'cohbans. "Be wary," she whispered. "There are many dangers in the mountains. You have to cross land belonging to other prides, so remember your manners. You are kin to the Firemaker, though, and should be shown respect. Know that once you leave the haven the taboos on your Firemaker powers are lifted, but not your debt of honor to the children of the White Gods."

Isabeau nodded. She knew her great-grandmother was telling her she would be allowed to use whatever powers she had to help her in her quest, but that she must not use her powers against any other Khan'cohban, no matter the provocation. The Firemaker was bound by a rigid code of rules and very rarely drew upon her powers in case she should offend. Isabeau had been confined by the same restrictions, which had sometimes chafed her unbearably, used as she was to drawing upon her witchcraft whenever she wanted.

Isabeau pulled on her boots and satchel, wrapped her coat around her, and gripped her tall wooden staff, the skimmer tied to her back. Any excitement she might have felt was totally overwhelmed by fear. She realized that all she really knew was that she had to journey across the harsh snowy wastes to the Skull of the World, where some gods she did not really believe in would somehow give her a new name.

As she walked toward the mouth of the cave, the pride all bowed to her and made the good luck gesture, and she wondered somberly if she would ever see any of them again. She cast a despairing look back and saw that both her teachers, the wise shaman and the stern warrior, were following close behind. Although neither gave her any smile of reassurance or comfort, she was both reassured and comforted, and left the dark, stifling warmth of the cave with a slightly lighter heart.

They led her around the side of the haven's valley and up the steep slope to the crown of the mountain. With the sun at their backs they faced the Skull of the World, which bit into the sky as white and sharp as the incisor of a saber leopard. Between them and the towering pinnacle were tier upon tier of sharp-pointed, ice-white mountains, their spreading roots hidden in gloomy shadows. Isabeau stared in cold dismay. How was she to climb all those mountains? How was she to find her path?

"The fastest route is not always the straightest," the

Soul-Sage said. She pointed to the north. "That way lie the snow plains of the Pride of the Fighting Cats."

"The glacier sweeps down from the Skull of the World," the Scarred Warrior said. "Although it has its dangers, it is much easier to cross than the peaks. There the slopes are smooth and one can skim for long distances before one needs to climb again."

"Are they not the enemy of the Fire Dragon Pride?" Isabeau asked anxiously.

"Remember you are on a sacred quest and therefore cannot be challenged by any you pass. They will see your feathered staff and let you alone," the Soul-Sage replied.

Isabeau nodded, staring out toward the north. "What do I do once I get to the Skull of the World?" she asked.

"You must be eaten, swallowed and digested," the Soul-Sage replied. "Only once the Gods of White have devoured you may you be reborn as an adult."

Isabeau stared at her. "Do you mean that literally or metaphorically?" she said, unable to prevent her voice from quavering.

The Khan'cohbans did not reply, their faces blank. Their language did not have such subtle distinctions. Isabeau grinned, feeling a little bubble of hysteria floating up her throat. Their expressions only darkened. Khan'cohbans did not have any sense of humor and abhorred any sign of levity in Isabeau. She controlled her face with difficulty and said, "How am I meant to know what to do?"

"Have you not listened to the wisdom of the storytellers? Their tales are not only told to divert but also to teach."

"But I mean how shall the White Gods tell me my name?" she asked in an exasperated voice.

"Speechless, you shall speak my name.

"Must you speak? Why then again,

"In speaking you shall say the same," the Soul-Sage said cryptically.

Isabeau repeated the words to herself, having to fight down anther gurgle of disbelieving laughter. The Khan'cohbans were very fond of riddles, proverbs and aphorisms, which often made for very tedious conversations. Isabeau had never been very good at guessing riddles, but she knew better than to demand an explanation.

The Soul-Sage crossed her hands at her breast, then swept them out, palms flat. The Scarred Warrior repeated the gesture of farewell, and then together they turned and made their way down the side of the hill without a backward glance, leaving Isabeau alone on the crest of the mountain.

Swooping and swaying, Isabeau reached the end of the valley and came to a halt with a little flourish of snow. She leaned on her staff, panting, and threw back the shaggy hood so she could see. All around her the rim of the mountains cut into the greenish sky like the jagged edge of an eggshell.

Below was another fall of white land, much broken with rocks and stands of trees. It dropped down to a great smooth sweep of ice, carving a path through the mountains like a giant's road.

Isabeau's heart lifted at the sight of the glacier, and she had no hesitation in setting off down the hill once more. Her body bent and swayed as she drove through the snow, having to leap or twist as natural obstacles bounded up at her. A branch whipped her across the face and she fell several times as her little sleigh skidded on ice or hit a concealed boulder. The euphoria of skimming was zinging in her blood, however, and so she merely swung herself upright again, using her staff, and sped on her way.

Soon it was too dark to see, but Isabeau conjured up a witch's light and sent it bobbing away before her, the sharp blue light revealing cracks, crevasses and concealed rocks much more clearly than daylight could. The owl took to the wing and flew before her, showing Isabeau the safest route down the mountain.

It was a swift, dangerous, heart-jolting journey, but Isabeau had thrown away all caution, the adrenaline pumping through her system like the sweet intoxication of moonbane. She should have been injured time and time again, but some sixth sense seemed to warn her of obstacles so that her body was swerving away even before her eyes discerned the danger. Many times her wooden skimmer launched off into the night sky as the slope fell suddenly away, but somehow she always managed to land squarely, her headlong pace only quickening. She skimmed so swiftly and skillfully that it was as if she took flight, following the owl on wings of crackling blue light.

The dark floor of the valley rushed up toward her, then suddenly her skimmer hit a patch of ice hidden by a light dusting of snow. Isabeau skidded sideways, spun out of control, then cartwheeled high into the air. She came down with a great crash into a bank of snow, all the breath knocked out of her.

Buba came down to rest by her face, hooting softly

in concern. The witch's light had winked out so all
was dark.

*Buba, dearling, I need ye to fly about for me and find
me somewhere to shelter,* Isabeau thought.

*Why can you-hooh not snooze-hooh through noon-hooh
as Owl should-hooh?* Buba grumbled.

But you ken I am no' an owl, Buba, Isabeau replied,
smiling despite herself. *I like to do things during the
day and sleep at night.*

*I do-hooh not know why-hooh. Under moon-hooh all is
cool-hooh, and Owl is queen, as mute-hooh as wind. It is
good-hooh.*

For you, maybe, but no' for me, Isabeau said with a
smile. *It is almost night now, though, Buba, and I need
your keen eyesight and your wings. I need to find somewhere to hide until the sun comes again.*

Haunt-hooh to snooze-hooh in, the owl said know-
ledgeably.

Aye, but somewhere big enough for all of me. Isabeau
smiled, remembering how the owl had found her a
hole in a tree the previous night, barely large enough
for Isabeau to fit her hand in.

Huge-hooh haunt-hooh then, the elf-owl said, staring
at Isabeau unblinkingly. Since the bird was no bigger
than Isabeau's hand, the young witch seemed enormous to her. Buba fluffed out her wings, rotated her
head around so she could see what lay in all directions, then took flight. The beat of her wings was
silent, her velvety feathers fringed to muffle the
sound. As white as the ground, the owl disappeared
from sight in moments.

Isabeau sat down on her skimmer to rest, then
began to poke around in the snow with her skewer,
looking for anything to eat. Although she still had

some supplies left, it would not take long to devour all that she carried. The cold and exertion always made her very hungry indeed.

If Isabeau had been a true Khan'cohban, she would have tracked down and killed a coney or bird for her supper, or dug a hole in the ice through which to fish. But Isabeau was no Khan'cohban. Her years as the ward of Meghan of the Beasts had formed her character and philosophy too fully for her to take another creature's life. So, despite the scorn and mockery of her pride, Isabeau continued to refuse to kill or eat meat.

Found by the old wood witch as a baby abandoned in the forest, Isabeau had been taught to revere all life and think of the woodland creatures as her friends. Her guardian had had a little donbeag as her familiar and Isabeau had been taught to speak the languages of animals as fluently as she spoke the language of humans. She could no more murder a coney than she could a trusted friend, and so during the cold dark months spent on the Spine of the World, she had subsisted only on what she could herself gather to supplement the stores of the pride. Most of the pride's gathering of grains, fruits and nuts was done by the children and old people in the summer months and stored in huge, stone jars in the haven. Since Isabeau left the pride in the summer to return to her family, she did not help in the gathering and so could not ask that she be given more than her fair share of the jealously guarded hoard. Winter was therefore always a hungry time for her, and she had grown adept at finding edible barks and fallen nuts to give her the protein she needed.

Digging through the snow for something to eat

made Isabeau miss her guardian keenly. Although Meghan of the Beasts was now Keybearer of the Coven, the most powerful sorceress in the land, Isabeau still thought of her as the grumpy old witch who had raised her. She had a sudden sharp longing to be back in Lucescere, toasting her toes by Meghan's fire and listening to her tales of the Three Spinners. When she had eaten her fill of Meghan's delicious little honey cakes, she could walk over to the palace to visit with Iseult and Lachlan, playing spillikins with the children while her oldest friend, the jongleur Dide, sang some wistful love song . . .

Isabeau had to swallow hard to dislodge the lump in her throat. *If I starve to death in the snow I'll never be going home*, she told herself sternly and bent once more to her task.

By the time the little owl had winged silently back to her shoulder, she had found only a handful of lichen and bark and a few small nuts and was looking rather forlorn. Buba kindly offered to hunt down some insects to share with her but Isabeau declined with a shudder. It was pitch-black in the valley and bitterly cold, and she gladly followed the owl along the frozen stream, sinking up to her knees in the snow, until she came to a massive old fallen hemlock.

Isabeau clambered around the roots, which were flung up into the air like hissing snakes, and jumped down into the pit where the roots had once dug into the soil. Looking about her she gave a little murmur of appreciation. If she could not have a cave, this little pit was almost as good. Not much snow had fallen into the hollow, which was protected by the upflung roots, and there was plenty of firewood close to hand.

She lit the fire with a snap of her fingers, blowing it into life and feeding it with scraps of bark and leaves until it was burning merrily. She then ground the nuts and bark into a handful of grain, threw in some snow and made herself a thick porridge for her dinner.

Leaving Buba to guard her sleep, Isabeau rolled herself in her furs. It was a clear night and she stared up at the luminous stars through the fretwork of pine branches, feeling a pleasant, euphoric fatigue.

The owl woke her only a few hours later. Isabeau opened her eyes unwillingly. Every muscle ached and the euphoria had faded into bone weariness. The bruises from her many falls were throbbing and she gave a little moan and tried to burrow herself back into sleep. The owl bobbed up and down on her chest, then, receiving nothing but another groan, pecked her sharply.

Isabeau sat up angrily. "What be the matter, for Eà's sake?"

Horned-hooh men pursue-hooh . . .

Isabeau rubbed her eyes and looked about her. All was still. One of the moons had risen and cast a pale radiance over the black and silver landscape. For a moment Isabeau thought her gaze was swimming and she rubbed her eyes again, only to realize that the black dots dancing across the landscape were the shadows of people, swiftly skimming down the glacier.

Dressed all in white, the Khan'cohbans themselves were invisible but the cold moonlight caused them to cast sharp shadows that swung and leaped as their skimmers sped down the slope in wide graceful curves.

Isabeau crouched down, trepidation filling her. No doubt the Khan'cohbans had seen her wildly swinging witch-light and had come to investigate. In her white furs, Isabeau knew she would be difficult to find. All she needed to do was curl up in the snow and the searchers could pass within a mere foot of her and not see her. She was a trespasser on the Pride of the Fighting Cats' territory, however, and concealing herself could be misconstrued as hostile or deceitful behavior. After a moment's thought she stood up, scouted around in the snow until she found a fallen branch and then caused it to ignite into a blazing torch. She stuck it into a cleft between two rocks and then sat cross-legged on her skimmer to wait.

The Khan'cohbans saw her fire and turned swiftly, converging on her like birds to a thrown scrap of bread. There were twenty or more of them and Isabeau had to breathe slowly and deeply to maintain her air of calm.

They stood in silence, regarding her. Although it was night, the moon rode high in the sky and cast a brilliant light over the snow. They should be able to see the feathers decorating her staff, even if they could not tell their color. Isabeau kept her eyes lowered and waited, though every nerve was strained in anticipation of violent movement.

Then one of the men stepped forward, pulling back his hood so she could see his thick, curling horns and the steep, dark planes of his face. One of his horns was broken and the thin line of his six scars gleamed against his olive skin. He swept two fingers to his high forehead, then to his heart, then out to

the view. Isabeau lifted one hand to cover her eyes,
the other hand bent outward in supplication.

Her response must have satisfied them for the warrior said curtly, "Come."

Isabeau nodded and gathered up her satchel and
skimmer. She followed them down through the copse
of trees until they came to a smooth open slope. The
Khan'cohbans strapped on their skimmers and glided
away quickly, with Isabeau following as fast as she
could.

The Khan'cohbans gave her no respite, only waiting long enough for her to catch up with them before
climbing up into a steep ravine with long strides that
left her panting along behind. At last the ravine came
to an end in a steep cliff. On either side were occasional clefts or caves, most quite shallow. Isabeau
could smell smoke, and the mouth of the largest of
the caves was illuminated with the uncertain light of
a fire. It was close to dawn and Isabeau was stumbling with weariness. She followed them up the steep
rocky path until they reached the mouth of the cave,
looking about her with interest. The leader of the
Scarred Warriors pointed at the ground. "Stay," he
said.

Isabeau nodded, though disappointment filled her.
She was cold, tired and hungry and had hoped for
a more comfortable resting spot than an icy rock
ledge. As the Kahn'cohbans disappeared inside the
cave she wrapped her damp furs closer about her
and squatted down in the shelter of a boulder. Buba
flitted down, silent as a snowflake, and perched on
her knee, the round golden eyes inscrutable. Isabeau
smoothed down the tufted ears with one finger, al-

lowed the owl to creep within her sleeve, then rested her head on her arms.

She was woken from an uneasy doze by the sound of someone approaching. Isabeau jerked her head up and saw a tall woman coming up beside her. The sky above the valley walls was pale, almost colorless, and the light had the peculiar clarity that dawn brings. Isabeau stared at the Khan'cohban warrior and felt a little shock as the woman bent down to speak to her.

"Iseult?" she said dazed, looking up into eyes as vividly blue as her own.

The Khan'cohban woman scowled, the blue eyes as cold as glacial ice. "Come," she snapped. "Old Mother has granted you audience."

Isabeau stared at her without moving for a moment, thoughts jostling through her mind. The Khan'cohban did not have blue eyes. Their irises were clear and pellucid as water. The Khan'cohbans did not have pale skin liberally bespattered with freckles. Their skin was swarthy with white shaggy eyebrows. This woman's brows were red and finely marked. Although her hair was hidden by her fur cap, Isabeau had no doubt it would be as red as her own. Yet her features were unmistakably those of a Khan'cohban, with strong, prominent bones, a beak of a nose, and heavy eyelids.

Isabeau followed the blue-eyed Khan'cohban into the cave, nibbling the tip of her glove thoughtfully. This must be a descendant of the Firemaker's sister, who had been rescued from exposure in the snows by the Pride of the Fighting Cats many years before. That would make her some kind of cousin to Isabeau and her twin sister Iseult. The apprentice witch had been without family for so long she could only feel pleasure at the idea of meeting a relative, but it was obvious the Khan'cohban regarded her with resentment and suspicion. Her back was stiff, her hands clenched by her sides, her gaze averted. Isabeau remembered the troubled history of the Firemaker's family and said nothing.

The cave was low and dank-smelling, lit only by the bonfire built toward the back. A heavy pall of smoke hung in the air, making Isabeau's eyes sting. Sitting around the fire in the familiar cross-legged position were the Old Mother and the council of Scarred Warriors. Further away from the fire sat the storytellers, the metalsmiths, the weavers and the Firekeepers. All cast her one quick glance then lowered their eyes to their hands, returning to their work.

Isabeau knelt before the Old Mother, not daring to scrutinize her face though she longed to search for a resemblance to her great-grandmother, the Firemaker. After a while the First of the Scarred Warriors demanded, "You have dared to cross our boundaries. What is your business here?"

Isabeau lifted her staff so they could see the red-dyed feathers and tassels. "I go in search of my name," she answered respectfully. "I beg leave to pass through your lands on my way to the Skull of the World."

The First of the Warriors said gruffly, "Those on the name-quest are under a *geas* to the Gods of White and are therefore under their protection. You may travel freely."

Isabeau made the gesture of thanks and raised her eyes. She saw a middle-aged woman with a high-boned face set in heavy lines of pride and temper, and sunken eyes that gleamed blue in the firelight. Her long red hair, drawn back tightly from her brow, was beginning to be dulled by gray. Isabeau could have been looking at a younger version of her great-grandmother, except this woman wore the tawny spotted fur of the native lynx, the totem of her pride. The broad head with its snarling muzzle and black tufted ears hung down her back.

The blue-eyed woman who had fetched Isabeau gave a sharp protest. "But she is the get of the Fire-maker!" she cried. "See her eyes, blue as the sky, and her hair, red as flame. She is one of the Red, sent to deceive us and spy on us. The Firemaker re-grets her overture of peace and seeks to disinherit us again!"

Anger and suspicion flashed across the Old Mother's face. She leaned forward and seized Isabeau's face in a painful grip, turning it so the firelight blazed upon it. Then the fur cap Isabeau wore was torn off so her abundant red curls sprang free. The circle of watchers muttered angrily.

"Never trust the dragon," the First of the Story-tellers said grimly.

The Old Mother nodded, her mouth compressed into a thin line. "We have always known the Pride of the Fire Dragon were our enemies," she said. "I have often pondered the meaning behind the Fire-maker's gesture of friendship these last few years. She has ever been jealous of her power, and though we hoped she spoke truth when she spoke of her acceptance of me as her rightful heir, often I have been beset by doubt. Now it seems as if this doubt has foundation."

Isabeau was dismayed. Carefully she made the gesture of respect and then said, "Old Mother, it is true I am of the Firemaker's get but I have no desire to disinherit you. I wish only to travel unhindered upon my naming quest. I was assured I would be given leave to cross your land since the Pride of the Fighting Cats and the Pride of the Fire Dragon are at peace."

There was a snort of disbelief from the blue-eyed warrior. "You lie!" she cried. "Do you think I do not remember you? It has been many winters since you received your name and your scars. I have often fought with you in the past and know you hate us as much as we hate you."

"Indeed, you are no mere child," the storyteller said. "You have the breasts of a woman grown and your eyes show you have seen more years than thirteen."

Isabeau made the gesture of agreement. "You speak with truth," she replied. Her impulse was to rush into explanations but her training held true and she said nothing more, lowering her eyes respectfully.

There was a long, charged silence, then at last the storyteller said reluctantly, "You say we speak with truth. How can *we* speak truth if what *you* say is true?"

"You ask of me a question. Do you offer me a story in return?" Isabeau said. There was another long pause, then even more reluctantly the storyteller made the gesture of agreement, saying gruffly, "I ask of you a question. Will you answer in fullness and in truth?"

"I will answer in fullness and in truth," Isabeau

answered, and raised her head, bringing her hands to lie upturned on her thighs in the traditional pose of the storyteller. "You, the First of the Storytellers of the Pride of the Fighting Cats, spoke truth when you said I was no child, for I have lived through twenty-one of the long darknesses. I am but a child in the eyes of my pride, however, for I have lived on the Spine of the World for only four years. I am therefore nameless and without status, and travel to the Skull of the World to hear what the Gods of White shall tell me."

There was a little stir of surprise at her words, and Isabeau's cousin made an impatient gesture of disbelief. Isabeau turned to her and said sternly, "You, though, who share the blue eyes like the summer sky and the red hair like flame that all kin of the Firemaker share, you do not speak truth."

Consternation and outrage flashed across the Khan'cohban woman's face, echoed in more subtle ways by the listening crowd. Isabeau went on steadily. "To understand why, you must know the story of my birth. I am the daughter of Khan'gharad Dragon-Lord, grandson of the Firemaker. It is known to you all how he traveled away from the Spine of the World to study with the wise ones among the humans. He met there a human woman and loved her and conceived with her twins."

Again there was a little shift and murmurs of shock and outrage. Isabeau looked around at their stern faces and said, "Evil had cast its shadow over the lives of the humans and there was much war and bloodshed. My mother fled to the mountains in search of my father's people but was overcome with the birth pangs. She would have died if it had not been for the intervention of the queen-dragon, who was in *geas* to my father for the saving of her daughter's life. She bore my mother to the palace of the dragons in her claws and there my sister and I were born.

"Knowing that twins were forbidden among the People of the Spine of the World, the queen-dragon bade one of her sons carry my twin sister to the north where she was left for the Firemaker to find. Another of her sons was told to carry me to the south, where a wise woman and Soul-Sage of the humans found me and raised me to adulthood. It was not until I met my twin sister that I knew I was kin to the Children of the White Gods and I came to the Spine of the World to learn the history and wisdom of my father's people."

Isabeau paused for a long moment, letting her words sink in. "I and my twin sister are as alike in face and form as the Firemaker and her sister must have been. Thus you could mistake me for her, and an honest mistake it is, though not the truth. So I tell you again, although it is true I am of the Firemaker's get, I have no desire to challenge you for the godhead. I wish only to travel unhindered upon my naming-quest."

She looked back at the Old Mother, whose face was expressionless, her eyes hooded. The First of the Scarred Warriors made a series of swift gestures to her and she nodded slowly. He turned back to Isabeau and said, "You have answered fully, though we have no way to judge the truth of what you are saying. How are we to know that you are indeed the twin of the one we know as the Firemaker's kin and not herself?"

Isabeau peeled off her glove to show them her left hand. The two smallest fingers were missing, ugly scars where they had once been. Involuntarily the Khan'cohbans recoiled, disgusted by her deformity. Isabeau pressed her lips together but said nothing, lifting one finger to stroke the triangular scar between her brows.

"My sister had won two of her Scarred Warrior scars," she said softly. "You can see I have not been so honored. Yet I am scarred in my own way. They say it is the scratch of the White Gods' claw."

The Khan'cohbans glanced at the scar and then glanced away immediately, too polite to stare. Only one man dared to examine her face intently, an old man with seven triangular scars on his cheeks and forehead. Dressed in the heavy furs of a bear, he wore an eagle's talon around his neck and at his waist was a pouch of skin that clattered slightly as he moved. Isabeau made a low gesture of respect and he reached out one long bony finger and touched her gently between her brows. "The stranger speaks truth," he said and turned to shuffle into the shadows.

"So be it," the Old Mother said. "You are under the protection of the Gods of White and may travel through our lands freely."

"Thank you," Isabeau said and bowed.

Her cousin was tense still, her hands clenched on her thighs. Her mouth was shut grimly but Isabeau knew she was restraining passionate words. It seemed the quick, impetuous temper that she and Iseult shared was an idiosyncrasy of the whole family. Among the Khan'cohban any strong emotion was

regarded coldly, and Isabeau wondered fleetingly
how her cousin had fared, growing up among such
austere people. She cast her a swift look of sympathy
but this acted like a lash to her cousin's lacerated
pride. The fists tightened and she leaned forward,
saying angrily, "It may be true that this stranger is
the twin to the one we know, but does that mean
she does not covet the godhead? I say she has come
among us to lull us into sleep while she discerns our
weaknesses. The peace between our prides is naught
but a scab over a suppurating wound. For many centuries the dragons and the fighting cats have clashed,
and we have suffered many times from their scorn.
Should we forget that so easily? Do the storytellers
not say, 'If you want peace, prepare for war'?"

Anger sparked in Isabeau's eyes. "Have you forgotten these caves you shelter in are in the fire dragon's land?" she cried. "The Firemaker has made
many overtures of peace to your pride, and given
you these caves so you need not suffer the full force
of the winter storms. She has named your Old
Mother heir to the godhead, disinheriting her own
descendants whose paths have led them away from
the Spine of the World. Does all this mean nothing
to your people?"

"Never trust the dragon," the blue-eyed warrior
said with heavy emphasis.

Isabeau sprang to her feet. "Do you accuse me of
lying?" There was as much incredulity as anger in
her voice, for the Khan'cohbans were bound by a
rigid code of honor that included an absolute taboo
on falsehood, particularly when replying to a direct
question.

Her cousin was on her feet in an instant. "I do,"
she answered, and made the rudest, most contemptuous gesture in the Khan'cohban language.

For a moment Isabeau was so angry she could not
speak, then she said in a stifled voice, "Is this how
the Pride of the Fighting Cats treats its guests? Have
you forgotten I am on my naming-quest and thus
due all honor and respect?"

"I say your talk of the naming-quest is naught but
a trick and a lie to lull us into false peace," her cousin
retorted, her freckles drowned in the crimson that
had swept up her throat and face.

The First of the Scarred Warriors made an abrupt
gesture of intervention, but the Khan'cohban woman
was too livid with rage to heed him. She drew her
knife in a swift motion and flung it at Isabeau's feet.
"I challenge you to prove your truth upon my body!"

Isabeau looked down at the quivering knife then
around at the faces of the Khan'cohbans, who had
all sprung to their feet at the first hint of confrontation. She knew such a gesture could not be ignored.
The rules of honor demanded that she accept the
challenge and defend her integrity. Such an accusation could only be answered in blood.

Yet Isabeau had no desire to fight her own cousin
and, although she had been trained in the art of the
Scarred Warrior, believed violence was no solution.
She looked up at her cousin and cold fingers of fear
clenched around her heart. This was no mere challenge to be decided by the first drawing of blood.
The Khan'cohban woman had murder in her eyes.

"She is only a child and crippled!" the First Storyteller cried. "You cannot challenge a cripple."

"She is one of the Red," the First Warrior replied

slowly. "And has her seventh scar. That means she must have some power."

The crowd stirred uneasily. Isabeau slowly bent and picked up the knife, then handed it back to her cousin, hilt outward. "We are kin," she said gently, "and I am on my naming-quest. I do not wish to answer your pride's hospitality with violence. I have told my story and your Soul-Sage has accepted the truth of my speaking. Will you not let me pass in peace? Once I have won my name and my scars I shall be returning to my own people and you will probably never see me again. I would like to think we could part as friends."

The young warrior scowled, seizing the knife and spinning it in her hand. "Is it because you are afraid or because you know you speak falsely that you refuse my challenge?" she jeered.

Isabeau saw mistrust and contempt on the faces of all around her and sighed. "It is because I do not want to be the one to break the peace between our prides," she answered. "I will not allow you to call me dishonorable, however. To doubt my honor is to doubt my teachers and the Firemaker herself."

She turned and bowed to the Old Mother. "If I must fight to prove the truth of my telling, so be it. Let it be clear to all who watch that I mean no ill to the Pride of the Fighting Cat nor to those of the Red."

The Old Mother bowed her head in acceptance of her words. Swiftly the watching Khan'cohbans moved back so a wide circle opened around the cousins. Isabeau slowly stripped off her shaggy coat and folded it neatly, placing it to one side with her fur cap. Just as deliberately she set aside her satchel and took off her heavy boots, knowing that her calmness was only inflaming her cousin's rage. The Khan'cohban warrior was taller and stronger than Isabeau and had won three scars, the two slashes on her left cheek indicating she was an accomplished fighter. Isabeau must win this fight, which meant she must take every advantage she could. Her only chance was to goad her opponent into making ill-considered moves.

She saw Buba's head peep out of the pile of furs and sent her a silent message to lie still. Her enemy must underestimate her. Seeing Isabeau was accompanied by an owl would make her cousin think twice; Isabeau wanted her to think not at all.

With her red-tasseled staff in one hand, she bowed low to the Old Mother and then to her enemy. The Khan'cohban warrior gave her the most curt of acknowledgments then attacked in a flurry of swift movements, her dagger in one hand, her sharp skewer in the other. Isabeau made no attempt to return the attack, merely swaying out of reach while she watched intently for any clue to her enemy's strengths and weaknesses. An icy calm had settled over her. She breathed slowly and steadily, ignoring her enemy's cruel jibes, her feints and pyrotechnics. The turning of the planet seemed to slow until each heartbeat was like the muffled pound of a drum, her enemy's spins and kicks and blows as slow as a stately minuet.

Isabeau felt as if she was one of the watchers in the dark cave, not one of the combatants. She was still, the maypole around which her enemy swung and danced. She felt she knew every tactic the warrior would use before she herself did. Not one blow had connected, yet the Khan'cohban warrior was fighting with all her skill and training. Floating somewhere beyond her body, Isabeau knew her enemy was growing both tired and desperate, only her anger fueling her savagery. She was blind and deaf with anger, her breath rasping in her chest, while Isabeau was using the minimum of energy to evade her enemy's attacks. Somewhere deep inside she was conscious of surprise at herself, for she had never been considered a skilled fighter. All her teachers' training had come together, though, into this one pure flame of being. Isabeau was at one with the coh.

Her enemy lunged at her recklessly and Isabeau sidestepped gracefully, so that the lunge turned into a stumble. Isabeau could have cracked her staff down on her cousin's back, but instead she stood back courteously, waiting for her to recover her balance. The warrior snarled at her, mad with rage, and flung her dagger straight at Isabeau's heart. Without thought Isabeau's hand came up and she caught the knife only inches from her breast. She was unable to help grinning with amazed pleasure, and tossed the knife out of the fighting circle. The warrior flushed red with humiliation and drew her little mace with a curse. Her attack grew more frenzied, and Isabeau had to move more swiftly to avoid being struck. Sighs or soft groans came from the crowd, a sign of their intent involvement.

The warrior detached the head of the mace from its handle and swung it round her head till it was a blur, then sent it whizzing toward her opponent. Isabeau ducked and it flew over her head and into the crowd, out of the fighting circle. Quickly the warrior dived toward Isabeau, trying to take advantage of her weak stance, the skewer flashing down. Isabeau rose from her crouch into a somersault that took her high into the air, over her enemy's head. The warrior crashed into the floor and lay for a moment winded. Isabeau waited patiently, both hands resting on her staff.

This time the warrior rose slowly, her face twisted with hate, and circled Isabeau warily. She no longer underestimated the apprentice witch. They feinted for some minutes, the warrior unhitching her eight-sided *reil* from her belt. Isabeau breathed deeply and calmly, her eyes fixed on her opponent's. She did not bother to watch her hands or her body, knowing her enemy's intentions would be signaled in her eyes. Suddenly the warrior flung the eight-sided star and it came curving toward Isabeau's throat with a faint hissing sound. In the same instant her enemy lunged forward, the skewer held low. Isabeau arched backward, the skewer sliding along her back without breaking the skin, the *reil* missing her throat by a whisker. The crowd gave an involuntary gasp for it had seemed impossible that Isabeau could have avoided both. She took her weight on her hands and flung her body over, landing again on her feet. Again her enemy stumbled off balance and again Isabeau took no advantage, waiting for the Khan'cohban to regain her equilibrium. The First Warrior smiled grimly.

The warrior picked herself up and looked at Isabeau with some puzzlement. She weighed the long skewer in her hand and called out gruffly, "Why do you not strike a blow? Do you not wish to prove yourself?"

Isabeau said gently, "You are my kin. I do not need to strike a blow to prove myself." Despite herself, there was a stress of pride in her intonation and the warrior flushed redder than ever and hefted the skewer over her shoulder, throwing it with deadly accuracy. Isabeau had to fling herself to one side to avoid being spitted, and she heard the wicked hiss of the *reil* as it spun toward her. She flung up her hand and caught it, and there was a gasp of astonishment, for such a thing was near impossible, given the shape of the weapon and the speed with which it spun. Isabeau tossed it out of the fighting circle and got to her feet without haste. Her enemy was standing staring at her with her mouth open in disbelief. Of all a Scarred Warrior's weapons, the *reil* was the most prized, for it returned to the warrior's hand as if it had a life of its own. It took great skill to throw and catch the *reil*, and no one had ever known it to be caught by its target.

There was fear in the warrior's eyes now, and consternation. Isabeau bowed to her, leaning lightly on her staff, and slowly her enemy unhitched her little axe and approached her warily, almost reluctantly. They engaged again, though this time both were on the defensive. Isabeau used her staff to block a blow, then heaved it upward so her enemy fell backward. The skewer clattered out of her hand, and Isabeau turned and pointed at it, and it slid across the floor and out of the fighting circle. Now her enemy had only the little axe, a tool more often used for hacking firewood and ice than for fighting. She got to her feet slowly, gathering together her will and her courage, and attacked Isabeau again. There was no rage or bravado left in her face or her stance now, only a sort of puzzlement. It took only a few seconds for

Isabeau to disarm her and toss the axe out of the circle, then they stood, watching each other, Isabeau's hands at rest on the head of her staff.

Without rancor, the red-haired warrior said, "You could have killed me." Isabeau nodded. "But you struck no blow at all."

"You are my kin and the heir to the Firemaker," Isabeau said softly. "I would not be the one to destroy the gift of the Gods of White to their children."

"So you do not want the godhead," Isabeau's cousin said. "I thought . . ." She hesitated a moment, then bowed to Isabeau, lifting one hand to cover her eyes, the other hand bent outward in supplication. Isabeau brought two fingers to her brow, then to her heart, then out to the sunlit day.

"I give you my apologies," the red-haired warrior said clearly. "I confess to fear, vanity and pride, worst of deficiencies. I was afraid the Firemaker regretted her acknowledgment of us, the descendants of Khan'fella, she who was left out in the snow for the White Gods. I wanted to be the only heir and thought to eliminate any threat to my position. I challenged your truth-telling in order to kill you without consequences to myself, knowing that to kill you outside the fighting circle would be to call the punishment of the Gods of White upon me. I ask your forgiveness and offer you the right to order my punishment."

Isabeau made the gesture of acceptance, then said, "Your challenge was honest, though, for you truly did not believe I was telling the truth. It was a fair challenge therefore, and I have proved my truth and my honor to you and your pride. There is no need for punishment."

"The stranger-child is merciful," the Old Mother

said harshly. The color rose in her daughter's cheeks and she bowed her head, saying, "What then is your will, Old Mother?"

"Your humiliation is punishment enough, I think," the red-haired woman replied, "for indeed I do not think any warrior of this pride has ever been beaten so shamefully. Many times I have warned you against conceit and quick temper, and at last you see the crevasse that can open beneath you as a result of such faults. Remember, though, that you are in debt to the stranger-child for she had the White Gods within her and could have killed you a number of times. Wait upon her now like a bond-servant and do what she orders, and know that one day the time will come when she will demand payment of the debt."

Isabeau's cousin bowed her head and made the gesture of acceptance, all her freckles drowned under her high color. Isabeau restrained a gesture of protest, for she knew the Old Mother had just given her daughter's life into her hands. Debts of honor were taken very seriously on the Spine of the World. She could order her cousin to throw herself from a cliff and she would have to obey. Isabeau had no wish to put her cousin under such an obligation, but she knew she had no choice. The Old Mother had spoken and the red-haired warrior had accepted her words.

"It is the seventh scar of the warrior you should wear upon your brow," her cousin said. "I have never seen such a fighter as you and the Pride of the Fighting Cats is famous for its warriors."

"I am no warrior," Isabeau said. "Truly the White Gods had their hand upon me today. I have never fought like that before and I never shall again."

"The White Gods must have some dread purpose for you, to guard and protect you so well," her cousin said in awe. Isabeau nodded, troubled and afraid.

"My name is Khan'katrin," her cousin said very low. "It means 'swift with a blow as the fighting cat'."

Isabeau was honored. The Khan'cohbans did not tell their names lightly. "I do not yet have a Khan'-cohban name," she replied, "but when I do I shall share it with you. I am called Isabeau in my own land. It means 'god is my oath'."

"Indeed, the gods do honor you," Khan'katrin said. "Come, you must be weary. I shall serve you and when you have eaten and rested, I shall fill your empty bag with grain and fruit and guide you to the edge of the Fighting Cats' land to make sure you do not go astray."

Isabeau thanked her and made her farewells to the council circle.

"May the White Gods aid you in your quest and keep the wolf from your path," the Old Mother said. Isabeau made the gesture of farewell and then followed her cousin out into the gloomy dawn.

Transformations

The wind blasted along the glacier, driving sharp needles of ice into every gap in Isabeau's clothing. Huddling her hood as close about her face as she could, Isabeau stumbled along, her vision filled with whirling snow. In her mind, she heard the words of the Soul-Sage's riddle in endless repetition.

"Speechless, you shall speak my name.
"Must you speak? Why then again,
"In speaking you shall say the same."

Although the verse became a sort of mantra, muttered in time with her dragging steps, the words became increasingly meaningless with each repetition. As the words' significance receded, so grew Isabeau's sense of hopelessness.

A thin, dark shape emerged from the whiteness, and Isabeau gave a little gasp of relief. A tree! She must be coming to the edge of the ice plain. Trees meant shelter and a chance to rest. On the plains the snow was packed so hard she had not even been able to dig herself a little ditch in which to crouch, even if she had been willing to risk being buried in snow.

She waited out the worst of the storm inside a lightning-blasted tree and woke to a deep, profound silence. After hearing nothing but the unceasing shriek of the wind for the last four days, the silence was a blessed relief. Isabeau dug herself out of the hollow tree and crawled out into a silver and black landscape. Overhead huge stars hung, while the untouched snow stretched in all directions, soft as velvet.

Isabeau smiled wearily and strapped on her skimmer. Although she knew the dangers of skimming at night, she could not pass up the first clear weather in days; besides, her night sight was exceptionally good. The snow slid past easily and her chilled limbs began to warm. Buba flew on ahead, the only motion in all that still, silent world.

They came over a slight rise and sped down the slope ahead, Isabeau's heart giving a little bound as she saw the dark peak of the Skull of the World rearing ahead. She had been afraid she had lost her way in the storm, having nothing but her intuition to guide her.

By the time the sun rose, the mountain filled most of the horizon, its tip wreathed in clouds. The glacier was narrow now, and steep. Isabeau had to turn and recross every few hours, gaining as much height as she could each time. Then it became too steep and she had to take off her skimmer and climb.

She crossed the ridge, the keenness of the wind snatching the breath from her mouth. The Skull of the World filled the sky, towering above the other peaks around it. She scrambled down the rocks quickly, seeing her destination so close, perhaps only a day's journey away. As she neared the snow again, Isabeau heard a strange keening sound, like a crowd of women sobbing and wailing. All the hairs on her body rose. She moved forward cautiously, straining to locate the source of the weeping. She came around a bulge of stone and saw, far below her, a river winding its way through a wide, deep valley. It ran swiftly over stones, a pure clear blue. Steam twisted above its ruffled surface, pale and thin as ghosts.

Isabeau smiled, recognizing the geography. She was in the land of the Pride of the Frost Giants, and that river was called the Lament of the Gods. She had often heard it described in the tales of the storytellers. The river wept, it was said, in grief for her lover the sun, whom the gods murdered in a jealous rage. Later, the gods were sorry and allowed the sun to be reborn once a year, but he could only travel the world for a few short months before again dying. Their love was still cursed, though, for when the sun came to kiss the river once more, the heat of his presence killed their daughter the mist.

Isabeau knew from the tales of the great naming-quests that she had to follow the Lament of the Gods to its source, but first she needed to find some way of getting down the cliff. It was growing dark so Isabeau began to look around for somewhere to spend the night. She left the path and scouted up one of the deep ravines that cut down from the mountainside. Buba flew ahead, almost invisible in the gloom.

The ravine had been cut by a fast-moving stream which dashed down the rocks in a series of little waterfalls. Here and there the stream widened into pools, wreathed with mist and bound all about with snow. When Isabeau paused to drink she was startled to find the water was hot and rather bitter on the tongue.

Suddenly she crouched down, unmoving, all her senses straining. Ahead she could hear guttural shouts and laughs, almost drowning out the snarl of some young animal which, high-pitched and desperate, spoke of terror and pain. Isabeau bit her lip, then quietly crept forward until she could peer over a pile of boulders to see what was beyond.

A snow-lion cub was crouched within a circle of squat, grotesque creatures who were tormenting it with their spears and clubs. The cub's white fur was wet and matted, and stained here and there with blood. One leg hung uselessly, but still it hissed and snarled, lashing out with its sharp claws at any of its tormentors that came too close.

With broad flat noses, slitted eyes, huge flapping ears, protruding yellow teeth, skin the color of a dead fish, and big feet with long, spreading toes, they were repulsive creatures. Isabeau thought they must be *uka*, a Khan'cohban word meaning "demon" and used to describe all the ugly, dangerous creatures of the mountains. In her own mind she named them goblins, for they looked just like an illustration in one of her old fairy books.

She knew she had to save the cub. There was no question of leaving him to be tortured to death by the goblins. The only question was how. Although short, the goblins were wiry and strong, and armed with a wide assortment of clumsy weapons. Isabeau chewed her thumbnail then, in a flash of inspiration, raised her hands to her mouth and gave the terrifying roar of a snow lion. The sound reverberated around the ravine, causing snow to slide from the rocks above and fall in a rattle of stones. The goblins stared around in terror. Poking a baby snow lion with their spears was one thing, facing an angry full-grown male another altogether. As Isabeau roared again, they gave a shriek of dismay and ran away up the ravine.

Isabeau ran out and gathered the cub up onto her lap, purring in reassurance. At first he cringed away from her human scent but she dragged off her glove and let him smell her hand, purring all the while. He sniffed suspiciously, his tail gradually stopping its lashing. She rubbed his head and he cuddled into her fur coat, kneading and purring in contentment. She looked about her swiftly, then stood up, staggering a little under his weight. Although only a baby, he was still heavy. Buttoning him up in her coat, she turned and hurried away down the ravine, knowing the goblins would come back as soon as their bravado returned.

Floundering through the snow, her arms aching with the weight of the whimpering, squirming cub, Isabeau followed Buba's soft hoots. At last the little owl found her a den under a fallen tree and she thankfully crawled inside. Conjuring a light, she examined the injured cub more closely and bit her lip in dismay. The goblins' spears had been filthy and even the most shallow of his cuts would become infected if she did not clean them properly. Reassuring the cub in his own language, she reluctantly built a fire, melted snow in her little pot, and crumbled a few dried herbs into the bubbling water. It took a lot of coaxing before the cub let her touch the wounds, and by the time she had finished, her hands were bleeding from innumerable scratches.

It was late and snow had begun to fall again. With the lion cub curled against her side, his little heart beating rapidly against hers, Isabeau drew her heavy coat closer about them both and fell immediately into a deep sleep.

The goblins found them just after dawn. Isabeau had thought they were safe thanks to the snowfall which had hidden her tracks. The lingering smell of her smoke drew them, however, and they came hollering and shrieking up the gorge, waving their weapons. Woken from her sleep by Buba, Isabeau peered out from under the fallen tree, remembering all the dreadful tales the storytellers told about the *uka*, who were said to consider Khan'cohban flesh a great delicacy, particularly if it had been well tenderized by a long, slow, painful death.

She scrambled back into the shelter of the fallen tree and drew one of the half-burned faggots out of the ashes of her fire. Pushing the lion cub behind her, she made the faggot burst into flame just as the goblins swiped their spears under the tree trunk. With shrieks of fear and rage, they leaped back and Isabeau thrust the burning torch at their faces. The goblins retreated and she gave one of the terrifying war cries of the Khan'cohban and chased after them. They ran squealing but circled around to jab at her from the rear. She swept the torch around, throwing a ball of flame at the nearest goblin with her other hand. Although he dodged, his coat of uncured animal skin took flame and he had to roll shrieking in the snow to put it out. A few more feints with the burning torch and the goblins retreated once more.

"Well, that's the goblins taken care o'," Isabeau said to the baby lion. "I must be on my way, though. What am I meant to do with ye then?"

He gave a little mew and she said consideringly, "I wonder where your parents are. Are ye an orphan? Or did ye just wander away? Ye were wet through. Had ye fallen in the stream? If so, ye canna have wandered far. Your den must be near where I found ye. Shall we go back there?"

He yawned widely, his pink tongue curling, then began to limp away down the gorge.

"So ye want to walk on your own four feet, then," Isabeau said. "Bide a wee, laddie! I'm no' quite ready."

The cub turned back to look at her, then sat with his fluffy tail curled around his paws. Isabeau let the jealous little owl crawl inside her sleeve, tied her skimmer to her back and thrust her supplies back in her satchel, then began to retrace her steps. The lion cub bounded along before her, hampered only a little by his bandaged paw.

They arrived back at the ravine and clambered along the rocky shore of the stream, keeping a close watch out for any more goblins. Although the sun shone in a blue sky overhead, the gorge was shadowy with many boulders and crevasses where the hideous creatures could hide.

Isabeau caught the sharp odor of lions and her step slowed, though the lion cub gave a little meow of excitement and bounded forward. Isabeau tested the breeze to make sure she was downwind, then crept forward, peering over a huge round boulder.

The gorge widened out into a sunlit corrie with caves in the walls and flat rocks around a little spring of water which bubbled too swiftly to freeze over, despite the snow that heaped the rocks all around. A lion was drinking at the spring, his thick white coat blending in with the mounds of snow. He was huge, with a magnificent black-edged mane and great golden eyes. Behind him three lionesses basked in the sunshine, their cubs playing by their side. To one side another lioness prowled about anxiously, sniffing the rocks.

As the injured cub rushed forward, she bounded down the rocks, deadly and graceful. She bowled the cub over with one heavy paw, then sniffed him all over. The smell of Isabeau's ministrations caused her to snarl and tumble the cub about roughly, and he whimpered a little and lay meekly under her paw, belly up. The lion raised his majestic head and walked ponderously over to where the lioness crouched over the cub. He sniffed the little lion all over and then lifted his lip in distate. Isabeau slowly crept away, glad to see the cub had found his parents but not willing to risk talking to them. Although she had been taught the feline dialect as a child, and the little lion cub had seemed to understand her, she had never before tested it on a real live lion.

Suddenly she heard the deep call of the lioness and the sound of swift motion. Terrified, she glanced over her shoulder and saw the cub's mother racing after her, golden eyes glowing, red mouth open. Isabeau screamed and fled. Then a massive paw struck her between the shoulder blades and she fell into the snow, banging her elbow on the rocks.

Shoulders hunched, arms over her head, she buried her head in the snow, expecting the agony of tearing flesh. When nothing happened she looked up cautiously. The lioness stood over her, warm breath clouding in the frosty air. Isabeau half rolled, trying desperately to purr, though her throat was dry with terror. The lioness bent her head and nudged Isabeau's shoulder. Then she delicately licked Isabeau's cheek, her tongue as rough as sandpaper. She was purring deep in her throat, the sound as loud and contented as a hive full of bees. Isabeau purred back and the lioness kneaded her shoulder briefly but painfully, then stood back, allowing Isabeau to gingerly get to her knees. Isabeau cautiously put up one hand and stroked the lioness's plush white fur, and she in turn rubbed her head against Isabeau's palm, purring still.

"It was my pleasure," Isabeau said huskily. "I'm glad I was able to help."

The lioness nudged her affectionately then turned and prowled away, her paws sinking deep into the snow. The cub frisked about her, attacking her black-tufted tail which swung gracefully behind her, and pretending to nip at her legs. Isabeau got to her feet, her throat thick with emotion, and saw the lion was watching her, his golden eyes inscrutable. She bowed to him and backed away, her legs shaking. At last she was out of sight and could turn and run, unable to shake off the fear the lion would decide she looked like a pleasant way of breaking his fast.

The sense that she was being followed did not dissipate as she hurried along the edge of the cliff, though she could hear nothing but the wail of the river and the occasional lonely cry of an eagle hovering far above. She turned often to scan the path behind her, but it was narrow and twisting here, following the bulges of the rock, so she could not see for any great distance. It began to angle downward sharply so she had to jump down the rocks in several places, once slipping on a patch of ice in her haste. Isabeau heard stones rattle behind her and quickened her pace.

She reached an open stretch of snow with a wonderful view down to the river but did not pause, though her stomach grumbled with hunger. Some irrational fear drove her on, glancing often over her shoulder. Then she saw movement on the path several bluffs behind her. She stared intently and recognized the squat figures of the goblins, running swiftly. There were twenty or more of them now and terror seized her. She broke into a run, casting around for somewhere to hide. It was difficult to run in all her furs, with the skimmer and satchel banging on her back. Soon she was panting and sweating. From her sleeve she heard Buba protest sleepily, but she blundered on. She came to a stand of pine trees and leaned against one, breathing harshly as she looked behind her. Then the goblins broke from the shadows and ran toward her, waving their clubs and spears, screaming with delight.

Isabeau threw down her satchel and skimmer and drew her axe from her belt. With a sweep of her hand she conjured a circle of flame about her. Maintaining fire with no fuel for it to feed on was exhausting work but she had no time to cut down dead branches from the trees. The goblins came to a halt beyond the flames, jeering and shouting and shaking their weapons. Then the biggest of them, a brute with a helmet made horribly from a dead wolf's head, began shouting orders. Quickly the goblins gathered up handfuls of snow in their great spades of hands and threw them on the fire. As Isabeau desperately fought to keep the circle of flame burning, one raised a slingshot and slung a stone through the hissing, dancing flames. It caught her on the temple and she fell back, keeping one off with her staff while swiping at the other with the little axe. Her concentration broken, the fire fizzled away and then the goblins were upon her.

Isabeau was in danger of falling beneath the onslaught, hideous hands with filthy, broken claws dragging at her furs, clubs falling on her shoulders and back. She shook them free and leaped high into the air, catching hold of the branch above her and swinging into the tree. Four began to quarrel over her satchel, tearing it open and spilling her precious grain into the snow, while wolf-head caught hold of the tree and began to shake it. The goblin with the slingshot peppered her with stones while the other goblins swiped at her feet with their spears. Isabeau clung tightly to the tree and tried to climb high, out of their reach, though the tree was shaking alarmingly. Her maimed hand was wrenched free and she fell, swinging from the other and trying desperately to regain her hold. Her dangling feet were hammered with blows before she was able to swing her legs up and grip the branch. Wolf-head jumped up and down, swiping at her with his spear. Isabeau felt the fur of her coat tear, then a sharp sting as the spearhead broke her skin. She winced away from the pain, managed to climb onto the branch and then swung higher. A spear was thrown at her but hit a branch and fell back into the goblins crowding around the tree.

Suddenly a roar reverberated around the glade. Isabeau almost fell in her shock and the goblins screeched with dismay. Wolf-head swung around and then gibbered as he saw the huge white lion bounding down the slope toward him. The lion's golden eyes were burning with rage and his mouth was wide open, his fangs gleaming. The goblins fell over each other in their haste to escape, but the lion was among them in seconds, claws ripping, great jaws tearing. Some fell screaming, the others all scattered and ran. Within moments the glade was still.

The snow lion sat and licked his bloody paw clean, staring up at Isabeau. Isabeau stared back. She watched the lion groom himself, wondering if he could climb and thinking unhappily that he probably could, faster and more easily than she could herself. He finished tidying himself up, wrapped his black-tufted tail around his paws, and settled down to staring at Isabeau with undivided attention.

Isabeau suddenly realized he was purring deep in his throat. She relaxed. He grinned at her, stretched, yawned and got to his feet. Every line of his body expressed satisfaction and pleasure. She watched his chest rise with his purring and longed to run her fingers through his magnificent mane and rub the velvet whiteness of his cheek. She was still too wary to come down, though, and so she watched in silence as he slowly padded back up the meadow and disappeared into the shadows. Only then did Isabeau climb down and shakily gather her things together, careful to avoid the bodies of the dead goblins.

The weather stayed clear and fine all day and Isabeau was able to make good time. She did not encounter any more goblins or lions, to her relief, though once she saw an ogre down in the river valley, crouched on the shore with a spear in his huge black hand. The cliff was not so steep or high here, with the land all about beginning to grow more gentle.

Late in the afternoon she rounded a bluff and saw a great wide sweep of snow running down to the river. Ahead the peak of the Skull of the World cut into the blue sky. The river wound down from the tall mountain, its waters running a pure blue-green and fringed on either side with copses of trees. All around were high cliffs and bluffs, while an eagle floated far above, wings black against the apple-green sky. Isabeau took a deep breath, unable to believe her journey's end was so close. The sun was sinking toward the mountain peaks and so she drew Buba out of her sleeve, cupping her in her hands and rubbing her tufted ears.

"Will ye find me a holt, dearling?" she asked. The owl blinked her great golden eyes sleepily, rotated her head then stretched out her wings. With a soft hoot she took flight over the broad slope. The apprentice witch strapped on her little sleigh and began to skim gladly down the slope toward the river, the owl gliding ahead of her.

Isabeau sped so swiftly the wind roared in her ears and tears sprang to her eyes. She gave a little cry of exultation and leaped off a high mound of snow so she could spin in the air. It had been some days since she had last been able to skim so freely. She landed with a hiss of ice flying, spun again and did a great swooping curve. From the corner of her eyes she saw something move, something huge. Her heart lurched. With a jerk of her body she came to a halt and pulled back her hood, shading her eyes with one hand.

Far above her a frost giant was lumbering down

the slope. Twelve feet tall, with a shaggy mane of hair and beard all stiff with blue ice crystals, he was dressed in a motley of white furs. Carrying a long ice spear in one hand, his eyes shone with a cold blue light. Each blundering step caused snow to slide down the slope with frightening speed. He shook his spear at her and bellowed, and cold fear shuddered in Isabeau's stomach. She took off, no longer swooping and swaying but fleeing straight down the middle of the slope. He leaped after her, gaining with every step, while a mass of snow raced ahead of him with a grinding, roaring noise as terrifying as his hoarse bellows.

There was a great whoosh. Isabeau ducked instinctively. The ice spear flashed past her, missing her by inches. It smashed into the hill before her, loosening another great chunk of snow. Isabeau swerved, her heart pounding sickeningly. She bent low, skimming as fast as she could, the ground rising and dropping below her. She risked a glance behind her. The avalanche was eating at her tracks, swallowing the sky.

Buba flew up into the air, calling to her desperately. *Soar-hooh,* the owl cried. *Soar-hooh high-hooh.*

Suddenly the world plunged away. The clamor of the avalanche rose up and engulfed her. Stars spun overhead. Although dusk had fallen, Isabeau could see clearly. The mass of snow was plunging down the mountain, drowning trees tiny as matches, sweeping out across the river and blanking its glimmer. The frost giant was swept away. Isabeau saw his agonized face disappear under the raging white torrent far, far below her. The world was tilting, a fiery rim of black mountains spanned by sweeping stars. The wind rocked under her like a river of cold fire. All was quiet. She was queen of the night, her wings binding the wind to her will, the stars streaming away behind her. She saw Buba glide before her, leading the way down into thick trees where the shadows gathered dark, but not too dark for her keen gaze to pierce. They came to rest on a branch.

I knew-hooh you-hooh were Owl, Buba said complacently.

Instinctively Isabeau's talons flexed and gripped and she shuddered her wings. Her mind shrieked a denial. She stared at Buba, the bird's round eye as big as the sun. The owl blinked once or twice and shifted from claw to claw. Isabeau looked around rather wildly. The branch they were sitting on was as large as an oak tree. The tree was like a tower. She could hear every sigh and murmur of the wind among the pine needles like the melody of an orchestra. She ducked her head down into her feathers, terribly afraid.

Why are you-hooh a-swoon? Buba asked. *We flew-hooh together through moon cool-hooh, soar-swooped together as owls should-hooh.*

But I am not really an owl, Isabeau replied shakily. *I do-hooh not know how to-hooh change back.*

Why would you-hooh want to-hooh? Buba said.

I'm not an owl, I'm a girl-hoooooh, Isabeau wailed. If she had had tear ducts she would have cried, but all that came out was a long mournful hoot.

Owl now-hooh.

Isabeau unclasped and clasped her talons anxiously. Buba huddled closer, rubbing her feathery head against her. *Come soar-swoop through moon cool-hooh,* the elf-owl said and took off into the darkness.

After a moment Isabeau spread her wings and flapped them. She was afraid to launch off as Buba had done. The ground was terribly far away. It would have been like jumping off the top of the Tower of Two Moons. She hooted anxiously and Buba materialized out of the darkness, white and silent as a snowflake. She landed beside Isabeau and, without warning, pushed her off the branch. Isabeau shrieked and flung open her wings. Effortlessly she glided through the darkness. A fretwork of twigs sprang toward her and she shrieked again and turned instinctively, narrowly missing a tree trunk. She ducked her head and flapped her wings, and her body obediently soared upward. Euphoria filled her. She was flying! She experimented, stretching one wing then the other, flapping them, holding them still. Through the dark forest she bumped and bounced, Buba gliding beside her.

At last they came to the edge of the forest, looking out across the river to the shoulders of the mountain. The Skull of the World towered at the head of the valley. Isabeau's euphoria faded abruptly. Here she was at her journey's end, and she was trapped in the shape of an owl. How was she to complete her quest and return to the pride as an owl?

I have to-hooh remember how-hooh I changed shape, she said to Buba. *If I can change shape once, I can surely do-hooh it again.*

The elf-owl only stared at her unblinkingly. Isabeau stared back. She would have liked to have rubbed her eyes and yawned, for she was very tired. It was hard to think, her head felt stuffed with feathers.

Noon for snooze-hooh, moon cool for soar-swooping, Buba said. *Snooze-hooh when sun comes.*

So-hooh snoozy, Isabeau said. She could hardly stretch her wings out and thought if she had tried to fly, she would have dropped like a stone.

Come, Buba said. *Creep inside tree and snooze-hooh. Owl shall pursue subdue for you-hooh.*

Isabeau obeyed. Within the bole of the tree was a snug little cave, lined with sawdust and pine needles. She huddled her wings about her and closed her eyes, sleep falling down on her like a giant hammer.

When she woke Buba slept beside her, head sunk into her ruffled-up feathers, a little pile of half-eaten moths and grasshoppers beside her. Once Isabeau would have been revolted by the sight. Now she felt a savage hunger awake in her and devoured the insects hungrily. Once her appetite was sated, she poked her head out of the hole in the trunk. It was daytime and the sun dazzled her eyes. She snuggled back down into the burrow, hunched her head down into her wings, her ear tufts erect. Just as she was dropping back to sleep, she involuntarily burped up a little hard pellet of undigested shell and wing. Feeling much better, she settled down into sleep again.

It was night when she woke. Hunger was gnawing at her once more and so she made no complaint when Buba led her out to hunt. They flew through the forest, snapping at moths and little night insects, searching out grubs under bark, and breaking open cocoons with their sharp hooked beaks. Isabeau managed her wings with some skill this time, though she did not have the same effortless silence as Buba.

When they were replete, the owls flew on through

the forest, flying for the sheer joy of it. They soared along the curve of the river and up the cliff, where two thin waterfalls created fantastical curtains of water, intricate as lace. As Isabeau soared up into the dark sky, a vague thought tugged at the back of her mind. She saw how the waterfalls streamed down on either side of a great yawning cave and said to herself, *The Tears of the Gods.*

She turned and swooped back, following the course of the falling water till she came again to the dark entrance of the cave. With her owl-sight she could see clearly in the darkness. With a great bulge of rock above the gaping cave and the two waterfalls streaming down from clefts on either side, the cliff face looked like a face contorted with grief. The entrance to the cave was like a mouth stretched into a howl. Memory came back to her, and with it a kind of horror. *The World's Mouth!*

Isabeau fled back to the sanctuary of the trees, owl-thought and human-thought jostling together. She crept into the burrow in the hole of the tree, though this time she did not sleep, just huddled there, her head nervously rotating to one side then the other. Buba crept in and snuggled down close for comfort.

I have to-hooh change back, I have to-hooh change back, Isabeau thought frantically. *How-hooh? How-hooh?*

Buba gave a derisive cry. *Why all this hooh-hooting? Just do-hooh it,* she said. *Not here-hooh though. Too-hooh huge for this nook-hooh.*

Isabeau calmed a little. *True-hooh.*

It was almost dawn and Buba was sleepy. *Snooze-hooh through noon-hooh, in moon cool you-hooh change, hooh-hooh?*

Hooh-hooh, Isabeau agreed, coughing up a little pellet and settling down to sleep.

In the pine-scented darkness Isabeau crouched on the ground, her head sunk down into her wings as she concentrated as hard as she could. Buba sat on a branch above her, rotating her head occasionally to scan the forest, her round eyes unblinking.

Isabeau had absolutely no idea how she had managed to change shape. One moment she had been fleeing down the mountainside, an ocean of snow crashing down upon her. The next moment, she had been soaring up into the sky, a tiny white owl. There had been no conscious decision, no setting of her will as was usual with the working of witchcraft. All she had felt was an urgent need to escape, to fly into the sky as Buba did.

Shapechanging was not something witches could usually do. It was magic out of fairytales and myths, magic against the natural order of things. It was not like conjuring fire, which shivered always in the air between sky and earth. It was not like whistling up the wind, which coiled and shifted around the world in constant motion anyway. It was not like Meghan's charm with animals, which came from loving them and understanding them, or Ishbel's ability to fly, which came from reversing the natural forces of the universe which caused a stone to fall to the ground and the stars to swing in their courses.

Yet Isabeau had seen tadpoles grow legs and lungs and become frogs. She had seen caterpillars spin themselves silken cocoons in which to sleep, gnawing their way free in the spring with new wings glued to their backs, transformed into butterflies. Nature was full of transformations.

And Eileanan was full of magical creatures that shifted from one shape to another. Isabeau had watched her friend Lilanthe shift into the shape of a tree many times, flesh growing leaves and bark and flowers in a most disconcerting manner. She had seen Maya the Ensorcellor metamorphose into her sea-shape, shining with silvery scales, her back curving down into a great finned tail like a fish. She had even watched as her father had been transformed back into a man after seventeen years trapped in the body of a horse. Thinking about those metamorphoses, Isabeau remembered what Buba had said. *Just do-hooh it.*

So Isabeau did. She imagined herself as a woman, her own well-known and comfortable shape, and concentrated all her will and all her desire on re-turning to that shape. And suddenly she was no longer a little white owl but a tall white woman, crouched shivering and naked in the forest.

It was bitterly cold. Isabeau hugged herself, her breath hanging before her face in frosty clouds. Above the forest the two moons sailed, one red as a blood plum, the other an ethereal blue. The sky itself was a midnight blue and strewn with stars and plan-ets that glittered with all the cold colors of crystals, white, green, amethyst, rose.

The wind flayed her like a whip. She had no idea what had happened to her clothes and supplies. No doubt they lay beneath mounds of snow, left behind as she had flown into the sky. Desperation filled her. Despite the clear sky, she would soon freeze to death without clothes or food. She could gather together firewood and build herself a fire, but even so it would be hard to keep herself warm. Already her feet were numb from the snow. It took only a few moments' hesitation before Isabeau changed back into an owl.

Buba hooted joyfully.

Too-hooh cool-hooh, Isabeau hooted back, ruffling all her feathers gratefully. This time she could tell the difference between human-sight and owl-sight. The moons were huge and pockmarked in the sky, but gray. Everything was gray, even the darkness. She could see the gradations of blackness clearly, able to discern the shape of twigs and grasses even in the darkest shadows. Her hearing was also much sharper and her ability to locate the source of the sound preternaturally precise. Since she was so much smaller, the trees were like towers, looming over her. She spread her wings and flew up to the branch where Buba perched, dancing a little in her excitement.

Together they flew through the trees and out across the river, which wailed and sobbed against the stones, shining oddly in the moonlight. Beyond was the wreck of the avalanche, roots and branches sticking up out of the mess of snow and stone. Isabeau's keen eyesight scanned the broken slope and she saw something metallic glint. Immediately they flew down and Isabeau transformed again into her own shape. She dug frantically and found the strap of leather with its metal buckle. She freed it from the snow and was relieved to find most of her tools still firmly attached to the belt. The mace was gone and the blade of the dagger had snapped but her axe and skewer were intact still.

Isabeau used the long skewer to poke through the

snow, ignoring the shivers wracking her naked body. The skewer knocked dully against something, and she dug with a bound of her heart. Happily she retrieved her skimmer from a deep drift of snow and knelt on it, though the wood was near as cold as the snow. Despite all her frantic searching, she could find no clothes or her satchel and so sat back on her heels with despair, her teeth chattering. She was so numb with cold she could hardly move; but she was reluctant to change back into an owl since she could not then carry her tools or skimmer away, or search through the snow.

Inspiration burst upon her. Isabeau shut her eyes, gripped her hands together and concentrated. She felt the change ripple over her, felt power and strength race through her like a draught of gold-ensloe wine. She opened her eyes and grinned as she saw furry white paws stretched before her. Gingerly she extended and retracted her wicked claws, lashed her black-tufted tail about, and turned around on the spot. It took a few moments to adjust but once Isabeau has grown used to the change, she stretched out her great strong body and leaped forward over the snow, intoxicated with her speed and grace. The owl flew before her, hooting mournfully, while far overhead a star died in a burst of silver fire, arching across the dark night sky.

Isabeau could have run and leaped all night, every muscle and tendon in her body working in perfect rhythm, her blood singing with the knowledge of her own magnificence. She rolled in the snow, licked her fur sleek once more, and explored the sudden acute sensitivity of her sense of smell.

In this way she found her coat, quite unexpectedly,

for she had merely been following the vague delicious smell of woman and *ulez*. With her massive
paws and sharp teeth, she dragged it free of the great
weight of snow covering it, and found some scraps
of torn cloth that had once been her shirt. A dim
memory stirred in her and she was able to sharpen
her focus upon what it was she did here, in this
snowy field under a frozen sky. She searched with
greater resolve, and found her leather leggings, with
the stockings still inside them, wet through. Then she
found one boot.

Joyfully she bounded about, searching for the
other, but it was nowhere to be found. At last she
gave up, sitting and licking her paws clean of snow,
conscious of having looked ridiculous bounding
about like a new-born kitten. When her coat was
clean and her poise restored, she rose and strolled
back to where the little owl was perched on the curve
of the skimmer, watching expressionlessly. It occurred to Isabeau the bird might be a tasty morsel,
for she was conscious of the emptiness of her belly.
The round golden eyes stared at her apprehensively
and Isabeau grinned. Immediately the round, white
bird spread its wings and flew up into the sky, hooting angrily. Isabeau told herself it would have been
like choking on feathers and followed a most delicious smell of dead meat instead.

She found its source, half buried in snow, and dug
at it hungrily. Although the meat was half frozen she
could still smell its slowly decaying reek and had
soon uncovered it, worrying at it with her teeth. It
was huge, an unwholesome bluish color, covered
with thick wiry hair and stiff as wood. Even exerting
all the strength of her jaws and neck, Isabeau was

unable to drag it free of the snow. She sat back, snarling, tail lashing. The huge digits clawed for the starry sky. Somewhere deep inside her she recognized it as a giant hand. Contradictory emotions warred in her, hunger and disgust. She soothed herself by tidying up her whiskers.

Overhead an owl hooted and Isabeau's ears swiveled. She watched the little white owl float down and settle on the massive dead fingers. Round eyes met slanted.

Moon-hooh go-hooh, the owl hooted, rather coldly. *Snooze-hooh soon-hooh?*

Isabeau was confused. Between her pride, her hunger and her disdain struggled a little thread of memory. The smell of the decaying frost giant's hand suddenly made her nauseous. She retched, and found herself on her hands and knees, red hair hanging over her face as she vomited into the snow. Her stomach was so empty only a thin bile burned her throat and coated her tongue with a foul taste. She swilled her mouth out with a handful of snow and looked about her blearily.

Seeing the giant's hand Isabeau scrambled away hastily, her stomach heaving again as she remembered dimly worrying at it with her teeth. She picked up her fur coat and huddled it around her, even though it was heavy and wet. She struggled into her leggings, the damp leather unpleasantly slimy. Buckling the belt around her waist she dragged on the one boot and shoved her dripping stockings into her pocket. She then pulled the skimmer along behind her as she slogged down the slope toward the river.

Soar-hooh? Buba called.

Isabeau shook her head. "I think I need to bide as a lassie a wee while," she replied grimly in her own language.

Why-hooh? The owl hooted.

"I just do," Isabeau replied, and slogged on, conscious that the sensation of cold in her bare foot was turning to a dangerous numbness. She reached the stony banks of the river and plunged her foot into its unnatural warmth. Life rushed back into the limb with a shock of pain, turning again to a fiery cold as she withdrew it. Gently she dried it on her coat, careful not to rub too hard, until her whole foot tingled with returning blood.

Isabeau looked about her wearily. Exhaustion lay on her, heavy as a mountain. She had to have shelter, fire and food, and quickly. The sky was beginning to lighten, and it had been a long, arduous night. She did not understand much of what had happened but until she had slept and eaten, she knew she could not puzzle it out.

There was a huge dead tree on the rocks, swept down in the spring floods. Isabeau gathered her will together and caused it to burst into flame. She had not much strength and the flame guttered quickly, but enough of the wood had caught for the log to begin to smoulder at one end. Isabeau could summon no more fire, but she fanned it and blew on it until little sparks began to fly. At last a small fire was burning and Isabeau could crouch before it, warming her chilled body. She passed into a half-doze, the damp coat huddled around her.

*   *   *

Isabeau woke some time later, shivering with cold. The sun was up but its light was thin with little warmth. She looked about her dazedly and immediately froze into stillness.

A young Khan'cohban boy was standing only a few feet away, his staff held before him. His horns were only just budding but his face was as stern and hard as any fully grown warrior, his long mane of hair as coarse and white. His staff was decorated with gray tassels and feathers, and beneath his shaggy coat Isabeau could see the same color stitched along his woolen shirt in the stylized shape of running wolves.

Rising slowly, Isabeau carefully and humbly made the gesture of greeting. He did not return it, looking her over suspiciously. Isabeau knew she must present a very odd sight, dressed as she was in only a shaggy coat, leggings and one boot, her red curls wildly tumbled and matted with leaves. Her bare foot was blue and mottled-looking, with white patches here and there showing frostbite was sinking its bitter teeth into her flesh. The skin of her hands was white and dead looking, her nails blue as the river. She could not feel her ears or her nose or much of her face. Isabeau knew she needed treatment fast.

Patience was needed with Khan'cohbans, however. She repeated the salutation, saying courteously, "Greetings to you, Khan of the Gray Wolves. I see you, like myself, are on your naming-quest. I hope that your path, unlike mine, has been free of frost giants and avalanches."

The Khan'cohban boy's face softened slightly. He gestured to her, saying: "But how can you be one of the Children of the Gods of White? Your hair . . ."

"You ask of me a question. Do you offer me a story in return?" Isabeau said.

There was a brief struggle between curiosity and the natural disinclination of any Khan'cohban to owe a story, then the boy nodded. "I ask of you a question," he said reluctantly. "Will you answer in fullness and in truth?"

"I will answer in fullness and in truth," Isabeau answered, and assumed the storytelling position. She told the story of her birth yet again, taking care to explain that she had no desire to inherit the Firemaker's position. Even though the lands of the Pride of the Gray Wolf were far away from the Fire Dragon's lands, the boy knew all about the Firemaker and accepted Isabeau's story with as much interest as it was polite for him to show.

She ended with an account of the attack by the frost giant. She made no attempt to explain how she had escaped the subsequent snow slide, despite her promise to tell the full truth, telling herself he had not asked the right question.

When she had finished, he hesitated then said gruffly, "What question do you wish to ask me?"

"I would gladly relinquish the question in return for some food and clothing," Isabeau replied, trying in vain to still her shivering.

He almost smiled then, and came to her side, setting down his gray-tasseled staff against the rocks and undoing his satchel.

He gave her flat bread and dried fruit, then threw down a brace of dead coneys he was carrying over his shoulder. Isabeau turned her body so she did not have to look at the poor little corpses, though she devoured the bread and fruit hungrily. He then relit her fire from the live coal he carried at his waist and began to cook them up some gruel from herbs and wild grains, roasting one of the coneys on a spit made from a twig. Isabeau wondered how it was he managed to have such a well-stocked satchel and remembered his pride owned the land closest to the Skull of the World. He had not had far to travel. It did not seem fair somehow.

While she waited for the porridge to cook, Isabeau hung her fur coat up to dry and ran naked over the stones to immerse herself in the river again. She knew from her training as a healer that the only way to treat frostbite was to return warmth and circulation to the affected area as quickly as possible. Strange as it seemed, the water of the snowbound river was hot and would warm her faster than anything else in this wilderness of mountains.

Isabeau chose her entry point carefully for the river was swift and powerful and the rocks sharp. She found a place where the water was calmer and slid thankfully into its buoyant warmth. Sweat sprang up on her face and neck, the water so hot it was almost unbearable. She bent her head back so all her hair flowed like ruddy water weed and the numb tips of her ears were submerged. She floated there, her hands and feet moving constantly to restore fluidity to her joints and to keep her close to the shore. Staring up at the blue sky, she felt pain thrill through the affected parts and rejoiced. Having lost two digits in the torture chambers of the Anti-Witchcraft League, she had no desire to lose any more.

She rolled and kept her face under the water as long as she could, then swam about gently, feeling warmer than she had in months. The horned boy

was watching her, gnawing on a coney leg, his face
trying hard not to show his amazement and fear.
Khan'cohbans never swam, Isabeau remembered. He
must think her very strange indeed, to show no fear
of the water and to swim as nimbly as any otter.

At last Isabeau swam to the shore and climbed out,
having to fight the force of the current. Immediately
the cold air lashed her but she ran over the stones
to the fire, shaking off the water and rubbing herself
dry with her companion's spare shirt. Her coat was
dry and warm now and she wrapped it around her
gratefully, then pulled on her woolen stockings and
the leggings, rather tight after being dried so close
to the fire. Her feet and hands were coming up in
blisters where the skin had been frostbitten and carefully she bandaged them in the torn pieces of her
shirt.

She then wrapped her feet in the damp shirt, having nothing else to keep them warm. The horned
boy shook his head and gently pulled her feet free,
wrapping them in his own shaggy coat. She looked
at him in surprise and he said, "The sun is warm
enough. Let the shirt dry by the fire and when you
are ready, you can give me back my coat."

"Thank you," she said and hungrily ate the bowl
of gruel he passed her. When she had finished, she
paused and then said tentatively, "You are very kind.
I am in your debt, for surely I would have died without your food and the loan of your clothes. I shall
remember."

He nodded, pleased. She leaned back against the
boulder, weary and replete. Hanging her head down
between her knees, she began to dry her hair with
her hands. The curls sprang up, red and bright, and

she shook them back, grateful for this trick which the Firemaker had taught her. It had always taken hours for Isabeau to dry her hair naturally, even in the warmer lands of the south. This way it took only seconds, though the first few times she had tried it she had scorched her hair, unable to control the heat evenly enough.

Feeling the boy's eyes on her she glanced up and immediately he looked away, embarrassed to be caught staring. "There are some advantages to being the get of the Firemaker," Isabeau said.

He said severely, "You will never make a good warrior with hair like that. It stands out against the snow like a flame. It is said a Scarred Warrior should move as swiftly and silently as the wind, be as unfathomable as clouds when hidden, and strike as suddenly and as fatally as lightning."

"I know," Isabeau said with mock humility. "My sister used to crop hers to the scalp and wear a white cap to hide it, but I do not wish to cut mine. I like it long. It used to hang down to my knees, but I do not suppose it will ever grow that long again."

"It would get in the way of skimming," he replied austerely, and she nodded, smiling.

"It does get in the way a lot, even braided. Still, I do not want to be a warrior so it does not really matter."

He was affronted. To be a warrior was the highest ambition possible for a Khan'cohban child. To sit on the pride's council of warriors was the only position of high status not passed down from parent to child.

He said coldly, "What is it that you wish to be that you so scorn the art of the warrior?"

"I want to be a sorceress," Isabeau said, and at his

blank look pointed to the scar between her brows. "A Soul-Sage." She knew there were many differences between the definitions of sorceress in her language and soul-sage in his language, but it was the closest she could come to making him understand.

Reluctant respect crossed his face. She saw he wanted to ask her more questions but his deeply ingrained politeness held him back. She pointed to the fire and it leaped up warm and golden. He warmed his hands, glancing at her enviously. "I can see why the Firekeepers were not pleased when the Firemaker was first given to the prides," he said. "It would be very agreeable to not have to guard my coal so carefully."

"It takes a great deal of effort to make fire, though," Isabeau replied, feeling her weariness pressing her down into the rocks like a giant fist. "If I am very tired or ill, I cannot summon it and then I must go cold, unless I too have a live coal. And if there is no fuel for the flame, then I must use my own power to feed it and that drains me of energy very quickly."

She flopped her head back and stared up at the sky. She saw a dark, bent shape hanging in the bare branches of a tree by the river. Idly she wondered what it was. A dead crow perhaps? Then her attention sharpened. She leaned forward, staring at it intently, and then grinned in delight. "This," she said, "is another useful gift." She held out her fingers and the dark, hanging thing twisted, tore itself free of the branches and flew to her hand. It was her missing boot.

"I must confess to envy," the boy said, "a vice indeed."

"Who knows, you may be able to do it, if you try

hard enough," Isabeau said. "Many people could do things they thought impossible if they gave themselves a chance. Does the *reil* of the warrior not return to their hand? If a *reil*, why not other things?"

She saw she had given him food for thought and leaned her head back again, closing her eyes. The sun was warm on her face and her stomach was full. She could sleep again. With difficulty she opened her eyes and said, "I thank you again. I am very tired for I had little chance to rest last night, and I wish to sleep and regain my strength before I face the World's Mouth. These stones are hard and cold, and it is too bright here, so I'm going to go back into the forest to sleep. I am in debt to you. Is there aught I can do or must I carry the *geas* until such a time as circumstances give me a chance to relieve it?"

He said rather shyly, "I walked up and down this river all day yesterday looking for some way to cross the river, for one must cross to climb up to the World's Mouth. Yet the river runs so fast and the stones are so sharp I can see no way. There are bones all along the shore and a dead girl . . ."

Isabeau was revolted. "Dead? Where?"

He pointed up the river. "On the rocks, near the cliff. At first I thought she was still alive but she has been dead a few days. She is all bloated . . ."

Chewing her thumbnail, Isabeau remembered the tales of the storytellers. *And in her grief, the river took into her terrible embrace many of the children of the Gods of White, for if her child could not live, why should the sons and daughters of the prides? And to the voice of her lament was joined the wails of the drowned, echoing forever through the Skull of the World.*

"Come, let me take a look," she said abruptly. "I

cannot teach you to swim in a morning but perhaps I can find the safest way across the river. It is only a small deed though, not to compare with giving me food and clothes."

"It will save me from joining the dead girl in the watery arms of the river," he said and she nodded.

The shore of the river was treacherous with rocks so they clambered back up into the meadows. The frost giant's hand still groped desperately out of the mess of snow, broken trees and rocks, and Isabeau gave a little shudder as they skirted the edge of the avalanche. The events of the night were like a nightmare, only dimly remembered yet constantly lurching darkly at the edge of her consciousness.

If she was to change shape, Isabeau thought, she would have to be careful not to let the beguilement of a particular shape work on her so that she forgot who she really was. As an owl she could fly the forest, swift and silent, queen of the night. As a snow lion she was strong and powerful and deadly graceful, sure of her own mastery. Even now she wished she could transform and fly up the course of the river instead of slogging through the snow, her skimmer banging on her back and her boots chafing her swollen and blistered feet. She could not take the horned boy with her if she flew, though, and so she made her way on her own two weary legs.

Luckily the snow was light near the river for the gorge was much warmer than the heights around it, thanks to the heat of the water. Many different trees grew, the gray branches of larches, birches and maples creating a fine tracery among the dark green spears of fir, native hemlock and spruce.

Although the sky was mostly cloudless, mist

drifted here and there over the sparkling river, looking so like the ghosts of dead children that Isabeau
could understand how the tales of the storytellers
came to be told. Dead trees littered the rocky shore
and groped out of the river itself, refuse caught in
their branches.

They rounded the bluff, and the cliff face rose before them. From this angle the resemblance to a
misery-contorted face was stronger than ever.

Below the cliff was a small shadowed loch, half
obscured by steam and spray, its surface roiling in
constant turmoil as the waterfalls plunged into its
depths. From this maelstrom came the river, running
hot and fierce over the stones and the broken trees.
There was a strong smell of sulphur, like the lake in
the dragon's valley. Like Dragonclaw, the Skull of
the World was a volcanic mountain, though it had
been many centuries since it had last erupted. Isabeau knew that for the water to run so hot even in
the midst of winter it must rise from deep in the
mountain where the rock was still molten. The further away from the mountain it traveled the cooler
it must become, but here at the source it was uncomfortably warm to touch.

The dead girl was lying face down on the rocks,
the lower half of her body still in the water so her
slack limbs jerked and rolled as the swift current
dragged at her. It looked as if she were trying to
crawl from the water but Isabeau could smell the
stink of putrefying flesh and see the discoloration of
her skin. Nausea sprang up in her throat and she
tasted again the bile of the night before. She had to
turn her face away and breathe deeply to avoid losing her breakfast.

"Should we not pull her out and bury her?" she said huskily.

"Why?" the boy asked. "The wolves will only dig her up, or the snow lions if they are hungry enough. She is embracing the earth as she should, and the Gods of White will have accepted her death as is fitting."

Isabeau remembered then that the Khan'cohbans did not bury or cremate their dead but left them out for the Gods of White. She swallowed and nodded, making the sign of Eà's blessing before turning away. She scanned the river and the long island of gravel that stretched out into the water at the base of the cliff. To climb up to the cave one had to reach that island, but the water roiled all around and rocks protruded from the foam like teeth. Even Isabeau would find it a difficult swim, with the waterfalls pounding from above and the strong currents dragging away down the river.

She thought a moment then said to the boy, "You will have to let the river carry you, not try and fight against it. Take off all your clothes for the weight will hamper you otherwise. Pack as much as you can in the satchel and pile it all on the skimmer. Then you must go in the river there, where the rock pushes out into the water. It is slippery from the falls so be careful. Push the skimmer in front of you and let your legs trail out behind so that you can propel yourself forward by kicking."

She lay on the ground and demonstrated and he nodded, trying not to show his anxiety. "All you need to do is reach that island. Angle across this way to avoid that submerged log. If you can, use the end of it to push off from, then kick as hard as you can.

If you miss the island you'll have to try and get to shore again and it is very rocky just here and dangerous. The skimmer will help keep you afloat and if you are lucky your clothes will not be too wet once you get out."

He nodded again and she said, "Try while I watch you. If you get swept away I shall do my best to save you."

He began to strip off his clothes. Isabeau did the same, then crouched shivering by the rocks as he clumsily entered the steaming water, gasping a little at its heat. The current caught him and dragged him downstream and Isabeau held her breath, shocked at its strength. His white head bobbed up and down in the rough water and several times he went under, but each time he managed to struggle free again, his hands gripping the skimmer tightly. Then the little wooden sleigh scraped the very end of the islet, slid and almost bounced back. The boy kicked mightily, then heaved himself out onto the gravel. For a moment he knelt there, head bent, panting, then he raised one hand to Isabeau on the far shore and got to his feet, shaking himself dry.

Thankfully Isabeau scrambled back into her clothes and then went to find a comfortable resting place. She would need to spend some time foraging and regaining her strength before she could face the World's Mouth. She wanted to have a full stomach herself before she was devoured by the gods.

EATEN BY THE GODS

It was black as Gearradh's womb inside the World's Mouth. Isabeau conjured a sphere of witch's light and looked about curiously as she made her way down a long tunnel, its walls black and glassy.

She could not help feeling uneasy. The air was full of moans and sighs, and a foul-smelling wind caressed her face with unpleasantly damp fingers. She reached her hand inside her sleeve to stroke Buba's soft feathers. The owl protested sleepily.

"Will ye no' come out and keep me company?" Isabeau coaxed. Despite herself, her voice was a mere thread of sound.

Snooze-hooh.

"It's dark as night in here," Isabeau whispered. "Your sharp eyes and ears would be most welcome." She added a plaintive hoot and felt the elf-owl sigh in resignation. Buba crawled out of her sleeve, flapped her wings, rotated her head around, then tried to crawl back inside the dark warmth of Isabeau's sleeve. Isabeau caught her around the body, just under the wings. *Please-hooh?*

Reluctantly the owl submitted to being placed on

Isabeau's shoulder, where she dug her sharp talons into the fur and huddled her wings around her. Buba was a creature of the forests and did not like this long dark tunnel with its glittering walls and unpleasant odor. She grumbled away in Isabeau's ear as the apprentice witch traveled down through the tunnel.

The deeper into the mountain they penetrated the stronger the smell became and the louder the noises. Sometimes they sounded like someone snoring, other times like the grumble and roar of an unsettled stomach. The heat became unbearable and at last Isabeau removed her heavy coat and carried it draped over her arm. Still her palms and forehead were prickling with perspiration and she knotted up her curls so they did not hang on her neck.

The tunnel was angling down quite steeply now and Isabeau saw an angry red glow ahead. The smell was so strong it choked her throat so she could hardly breathe. Forcing herself on, she rubbed her stinging eyes and saw the tunnel floor was split by a glowing fissure. Her heart sinking, she crept close to its lip and peered over. The fracture in the stone plunged as far as she could see, bubbling with black fumes and burning with that sullen red light. Then an arc of boiling stone flung itself up as if reaching for her. She threw herself backward. Heart pounding, she stood pressed against the wall, almost overcome by the fumes and her own fear. The far side seemed a mile away, though if it had been a little burn of clear water dancing along below her Isabeau would have leaped the gap gaily and without a second thought.

She could have transformed into an owl and flown

across the flickering red gap, but that meant leaving behind her furs, her skimmer, and her limp satchel with its handful of nuts, bark and lichens. No matter how scanty her supplies, it had taken Isabeau the better part of a day to collect them and she had no desire to emerge on the far side of the mountain naked, cold and hungry.

So she gathered together her strength and her courage, ran down the corridor and leaped the fissure, landing on the far side with space to spare. Her legs gave way beneath her and she stumbled and rolled in a tangle of fur, wood and flesh, lying still at last, rather shaken and bruised but alive. Buba flew down to rest on her hip, hooting in amusement.

"It's grand for ye," Isabeau said crossly. "Ye can just spread your wings and fly but I have to rely on my own two legs."

You-hooh could-hooh swoop-soar too-hooh, the elf-owl replied smugly.

"Only if I left behind all my stuff and I dinna wish to do that!" Isabeau pushed the owl off her hip, got up rather gingerly, and rearranged the skimmer and satchel so they no longer banged together around her neck but hung down her back as they should. She then set off down the tunnel again, limping slightly and wishing her furs were not so heavy.

It had been early morning when Isabeau had entered the World's Mouth and by the grumbles in her stomach she judged it must now be nearing lunchtime. The tunnel had widened out into a series of small caves, some with odd structures like smooth stalactites hanging from the walls. She spread out her coat and sat down for a rest, rummaging through her satchel for something to eat. The contents were

most depressing to a young woman with a healthy
appetite, but she chewed away on what she had,
stroking Buba's feathery head as the owl settled
down for a snooze. Then on into the darkness she
went, every fiber of her being longing for blue sky
and a fresh cool breeze once more.

The caves grew larger and more spectacular. She
came to one with a small loch in its center, the water
bubbling and hissing and wreathed with steam. As
Isabeau made her way around its shore, all pitted
and stained with gray ash, a sudden fountain of boiling water shot up into the air, spraying her with
sizzling hot droplets. Instinctively she flung up her
arm with its drapery of shaggy fur, which took the
brunt of the spray. Nonetheless one cheek and the
back of one hand still stung and she had to fight
back tears of shock and pain. She hurried away from
the pool, almost tripping over the body of a young
Khan'cohban boy who had not escaped so lightly. He
had not been dead for long, horribly disfigured by
the steam which had doused him. Isabeau saw with
some relief that he was not the boy who had helped
her. She drew the crossed circle, the sign of Eà's
blessing, upon his blistered brow then moved away,
her legs trembling. She crouched against the wall, as
far away from the sinister pool as she could get, and
dug around in her pack, until she found the little pot
of healing salve she carried there. She tended the
burns as well as she could with her maimed hand,
then quickly hurried on, feeling a growing hatred for
this dark journey.

A stream now ran down one side of the tunnel, its
waters hot and stinking. Isabeau followed it down
into a great cavern, deep in the bowels of the moun-

tain. It stretched as far as the eye could see, the stream widening into a chain of pools and small lochan that wound about among piles of gray ash and cinders. It was a most desolate scene, without the eerie beauty of the caves Isabeau was used to. The air was thick with fumes and she could see quite a few tunnels leading away, some glowing fiery red with puffs of evil, black smoke gusting out as if dragons slept within.

She did not know which way to go. Until now the route had been clear, for the tunnel had run down without any branches. Now Isabeau had to pick her way through the pyres of gray-black ashes, exploring each antechamber and tunnel in turn. Instinctively she kept away from the ones spitting sparks, choosing those that seemed safer. Buba flew ahead of her, saving her much time by discovering many dead ends. Some of the corridors ran for some distance before ending. In one Isabeau found a skeleton still dressed in rotten leather and fur, his horned skull fallen onto his chest as if the pile of bones merely slept, his staff resting between the bones of his hands.

She made the sign of Eà's blessing, the fingers and thumb of her left hand meeting in a circle, and crossed with one finger of her right. Then she hurried back down the tunnel, hoping she would find her way free soon and without any more horrible discoveries. The Khan'cohban children had been making the dangerous journey through the mountain for many years however, and there were remains of those who had failed everywhere. Some were recent and these were the most shocking. Isabeau found panic was welling up in her throat, clouding her judgment and making her hasty and anxious. She had to force herself to rest and eat again, and drink tea made from the hot, bitter water, and find somewhere safe to sleep.

She slept uneasily and woke in a sweat of terror. As there was no difference between night and day in the darkness of the caves, Isabeau got up and kept on walking, desperate to be free. She found a tunnel without obstacles or dead ends and her pace quickened. Buba was also uneasy and flew ahead, hooting occasionally in distress. The sound of her hoots echoed alarmingly and Isabeau had to bite her tongue to stop from snapping at her to be quiet.

The caves were different now, the walls of coarse granite and much broken. It was cold and the breathing sounds had changed, become recognizable as the roar of water. Isabeau's step quickened till she was almost jogging. She came out in a wide low cavern with a river that pounded through in a surge of foam and roiling gray waters. Isabeau's witch-light looked frail and small in that immense darkness. She saw, far away, a bobbing ball of orange flame and knew someone else was ahead of her, scrambling over the rocks in a desperate attempt to be free of the mountain. She followed the flaming torch and saw it pause as its carrier became aware she was there.

It was her friend from the river, the horned boy from the Pride of the Gray Wolf. His grim dark face lightened when he saw her and he made the gesture of greeting. "You have survived the eating by the gods then?"

"So far," Isabeau replied in his language and sat down beside him with a sigh. "Though I hope we are near the end for I fear I shall go stark staring mad if I do not see daylight soon."

He was uncomfortable, not recognizing the mordant humor of her words. "It has been known for madness to affect the name-questers but I hope this does not happen to you."

"So do I," Isabeau said, too tired to smile. He shared some of his bread and dried fruit with her and she ate gladly, sick of the bitter taste of bark and winter nuts. It was comforting to have company in that roaring darkness, and so they sat in silence for some time, half dozing despite the discomfort of the rough, wet rocks and the noise of the river.

"We should go on," she said after a long while. "I feel as if air and light are very close."

He nodded, his horned head casting strange shadows over the rocks. "I have not much light left," he said and she saw his torch was indeed flickering very low. He helped her up with the grave courtesy of the Khan'cohban and together they went wearily down the side of the river. His eyes dilated a little as Buba crept out of Isabeau's fur coat to lead the way, but he said nothing.

At last a dim gray light began to filter through. The torrent of the river filled most of the cave, so that they clambered along the walls, slipping and stumbling, sometimes falling to their knees. They saw the rocks grow close all about, the river bursting from a gap in its walls. Together they knelt and peered out, despair filling them as they saw the water plunging down the side of a steep black cliff. Down, down, into a deep ravine the waterfall plunged, flinging spray high into the air where it gleamed like diamonds in the light of the rising sun. There was no way out except down that raging torrent.

Isabeau looked at the horned boy. He was pale,

his mouth firmly compressed so two white dents appeared on either side of his mouth. "We have come the wrong way," he said. "We must go back."

"I canna!" Isabeau cried wildly in her own language, then controlled herself with an effort. "I do not think I can," she said then in his language, her hands gripped into fists. "I cannot stand the dark, and the smell, and those noises . . ."

"We shall die if we try and go out this way," he said reasonably. "Not even you who flies through water like an eagle through the air, not even you could survive that fall."

He was right, Isabeau knew it, but she stared out at the day longingly. "There must be some way," she whispered.

"There must, for many find their way free in the end," he answered, rather stiffly. She nodded and followed him back up the course of the river, despondency weighing her down.

Suddenly there was a sharp cry as the horned boy slipped and fell into the river. Immediately he was dragged down, his face disappearing beneath the tumult. Isabeau dragged off her skimmer and boots and dived into the water after him. The power of the current took her by surprise. She had trouble keeping her own head above the water, which was cold as ice. Isabeau felt her strength being sapped away and she struck out, searching desperately for any sign of her companion. Then she saw his white head break through and plunged after him. Her fingers brushed against the wool of his shirt. She gripped tightly and tucked one arm about his neck, keeping his face above the water. He was incredibly heavy, dressed as he was in furs and heavy boots, with his skimmer

still strapped to his back and banging against Isabeau
with every stroke. She would have freed him from
his burdens if she could but there was no time and
so she merely struggled to hold him afloat, using the
buoyancy of the wooden skimmer as much as she
was able.

Kicking as strongly as she could she struck out for
the rocks, racing past at an incredible pace as the
river dragged them toward the falls. At last she was
thrown against the shore and managed to wedge her
legs against a rock long enough to heave him halfway out of the water. Her legs slipped and she was
dragged back into the torrent but Isabeau was a
strong swimmer and managed to kick her way back
to shore, dragging herself out some feet downriver
from where the horned boy lay, half in, half out.

She was sick with weariness but she knelt beside
him and managed to drag his slack body from the
river, pressing the water out of his body with both
hands on his chest and breathing her own breath into
his lungs. He coughed and vomited, and she rubbed
his cold limbs and squeezed the water out of his hair
and clothes, trying to draw upon her powers to dry
them. Her strength was all gone, though, and she
could not summon even a glow of warmth to comfort them.

There was nowhere to rest beside this cold, roaring
river and so together they stumbled back up the great
length of the passage and into the warmth of the
cavern above. Isabeau hung their clothes out to dry
at the mouth of the largest tunnel, where hot air
gushed out in a surge of smoke and flame. She made
them a thin porridge with her nuts and herbs, his
wild grain and the water from the bubbling pool,

wishing she had some honey to sweeten its salty bitterness. Then they cuddled together in the warmth of Isabeau's fur coat until at last their shivering ceased.

"I thank you," the horned boy whispered. "I am in your debt."

Isabeau shook her head. "You saved my life out on the mountain; now I have saved yours. There is no debt."

He nodded, and they leaned their naked bodies together, taking comfort in the closeness. All around them the darkness breathed and gurgled and fire leaped in the corners, illuminating for a few seconds the bizarre shapes of the ash piles. Buba slept on Isabeau's knee, her tufted ears sticking straight up, her head hunched in her wings.

Isabeau woke again some hours later. Only the red glow of the fiery tunnels cast any light and she lay and watched their sullen flicker with her throat all choked. Between them, she and the horned boy had tried all the other corridors and Isabeau knew they now had to brave the more dangerous routes. Her companion woke some time later and they packed up their things in a depressed silence, crossing the cavern with barely a word spoken.

"We may as well take that one," Isabeau said with a gesture toward the brightest of the glowing tunnels. "We have tried all the safe and easy routes, we should just bell the cat and have it over and done with."

Although he did not know the phrase, the horned boy understood the intonation and gave a little shrug. No Khan'cohban warrior-to-be would ever allow himself to appear less bold and courageous than another, particularly one that was not even a true Khan'cohban. So despite the ferocious redness of the light, the puffs of black smoke, the whole menace of the yawning tunnel mouth, he led the way without hesitation.

Heat struck them like a blow as soon as they entered. Fiery shadows danced all over the walls and ceiling and their eyes streamed with the fumes. Isabeau immediately regretted her rashness but she could not turn back now, as proud in her own way as the Khan'-cohban boy. Carefully they made their way forward, the ground rent here and there with fissures that groaned and smoked and sizzled. Even through the thick soles of her boots Isabeau could feel the scorching heat of the ground. Every breath of air was like swallowing ashes. She covered her mouth with a strip torn from her shirt and after a moment her companion followed suit.

They came to a fiery pit, seething with molten rock. Black on the surface, it heaved and bubbled like burned porridge, here and there pockmarked with red blisters that popped in a spray of white-hot fire. There was only a thin lip of rock around the edges which they had to creep along, gripping the smooth ridges of the walls with fear-stiff fingers. Somehow they made it safely around the cauldron of lava, and were able to hurry away down the tunnel with stampeding hearts. Behind them they heard a giant hiss and looked back to see an arc of fire leaping up like the lash of a burning ship. Had they still been edging their way around the rim of the lava bowl, they would have both been killed.

The tunnel ran smoother and cooler, the fiery cracks in the rock becoming smaller and less frequent. Both Isabeau and the horned boy walked swiftly, despite their fatigue, while Buba floated before them like a blown scrap of ash. They saw a glare of light ahead and broke into a ponderous run, weighed down by their furs and skimmers and their weariness. The tunnel led down into a cave, all grooved and ridged like black ice, with a small crack where daylight leaked in. They had to crawl on their hands and knees to get out, their skimmers catching on the rock and having to be freed. Then they were outside, breathing in great gulps of fresh air, tangy as greengage wine, their eyes dazzled with light.

They were standing on a snowy slope that swept down in soft white folds as beautiful as a banrìgh's wedding gown. The sun was in their eyes, rising into a sky all blue above, with clouds heaped along the horizon like another range of mountains. All was quiet.

"We have been devoured by the gods," the horned boy said with awe in his voice. "Now what do we do?"

For the first time in days Isabeau remembered the enigmatic riddle the Soul-Sage had told her.

"Speechless, you shall speak my name.

"Must you speak? Why then again.

"In speaking you shall say the same," she quoted. They looked at each other, then the boy said, very slowly, "I think we had best part, so we can hear what the White Gods must say to us in solitude."

Isabeau nodded. They gripped each other's forearms in the way of the Scarred Warrior, then made the gestures of goodwill and farewell. "I shall not forget you," he said.

"Nor I you," Isabeau replied. "I wish I knew my name to tell you."

"Perhaps we soon shall," he replied in a puzzled,

rather anxious way. Both knew they had passed their initiation. Where, then, was the voice of the White Gods telling them their name and their totem?

Isabeau watched him slog his way down through the snow then followed suit, too tired to bother strapping on her skimmer. She came to a little copse of trees and sat with her back against one, looking out over the valley. Winding its way down through the valley was the Lament of the Gods, but she was too far away to hear its wailing. All was quiet.

"Speechless, you shall speak my name.

"Must you speak? Why then again,

"In speaking you shall say the same."

Isabeau spoke the words aloud, though softly. Buba perched on her knee, blinking her eyes sleepily. Isabeau repeated the riddle. What name is it that is said without speaking?

It is so lovely and quiet, she thought rather drowsily. No bird sang here in the wilderness of snow, no insect chirruped. There was only the silence of snow. "Be as snow," her Scarred Warrior had told her many times. "Snow is gentle, snow is silent, snow is inexorable." *Like the White Gods*, Isabeau thought. *Cruel and cold and without voice. Why do they no' speak to me?*

Her thoughts drifted. She wondered rather crossly why the Khan'cohbans were always wrapping things up in riddles. It was like Brun, the little cluricaun that had helped save her life after she had been tortured. He too had loved to speak in riddles. Isabeau wondered with an odd little tremor of laughter whether the cluricauns and the Khan'cohbans were related. One so tall and white and grim, the other little and hairy and bubbling over with mischief.

Buba crept into Isabeau's sleeve to sleep, murmuring a little in her soft owl voice. Isabeau rested her head on her arms, closing her eyes. She was very tired. *Why do the White Gods no' speak?* she thought with a thread of panic. *I canna return to the pride if I do no' find out my name . . .*

The odd thing about the cluricaun was that so many of his riddles had proved to cut right to the very heart of things. At the time they had seemed like nonsense but later he had proved to speak with rare insight and clarity. Were the Khan'cohbans' riddles like that?

The First of the Storytellers had said, "When you seek, you cannot find." It had made Isabeau laugh at the time. It had seemed so typically meaningless. Yet here she was, seeking the meaning of the riddle, seeking her name and totem, seeking desperately for some vision or voice that would tell her what she wanted to know. Seeking and finding nothing. Nothing but silence.

Something seemed to connect in her mind. Isabeau opened her eyes and looked up at the pure, empty sky. *What name was it that was said without speaking? What name was it that was said with silence? Silence itself, o' course.*

And so the White Gods truly were voiceless, if they spoke with silence. How then was Isabeau to find out her name?

She remembered her guardian Meghan saying a long time ago as she had set out on her first quest: "The journey itself will be your first lesson." That had surely proved to be the truth. Isabeau had learned much about herself and the world on that first difficult journey down to the sea. And she had learned a great deal on this journey too. She had discovered strengths in herself she did not know she had. She had found her true Talent.

Excitement suddenly thrilled through her. She scrambled to her feet, ignoring the soft murmur of protest from her sleeve. Tiredness dropped away from her like a cloak. She knew now what her name was. Khan'tinka, She of Many Shapes. Isabeau the Shapechanger.

That afternoon, as she came down toward the river, Isabeau saw a great clenched talon protruding out of the snow, just like the frost giant's hand had out of the avalanche that had almost killed her. She knelt beside it and saw it belonged to a dead blizzard owl. Half buried in the snow, its round head was bent at a strange angle, its eyes closed. She took the broken knife from her weapons belt and carefully cut off the owl's talon. As large as her own hand, it was fringed with white feathers with four hooked, black claws. Under the pressure of her knife, the bone snapped cleanly and she hung it around her neck with a length of plaited cord.

As she rose to go she saw the owl's talon had been resting upon a great stone of white quartz crystal. Wonderment filled her. She lifted it up and felt her palm tingle as it came in contact with the stone. She stood for a long time, turning it in her hands. It was perfectly symmetrical, with twelve faces that flashed with color as the light glanced off the edges. She had only ever seen such a perfectly formed uncut crystal once before. That had been mounted on feet shaped like claws and was one of Meghan's most treasured possessions. Carefully, with a sense of fear and awe, Isabeau wrapped the stone in the remains of her old shirt and tucked it into her satchel. Indeed the White Gods had spoken.

The journey back to the haven took Isabeau over a month. She followed the course of the river most of the way, finding a greater variety of foods growing near the warmth of its waters. She stayed for a few days at the haven of the Pride of the Gray Wolf, feasted and honored by the family of her young friend. He wore with pride the shaggy gray skin of a timber wolf, which he had fought and killed the afternoon of their escape from the mountain. He was named Khan'moras, meaning "swift and cunning as the wolf." On his left cheek was the bloody red line of a newly cut initiation scar.

Her satchel filled to bursting with fresh supplies and new clothes to replace the ones she had lost, Isabeau at last left the warmth and shelter of the Gray Wolves' cave and set out on her journey home. Although she could not skim along the shore of the river, it was swift and easy walking and she made fairly good time. Buba was happier in the river valley, for there were many trees in which to roost and many varieties of insects on which to feast. Isabeau was happier too, able to swim in the warm waters and rest in the sweet-scented dimness under the pine trees.

Finally she had to leave the river and climb up into the mountains again. It was slow and difficult progress, hampered by the foul weather and the steepness of the terrain. At last she crossed the moun-

tain height and was able to skim down toward the
haven of the Pride of the Fire Dragon.

She slogged wearily up the slope to the haven late
one evening in the last few days of winter. The sun
had set and it was very cold, but Isabeau was too
eager to reach home to look for somewhere to camp.
She was challenged by one of the sentries and had
to shout the password to avoid being shot with his
crossbow. Once he realized who she was, though, he
brought her in speedily to the Firemaker and she was
greeted with more warmth and excitement than she
had ever seen any Khan'cohban demonstrate.

Isabeau had not been the only child of the pride
to be sent on her initiation journey that winter, but
she was one of only three to return and the last. They
had given her up for dead and Isabeau was rather
shocked at the ravages her long absence had made
to the Firemaker's face. Her great-grandmother
seized her in her arms and held her against her heart.
Isabeau was shocked to see tears reddening the
heavy eyelids.

At last the Firemaker let her go and Isabeau knelt
before her, hands folded on her lap.

"I would ask of you the story of your name," the
old woman said with great ceremony. "Will you answer in fullness and in truth?"

"You ask of me my name. Do you offer me your
name in return?"

"I do," the Firemaker replied. Isabeau bowed her
head and crossed her legs, her hands upturned on
her thighs. She was weary and cold, and all her
clothes were still damp from the snow, but she took
her time over the telling as she ought. Only the Firsts
and the Council of Scarred Warriors were there to

hear her story and they listened with great interest, occasionally commenting to each other with a guttural word or emphatic gesture.

When she told of her transformation into an owl, a stir of surprise ran over them. Isabeau saw the Soul-Sage smile and finger the withered talon that hung around her neck. Isabeau described her difficulty in changing back into her own form and then her hunt through the snow in the shape of a snow lion. This time the stir of amazement was more marked.

At last Isabeau reached the end of her story. She showed the assembled listeners the owl's talon that hung between her breasts. They were all impressed, even the Scarred Warriors who had at first glanced at Isabeau with some disdain for she had not worn the freshly killed pelt of some predatory animal. It was not unknown for questers to return without a new fur cloak. Isabeau's own father had returned with a live dragon to show his mastery over a beast of power and prestige. He had been one of the greatest warriors the pride had known, even though he had not worn the skin of his totem. An owl's talon was a sign of great power, though, and so they looked at her with new respect and even awe.

"So it is that I am named Khan'tinka, She of Many Shapes," Isabeau finished, "and can fly with the owl, queen of the night, messenger of the gods."

She bent her head and silence fell over the circle of listeners. Then the Firemaker said, very softly, "Welcome to the pride, Khan'tinka. I am Khan'lysa, proud and strong as the snow lioness."

The First of the Scarred Warriors repeated her words and then told his name: Khan'derna, brave as the saber leopard. The Soul-Sage was next. She was named Khan'deric, swift as the falcon. One by one the council of warriors told her their names in strict order of their hierarchy. Isabeau's Scarred Warrior teacher was named Khan'bornet, meaning "powerful as the bear."

When all had told her their names, she was brought a mug of a heady brew of fermented berries called *ika*. She drank deeply, almost choking as it scorched its way down her throat and into her belly. Heat spread out through her limbs, bringing with it light-headed euphoria. One by one the others all drank, calling the blessing of the White Gods down upon her. Then the Soul-Sage came toward her, her sharp dagger in her hand.

Isabeau had only time for a flash of fear then the Soul-Sage had slashed her left cheek with two swift movements. There was a brief burning sensation, then Isabeau felt the warm blood gushing down her face. She put up her hand and it came away bloody, though she felt little pain. They gave her more *ika* to drink then brought ice to press against the wound. After a while Isabeau felt her cheek throbbing but the *ika* had brought her a pleasant floating feeling and she hardly noticed the pain.

Then she was presented to the rest of the pride, though her name remained a secret, known only to those who had heard the full story. There was a feast in honor of her return and Isabeau was served first, much to her pleasure. Child no longer, she would never again have to wait with the little ones for the scrapings of the pot. Among the Khan'cohbans, drink and food were never taken together, but after they had all eaten their fill the *ika* was offered around

again, and there were mock wrestling matches and
displays of acrobatic finesse. Isabeau's head was
swimming and she sank into an exhausted sleep even
while the Khan'cohbans still leaped and somersaulted around the cave.

She woke in the morning with a pounding head,
a dry mouth and thick tongue, a heaving stomach,
and a cheek that throbbed like a burn. All she could
face was melted snow before burrowing back into
her furs to sleep again. When she woke the second
time she gingerly felt the cut on her cheek, which
was stiff and sore, then bent over one of the pools
of water so she could see her face. Dimly she saw
the shape of a triangular scar slashing her left cheek.
Carefully she rubbed in healing salve, ate a little
bread and fruit, and crawled back into her furs to
sleep again.

It was morning once again when she woke and the
cave was virtually empty, the children all out tending
the *ulez*, the hunters in search of game. The Soul-
Sage sat beside her, eyes shut in meditation. As soon
as Isabeau sat up, hand to her dizzy head, one hand
groping for her wooden drinking cup, the shaman's
eyes snapped open. She passed Isabeau the mug
filled with cold water. Isabeau drank thirstily, wondering how she could still feel like a wrung-out rag
two days after the feast. The Soul-Sage smiled grimly.
"*Ika* makes even the strongest warrior wish for the
peace of death the morning after," she said. "Show
me your stone."

Isabeau glanced up at her, wondering how she had
known about the crystal. She had meant to bring the
glittering stone out to show around proudly but
somehow it had slipped her mind. Isabeau had not

thought of it again. She showed the quartz rock to her teacher, who examined it closely though she did not take it into her hands.

The wise woman nodded slowly, then said, "They call this the icestone. It is believed to be fossilized ice. A stone of power for clear-seeing, future-seeing, far-seeing. It is a mark of great favor from the gods of ice and snow. Guard your first stone well, Khan'tinka."

It gave Isabeau a little thrill to be called by her new name. Shapechanger. She wondered what Meghan would say when she knew. A great longing woke in her to see her old guardian and share with her the tale of her adventures.

"It's time for me to go home," she said abruptly.

The Soul-Sage nodded. "Many long journeys before you are worthy of the seventh scar," she said, tracing the mark between Isabeau's forehead with one long, multi-jointed finger. "The White Gods have shown you favor so far. You are in their debt. In time they will ask for payment. In the meantime, remember what you have been taught. Learn and keep silence."

Isabeau nodded. "I shall," she promised and knew that was a *geas* in itself.

THE CAVE OF A
THOUSAND KINGS

The Cave of a Thousand Kings arched high overhead, ripples of reflected light wavering all over the smooth gleaming walls. Light struck down from an aperture high overhead, penetrating deep into the sea-green water that surged and swayed against the rocks. At the far end of the great cavern a waterfall fell down in silvery cascades which flung up a haze of steam and spray. Rising from this mist was a tall, sparkling throne, built on the pinnacle of a rock that thrust up through the tumult of foam at the waterfall's foot. Carved from crystal, the throne caught the wide ray of light and refracted it into sparks of icy color that dazzled the eye.

Reclining on the crystal throne was the Fairgean king. As sleek and muscular as a tiger shark, his skin had the same opalescent shimmer as the sheets of mother-of-pearl shining in the rock. He wore nothing but a cloak of white seal fur and a jeweled skirt of seaweed, the waistband hung with daggers of both steel and fretted coral. Around his burly neck hung a great many necklaces of dried seaweed hung with coral and jewels, and he wore a coronet of pearls and diamonds. Set in the center of the crown was a black pearl the size of a storm petrel's egg, which gleamed with mysterious and subtle color. His hair flowed down from beneath the coronet like a curtain of black silk, and two thick, notched tusks curved out from either side of his lipless mouth. It was a cruel face, contemptuous and unforgiving.

At his feet sat his three favorite wives, all with eyes as silvery-pale as moonlight on sea foam, and blue-black hair tied back with pearls and white coral. A human concubine was chained to the very base of the rock, her matt skin almost as blue as theirs with cold, her fair hair as elaborately arranged. There was nothing but hopeless despair in her eyes, though, and she cringed down whenever the King's voice rose in a roar, which it often did. She was not chained to prevent her from trying to escape but to stop her from trying to drown herself.

The King's seventeen sons rested on rocks on either side or wrestled together in the icy-cold water. Although the waterfall which cascaded down from the higher caves was steaming hot, the depths of the pool in the Cave of a Thousand Kings had never been plumbed. It was as cold as the sea outside where icebergs drifted.

The many tiers of the cavern were crowded with Fairgean warriors, talking, gambling, listening to the songs of the concubines and the eerie wail of the conch choir. There were three hundred in all, the elite of the Fairgean martial force, resting safe and warm from the ice storms that howled outside.

Nila, the seventeenth son, sat as far away from the throne as he could get. Unlike his brothers he did not wear a great number of necklaces and bracelets twisted with coral, turquoise, amethyst or sea-diamonds. He wore only the black pearl he had found in the summer seas, hanging from a fine sealskin cord.

Fand came and knelt beside him, offering him a tray of delicacies. He accepted a slither of raw fish heaped with fish eggs without looking up from his game of sea-stirk knuckles. Another slave refilled his goblet with sea squill wine. Fand waited for her to move away before saying, very softly, her hair hanging over her face: "Beware. I feel cold currents of evil intent. Watch yourself."

Nila bent back his head to toss the morsel of food into his mouth. As he swallowed he glanced around the cavern. At least three of his brothers were watching him, their lipless mouths stretched in pleased anticipation. As his eyes moved over their faces, they glanced away, trying without success to subdue their smiles. Nila felt all his muscles tighten. It took an effort of will to turn back to his game without letting his expression change. He cast his sea-stirk knuckles, then lifted the goblet of wine to his lips. If all his senses had not been strained to the limit he may never have noticed the faint tingle in his lips as he drank. He did notice, though, and every nerve and sinew in his body jangled. Involuntarily he spat his mouthful out, causing those about him to glance at him in surprise.

"That sea squill must have been past its prime," he managed to say. His tongue felt stiff.

He got to his feet with a bow and a quick word of excuse and made his way to the back of the Cave

of a Thousand Kings. Steps led up past the cascades
and into the dark labyrinth of tunnels behind called
the Fathomless Caves. Stumbling a little, he climbed
out of sight then bent and washed his mouth out
again and again. The inside of his mouth and throat
were completely numb. Once or twice he retched,
though he managed not to succumb to the waves of
hot sickness beating through him. At last Nila
stopped, his head hanging, trembling with delayed
shock. If he had swallowed that mouthful of wine,
he would have died an agonizing death. He would
be dead now, and all his brothers smiling to themselves.

At last he got up and found his stumbling way to
his cave. Although it opened out onto the side of the
cliff, the cave entrance was sealed over with ice now
and inside all was dark and silent. He carefully shook
out his seal furs, then curled up inside their warmth.
Inside he was still shaking.

It was many hours before the numbness in his
cheeks faded to a burning tingle that almost drove
him mad. He was parched and dry, his limbs weak,
his stomach uneasy. Even though he had not swallowed the poisoned wine, enough had seeped
through the pores of his skin for him to be made
exceedingly uncomfortable. At one point he became
aware of a cool hand on his brow, then Fand was
lifting his head and feeding him slivers of ice. He
slept then, though he was much troubled with fevered nightmares. He woke with a jerk much later,
to find her still there with a goblet of icy water to
soothe his inflamed throat.

"You should not be here," he managed to say.
"They will suspect . . ."

"I have been and gone," she whispered. "Lie still, sleep. I will watch over you."

He woke sometime during the night to see his father standing over him, a priestess holding a nightglobe high so its greenish, luminous light cast peculiar shadows over the fur heaped bed. His father was frowning heavily.

"What ails you, boy?" he asked.

"Must have been something I ate," Nila managed to reply.

The King looked at the priestess and she grinned. Her teeth shone oddly in the luminescent green.

"Loreli poisoning, my blessed liege," she said in the sibilant tones of the Priestesses of Jor.

The King roared with rage. "My stupid, weak-willed, cowardly sons!" he shouted, striking his palm with his fist. "Do we not have enemies enough without the sons of my loins quarreling like boxerfish? Do they not see we need all of our strength if we are to grind those Jor-cursed humans to sand? What have I done to be worthy of such blind, ignorant, jelly-spined children?"

"Your seventeenth son, the least of all the princes, has been foolish enough to flaunt a black pearl upon his breast," the priestess hissed.

The King smiled thinly. "So I had observed. Pride and ambition have always been the defining characteristics of Those Anointed By Jor. Yet if my seventeenth son thinks to sit upon the Crystal Throne, it is his brothers and I who should be giving our wine to the Cupbearer to taste. Yet somehow I do not fear. This tuskless boy is too feeble and soft to dare squeeze the loreli fish into my wine or hide a sea urchin in the beds of his brothers. He is nothing but a bawling babe, weak as sea anemones' piss."

Nila lay stiff and silent, pricked with humiliation that the King should speak of him so before a woman, even if that woman was a Priestess of Jor. The King laughed contemptuously, prodded Nila with one wide-webbed foot, and said, "Do not sleep too deeply, my son." He turned and left, his necklaces and bracelets rattling.

The priestess hung over him for a while longer. The viperfish in the glass orb swam about lazily so the light shed by its luminescent organs flowed over his face in soul-troubling rhythms. Although he could not meet her eyes, he saw her grin and then she too was gone in a swirl of sealskin.

When Nila was sure they had really left, he lifted his bedcovers so Fand could crawl out. It was too dark in the cave to see her face but he could feel how she was trembling. He held her close but she resisted him. "What if they had caught me, Nila?" she said in a scared little voice. "I could feel her eyes on me through the furs like hot suns. I know she knew I was there."

"What of it?" Nila asked. "She would just have thought you my concubine. Even the lowest of the King's sons may take a woman to his bed if he so desires." There was a trace of bitterness in his voice.

Fand shuddered. "I do not know why, but my skin is crawling. When I saw the glow of the nightglobe and heard their footsteps down the hall, I knew I had to hide. My heart was hammering the whole time and I could hardly breathe . . ."

"The priestesses make us all feel like that," Nila

comforted. "There is no need for you to fear them, though. You are one of the King's slaves. They will leave you alone." He pulled her down to rest within the circle of his arm, and she nestled her head into his shoulder. "I should not stay," she whispered. "Someone will notice . . ."

"Let them," he replied tersely and felt her warm breath against his skin as she sighed.

When Nila appeared in the Cave of a Thousand Kings the next morning, he was immediately aware of the undercurrents of malice flowing around him. He allowed the slaves to serve him with little crustaceans still wriggling with life and ate with every sign of enjoyment, washing his repast down with sea-grape juice. A few of his brothers asked him how he was with spurious concern in their voices. To all of them he answered blandly, "Very well, thank you."

It was over a week before he at last felt safe enough to meet with Fand. It was difficult to sneak away from the cave with so many eyes watching his every move but at last he managed it, knowing Fand would sense his intent and meet him in the ruins aboveground. There they would be safe from prying eyes, for none dared make their way through the darkness of the Fathomless Caves. The steps to the old witches' tower were far beyond the usual passages and caverns used by the royal family and their retainers, and only kelp ropes marked the passages where natural light did not fall.

Although the Fairgean royalty had occupied the Isle of the Gods for many thousands of years, the labyrinthine cave system that riddled the old volcano had never been fully explored. Most of the caverns were hidden far away from the surface, where no light could penetrate. Since only the Priestesses of Jor carried nightglobes, this meant the Fairgean went only where rifts in the cave walls let in natural light or where bygone explorers had left kelp ropes to show the way. In the lower caves lurked many terrible monsters whose appetite for warm blood was never satiated. There were holes in the floor where jets of hissing steam exploded without warning and many caverns were flooded at high tide, the dark angry sea rushing in at breakneck speeds. Jor himself, the God of the Shoreless Seas, was said to have been born in the Fiery Womb, deep within the island.

When the human invaders had come, they had driven the Fairgean out of their hallowed caves with swords of steel and flaming torches. These burning brands had illuminated caverns where no light had ever before fallen. Aghast at such sacrilege, the Fairgean had defended the sacred mystery of the Fathomless Caves with all their strength, but they had had no recourse against fire and metal. Many hundreds had died.

The tailless intruders had moored their ships in the Cave of a Thousand Kings, used the royal bedchambers to store their barrels and sacks, and had carved a staircase to the sky out of living rock. On the pinnacle of the Isle of the Gods they had built a great fortress, where their witches had lived and studied new and terrible ways to kill the faeries of the sea. This fortress lay in ruins now, open to the icy winds and occupied only by seabirds and ghosts. It was to this haunted pile of stones that Nila now climbed, his eyes wide open and anxiously searching, though all he could see was impenetrable blackness. Although he and Fand had first discovered the way to the old tower some years ago, the young prince was never able to shake the terror that he would wander from the path and be lost forever in the Fathomless Caves.

At last, with a little gasp of relief, he saw a glimmer of gray light. He climbed the steps quickly, the rough stone scraping his webbed feet. Snow whirled against his face, stinging his skin with cold, and he drew his sealskin cloak closer about him.

He emerged in the midst of a heap of gray stones, all blanketed with snow. Here and there a broken arch rose in a graceful curve against the leaden sky. Most of the building lay in great piles, however, smashed beyond repair. Fand waited for him in the meager shelter of one crazily leaning wall, shivering with cold. She was dressed only in the tattered skins of a slave and her skin was mottled blue and purple. He wrapped his arms and cloak about her, and they coupled quickly against the wall. There was desperation in their haste, a recklessness that took no heed of the bitter cold. When they were done, they leaned their heads into each other's necks, panting and close to tears.

"I cannot go on like this," Nila said. "I want to have you for my wife, without fear."

He felt her take a shuddering breath and then she said, without scorn, "Do not be a fool. You know that can never be."

He pressed his mouth against her soft, unscaled skin and said nothing. For a long time they stood together, leaning against the cold stone, then at last she pushed him away, saying miserably, "I must get back. There is work to be done."

"Next summer we shall flee the winter seas," he

whispered. "We shall find ourselves an island in the sun and be together forever and happy." She nodded. "We shall make a beautiful little baby together and you shall sing to him and I shall spear fish for you both and we shall make love in the warm ocean and I shall make you a crown of pearls . . ."

"And I shall gather sea quills and make us sweet wine," she whispered and he kissed her, long and lovingly.

"I need to be able to dream of a future," he said when at last he moved his mouth away. She nodded, though her face was averted, her sea-green eyes wet with tears.

The falling snow thickened. "We should get back," Nila said, unable to repress his loathing at the thought of returning to the royal court. Fand nodded and together they hurried back to the gaping dark mouth of the stairwell.

They made their slow, anxious way through the tunnels hand-in-hand, sliding their feet over the rough ground to avoid falling into any of the many pits. At last their groping fingers met a rusting metal chain that the witches had hung up many years ago. They sighed in unison and hurried on, their steps sure now in the darkness. At last they came into a long, low passage illuminated dimly by a crack in the roof, and they were able to move with more confidence.

Fand left him at the beginning of the Scalding Falls and Nila made his way down the side of the chain of bubbling pools and cascades toward the Cave of a Thousand Kings, his step heavy. As he came toward the first of the long falls, Nila heard a swish behind him and half turned. He saw a swift down-

ward movement, a fur cloak swinging. Instinctively
he threw up his arm. The blow that was aimed for
his head hit his forearm instead, cracking bone. He
cried out. Another blow caught the side of his temple, then he was punched hard in the stomach. He
doubled over, choking. A hail of blows hammered
him down to the ground. He slid helplessly into
unconsciousness.

Nila woke to darkness. He was lying half in, half out
of icy-cold water, his breast and face against wet,
slimy stone. His body was aching and bruised, his
forearm throbbing. When he shifted his weight, a
sharp agonizing pain shafted through his flesh. He
cried out involuntarily and his voice echoed and
echoed. Nila's heart shrank with fear.

Painfully he crawled further out of the water, nursing his broken arm against him. The water heaved
and fell about him. Something slimy brushed against
his leg and Nila recoiled with a shriek. He managed
to scramble further up the slippery rock but felt a
thick tentacle wrap around his ankle. Desperately his
hand sought his dagger but his belt was empty. Another tentacle groped up his body and wrapped
around his waist, innumerable suckers seizing his
flesh in an unbreakable hold. Slowly, inexorably, he
was dragged back down into the sea. He screamed
for help but heard only the thin echoes beating back
at him.

The dark water closed over his head. Nila clamped
his mouth and nostrils shut and let his gills flutter
into life. With his uninjured hand he grasped hold
of a rock ledge but his fingers were torn loose. What-

ever terrible creature had hold of him was very
strong. Despairingly he twisted and fought but felt
the pressure of deep water as he was dragged down
toward the monster's lair.

Then he saw, far above, the glimmer of green light.
Suddenly the surface of the water was smashed into
foam as divers plunged after him. The green lumines-
cence struck down all about him and he saw, for a
mere instant, the dreadful gaping maw and the groping tentacles of the giant octopus that had him in its
toils. Then the warriors were all around him, striking
at the octopus with their daggers. A filthy colored
liquid spurted out, blinding them and paralyzing
their gills. For a while all was a confusion of thrashing water, thick tentacles and slender, scaled limbs.
Then spears were flung into the water from above,
striking the octopus in its vulnerable mouth. It released all its suckers and shot down into the water's
inky depths.

Choking for breath and unable to see or hear or
move, Nila and the warriors sank down in its wake.
Then the King himself plunged into the water, seizing Nila and two other tall warriors in his strong
arms and towing them to safety. As they lay on the
rocks, coughing and gasping, the King again plunged
into the turbulent depths, seeing more of the para-
lyzed warriors. At last all lay safely on the rocks, the
weird green light of the viperfish sliding over them,
two Priestesses of Jor gazing down at them with
contempt.

Nila came back to full consciousness only slowly.
His vision swam. He lay facedown and stared
blankly for quite a long time before he realized a
pair of bare human feet were standing between the

priestesses' webbed ones. His heart jolted. He looked up and saw Fand, her shadowed eyes piteous.

Nila stared at her and she gazed back. He saw both priestesses had their hands clamped hard on her upper arms. They were smiling.

"It seems this halfbreed slave has talents that will be of use to the priestesses in their service to Jor, god of whirlpools and tidal waves," one said with a sibilant hiss.

"She is a very fortunate girl," the other said. "We are to release her from her bondage and take her into the priestesshood as one of our sisters."

"She shall be enlightened into the mysteries of Jor."

"Taught to harness all that raw human power."

"Discipline her weak human emotions."

"Discover strength of will and purity of purpose."

"Put to work."

"In the service of the priestesses."

"In the service of Jor," the first said with a light stress of reproof in her voice.

"In the divine service of almighty Jor, God of the Shoreless Seas," the other said.

Nila stared at Fand. There was terror on her face. She strained against their hold, trying to reach him. Their hold tightened until her mouth twisted with pain, though there was no change on the gloating faces of the priestesses.

"No!" He jerked upright, fighting his dizziness. They smiled and he had to subdue his terror. "You are mistaken," he said through stiff lips. "She is only a stupid halfbreed, not worth the toss of a sea-stirk knuckle. She has no power, no talents."

"She had the temerity to accost me on my own

throne and beg me to save you," the Fairgean king said, amusement in his voice. "When we asked her if she had seen you being attacked, she tried to lie and say that she had . . ."

"But only fools lie to a Priestess of Jor," one priestess hissed.

"It did not take her long to confess that she had *sensed* the attack on you," cried the other.

"She was able to lead us here through all the Fathomless Caves," the King said. "It would seem she is like so many of these misbegotten halfbreeds and has very powerful talents indeed."

Nila sought desperately for words. "She is my concubine . . ."

"There are many halfbreed slaves," the King said indifferently. "If that sort of meat is to your liking." He waved his webbed hand and the priestesses bowed low before him; they gave Nila a far shallower obeisance, then turned to leave, Fand straining against their hold.

Nila scrambled to his feet. "No!" he cried. "Leave her! You cannot take her. She's mine!"

"Actually," the King said, smiling, "she's mine."

He gestured and the warriors clamped their hands upon Nila's arms as he struggled to reach Fand. Though he fought against them he was helpless against their strength. Fand did not struggle. Her head bent, her hair over her face, she allowed the priestesses to lead her away. The glimmer of the priestesses' nightglobes sank away into darkness.

The Warp and the Weft

DRAGON FLIGHT

Spring was casting its warm green veil over the forest when Isabeau at last reached the Towers of Roses and Thorns. Although there was still snow on the mountain heights, she felt the warmth of the wind on her skin and rejoiced. The spring was the herald of a new season and a new life for Isabeau, free at last from the queen-dragon's *geas*.

The bare branches arching over the road were sprouting with new leaves, while the rose briars trained over pergolas were budding. Isabeau was glad to see the neatness of the gardens, which had been completely overgrown when she had first come here five years earlier. Floyd Greenthumb, the head gardener, leaned on his spade, calling to her, and she went over to greet him.

He had been among many who had sought a new life up in the mountains, away from the ravages of the wars which had so devastated southern Eileanan. The Rìgh, Isabeau's brother-in-law Lachlan, had arranged for five hundred refugees to accompany Khan'gharad and Ishbel back to the Towers of Roses and Thorns. These included stonemasons and carpenters to help rebuild the ruined towers; gardeners and farmers to plant the land about with grains and vegetables; weavers, seamstresses, cooks and house servants to help in the running of the castle; scribes and apprentice witches to study in the library; and miners to look for lodes of precious metals in the mountains. There was also a retinue of the younger sons of the nobility eager to carve out a life for themselves in service to the newest of the prionnsachan.

It had taken the refugees almost a year to travel to Tìrlethan through the mountains, for they had brought with them many supplies and livestock. The ancient road that had once connected Tìrlethan to Rionnagan had virtually disappeared and the immigrants had had to rebuild it as they traveled. Consequently they had arrived only a short time before Isabeau had had to leave the valley to stay with her great-grandmother on the Spine of the World. She was most impressed with the changes to the valley in the months she had been gone. The meadows all about were busy with men and women ploughing, building walls and ditches, cutting back thistles and weeds, rebuilding ruined cottages that had been reclaimed from the forest, and tending goats, sheep and horses.

From an abandoned pile of stones, hung with cobwebs and occupied only by rats, owls and ghosts, the Towers of Roses and Thorns had become a bustling residence, well tended and self-sufficient, as it must have been in the days of the first Red Sorcerers a thousand years before.

"What news, Floyd?" Isabeau asked.

He shook his head lugubriously and sucked at his empty pipe. " 'Twas a hard winter indeed, many storms and days when we could no' set toe outside the doors for fear o' being lost in the snow. I was worried indeed about the frost killing all my new trees, which I knew should have been planted earlier . . ."

"What o' my mam?" Isabeau asked. "Is she well?"

"Huge as a blue whale," the head gardener replied succinctly, "and in no guid humor, that I have heard."

"So the babes have no' yet come?" Isabeau exclaimed in relief. "Thank Eà!"

"Aye, thank Eà," he replied. "Although auld Dimpna says she's brought many a bawling babe into the world, I'd no' be trusting her myself."

Isabeau only smiled and bade him goodbye as she turned back to the towers, which soared gray and tall into the sky. Once they had been so entwined with rose briars and brambles they could hardly be seen, but now the gray bulk of the buildings rose uncluttered from the gardens, their great flying buttresses, cone-topped turrets and the graceful shape of arches over the river clear in the sunlight. The lawns swept down to the loch, where the reflection of the twin towers stretched out as if to touch the reflection of the twin peaks, cutting as sharply into the sky as the pinnacle of the Skull of the World. It was a scene of great peace and beauty and Isabeau was smiling to herself as she leaped up the steps and into the great entrance hall of the first tower.

Ishbel had seen her coming through the garden and was hurrying down the spiral staircase to meet her, both hands outstretched. Dressed in a voluminous white gown she was indeed huge, the swell of her pregnancy preceding her like the crest of a wave. Isabeau's eyes widened a little at the sight of her. She was even bigger than Iseult had been during her two pregnancies, and Isabeau had thought then her twin must surely burst before she could carry her babes to term. Isabeau had assisted her sister through the birth of her twins, Owein and Olwynne, a year earlier, as well as through the birth of Donncan, the heir to the throne, and his stillborn sister five years before that. The experience had been enough to make Isabeau rather glad it had been prophesied that she was never to have children of her own.

Mother and daughter embraced awkwardly, and Ishbel gestured down to her swollen abdomen with a grimace. "Why oh why did I have to fall in love wi' a man predestined to breed up twins?" she lamented. "Have ye ever seen such a sight!"

"Ye must be uncomfortable," Isabeau replied, slipping her arm through her mother's and helping her to waddle back up the stairs. Ornately decorated with carvings of single petaled roses entwined in thorns, the staircase was broad enough for seven people to walk abreast.

"Uncomfortable! What an understatement! I canna sleep at night, the babes spend all night dancing jigs and reels, and I need to crawl to the privy every few minutes to squeeze out only a few drops o' water. My feet and ankles are so swollen up I canna fit into any shoes or into any o' my rings, and it takes all my energy just to get downstairs in the morning. Why do I have to live in a draughty auld tower with so many flights o' stairs, for Eà's sake!"

"It could be worse, ye could be giving birth in a dragon's lair again," Isabeau said with a smile. Ishbel gave a theatrical shudder and sank down on a couch in the grand drawing room. Isabeau looked about her with approval. The weavers had spent the winter making tapestries, cushions and embroidered upholstery which gave the room a cheer and comfort it had certainly lacked before.

"I'm so glad that ye've returned in time for your birthday, dearling," Ishbel said once she had recovered her breath. "I was afraid ye might have to celebrate it alone again and ye ken I have promised never to let that happen again."

"I just wish Iseult and I could one day manage to celebrate it together," Isabeau said wryly. "We always seem to be leagues away from each other."

"Aye, happen the day will come when we can all be together at Candlemas. Ring for some wine, dearling, and send someone to fetch your *dai-dein*, he's been longing to see ye. He wants to ken if they found ye fit for your initiation."

Isabeau's hand touched her cheek. Her scar was fully healed, thanks to her salve, but still rather red. Ishbel said quickly, "I can see ye have, ye poor dearling, but wait till your father comes afore telling me the story."

Isabeau nodded and pulled the bell cord. While they waited she asked Ishbel for news of Lucescere and was regaled with stories of the twins' beauty and cleverness, Donncan's mischief and precocity, raids by pirates, the belligerence of the Fairgean, the stupidity of the lairds, and Meghan's increasing frailty. Ishbel had been Meghan the Keybearer's apprentice when she was only a girl herself, and she loved the old sorceress as dearly as she loved anyone. Real concern was in her voice and Isabeau frowned in sudden anxiety.

"Does a Mesmerd still follow her everywhere?"

she asked in a low voice and Ishbel nodded, her swollen face creasing in fear.

Isabeau sighed and twisted her fingers. "I must go back to Lucescere," she said to herself.

Ishbel cried out in distress. "Nay, why must ye? I've been hanging on in the hope ye'd get here afore the twins were born so ye could help me through. Why must ye be going again so soon?"

"I will no' go just yet," Isabeau reassured her. "I shall stay for the birthing, fear ye no'. It is no' every day I get a new brother and sister! Nay, I shall go once I ken ye and the babes are fine. Ye have plenty o' people here to help ye now and I must see Meghan and take up my studies again. I have lost too much time as it is."

Ishbel sighed and resettled her weight in an attempt to get comfortable. "But why can ye no' stay here and study in the library as ye have the past few years?"

"I need a teacher," Isabeau replied gently. "I am near auld enough to sit my Third Tests and be allowed to enter the Coven. I should have spent my apprentice years sitting at Meghan's feet and learning from her but instead I've been either here or on the Spine o' the World. I've learned a great deal but no' enough, I think, and probably no' the right things. The lore o' the Soul-Sage is different indeed to the lore o' the witches."

Ishbel nodded rather reluctantly.

"Besides," Isabeau said, half to herself, "I may no' have much time left with Meghan."

"Ouch, she's a tough auld boot!" Khan'gharad cried, coming in through the door. He was a tall, strong-looking man with vigorous red hair tied back with leather, and the thick, curling horns of the Khan' cohbans. His stern face was marked with the seven scars of the Scarred Warrior and he wore a weapons belt around his lithe waist, the eight-pointed star of the *reil* hanging conspicuously in front. Dressed in rather shabby, dirty clothes, he was covered in dust. "Do no' fret for Meghan o' the Beasts, lassie. She's lived this long, I do no' think ye need to fear for her health now all is at peace."

Isabeau did not reply, though her face was troubled. Khan'gharad bent and kissed his wife, who made a little sound of protest at his dirt and sweat.

"I've been working, *leannan*," he replied. "I canna help mend a ceiling and no' get a wee bit dirty."

"But why must ye help the laborers?" Ishbel asked rather fretfully. "Are ye no' acknowledged as the Prionnsa o' Tirlethan now, and laird o' the clan? Why can ye no' bide a wee wi' me in peace and quiet?"

"A good laird works wi' his men," Khan'gharad said rather sternly, then looked Isabeau over with a keen gaze. "The mark o' the Soul-Sage, I see. Well done! Will ye tell us the story o' your name?"

"But that's hardly fair," Isabeau replied, laughing, "when I've heard the story o' your name quest so many times I could recite it in my sleep. What story shall ye tell me in return?"

"Any story ye wish to hear," he said with a grin. "Come, Isabeau, we have been anxious indeed about ye. Your mother has had nightmares o' ye being swept away by avalanches and drowned in raging rivers. Can ye no' tell us the tale?"

"Ye ask o' me a question. Do ye offer me a story in return?" Isabeau said, only half jesting, and her father bowed and replied ritualistically.

As she told them her story her mother groaned and shuddered at every twist of the tale. Occasionally her father frowned and once he smiled rather grimly, but otherwise he was silent, as a Khan'cohban should be.

When she told them how she had changed shape her mother clapped her hands in delight. "Isabeau! What a Talent! I can hardly believe it. Where could such a Skill have come from? I've heard stories o' witches being able to cast a glamourie so they look like an animal but to actually transform . . ."

"Sssh, *leannan*," Khan'gharad said. "She has no' yet told the end o' er tale. It is rude indeed to be interrupting."

Isabeau smiled but continued on without breaking the measured pace of her narrative. When at last she had finished, Ishbel caught her hand and squeezed it, the ready tears flowing down her cheeks. "Och, my wee lassie, to think o' ye facing such dangers! And such a Talent! Ye shall be a powerful sorceress indeed. Can ye change shape into any animal ye please?"

"I do no' ken," Isabeau said. "So far I have only transformed into animals wi' which I have a close affinity." She heard, deep in her mind, the resonating memory of the queen-dragon's voice. *To understand any living thing thou must creep within and feel the beating of its heart. To understand the deeper secrets of the universe thou must feel its heart beat too.*

Khan'gharad made the Khan'cohban gesture of congratulations. "Khan'tinka," he said slowly. "Indeed a powerful name, if a somewhat unusual one. I think they will now be telling the tale o' your

naming quest around the fire more often than they
tell mine."

"Yours is still the favorite o' the storytellers," Isabeau reassured him with a laugh.

"And did I no' tell ye I had dreams o' Isabeau
being caught by an avalanche?" Ishbel said, catching
Khan'gharad's big hand with both of her small ones.
"When will ye admit that my dreams are true
sendings?"

"I'll admit it now that Isabeau is safe home wi' us,
leannan," he said with a rare smile that transformed
his stern face. "Come, Isabeau, ye must be weary.
Why do ye no' go up to your room and have a rest?"

"I'd much rather see all ye have done to the towers
while I've been gone," Isabeau said and stood up,
stretching till all her joints cracked. "Ye should have
a lie down though, Mam, ye look weary indeed."

"Weary o' carrying around these babes, that I will
admit to," Ishbel said and let her husband pull her
to her feet. "I pray to Eà that they come soon."

Eà answered her prayers, the twins being born the
following evening. It was Candlemas, and Isabeau
and Iseult's birthday. Instead of celebrating the turn
of the seasons at dawn as she did normally, Isabeau
spent the whole night and day in Ishbel's room for
it was a long and difficult birth. The firstborn, a little
girl with a mass of coppery hair, was called Heloïse,
with her younger brother, smaller and fairer,
named Alasdair.

"Heloïse was my mother's name and Alasdair was
my father's," Ishbel whispered, very pale and tired.
"I'm glad to be able to remember them, for both died
when I was very young."

"Whom did ye name me for?" Isabeau asked,
smoothing back her mother's sweat-darkened hair
and bringing a cup of restorative tea to her mouth.

Ishbel swallowed weakly then said, "Ye and Iseult
were named for both my grandmothers. Isabeau Nic-
Aislin was my father's mother and Iseult NicThanach
was my mother's mother, so ye see ye are related to
both the MacAislins and the MacThanachs, which
may explain why ye feel such an affinity with the
earth and the forest." She sank back on her pillows,
looking down at the two heads nestled close beside
her with a sort of amazement on her face. "They are
such wee bits," she whispered. "I had forgotten . . ."

Isabeau smoothed back the downy hair of little
Alasdair, who was sleeping. "Well, it is twenty-two
years today since ye gave birth to Iseult and me. Odd
that they should be born on our birthday."

"And what a difference," Ishbel said with a shudder that caused Alasdair to whimper in his sleep and
Heloïse to look up with smoky blue eyes. "Och, it
was a nightmare, your birth. Dragons all around me,
wi' the smell o' smoke and fire and the shadow o'
their claws on my face . . . I do no' want to even
think o' it."

"Nay, go to sleep, Mam," Isabeau said gently.
"That was a long time ago and ye are safe here and
your wee babes are strong and well."

Ishbel nodded and smiled, tears leaking out from
under her bruised looking lids. "Aye, thank Eà," she
murmured. "And thank ye too, dearling. I'm glad ye
were home in time."

Ishbel did not awake from her sleep for seven days
and seven nights. Despite the wails of her hungry
babies, she floated peacefully about the bedroom, her

silver gilt hair weaving itself into a cocoon about her. Vigorous shaking, pinching, shouting in her ear, dashing cold water over her, and bringing the babies to scream lustfully beneath her did nothing to disturb her slumber.

There was no one at the towers who could act as the babies' wet nurse and so Isabeau had to feed the babies on watered down goats' milk reinforced with strengthening and nourishing herbs. She had great difficulty in getting the milk into the children, having to teach them to suckle from an adapted wine gourd. For two such tiny scraps of humanity, the twins had extremely strong lungs. No one in the castle got much sleep, except for the twins' own mother. Exhausted, stressed and worried, Isabeau was irresistibly reminded of the days when she was nursemaid to Bronwen MacCuinn, the Ensorcellor's daughter.

Thinking of Bronwen made Isabeau eager to leave the Towers of Roses and Thorns and return to the capital. She had been away so long she really had no idea how Iseult and Lachlan were doing in their endeavor to bring peace to Eileanan. Ishbel's stories of increased activity by the Fairgean had made her uneasy for she knew the sea faeries felt a great hatred for all humans and wished to destroy them utterly.

Isabeau had developed a peculiar friendship with Maya the Ensorcellor, who was the daughter of the King of the Fairgean and a human concubine. Even though Maya was the implacable enemy of everyone Isabeau loved most, the young apprentice witch had been unable to help feeling a strong connection with the former banrìgh.

Since Lachlan had won the throne, he and Iseult had been engaged in bringing peace and order to

Eileanan and rebuilding the towns and cities which had been destroyed by the long civil war. Isabeau knew, however, that Lachlan would soon have to raise arms against the Fairgean once again. And she knew more about the sea dwellers than any other human, thanks to her friendship with Maya and her care for the little Fairge banprionnsa. So she was determined to travel to Lucescere as soon as she was able, to help in the struggle.

Isabeau was terribly afraid, though, that her mother would not wake from her strange enchanted sleep. Ishbel had slept for sixteen years after she and Iseult had been born. If Ishbel slept on, Isabeau would have to stay and care for her baby brother and sister, giving up her dreams of studying at the Tower of Two Moons and becoming a sorceress. She could not leave the little babes to be brought up by old Dimpna, who was rather too fond of a wee dram for Isabeau's liking. Khan'gharad, the stern warrior, was helpless before the rage and hunger of his two tiny newborns. A look of absolute terror would cross his scarred face whenever Isabeau thrust one at him, and he would hold the babe awkwardly in his huge, hard hands, as if the child was made of eggshell and would break with the slightest pressure. So it was with a feeling of utmost relief and joy that Isabeau woke from an uneasy sleep seven days after the twins' birth to see her mother standing over the cradles, her blue eyes shining with tenderness, her pale cheeks touched with color.

Well rested after her week's repose, Ishbel was happy to try and suckle her hungry babes, who went to her breast like bees to honey. Within moments the red-faced screaming demons who had tormented

Isabeau for seven days and seven nights were sleepy, contented little cherubs. Isabeau was able to crawl into her own neglected bed and sink fathoms deep into sleep.

When she woke it was midafternoon and all was quiet. She lay thankfully still, looking about her room with its tall mullioned windows and the stone fireplace carved with roses and thorns. When Isabeau had first come here it had been a cold, austere room with only a chest and a tall wooden candlestick to relieve the severity of the stone walls. Now it was hung with tapestries and decorated with beautiful artifacts which she had found while cleaning out the towers. The diamond-paned windows sparkled in the sunshine and the dragon carved over the fireplace seemed to dance in the reflections of light.

A smile curved Isabeau's mouth. Now her mother was awake, she was determined to set out for Lucescere as soon as she could, but the journey would take many months by foot. Isabeau really did not want to spare the time. She glanced up at the curved wings and raised claws of the dragon on the wall and her smile deepened. It might be time to call the dragon's name.

Isabeau had flown to Lucescere by dragonback twice before and there was no swifter or more spectacular way to go. The young dragon-princess Asrohc was not always amenable to allowing a human to cross their leg over her back, however. Isabeau had not seen her for some months and was not at all sure the great flying beast would wish to take her such a distance.

Isabeau leaped out of bed, washed her face and hands, and dressed in her shabby old breeches. Buba slept, crouched on the back of the ladder-backed chair, her ears sticking straight up, her eyes shut. Isabeau let the elf-owl be, digging around in her chest and pulling out a massive leather halter, so heavy she could hardly carry it. Hanging it over her shoulder, she went down the corridor, marveling anew at the new tapestries and chairs, the polished silver jugs and candlesticks, the gilded mirrors and ornaments that graced the walls. Ishbel and her team of refugee women had worked wonders in turning the long-abandoned towers into a home.

She popped her head around the nursery door, to see her mother and the babes sleeping and a chambermaid ensconced by the fire with a pile of mending. Feeling freedom heady in her veins, Isabeau bounded down the stairs. Grabbing some bannocks on her way through the kitchen, she ate hungrily as she ran down through the garden to the loch. Even though the sun was shining, Isabeau had pulled on her tam o' shanter and had her plaid draped over her arm. It was bitterly cold on dragonback.

Isabeau stood on the shore of the loch and looked up toward the twin mountains the Khan'cohbans called the Cursed Peaks. She felt excitement and anticipation quickening her blood. There was no greater thrill than flying the dragon's back. Even flying in the shape of an owl was no comparison, for the dragon could soar above the clouds, so high the curvature of the planet could be seen. Besides, the dragon was the greatest of all creatures, the wisest and the most dangerous. Few people had the chance to even see them, for they lived in the most remote mountain heights, far away from human civilization.

To have the right to call the dragon by name and fly the skies on her back was a rare and precious privilege.

Caillec Asrohc Airi Telloch Cas.

She did not say the name aloud but thought it, each strange syllable throbbing through the chambers and tissues of her body. For a long moment afterward there was a sort of sickening echo that made her ears ring. Then Isabeau saw an immense winged creature rise from the heart of the Cursed Peaks, serrated wings spread wide. The dragon's gilded green body shone in the sunshine, dazzling Isabeau's eyes. She raised her hand to shade them, watching as the dragon soared down the snow-patched slopes and over the loch, her sweeping shadow blotting out the turquoise color of the water. All the birds stopped singing, and the insects stopped chirping. There was an impression of stillness, as if all the busy life of meadow and forest had crouched down in terror. Then the black shadow of wings fell upon Isabeau's face and she had to fight down the instinctive urge to run for her life.

Gracefully the dragon landed on the shore beside Isabeau, folding her wings along her burnished side. Rather dazedly Isabeau thought, *How big she has grown. How bright.*

Greetings, little human. Is it not a beautiful day?

Aye, bonny, Isabeau replied, approaching on rather shaky legs. The dragon towered over her, tall as a castle. Her scales were as smooth and shimmery as silk, her angular head with its crown of sharp spikes and narrow golden eyes seeming more menacing than ever. Her long crested tail, sinuous as a snake, writhed gently back and forth.

So thou wishest to fly, little human. Dost thou dare to trust the dragon?

Isabeau stopped her approach, feeling unaccountably apprehensive.

Dost thy Khan'cohban relatives not say one can never trust the dragon? Dost thou believe them?

Aye, Isabeau said with a mental smile. *The Khan'-cohbans are wise indeed.*

Yet still thou dreamest of soaring the skies. Art thou brave or art thou foolish?

Both, probably, Isabeau said and reached out a tentative finger to stroke the cream silk of the dragon's forearm. A vein raised the silken skin, pulsing. The dragon-princess reared back, her wings spreading and that long muscular tail thrashing. Isabeau scrambled backward, alarmed.

Do ye no' wish me to cross my leg over your back?

The dragon sat still, coiling her tail over her claws. *It is not that I do not wish to speak with thee or fly with thee,* she answered in a rather puzzled tone of voice. *I feel very restless today. I wish to fly. I wish to fly very far and very fast. Thou mayst fly with me if thou so wishest.*

I would like to, very much, Isabeau replied, still hesitant to approach for the tip of the dragon's tail was twitching and she could see muscles bunching in the dragon's neck.

Then cross thy leg, for I grow impatient. Choose. Dost thou wish to fly or stay on the ground and merely long to fly?

I will fly, Isabeau replied, coming forward with the leather harness. The dragon submitted to having the bridle fastened around her head and shoulders and crouched down so Isabeau could clamber up on to her back, settling herself between two of the great spikes that crowned her spine. Isabeau was hardly in place before Asrohc launched herself into the air, bugling loudly. Isabeau clung on, the sound of that cry chilling her to the very marrow. It was a cry of challenge, of triumph, of excitement, and Isabeau had never heard the young dragon-princess make such a call before.

They soared over the mountains, heading west. Isabeau saw the Spine of the World below her, that great range of peaks which cut Eileanan in half. Far, far below she saw the blue winding ribbon of the Lament of the Gods and marveled that they had traveled so far, so fast. The journey that had taken her so many weeks had been accomplished in minutes.

The dragon screamed again and folded her translucent wings. They plunged, the world below blurring into a swirl of blue and icy white. Isabeau clung to the leather straps, her long hair dragged from its plait and twisting behind her like the fiery tail of a meteor. As the snowy ground rushed up toward her, she shut her eyes and bit her lip, determined not to give the dragon the satisfaction of hearing her scream. Without warning the dragon suddenly twisted and soared, and a cry was forced from Isabeau's lips as her crouched body was flung clear of the dragon's. She gripped even tighter to the leather straps and grunted as she again thudded into place between the spikes of the dragon's crest.

"Ouch!" she cried. *Asrohc, do ye have to do that? Your spine is bloody hard.*

The dragon laughed and writhed sinuously so that

Isabeau was almost flung clear again. *Art thou afraid I shall let thee fall, human? It is a very long way down for one who has no wings.*

That is why I wear all these straps, Isabeau replied, clinging tighter nonetheless. *I do no' trust ye for a moment.*

The dragon turned her head to regard Isabeau with one huge, golden eye, nearly as tall as Isabeau herself. *I always thought you were wise for a human,* Asrohc answered sardonically. She rolled, her wings folded along her side. Isabeau's hair hung straight down, the sky arching blue above the dragon's bright green body, then she was swung upright again, screaming despite herself.

Asrohc! What's wrong with ye today?

I feel . . . odd. Restless. I want . . .

Suddenly the dragon-princess bugled again and soared into the sky. Isabeau was blinded by tears as the bitterly cold air rushed past her face. She raised one gloved hand and rubbed her eyes, then tried to secure her hair into a knot at her nape. She saw a flash of bronze-gold from the corner of her eye and turned. Another dragon was chasing them. By the deeper cast of his skin, Isabeau knew he was male. With fingers suddenly rigid with fear, Isabeau clung to the harness. Asrohc bugled again and this time her call was answered. Another male, far bigger than the dragon-princess, was coming up from the south. He was flying with great, powerful beats of his sail-like wings. The two males saw each other and bellowed in rage. Asrohc mocked them, turning and rolling so her pale belly was exposed, then soaring up far into the sky.

They shall never catch me, she said complacently.

Asrohc, why are they chasing ye? Why are ye putting on such a show for them? Asrohc, I think I want to get down!

The dragon princess only bugled mockingly, then folded her wings and plummeted like a stone, falling past the big bronze males who twisted midair trying to catch her. Isabeau saw to her horror two more dragons on the horizon, flying to join in the chase.

Asrohc, are ye on heat? Isabeau asked frantically. *Are ye ready to mate?*

Is that why the males all follow me? Asrohc asked with a dragonish laugh. *They think to mount me, daughter of the queen of them all? Arrogant fools! So big and clumsy they are.* She bugled a challenge that was met with four deep-throated bellows. Isabeau saw with absolute terror that the dragons were now all soaring and swooping in Asrohc's tail wind, their eyes gleaming like jewels, their red cavernous nostrils spread to catch her scent. Two were so huge their shadows darkened entire mountainsides, their coats so dark a bronze as to be almost black. Beside them Asrohc seemed very small and very bright, but she darted and danced ahead of them like a dragonfly. Again and again the males lunged for her, seeking to close their jaws upon her neck. Isabeau said aloud, "I do no' think I want to be here. Asrohc! How could ye let me fly wi' ye today o' all days?"

How was I to know? the dragon-princess replied with a little shudder that had her whole body undulating. *All I knew was that I wanted to fly . . .*

A small, lithe copper-colored dragon tangled his wings with hers. For a moment Asrohc let him grasp her with his strong forearms and the two dragons fell toward the earth, their bodies pressed together.

Isabeau crouched as close to Asrohc's neck as she could, the weight of the male dragon's great body pressing against her, crushing the breath from her body. Then Asrohc shook him free contemptuously, bugling again. The dragon-princess spread her wings and glided away, the male screaming in frustration.

Isabeau bit her lip. Carefully, wondering if she was a fool, she unfastened the straps around her waist. Asrohc wheeled and soared, and then the shadow of a dragon fell upon them. Isabeau glanced up and saw a bright-winged bronze falling down upon them out of the sky, claws extended, wings spread against the sun. She screamed and let go.

The earth rushed up toward her at a sickening rate. The wind thundered in her ears. Isabeau shut her eyes and concentrated. For a moment she thought her Talent had failed her and she was falling to her death, then suddenly the wind was knotted to her will. She beat her wings and opened her eyes, giving the harsh, triumphant scream of a golden eagle. The wind held her, rocked her, obeyed every minute adjustment of her wings and tail. She soared up, watching impassively as a majestic bronze dragon closed his jaws upon Asrohc's neck and twined his tail with hers. The two great winged creatures fell together, screaming hoarsely.

Isabeau tilted her wings and spiraled away. All her clothes were falling like little rags in the wind. She caught a falling square of white fabric in her cruel curved talons and used it as a net to catch the small glittering rings tumbling down through the air. Even as an eagle, Isabeau knew she did not want to lose her rings and plaid. The owl talon on its leather thong still hung down upon her feathered breast, much to her relief.

It was a long flight back to the Cursed Valley, and even with the strength of a golden eagle's wings, Isabeau was worn out by the time she at last glided down toward the towers. She had no desire to run naked through the halls so she came down to land on the sill of an open window on one of the top floors. She transformed back into her own shape and almost fell from the window, so deep was the exhaustion which swept over her. She managed to scramble through, bruising her knees as she dropped to the floor. Wrapping her soft woolen plaid about her, Isabeau was relieved to find it was still fastened by the brooch Lachlan had given her, the stylized dancing dragon with the golden jeweled eye. It was one of Isabeau's most precious possessions, along with the plaid itself which had been woven for her by the Keybearer Meghan herself. White crossed with soft bands of red and blue, it was the MacFaghan tartan and the mark of Isabeau's royal heritage. Although she was sorry to have lost her favorite breeches and tam o' shanter, she would have been distressed indeed by the loss of plaid and badge.

"I can see I'm going to have to work out some solution to this problem o' losing my clothes all the time!" she said to herself as she thrust her two rings back onto her fingers. She then hurried through the corridors to her own room, managing to avoid being seen by any of the servants.

Isabeau had studied a great deal of dragon lore during her time at the Towers of Roses and Thorns. For her first three years there she had had Feld of the Dragons as her teacher and mentor, and after he had died, she had continued her studies alone. Feld had catalogued all the books and scrolls in the library with references to the dragons and Isabeau had systematically read her way through them. She knew that Asrohc would soon lay an egg which she would guard jealously for the next three years as the little dragon embryo within grew and developed. According to the textbooks, a newly laid dragon egg was quite small but over the three years slowly swelled until it was large as a sleeping horse. It would take a hundred years for the young dragon to reach its full size and maturity. Asrohc herself was only a century old and the youngest by far of all the dragons. If she could keep her egg safe, and if the newly hatched dragonet proved to be female, the slow dying-out of the dragons might be halted.

Isabeau could only be happy at the thought, even though Asrohc's coming of age presented her with what seemed like an insurmountable problem. There was no possibility of the dragon-princess flying Isabeau down to Lucescere now. She would be busy building a nest before the egg was laid, and busier still keeping it warm and safe from ogres, goblins, frost giants and the other vicious scavengers of the mountains. Her mate would hunt for her and take turns to rotate the egg and keep it warm. Dragons mated for life, Isabeau knew, and only if their mate died could they be persuaded to take another.

Although Asrohc was not the only dragon to live in Dragonclaw, she was the only one to allow humans to fly her back. Asrohc had been saved by Khan'gharad when he was only a boy himself, and she felt some friendship toward his family as a result.

Isabeau could no more ask Asrohc's haughty brothers to fly her down to Lucescere than their ancient and powerful mother, the queen-dragon herself.

All that evening Isabeau worried about how she was to get to Lucescere. She could transform into an eagle again and fly down, but that would mean arriving at the royal court naked and without any possessions. She wanted to take her plaid and brooch, her rings, her owl's talon, her quartz crystal, her witch's knife, her belt of tools and weapons, her satchel of herbs and medicines, not to mention a few essential items of clothes. Far too much to be carried in the talons of an eagle, no matter how large and powerful.

She could set off on foot, as she had done when she had first left the safety of Meghan's secret valley on the night of her sixteenth birthday. That had been a long and dangerous journey, though, and Isabeau had no real desire to repeat it.

So, that night at dinner, Isabeau leaned over to her father and said softly, "Do ye remember when we first came to the Cursed Valley?"

They were sitting together at the high table in the grand dining room, with Khan'gharad's newly appointed squire serving them. The gentlemen and ladies of the household sat at the lower table, served by either their own personal servants or by the footmen who, having only recently been promoted, were still rather clumsy. There was a loud buzz of conversation which effectively screened Isabeau's voice.

Her father shook his head. "No' really," he answered softly. "My years as a horse seem like a nightmare now, vague and horrible. I remember they had hobbled me and ye came and cut the hobbles."

"Ye brought me and Bronwen here by the Auld Way," she said.

"Aye, that's right." Khan'gharad's voice was reserved.

"How did ye ken how? Are the Auld Ways no' the Celestines' roads? Meghan has been friends with the Celestines for centuries and they have never shown her the secret o' the hidden roads."

"Happen she never asked them."

"Nay, she would've. Meghan always wants to ken everything about everything."

"Happen they did no' want to reveal their secrets to one o' humankind."

"But ye are half human."

"I am also Khan'cohban."

"So do the Khan'cohbans ken the secret o' the Auld Ways?"

"Why all these questions? Are ye offering me a question in return?"

"If ye wish to ask me questions, ask me," Isabeau replied impatiently. "We are no' on the Spine o' the World now."

"Rudeness is rudeness anywhere."

Isabeau sighed. "I'm sorry if ye think I have been rude but indeed I have a reason for my questions."

"And what is that reason?"

"Now the babes are born and Mam is on the mend, I wish to be returning to Lucescere. Ye ken I can be o' help to them there, and besides, I want to study at the Tower o' Two Moons. I'm way behind the rest o' my peers now, and if I want to take my Tests and join the Coven, then I need to be working hard and catching up."

"But Ishbel tells me this ability to take on the form

o' different animals is a powerful Talent indeed, that ye are already a sorceress o' uncommon ability. Why do ye need to study and take Tests?"

"If I want to reach my full potential I need to be in complete control. I do no' really understand what it is I do or how. Besides, there are many, many Skills I do no' have. I've had only a wee bit o' instruction in the powers o' air and water and earth, though my fire Skills are quite good thanks to Latifa. A witch needs to learn as much as she can about all the elements if she is to gain the High Magic. Normally an apprentice spends eight years doing naught but studying afore she is thought to have enough understanding o' the One Power to even be admitted to the Coven as a witch. Then there are many years more specializing in one element or another afore ye can win your sorceress rings. Ye must ken all this, *Dai-dein*, ye went to the Tower o' Two Moons to learn what ye could. I remember Meghan saying ye came to learn from the witches once ye had mastered all that the Khan'cohbans could teach ye." He nodded. Isabeau went on, "Ye ken it is no' that I do no' want to be with ye and Mam, but ye have the babes now and ye are both busy restoring the castle and setting up trade opportunities. I need to find my own place in the world."

He nodded again.

Isabeau sighed inside. Her father had all the more irritating Khan'cohban traits. She wished he was not so reserved and taciturn. She subdued her impatience and said very deliberately, "I have answered your question in fullness and truth, now will ye answer mine?"

His eyes widened a little and he leaned back in his

chair, goblet in one hand. She watched him thinking
back over their conversation. Then amusement flickered on his hard face and he inclined his horned
head.

"I asked ye how it was that ye knew the secret o'
the Auld Ways but ye were reluctant to answer me,"
Isabeau said with the appropriate Khan'cohban gestures. "I respect your reticence and ask ye instead if
ye will tell me how I may travel that way."

"It is no' my secret to reveal," he answered. "The
Auld Ways are dangerous indeed and no' to be traveled lightly."

Isabeau remembered their journey along the magical road and gave a little shudder. She knew her
father spoke the truth. She was anxious to reach Lucescere though and knew no faster way. She sipped
her wine to give her time to think, then said, "When
I told ye the story o' my naming quest, ye offered
me a story o' my choice in return. Ye ken that the
secret o' one's name is the most carefully guarded
tale o' any Khan'cohban yet I told ye mine willingly.
I have now asked ye the question o' my choice. Do
ye refuse to answer?"

He stared at her, anger in his eyes. His mouth was
set grimly. "Ye ken I canna do that," he answered in
a hard voice. "It would be dishonorable indeed and
though I may have left the Spine of the World afore
ye were born, I am still a Khan'cohban and a
Scarred Warrior."

"Well then," Isabeau replied.

He stared at her for a long time then bowed his
head. "The secret o' the Celestines' road is no' one
easily told," he said harshly. "I shall have to show
ye. I warn ye again about the dangers o' the Auld

Ways. It is easy to wander astray. Once ye ken the way o' it, ye must promise me no' to use it lightly. Ye could end up in places ye could never have imagined."

Isabeau nodded, her blue eyes brilliant with excitement. He rose abruptly, saying, "We must be at the ring o' stones by dawn so ye shall have to wake early."

"I am no' sure I'll be ready to leave so quickly, I—"

"Do no' be a fool," he snapped. "Do ye think ye can learn to travel the Auld Ways in a single morning or that ye can go on any auld day? Nay, if ye are to travel to Lucescere ye would be best waiting till the night of the spring equinox, when the Celestines shall sing the sun to life and the running o' the summerbourne cleanses the lines o' power. Even so, ye shall have to run fast."

Isabeau nodded again, though the light in her eyes had quenched. Many in the room were looking at them, startled by the harshness of Khan'gharad's tones. He bent his horned head and said softly, "The Auld Ways are one of the Celestines' most magical mysteries. Since I am forced to reveal it to ye, ye must promise me to never betray my confidence and tell it to anyone else, no matter what. Do ye promise?"

"Aye, by the stars, the moons and Eà's green blood, I promise," Isabeau replied and he nodded curtly, satisfied.

THE FAERY ROAD

Isabeau stood within the Celestines' circle of stones, the elf-owl perched on her shoulder. The shadows of the great crags stretched long over the grass, her own shadow dwarfed between them. A cool wind riffled the curls that had escaped from her plait and blew the edges of her plaid about.

It was the night of the spring equinox, when the tides of the seasons turned and the elemental energies ran strong. It was a time of great power, when witches celebrated the coming of summer and at dawn, the Celestines sang the sun to life.

The sun slipped down until only a thin fiery crescent showed above the dark peaks. A single red ray lit the tall stones on the hill with glowing color. Isabeau stepped forward and laid her hand on one of the symbols carved deep into the south-facing crags. A fierce shock ran up her arm and she had to fight to keep her hand pressed against the symbol.

A glinting curtain of silver-green fire materialized from nowhere. Isabeau took a deep breath and stepped through, the elf-owl taking flight from her shoulder. The curtain brushed her skin with an icy shock that caused Isabeau to cry out in pain. Then she was running down a long glimmering tunnel that stretched as far as her eyes could see. All around her the silvery walls and floor undulated with raw energy, like sheet lightning irradiating a stormy sky.

She could see the outside world through the glinting walls, but with every difficult stride the scene lurched. It was as if each step covered many leagues at once. One moment she saw the dark shapes of trees looming over her, the next a cliff face was leaping at her. Then she was inside the mountain, stalactites stabbing toward her. Then she was beyond and a waterfall was pouring past, the starlit foam white in the darkness. Then a dark forest, the groping, writhing branches all hung with gray moss, growing close about a high bare hill crowned with a circle of blazing pillars.

An eldritch shriek echoed through the tunnel and Buba hooted fearfully. Isabeau's heart jerked sickeningly. She well remembered the ghosts that had chased her along this pathway when she had last traveled it. From the corner of her eye she saw a menacing shadow swooping at her heels. Isabeau did not look back, sprinting as fast as she could down the road. There was a rush of icy wind upon the back of her neck, an unearthly wailing that almost caused her step to falter.

She must not let her concentration lapse. Any misstep and she could find herself traveling to another world or another time. Khan'gharad had impressed the dangers of the Celestines' road upon her forcibly.

In the past two months he had done his best to explain to her the nature of the faery roads, what the

Celestines called the Old Ways. The more Isabeau learned, the more afraid she had become and the more eager to learn their secrets.

The Celestines had built their rings of stones in places of power, places charged with energy. Called the Heart of Stars, these centers of energy each radiated seven invisible lines of power that connected with each other across the entire planet, like an immense yet delicate spiderweb of knots and rays. These lines of power followed the swing of the sun, the moons, the stars and the planets across the land, converging into spirals of primary energy where the magnetic forces of the earth and the universe knotted together into sources of immense power. Each Heart of Stars acted as a focal point for this energy, like a magnifying glass concentrating sunshine into a ray of light that could burn a hole in paper.

Isabeau had heard of lines of power before but she had never realized that the Celestines could travel along these lines as if they were a road. The journey along the faery path was not one to be taken lightly, however. Apart from the strain it placed on the traveler's body and mind, the lines of power existed in a warp of space and time. Khan'gharad said it had been known for people from another time or another world altogether to step through the standing stones and find themselves stranded in Eileanan, unable to make their way back to their own existence.

Such sudden and peculiar arrivals were rare though. The primary danger to traveling the faery roads was that they attracted emanations of psychic power, some of them very spiteful. Few ghosts could muster enough strength to physically harm a living being, but those of particular malevolence could sometimes overwhelm you with their negative energy, swamping you with darkness, depression and madness. Isabeau knew she was particularly vulnerable to such forces, having had to fight periods of melancholy ever since her torture six years earlier. So she did not look back. She forced her body forward against the roiling billows of energy surging around her legs, her heartbeat pounding like a drum in her ears.

She could not run all night. Soon she stumbled in exhaustion and slowed to a walk, hardly able to breathe, her lungs on fire. On she plodded, forest blurring past her. Twice more ghosts came at her, mere shreds of mist and shadows with wailing faces and outstretched hands. Each time she somehow found the strength to outrun them, though all her joints were screaming.

Suddenly someone was there beside her. She tried to run but a soft humming sound reassured her. It was a Celestine. All three of his eyes were open, the one in the center of his forehead as black and fathomless as a well, the two below as translucent as crystal. New energy spread through her with the touch of his hand on her arm. Side by side they walked, and Isabeau found her stride lengthening once more, the muscles in her thighs and calves forgetting the many miles she had run.

Dark, twisted shapes with malevolent faces writhed out of the walls and floor but the Celestine sang them away. Then another Celestine joined them, then another, stepping through the walls seemingly from nowhere. Isabeau began to understand how it was that one could stray from the road when there was no indication in the walls that a junction of paths was near.

Soon there was a procession of white-clad Celestines walking the road, Isabeau in their midst, the owl floating ahead like a snowflake blown in the wind.

Isabeau heard a soft crooning rise almost imperceptibly out of the rush and billow of sound that continually shook the tunnel of green fire. The crooning grew and grew till Isabeau heard cadences in it, a melody of such depth and timber that all the hairs on her arms rose. The Celestines all around her were humming deep in their throats, yet the sound was much greater than could be produced by these few. It rang all down the road, sparks of silver fire racing through the iridescent walls, igniting and exploding into fireworks of unimaginable beauty. Brighter and brighter the tunnel grew, until all was blazing with silver light. Isabeau could feel the song thrumming through every vein and artery, shuddering up her legs and down her spine, her skin tingling with it. It was like a storm wind, green with lightning, that flowed over her and into her, purifying her blood and filling her with a joy so keen it was akin to grief.

Through the silver-shot walls she could see the crowded streets of Lucescere, then the trees and lawns of the palace gardens, then the dark fretwork of the labyrinth. Her step quickened in anticipation. Ahead was the Pool of Two Moons, surrounded by a blazing ring of pillars and arches. A fountain rose in the center of the pool, the water shining as if a light was hidden within. One by one the Celestines stepped through the archway, then Isabeau stepped through too, the owl fluttering down to rest on her shoulder.

It was dawn. The sky was the color of pewter, the dark spears of the cypress trees stabbing upward. The relief from the tingling pain in her joints and fingertips caused Isabeau to stagger, then fall to her knees. She looked up, dizzy and sick. Lachlan stood over her, naked as the day he was born, his wings spread wide, singing. He stared at her in astonishment but did not falter, his voice ringing out pure and strong. He was holding hands with two Celestines, a great ring of faeries standing around the pool, humming the sun to life. The faeries who had traveled with Isabeau along the Old Way joined the circle, their deep crooning like the thrum of an organ. Isabeau sat back on her heels and watched them, so tired she thought she would faint, so happy she thought she would cry.

Lachlan met her gaze, his golden eyes very bright against his olive skin. Isabeau shut her eyes, listening to the deep reverberations of the Celestines' voices. Lachlan's clear harmonies wove all through it, like the gold of celandines through grass. The very ground beneath her feet thrummed with the sound of it, running up her legs and spine and into her brain so that all of her quivered and thrilled in response. She clenched her jaw, her hands clasped in her lap.

The song shivered into silence. Isabeau opened her eyes. The sun had lifted above the horizon, a blazing orb of golden light, and birds were singing joyously. Lachlan released the faeries' hands and bent down his own, large and warm, to help Isabeau to her feet.

"By Eà's green blood, how do ye come here?" he

cried. "Ye just stepped out o' thin air, Isabeau! I almost broke the song, which would've been an ill omen indeed."

Celestines clustered all about, lifting their four jointed fingers to touch Lachlan between the eyes. Isabeau smiled and shrugged, stepping back, and he submitted to the faeries' touch, mouthing, "Later!"

Behind the faeries a circle of witches sat around a fire, naked, their hair unbound, their fingers loaded with jewels. On their heads they wore wreaths of yew and rosemary, and the herb-scented smoke of the fire drifted about the garden.

Isabeau crossed the lawn to the fire, smiling and raising her hand in greeting to the witches who were all stretching in relief, stiff after the long night's Ordeal. She put down her hand for Meghan and helped her to her feet, the old sorceress groaning as all her joints protested. She looked very gaunt beneath the curtain of snowy-white hair, her breasts hanging flat and pendulous over her ribs. Isabeau wrapped her hurriedly in her own plaid.

"What are ye doing sitting up all night with no' a stitch o' clothing on!" she scolded. "Ye'll be catching your death o' cold."

"And what kind o' Keybearer would I be if I stayed in my bed for the vernal equinox!" Meghan snapped. "I may be auld but I've no' yet heard death's bell, I'll have ye ken, Beau!" Suddenly she softened, kissing Isabeau's brow. "Though the sight o' ye stepping out o' thin air was almost enough to make me die o' shock! It was strange enough seeing the Celestines materialize that way, but ye!"

Isabeau felt a hand on her arm and turned to see Iseult standing beside her, smiling. As usual she was dressed very simply in white, with her red hair bound back at the nape of her neck and covered with a white linen cap. She carried a baby girl on her hip, a five-year-old boy clinging to her skirt. Behind her stood a fair-haired nursemaid with round, pink cheeks, another baby in her arms.

The twins embraced warmly. "Och, it is so good to see ye all!" Isabeau cried.

"But where did ye spring from?" Iseult asked. "Ye seemed to step out o' nowhere."

"I traveled the Auld Way," Isabeau replied.

They all stared at her in amazement and Lachlan turned sharply. "The Auld Way!" he cried. "All the way from Tìrlethan?"

Isabeau nodded. "And I'm sick with weariness now and aching all over. I'll be glad o' a bed, I promise ye."

"But how do ye come to ken . . . ?" Meghan cried.

"O' course, your father." Isabeau nodded.

Lachlan came up behind his wife and said softly in her ear, "The Auld Ways! I wonder if they run to the Bright Land? We could save Dide and Enit a long and dangerous journey if they went that way instead o' facing the danger o' the seas, *leannan*."

Iseult replied, just as low, "It's a possibility at least."

When Lachlan became aware of Isabeau's curious regard, he turned away so she could not see his face but still she heard him mutter, "We'd best no' speak o' it here. Too many people. Later."

Iseult nodded. She said to Isabeau with a smile, "Come and break your fast and tell us all your news while I have the servants make up a bed for ye. Ye look worn out."

"I feel worn out," Isabeau said with an attempt at a laugh. "That's no' something I'll do again in a hurry."

She helped Meghan put on her long white robe trimmed with silver to show her standing as the Keybearer of the Coven. The sorceress lifted out the talisman she wore around her neck so it hung outside her robe. Inscribed with runes of power, the Key was wrought in the shape of a six-sided star enclosed within a circle. To Isabeau's trained witch senses, it seemed to thrum with power, giving off a smell like thunder-charged air. The sight and smell of it was enough to fill Isabeau with jealous longing. She had carried one third of the Key for five months, long enough for it to take hold of her heart and her imagination. Isabeau had to fight back the urge to snatch if from Meghan's breast, and clenched her fingers into fists, her face schooled to impassivity. Meghan knew her thoughts, however, and frowned at her, one hand rising involuntarily to wrap around the magical talisman, hiding it from view.

Isabeau touched her arm in reassurance, and the stern look on Meghan's face softened. The little donbeag Gitâ unrolled from his tight ball by the embers of the fire, stretched sleepily, then unfurled the little sails of skin between his paws and flew up to Meghan's shoulder. With one paw on her ear, he chittered an excited welcome to Isabeau, who chittered back. The other witches were standing by to talk to the Keybearer so Isabeau left her side and turned back to Iseult, who was chatting to her nursemaid Sukey while Lachlan dressed.

Sukey was an old friend, so Isabeau greeted her

warmly. "How are ye yourself? The twins are no'
running ye ragged?"

"Aye, my lady, keeping me on my toes, as ye can
imagine," the nursemaid replied ruefully. "I thought
Donncan was as artful as a bagful o' elven cats when
he was a laddiekin, but Owein and Olwynne beat
him hollow. Wee Olwynne may no' have wings like
the laddies but she's swift as a snake and twice as
cunning."

Isabeau lifted the little girl from Iseult's arms and
cuddled her close. "This bonny lassie? I dinna believe
it. She looks as if butter wouldna melt in her mouth."

Olwynne stared at her with suspicious black eyes,
then reached out one fat little hand, seized the owl's
talon hanging around Isabeau's neck, and smiled
blissfully.

"Och, she's a wicked wee lass but sweet as honey,"
Iseult laughed, tousling her daughter's bronze-red
curls.

"It doesna seem fair that the two boys should have
Lachlan's wings but not wee Olwynne," Isabeau said.
She glanced at Donncan, who was swooping around
his father's head, his wings the same burnished gold
as his curls. Owein, as red-headed as his twin, was
bouncing up and down on Sukey's hip, his bronze-
colored wings spread and testing the air. All three
children had the distinctive white lock of the Mac-
Cuinns springing from their brow, a sure sign that
they had bonded with the Lodestar, the magical
sphere that responded only to the hand of a Mac-
Cuinn.

"Och, no doubt she'll have Talents o' her own,"
Meghan said, coming up beside them. She reached

out one gnarled finger, hooting softly, and Buba
rubbed her ear tufts against it, hooting back. "How
can she no' with two such Talented parents?"

They all began to walk down the garden, talking
companionably. Behind Lachlan walked his squire,
Dillon. Isabeau hardly recognized the sturdy, freckle-
faced lad she had known in this tall, powerfully built
young man. He was dressed in the blue kilt and
jacket of the Rìgh's own bodyguard, the plaid secured over his shoulder with a silver brooch de-
picting a charging stag. At his waist he wore a long
sword with an intricately coiling hilt.

Behind them came the other witches, dressed now
and their hair bound back as usual, with the Celestines all streaming behind them. The marks of their
footsteps were dark in the dew-laden grass. The
white-clad procession left the garden and plunged
into the narrow hedge-lined corridors of the maze,
the walls of yew high above their heads.

"I see ye are newly scarred," Iseult said softly. "I
would ask o' you the story o' your name."

"I will gladly tell it," Isabeau answered in the language of the Khan'cohbans, sweeping her fingers to
her brow, then to her heart, and then out to the tall
yew hedge.

"Wait until we are alone," Iseult said softly.
"There are many listening ears in the palace."

Isabeau nodded, casting her twin a quick glance.

A feast to celebrate the spring equinox had been
set up in the great hall but to Isabeau's relief she was
not expected to sit down with a horde of strangers.
Sukey took her up to the royal suite and fed her
bannocks with bellfruit jam and told her amusing

tales about the children until Iseult and Lachlan could escape and join her.

When she had eaten Isabeau curled up in a big chair by the fire to rest while Sukey put the twins to bed. Although Iseult had ordered a room to be prepared for her, Isabeau was eager to tell the story of her adventures and planned to wait for the others before seeking her own bed.

It was quiet and peaceful in the royal drawing room, however, and so Isabeau soon slipped into sleep. She was woken some time later by the soft murmur of voices. Her eyelashes fluttered open.

Meghan was sitting in the armchair opposite, her hands resting idle on Gitâ's brown fur. Iseult had drawn up a chair beside her, while Lachlan was pacing up and down the room in his usual restless way, his kilt swinging.

"It is so hard to ken what we should do first," Lachlan was saying. "We have spent all winter building a fleet o' ships and now I am afraid to send them out in case they end up on the bottom o' the ocean like every other ship that has left safe harbor these past ten years. The Ship Tax has been unpopular indeed and I canna risk all the money we raised going on naught."

He paused to stand before the fire, lifting his kilt to warm his behind. Isabeau hastily shut her eyes.

"And o' course, everyone wants us to do something different," Lachlan continued. "Linley Mac-Seinn wants us to send the ships around to Carraig and win back the Tower o' Sea Singers from the Fairgean, the merchants want us to wipe out the pirates and keep the trade routes free from sea serpents, and

Iain and Elfrida want us to attack Bride. No matter what we do, *someone* is going to be unhappy. I just canna see my way clear, Meghan. Can ye no' advise me?"

The sorceress stroked Gitâ's fur, her face troubled.

"Happen we should try and find out who it is that is betraying us," Iseult said, her voice very cold. "It be no point making plans if our enemies ken them as well as we do ourselves."

Meghan sighed and Lachlan began to pace again. "I feel like a wounded sheep with a shriek o' gravenings circling over me," he said then, his voice moody. "No matter what I do, I am beset by enemies on all sides. We cut off the head o' one faction and it sprouts two more, like a harlequin hydra . . ."

"The harlequin hydra. Symbol o' insurmountable opposition," Meghan said softly. "Cut off one head and another two grow."

Lachlan sat down heavily, his head in his hands.

"Och, we shall just have to overcome the harlequin hydra like your namesake, Lachlan the Navigator," the old sorceress said. "There is no point in falling into despair, lad. Iseult is right. If we discover who the spy in our ranks is, we may have a better chance in overcoming our other obstacles."

Lachlan made an impatient gesture. "Do ye think we have no' tried? Once we exiled Finlay, I thought we had done with spies and betrayers. Yet every time we move against the Bright Soldiers, they're waiting for us. I've lost so many good men in their bloody ambushes! And as if that was no' enough, every ship we send out has been lost because the blaygird pirates knew exactly what route we planned to sail. It's uncanny!"

"I ken all that," Meghan said, just as impatiently.

Lachlan got to his feet. He wandered around the room, fiddling with ornaments on the dresser, twitching aside the curtain and glancing outside, straightening a picture. Suddenly he came and sat back down again, looking directly at Isabeau. The color rose in her cheeks.

"So, we've woken, Beau," he said. "Why do ye no' tell us your news?"

Isabeau busied her hands by pulling at Buba's ear tufts, though the owl grumbled sleepily in protest. "I hardly ken where to start, so much has happened."

"Tell us about the Auld Ways," Lachlan commanded, just as Iseult said, "Tell us your new name!"

"Starting at the beginning is always a good idea," Meghan said.

It was far more difficult telling the story of her name quest this time, because both Lachlan and Meghan interrupted constantly with questions and exclamations. When Isabeau finally reached the part where she changed shape, both leaned forward, exclaiming with amazement. Lachlan was incredulous then excited, while Meghan's whole face glowed with pride and satisfaction.

"That's all there is to tell," she said at last. "I could no' fly down to Lucescere with Asrohc building her nest, so I made *Dai-dein* tell me how to travel the Auld Ways and came home that way."

"How did ye manage that?" Iseult said wryly. "I canna imagine a warrior o' the seven scars being made to do anything by a mere child."

"Child no longer," Isabeau cried, lifting her hand to trace her initiation scar.

"Still," Iseult said.

Isabeau grinned. "I tricked him into it."

"But ye have no' said much about the Auld Ways, Beau, only that Khan'gharad showed ye the way o' it. Canna ye tell me more?" Meghan asked.

Reluctantly Isabeau shook her head. "I am sworn to secrecy."

Irritation flashed across Meghan's face. "Surely, Beau, ye can tell me more than that. What are they? How do they work? Where do they run?"

With both Lachlan and Meghan's imperious gazes focused intently upon her face, the color rose high in Isabeau's cheeks but she shook her head again. "I'm sorry, but I swore a sacred oath. I canna tell."

"What do ye mean, ye canna tell?" Lachlan exclaimed. "Who is your loyalty to, Isabeau the Red?"

"It is no' my secret to tell," Isabeau protested, her cheeks scarlet. She glanced rather wildly at Meghan. "Why do ye no' ask Cloudshadow if ye are so desperate to ken? She is the one to ask, no' me."

"Cloudshadow will no' tell me either," Meghan snapped. "I have begged her many times to reveal the secret to me but she never will."

"So how can ye ask me to?" Isabeau cried. "It is a mystery o' the Celestines and I have no right to ken it myself. Humans have betrayed Celestines before, ye ken that better than anyone, Meghan. Ye shouldna be asking me!"

"Yet ye say yourself ye tricked your father into revealing the secret to ye," Lachlan said scornfully. "What right have ye to be so mealy-mouthed?"

"Happen it could save us all from much danger and trouble if we could use the faeries' roads," Iseult said persuasively. "Will ye no' help us, Beau?"

"I canna, I promised," Isabeau cried, tears very close to the surface.

"Do ye no' realize that your auld friend Dide may die because ye refuse to tell us!" Lachlan bent over her, his dark face suffused with anger and frustration.

"Why? Where is it that ye're sending him? Ye said before a dangerous journey—what dangerous journey?" Isabeau had to fight not to shrink back in her chair, intimidated by the great bulk of a man bending over her, his burly neck and chest, his great black wings, all his strength and regal power.

To her surprise and relief he stepped back, dropping his gaze. Then he said sullenly, "How am I to ken ye can be trusted, Isabeau?"

Cut to the quick, Isabeau could only stare at him. He went on inexorably. "Why should I tell ye our most secret plans when ye will no' tell us what ye ken? Ye were the one to befriend the Ensorcellor and offer her shelter. How do we ken she has no' cast her charm over ye and compels ye to do her bidding?"

Iseult protested but Lachlan would not be stopped. He said loudly, with a cruel edge to his voice, "We ken the spy must be someone close to us, for they are privy to all our most secret plans. Who is to say it is no' ye, Isabeau?"

Meghan cried, "That's enough, Lachlan!" and Iseult leaped to her feet, her face white with anger. Isabeau said with a tremble in her voice, "But I have no' been here."

"Nay, ye have no', have ye?" Lachlan replied coolly. "While we have been here fighting impossible odds ye have been off, safe in the mountains, riding dragons and playing with owls. We ask o' ye just one wee thing to tell us something that ye ken could help us enormously, and ye refuse to help."

"But I swore an oath," Isabeau said helplessly, tears rising in her eyes. Gitâ soared over to comfort her, chittering in distress, while Buba hooted softly and rubbed her head against Isabeau's hand.

Iseult knelt next to her and took her hand, saying over her shoulder, "Lachlan, how can ye say such things? Ye ken Isabeau is loyal and true."

"Nay, I do no'," Lachlan answered, his angry color beginning to fade. "I thought Finlay loyal and true, I thought all my men were. Now I can believe treachery o' anyone. I meant what I said about Maya. Isabeau sheltered her for close on a year. We ken the cursehag has the strongest and most subtle compulsion o' will o' any witch we've ever kent. How can ye be sure Isabeau was no' ensorcelled by her?"

To Isabeau's dismay no one said anything. She knew they were thinking of Latifa and Lachlan's brother Jaspar, both of whom had succumbed to Maya's charm despite their own strength. Isabeau pushed away Iseult's hand and got to her feet, her vision so obscured by tears that she could hardly see straight. "I only sheltered Maya so I could break the curse she'd cast on ye," Isabeau said, knowing as she said this that it was not the entire truth. "I do no' ken where she has gone or what she is doing now. I have had no communication with her since she left the secret valley. And even if I had, I would never do anything to betray ye or the Coven." Her voice broke.

"Oh, Beau," Meghan said gently. "Lachlan . . ."

"I ken, I ken," he answered in exasperation. He put out his hand and grasped her arm, keeping her still. "I'm sorry, Isabeau. Do no' be so much upset. I was simply trying to make ye see, make ye all see . . ."

The touch of his hand on her arm undid her. Worn out by the exertions of the night, Isabeau was unable to control the shuddering sobs that rose up and choked her. "Ye . . . think I . . . I would never . . . How could ye . . . ?" She could not get the words out.

Lachlan pulled her close. Isabeau could not resist the temptation to rest her head against his shoulder, muffling her sobs against his shirt. Under her cheek his muscles shifted, the soft silk of his midnight-black feathers brushing against her. "I'm sorry," he said awkwardly, lowering his head to try and see her face. "I did no' mean to hurt ye. Please stop greeting. Canna ye see I was just trying to prove a point?"

Isabeau rubbed her face with one hand. "I would never . . ."

"I ken, I ken." He patted her back. "I'm sorry. I shouldna have said anything. I was angry. It was just that ye ken something that could make such a difference to us and ye will no' tell. I shouldna have lost my temper, though. I'm sorry."

Isabeau looked up at him, her hand resting on his chest, then suddenly she pushed herself away. She wiped her face with her fingers, turning away so they could not see her face. "I'm sorry too," she said, trying to swallow her tears.

Lachlan had turned away also, staring moodily into the fire. "I did no' mean to sound as if I thought ye were the spy, Isabeau," he said curtly. "I ken it canna be ye anyway. Ye do no' ken any o' our secret plans."

Isabeau sank down on to her chair, hurt and unhappy. Buba crept into her hands and she cuddled the little owl close.

"Come, Isabeau," Meghan said, getting to her feet. "We are all tired after our long night and happen none o' us are seeing clearly. Why do we no' all go and rest and recuperate our strength and we can talk again in the morning."

Isabeau nodded, even though she was afraid they would again press her to tell the secret that she had sworn on Eà's green blood never to reveal. "Where am I to sleep?"

"The maids have made up your auld room for ye," Iseult said, rising to her feet.

"Nay, ye must come to the Tower," Meghan said decisively. "Ye've been away from us far too long. Are ye no' meant to be my apprentice? Some apprentice ye've been, spending all your time away from me."

Isabeau was too tired to recognize Meghan's humorous inflection. "But, Meghan, ye ken I . . ." she began in some distress.

Meghan patted her hand, smiling. "No need to fret, dearling, I was only teasing ye. I ken the queen-dragon told ye ye must learn what ye could from your father's people, but now ye have won your scar it is time for ye to settle down at the Theurgia and start studying in earnest. Such a hotchpotch education ye've had!"

"Aye, that be the truth indeed," Isabeau said with a faint smile. She made to rise to her feet and was rather disconcerted when Lachlan bent and grasped her arm, pulling her upright. "Thank ye," she said, not looking at him.

As she walked slowly along the avenue with

Meghan, they heard the sound of children's shouts and laughter, then came out into the square before the Tower of Two Moons. Rebuilt to its former grandeur, the massive building dominated the western end of the palace gardens. Great flying buttresses held up four towering spires, one at each point of the compass. A broad terrace ran the length of the building, planted with the seven sacred trees in huge square pots marked with the sign of the Coven. Under the trees' shade children squatted, tossing sheep's knuckle, or ran, screaming with excitement. A few young men or women strolled, dressed in the flowing black gowns of apprentices, their heads bent in earnest discussion. As Meghan and Isabeau mounted the three wide stone steps to the terrace, the students bowed or curtsied respectfully. A few murmured humble greetings and Isabeau was astonished when they called her Highness.

She looked at Meghan in some surprise but the sorceress gave a little shrug. "The Theurgia tittle tattles will soon spread the truth o' it, Beau. Few here ken ye, remember."

So Isabeau just nodded and smiled and accepted their respect. Soon enough they would know she was only the Banrìgh's twin sister and a student like themselves.

They passed from the warmth of the terrace into the cool hush of the main building. Isabeau looked about her with interest. She was unable to correlate the grand hall within, the walls hung with tapestries and the hollowed stone softened with rugs, to the smoke-stained, ghost-haunted ruin she had seen six years earlier.

Meghan read her thoughts. "Children's laughter

does more to help the ugly memories fade than any other form o' exorcism I ken," she said, her face softer than Isabeau had seen it since she had arrived. "I hardly feel the ghosts now."

With the Keybearer by her side, Isabeau was taken swiftly through the formalities of acceptance into the Theurgia. She accepted the flowing black gown they gave her and let Daillas the Lame, the head teacher at the Theurgia, pile her arms with books and scrolls. The old sorcerer was determined that Isabeau catch up for lost time as quickly as she could. Isabeau submitted willingly, eager now to prove herself to her teachers. She had studied with Daillas when the Theurgia had first been set up in the days after the Samhain rebellion, and was fond of the old man who had been as cruelly tortured by the Awl as she had.

Aware of some sort of peace settling over her, she followed meekly in Daillas and Meghan's wake as the two most respected witches in the land led her up to her new room.

Isabeau had been assigned a tiny room in the apprentice wing of the Theurgia. It was only large enough for a small white bed, a chest, a writing desk and a bookshelf, but it was considerably larger than her room in the tree where she had grown up. Through the mullioned glass of her window she could see the green leaves of the oak tree growing on the terrace. She dumped her armful of books on the desk and stood watching the children play as Daillas and Meghan stood in the open door behind her, discussing what lessons she should take and who she should study with. Buba fluttered down from Isabeau's shoulder to perch on the back of the chair, her head rotating as she stared about with round-eyed interest.

Taken by surprise by an immense yawn, Isabeau opened her watering eyes to find Daillas peering at her sympathetically. "Ye must be weary, lassie. Why do ye no' rest and restore your strength, and we shall save planning your lessons till the morrow. None should study on the day o' the vernal equinox."

Snooze-hooh? Buba hooted hopefully and Isabeau hooted back softly in reply. She saw both Daillas and Meghan smile, then with a fond pat of her hand and a gentle, "May Eà bless your sleep," they left her. She was alone at last.

It was dusk when she woke. She lay still for a long time, unable to recognize the dim shape of the furniture about her or the smell of wood polish, lavender and old leather. Feeling an instinctive clutch of terror, she let fire blossom in her hand. As the room sprang into brightness, she realized where she was and all her tension drained away, leaving only a feeling of contentment.

She lay quietly, smiling. Isabeau was very glad that she was here in the Tower of Two Moons and not at the palace. Here she had a chance of making her own way, independent of her sister the Banrìgh. Much as she loved Iseult, Isabeau had no desire to be a mere hanger-on at court. All her ambition to be a sorceress was hot and eager in her, and she was happy to be once again close to her beloved Meghan, able to see her every day, listen to her stories and learn her wisdom.

Isabeau swung her legs out of bed, and pulled the

black gown over her head with a little quickening of
pleasure in her veins. Somber in hue and in cut, it
hung loosely on her, without a single pleat or bow
to relieve its severity. She pulled her unruly red curls
back from her brow and plaited them swiftly into a
thick braid that hung down to her waist. There was
no mirror but when she hooked back the curtain she
could see her reflection in the window, broken into
an intricate jigsaw by the many panes of glass. All
she could see was a pale, serious face floating above
a sea of darkness, haloed with the fiery glint of the
curls that refused to be subdued by the plait. The
sight pleased her and she smiled again.

Buba slept still, her head sunk down into her feathers, her ear tufts sticking straight up. Isabeau rubbed
one finger on the white head lovingly and the round
golden eyes opened, blinking sleepily. "I'm going
out, Buba, do ye wish to come?"

Snooze-hooh, Buba replied and shut her eyes again.

Smiling, Isabeau let herself out her door. Beyond
was a wide balcony, bounded by a colonnade of slim
gothic arches that supported a high vaulted ceiling,
fringed by an intricate frieze of stars and moons.

The balcony looked down onto a central garth of
smooth green lawn, lined with cypress trees and with
a fountain in the center. The only sound was the
tinkle of falling water, the singing of birds and the
muffled chanting of incantations.

Isabeau found the Keybearer in her rooms in the
main tower. Meghan was writing in *The Book of Shadows*, a massive thick book with a heavily embossed
cover of red leather. It contained all the history and
lore of the Coven of Witches and it was the duty of

each Keybearer to record within its pages all of note that occurred in Eileanan.

"I am just writing the tale o' your adventures on the Spine o' the World," Meghan said with an affectionate smile. "Come tell me once more, Isabeau. It gladdens my auld heart indeed to hear ye tell it."

So Isabeau told her tale again and Meghan inscribed her words carefully, often asking her to pause so she could catch up. Isabeau saw how much Meghan's hand trembled and how thin and wavering her handwriting was and offered to act as her scribe. But Meghan just shook her snowy-white head and wrote on. As she reached the end of the last page in the book, she shook sand over it carefully, shut the book for a moment and then reopened it. A fresh white page stood where a moment before there had been none. Meghan smiled at Isabeau, who took up her story once more, the old woman laboriously writing down every word.

At last Meghan had finished and she shut and locked the book with a silver key as long as Isabeau's finger. Carefully she put *The Book of Shadows* back on the shelf.

"What a tale!" she sighed, pouring out two goblets of goldensloe wine. "Indeed, I do no' think I've heard one like it. I always kent ye had a powerful Talent though, my Beau, ever since ye were naught but a wicked lass."

Isabeau only smiled, sipping her wine and hungrily devouring, one by one, all of Meghan's little honey cakes.

"How ye puzzled me as a bairn," Meghan mused. "Ye had such a link with the beasts I often thought

ye'd follow in my footsteps and be a wood witch,
yet ye had little understanding o' the other powers
o' earth. It was strange. Fire was clearly your strongest power, yet fire and talking with animals does
no' usually go together at all. And ye were always
one for making up games and pretending to be what
ye were no', a tendency that troubled me sorely."
She sipped her wine, the firelight playing over the
deep wrinkles so that she looked ancient indeed.
"It all makes sense now," she said softly. "Indeed
it does."

"Latifa said fire is the element o' transformations,"
Isabeau said.

"Aye, indeed, she was right. I am glad I sent her
to ye. She taught ye well."

"No' just about fire magic." Isabeau spoke cheerfully, wanting to banish the melancholy darkening
Meghan's face. "Ye'll be glad to ken she taught me
to cook as well."

Meghan smiled briefly. "Well, that was more than
I could ever do."

"Aye, but was that because o' the limitations o'
the apprentice or o' the teacher?" Isabeau replied
cheekily.

Meghan smiled again but the shadow of melancholy on her face did not lift. "Can ye show me?"
she said suddenly. "Shapechange for me."

Isabeau felt a little sink of her spirits, but she nodded. "I'll try," she said. "I am still no' altogether sure
o' what it is I do."

Isabeau gathered together her strength, looking
down at her hands clasped together tightly in her lap.
She flexed them, imagining them talons. In her mind's
eye she could clearly see herself as owl, white feathers

faintly speckled with brown, golden eyes inscrutable. There was the odd dislocation of the world that came when she was changing, the bending and lengthening of shapes, the draining away of color, the springing out of detail, sharp and precise. Then the transformation was complete. She looked up at the old woman, now so huge and frightening, her human smell causing Isabeau to cower down instinctively.

So-hooh, you-hooh see-hooh, she managed to hoot.

I do-hooh see-hooh, the human hooted back. Isabeau was aware of the kindness of her dark eyes, the waves of reassurance and understanding that beat from her, palpable as the scent of pine resin on a warm day. She relaxed a little, her feathers smoothing down, her ear tufts sinking. The human smiled gently, holding out her hand, willing Isabeau to come to her. After a moment Isabeau opened her wings and swooped across, alighting on the human's twig-like hand. They regarded each other thoughtfully, the human turning her hand this way and that to examine Isabeau's claws, her feathers, the cryptic pattern of gray-brown speckles and stripes that was only visible when she crouched down to hide. Isabeau's head rotated first one way then the other as she kept her huge round eyes fixed on the human's deeply wrinkled face. One gnarled finger came up and gently stroked Isabeau's ear tufts and once again Isabeau let herself relax.

You-hooh are true-hooh owl-hooh, the human hooted.

Isabeau hooted back crossly and fidgeted her feathers.

No-hooh slur-hooh meant-hooh, the old human apologized. *You-hooh may change-hooh back.*

Isabeau regarded her for a moment, then suddenly shook herself and transformed back. Immediately she fell to the floor with a jolt, bruising her bottom and knocking the wind out of her. Meghan was nursing her hand, which had for a second borne all of the weight of Isabeau's tall and muscular figure. "Ye silly lass!" she cried. "Could ye no' have flown to the floor first? I think ye have broken my hand."

"I did no' think o' it," Isabeau replied sulkily, rubbing her bare bottom and getting to her feet rather shakily. All the energy that the wine and cakes had given her was gone. She felt as if she had run the entire distance of the Old Way once again. For a couple of seconds she swayed, her sight obscured by a wave of dizziness, then she was able to sit down and sip her wine and rest her head on her hand, drawing her plaid about her.

"It is incredible," Meghan was saying. "Indeed ye were an owl, no doubt o' that. It was no mere illusion, I felt your feathers and claws, and your mind, your thoughts, they were the thoughts o' an owl, no' the silly lass I ken."

Isabeau said nothing, just held out her goblet for more wine. Meghan poured her some more, still talking excitedly.

"So ye have taken on the form o' an owl, a snow lion and a golden eagle. All very different indeed. Can ye do anything else?"

Isabeau drained her wine and took a deep breath. In her mind's eyes she imagined herself as a donbeag, as bright-eyed and plumy-tailed as Gitâ who was perched on Meghan's knee, watching with interest. She had grown up with donbeags, she knew their every quirk and mannerism. With a thought she changed shape.

Suddenly the world was huge and dark and filled with stealthy sounds that had her quivering with fear. She gripped the wood with her claws, looking about her, her large round ears twitching back and forth as she listened for any sound of danger. The unsettling odor of humans caused her to spread her sails of skin a little in preparation for sudden flight. She smeled donbeag too, which reassured her. She heard an excited chitter of welcome from across the room and peered that way.

A hugh white hand descended toward her. She took flight, her tail spreading wide. A wall of wood collided with her, she fell, shrieking. A human voice like the crash of thunder. All her nerves jangled, causing her to startle. A peculiar desire to trust the voice fought against all her instincts, all her natural fear. The voice boomed about her. Somehow she recognized something in the thunderous sound. She turned, tried to answer. For a moment she was not sure whether she was owl, donbeag or woman. The room spun, she fell back into her own skin, naked, shivering and sick.

For several long, horrible moments she retched helplessly, vomiting the honey cakes and wine upon Meghan's fine blue carpet. Her ears rang and the world whirled about her. Long after her stomach was empty she retched still, Meghan's cool hand supporting her. At last she was able to lie back, limp as a scullery maid's rag, her vision oddly blurred. Vaguely she heard Meghan moving about her, wringing out a cloth to lay on her forehead, giving her cool water to sip, stroking back her sweat-tangled hair.

"Sorcery sickness," the Keybearer said softly. "Have ye found yourself sick and weak after changing shape before?"

Isabeau nodded, then wished she had not, for stabbing pain shot through her temples and the world sank away into a fizzing darkness once more. She came close to fainting but at last the whirling sickness subsided and she could try and concentrate on Meghan's words once more.

"Ye must no' change shape again till I give ye leave," the Keybearer was saying with great emphasis. "Sorcery sickness is dangerous indeed. It can leave ye mad as a March hare or foolish as a babbling babe. Even worse, it can twist all your reason so that you use your Talents for evil or self-advancement, which as ye ken, all witches o' the Coven swear no' to do. Isabeau, are ye listening to me?"

Isabeau jerked her head up. "Aye, Meghan," she said, and heard her words thick in her throat.

"Beau, are ye well? Can ye hear me?"

"Aye, Meghan, I hear ye," Isabeau replied, holding her head straight so it would not fall off her neck. It sounded as if she spoke through a thick woolly plaid and she shook her head to try and clear it. At once the world spun down into darkness again and she reached out her hands for anything to grip onto, anything to hold her still in all this giddy, spinning, roaring darkness. Something hit her hard. She saw the edge of Meghan's white robe sweep close, and then nothing but darkness.

Isabeau woke much later to find a pair of round golden eyes staring unblinkingly into hers. She stared back, feeling very light and thin, as thin as a bellfruit seed dangling in the wind.

You-whoo well-whoo?

"I'm no' sure," Isabeau answered. "How long have I been asleep?"

The owl gave an expressive little shrug of her wings. Clever as owls were, they could not count very high. Isabeau had a vague memory of easing in and out of a fevered sleep, and thought she must have been unconscious for quite a long time.

"Three weeks," Meghan said softly. "We have all been worried indeed about ye."

"Three weeks!" Isabeau echoed. "How . . . ? I mean . . ."

"Sorcery sickness can take ye like that," Meghan said, smoothing back Isabeau's hair. "I blame myself. Ye had walked the Auld Way only that night, and who kens the toll that takes on your mind and body? And ye have no' been properly trained in the High Magic, ye do no' ken how to prepare yourself or conserve your strength. And for me to be asking ye to perform for me like a dancing bear in a traveling circus! I o' all people ken the cost o' such sorcery and should never have asked ye to overextend yourself like that. Please forgive me, Beau."

"O' course," Isabeau replied rather dazedly, glad to let her head sink back into the pillow. After a moment she said, "I think I'm hungry."

"Och, that's a good sign," Meghan said encouragingly. "I'll ring for some soup for ye. Lie still, Isabeau, do no' try and sit up yet. And do no' even think about summoning the One Power! It'll be some days before we'll even let ye light a candle for yourself, and months before we allow ye to try and shape-change again."

She caught Isabeau's expression and said sternly, "It'll do ye good, my bairn. Rest now and when ye are well and strong again, then we'll begin to teach ye the ways o' the High Magic. Ye must be patient."

Isabeau lowered her eyes. "Aye, Keybearer."

Meghan glared at her suspiciously for a moment, clicked her tongue against her teeth as if in annoyance, and went swiftly out of the room.

You-hooh snooze-hooh, Owl guard-hooh you-hooh.

Thank you-hooh, Isabeau hooted back, and turned her cheek into the pillow.

As spring warmed toward summer, Isabeau settled happily into her new life at the Tower of Two Moons. She wore with pride the loose black gown of an apprentice and studied hard with the other students. Most of her lessons were in mathematics, history, alchemy and the old languages, but she was also given a thorough grounding in the many basic skills that all witches must learn—the manipulation of the forces of air, water, fire and earth. To her great pleasure she also studied the element of Spirit with Arkening the Dreamwalker, learning much about the use of her witch senses, the uncanny insight into the minds of others that most witches seemed to possess.

To her surprise this did not merely involve the use of her third eye, though this was growing clearer and sharper every day. The training a witch received at the Theurgia was designed to increase their natural powers of perception, intuition and logic to such a degree that many so-called Skills required no use of

the One Power at all. Isabeau was taught to interpret
the slightest change in expression and intonation, the
flicker of a glance, the flutter of the fingers. Her
memory was honed to a preternatural extent so that
she carried with her all that she saw and heard and
read. And over and over again she was taught the
lessons of humility, sympathy and compassion.

"If there is naught else to learn from the lessons
o' history," Arkening said dreamily, "it is that
witches can grow arrogant and, worse, manipulative.
Because the motives and emotions o' the common
folk seem transparent to us, and their messy mud-
dling ways downright foolish, it is not uncommon
for a witch to begin to feel she is superior in every
way. But we are mere humans ourselves, and as
prone to self-deception as any other human."

Isabeau nodded, knowing how true this was. Arkening leaned forward, her eyes for once losing their
vagueness. "Ye must remember that the Coven is
here to help and heal and teach, to try and guide the
rest o' the world toward an ideal o' wisdom and
kindness. That is why we swear to the Creed, to remember that all people must choose their own path
and tread it alone. Witches o' the Coven must always
remember their oath—to speak only what is true in
their heart, to never use the Power to ensorcel others
or change their destiny, to only ever use the One
Power as is needed, and then with a kind heart, a
fierce and canny mind, and steadfast courage."

"May my heart be kind, my mind fierce, my spirit
brave," Isabeau replied with fervor, and the old sorceress smiled at her and patted her hand.

Soon after this conversation Isabeau was allowed
to begin studying with Meghan herself, a sign of how

quickly she had learned. Once a day Isabeau climbed the stairs to the Keybearer's own rooms. Surrounded by all the familiar objects of her childhood—the spinning wheel and lap-loom, the piles of books and scrolls, the globe of another world, Meghan's sphere of shining crystal—Isabeau was taught to draw upon the One Power, and to wield it with increasing subtlety and control.

Isabeau loved her lessons in magic. She loved the feeling of euphoria as her body was filled to brimming with the One Power, the delicious quivering tension, the urge to release it all in one white blaze, the struggle to contain it as she brought her will to bear upon the world around her, the gratification and relief as what she willed came to pass. There was no feeling to match it, no sensation so exquisite, no experience so fulfilling.

She climbed the stairs to Meghan's room with eagerness every day and left it reluctantly, no matter how exhausted she was or how highly strung. Working magic left one overwrought, all one's senses too highly attuned, all one's nerves exposed. Isabeau came to understand how it was that great acts of magic left her limp and wrung out like a scullery maid's rag, unable to find the strength to light a candle flame. And so at last she understood why it was that Meghan and the council of sorcerers had forbidden her to practice shapechanging.

At first she had resented this dictum deeply. Many times she was tempted to break the rules and fly the night with Buba in the shape of an owl. Always she managed to resist, knowing how harshly Meghan and the council would view any transgression. This was the time for Isabeau to practice all the humbleness and reserve taught to her by the Soul-Sage, to keep her mind on her books and her thoughts to herself. For the more Isabeau learned, the more ignorant she felt. She was finally understanding what Meghan had told her so many times—that to master the One Power she needed to understand the immutable laws of nature and the universe. That was not something to be learned easily.

When Isabeau was not studying she wandered in the gardens or walked down to the palace to see her sister and play with her niece and nephews. Sometimes she accompanied Meghan to the council meetings, though she always found it hard to face Lachlan with any degree of composure.

Despite his words of apology, Isabeau found that the young Rìgh kept a wall of reserve up against her, and that troubled her very much. At first she had been hurt that she was not taken into his and Iseult's confidence, but as time went on, she came to realize that she was not the only one to be excluded from Lachlan's inner life. He seemed to trust only Iseult, Meghan, Iain of Arran and Duncan Ironfist, the captain of the Blue Guards. Only with them did his air of regal reticence drop away into warmth, merriment and affection. Only with them did he discuss his plans and strategies for dealing with the many problems that beset the new order.

The rising of the spring tides had brought the Fairgean in greater numbers than ever before. The sea was teeming with their sleek black heads as the sea-warriors swam in the wake of the great blue whales, while the soft beaches of the south grew crowded with the Fairgean women, many swollen with pregnancy. Despite all the arguments of the lairds and merchants, the Rìgh would not launch an assault against them, saying tersely that the Fairgean must be offered the chance to sign the Pact of Peace as all the other faery kind had been.

This proposal was met with hoots of scorn and cries of dismay by the council, but Lachlan was adamant. "For a thousand years we have sought to force the Fairgean to submit to our will, but always they have risen again. We shall never gain a lasting peace unless we can come to terms with them," he said, frowning down into the lambent glow of the Lodestar, which he held cupped in his hands. "There has been much evil done on both sides and unless we can learn to forgive each other, this war will go on until all o' us are dead."

"No' if we destroy all the Fairgean first!" Linley MacSeinn, the Prionnsa of Carraig, cried furiously.

"By trying to destroy them, we may destroy all chance o' a true peace," Lachlan replied, but the prionnsa cut across him impatiently.

"Their concubines loll in comfort on our beaches, ready to bear litters o' the foul black-blooded creatures. Why do we no' attack them while the bulk o' the warriors are swimming south to hunt the whales?"

Lachlan glanced his way, his dark face softening in sympathy. "Linley, I ken ye lost most o' your family in the Fairgean invasion o' your homeland twelve years ago, but ye are asking me to send soldiers against women heavy with babe. I canna and shallna do it. I canna believe that Eà would wish me to have the blood o' innocents on my hands . . ."

"Innocents! No Fairgean is innocent!" the MacSeinn retorted, his face white with fury and grief.

"Did they no' murder my wife and my son? Did they no' massacre my clan till I have naught but a few hundred men left?"

"Aye, they did," Lachlan said, "and that is no' something to be forgiven lightly—"

"I shall never forgive, never," the MacSeinn shouted, his voice raw with grief. "Do ye forgive the murder o' your brothers so easily, Lachlan the Winged?"

The Rìgh's face froze and his fingers tightened convulsively on the Lodestar so that it flashed with silver fire. "I do no'," he said in a cold voice.

"Or your father, Parteta the Brave, who was murdered by the sea demons' king on the very beach where his concubines now lie fat and idle?"

"I do no' forget my father." Lachlan's face was tight with anger and a bitter grief.

"Then how can ye speak o' innocents? How can ye waste the lives o' our men trying to subdue Tìrsoileir when the Fairgean have us trapped like coneys in a cornfield, too terrified to set our noses outside the harbor? My clan have been loyal to yours for a thousand years, yet ye make no move to restore *my* throne to *me*! It is the lands o' the MacFóghnan and the NicHilde that ye fight to regain, when they have been your enemies for centuries! Where is the justice in that?"

"Linley, ye ken we canna launch a strike against the stronghold o' the Fairgean just now." Lachlan tried to control his temper but his voice and his body were trembling with anger. "We have no' the men nor the money. If we can win Tìrsoilleir back for the NicHilde, then she will pay us well for all the damage the Bright Soldiers inflicted upon our lands. Better still, we shall have access to a whole army o' highly trained soldiers. We shall be able to march on Carraig from both the west and the east, aye, even from the south with the Khan'cohbans' help. Then we may have some chance o' winning back your lands for ye."

"By that time the Fairgean will have swelled their numbers even more with all these newborn pups," Linley cried with disgust. "Why let them bear their young now if we plan to kill them all later?"

"Happen we will no' need to kill them all," Meghan said, her voice very stern. "If we can parley—"

"Parley! Faugh!" The MacSeinn made a sound of disgust. "Parley with the Fairgean? Your brain has grown soft with age, Meghan Keybearer!"

There were cries of outrage from the council, but most of the room remained silent. Fear and hatred of the Fairgean ran deep.

"And is my brain soft with age too, Linley?" Lachlan said, his voice very cold. He got to his feet and advanced on the MacSeinn, his wings raised so he was surrounded by darkness like a storm cloud. The prionnsa from Carraig shrank a little, despite all his attempts to stand firm. "Do ye think I do no' understand the threat o' the Fairgean? For twelve years they have rampaged unchecked, growing in strength and numbers every year. We are indeed trapped like coneys in a cornfield, unable to sail the seas, unable to send out our fishing fleets to harvest the ocean's riches, unable to even water our herds at the rivers in fear o' a webbed hand reaching out to drag us in. Do ye think I do no' hate them too? My father died trying to repel them, all three o' my brothers died at the hands o' Maya the Ensorcellor, their wicked deceitful daughter. I have lost all my family and many o' my friends because o' their sly stratagems . . ."

He paused and took a deep breath, stepping back so he no longer loomed over the prionnsa of Carraig. He stared into the Lodestar and some of the angry color left his face. For a long moment he seemed to listen, and then he looked up, holding out one hand appealingly to the MacSeinn.

"We have so few men," he said simply. "Our losses in the Bright Wars were heavy indeed, and ye ken the lairds are reluctant to commit more men to our cause when they need so many to rebuild their ruined lands. Will ye no' be patient a wee while longer?"

"Patient!" Linley MacSeinn shouted, his face suffused with rage. "For twelve years I've possessed my soul in patience, I've served my Rìgh loyally, and for what? For what? My home lies in ruins with those blaygird sea demons swarming through its heart like maggots through dead meat, the ghosts o' my loved ones haunt my sleep, and ye, ye wish to parley with them. Are ye mad or merely a fool? The Fairgean will never come to terms with ye. They hate us, and they will never rest until we are dead, every last warm-blooded one o' us."

Lachlan tried to speak but the MacSeinn threw his goblet across the room, splashing wine across the gilded walls like a stain of blood. In the shocked silence that followed, the MacSeinn strode out of the room, his unhappy son following with a shy glance of apology. Lachlan stood silently, his face heavy with trouble, his jaw clenched tight. Isabeau had to fight down an urge to comfort him, to smooth away

the lines graven between his brows. She watched her
sister lay her hand on the back of his neck and saw
with a strange little twist beneath her breastbone how
his tension eased.

After a moment Lachlan said with great authority,
"We do no' send soldiers against pregnant women
and boys, no matter the bloody history that lies between our people. We shall attempt once more to
parley. A messenger must be sent to the Fairgean
king with an offer to discuss terms o' peace. We are
creatures o' the land and they are creatures o' the sea.
Surely there is some way for us to live side by side?"

Three weeks later the Rìgh's messenger was flung
down from the back of a sea serpent by one of the
Fairgean princes. The messenger's hands and feet
had been hacked off, his eyes gouged out with coral,
his tongue torn out by the roots. There would be
no peace.

Fand crouched in the darkness. Her arms were
wrapped tight about her knees, her head burrowed
down in their meager shelter. She was naked.

It was freezing in this tiny dark hole. Her limbs
twitched uncontrollably. She bit her lip and the blood
that ran down her chin was hot. She concentrated on
that heat, trying hard to find the strength to keep her
body warm, as she had for so many years. For after
only three minutes in the icy seas of the north, the
human body began to shut down. Respiration failed,
circulation stopped, the fiery track of nerves ceased
their urgent pulse. The body's frail thrashing would
slow, surrendering to the cold. Slowly it would sink

below the waves, only to resurface again stiff and blue, many miles distant, many months later.

Fand, however, had survived for more than twenty years in these freezing seas, willing her blood to run hot and fast. Twenty years and she had not once succumbed to the temptation of drowning, not once let the cold defeat her.

But now the little spark of stubbornness was sunk down to nothingness. She could find no reason for living. Her mind wandered, traveling down well worn tracks. Fand rocked slightly, her eyes shut, her mouth shaping words and names that had almost lost meaning. It seemed she heard the sibilant hiss of voices slithering around her, searching to know what she knew, to make her speak those names, those words. She bit her lip harder and the blood ran into her mouth, sour as the taste of metal.

"Who? Who?" the voices hissed. "Who do you love? Who do you hate?"

Days before she had screamed. "You! I hate you! Leave me alone."

Now she merely rocked and mumbled, the sounds without form or meaning. The blood froze on her chin, and her eyes were sealed shut with icicles of tears.

Suddenly they were all about her, lashing her with doom-eels that stung her into screams of agony. She ripped her eyelids open, seeing only the laughing, gloating faces of her tormentors, their skin livid in the strange shifting light. The tails of the doom-eels shone blue-white. She twisted and turned, trying to avoid the shock of their touch. Each strike lacerated her frozen flesh so blood welled up, horribly black in the phosphorescent gleam of the nightglobes.

"Weak, sickly, stupid, halfbreed scum," the priestesses hissed. "Puny, useless, half-witted human, worthless as sea cow's offal. What use are you? What can you do? Can't even grow a tail. Any worthless concubine's get can do that. Can't even breathe underwater. Pathetic girl slave. No use even as a footstool. Can't skin her to keep warm, no flesh on her to eat, no blood in her to drink, no fire in her to keep us warm, feeble as sea anemones' piss, useless as spawn jelly."

Fand closed her eyes and did not listen, the slap of the doom-eels tails' no longer enough to jerk her into consciousness. For a long time she floated in darkness, pain occasionally twisting through her, damp and frail as the touch of seaweed against the leg. It was too tenuous to rouse her. When she did at last wake, it was to silence. She had difficulty remembering who she was or why her whole body was twitching with the memory of white searing pain.

"Fand," she said and remembered the mother who had named her.

"Fand," the voices hissed. Faces floated out of the blackness, lit from beneath with sickly green light that flowed and changed, causing eyes to sink back into cavernous sockets, teeth to gleam, hair to writhe and grope. "Fand," they mocked, circling her. She shrank back into herself and found, unexpectedly, a tiny guttering spark. She hid herself within it.

At last they left her. Fand rocked back and forth, weeping a little in despair. *Nila, Nila, Nila, Nila.* A movement nearby caused her to freeze, desperately afraid they had heard her silent plea. Someone knelt beside her, fed her raw fish and some bitter drink made of seaweed.

"You should do what they ask of you," the voice said softly, gently. "Why do you fight them? You cannot win. You should do as they ask."

"I can't, I can't." Fand found words. "I can't, I can't." Her voice grew stronger.

"Of course you can," the voice hissed in her ear. "Of course you can, girl human."

Then Fand was alone. The silence and the darkness shook around her. The cold was like fire. It bit into her very marrow. She shook and shuddered. Tried to rub her body warm with her hands, but could not even feel the scrape of her flesh against flesh. Teeth chattered. *I am Fand. Nila will come. I am Fand. Nila will come.*

But he did not come.

MIDSUMMER MADNESS

Isabeau sat cross-legged in the garden, naked, her hair flowing down her back in a mass of unruly curls. Her eyes were shut and her face calm and empty of all expression. The clouds of stinging midges did not seem to bother her, nor the occasional low growl of thunder in the south. She sat as still as if she had grown from the rock itself.

Slowly the darkness lifted. Isabeau opened her eyes, swept one hand out then the other, stretched her arms overhead and rose to her feet. Gracefully she went through the thirty-three stances of *ahdayeh*, warming her muscles and keeping her focus still and small. *Ahdayeh* was meditation in movement, as her previous trance had been meditation in stillness. Both enabled her to reach a plane of heightened awareness, a sense of being both in the world and apart from it. It was in this plane that the One Power could be seized and wrought to her will.

When she had finished the last difficult ritualistic move, Isabeau picked up her satchel and walked slowly and steadily toward the Tower of Two Moons. She came to a small garden near the entrance to the labyrinth, surrounded by high hedges and planted with the seven sacred trees in a circle, their branches intermingling.

The trees were incredibly ancient, their trunks so thick two men could not have touched hands around them. Within the circle of overreaching trees was a stretch of smooth turf where five witches sat, their eyes closed in meditation, their long gray hair flowing down their bare backs. Firelight danced over their old faces and sparkled from the rings that loaded down their gnarled fingers.

Isabeau stood in the dimness, trying to calm her nerves. She breathed deeply till she was serene once more, then stepped into the glade. In the brightening light she could clearly see the shape of a circle and six-sided star scored deeply into the earth. The witches' staffs had been driven into the soil to mark where the six points of the star and the circle met. There was a gap of about a foot in the circle and without saying a word Isabeau walked around the outside of the circle until she came to the gap. She paused, made the sign of Eà's blessing, and stepped inside the circle.

At once the witches' eyes opened. Isabeau bowed to Meghan, who sat at the northern point of the star, a small pot of soil set before her. The old sorceress wore nothing but her rings and the Key, dangling down between her breasts. Meghan bowed back, unsmiling.

Isabeau then bowed to the other witches. At the southern point of the hexagram sat Daillas the Lame, his face heavily seamed with age. One leg hung thin and useless, withered as an old stick. He held a ceremonial dagger in his hands, its dark blade inscribed with magical runes.

On Meghan's left sat Gwilym the Ugly, a dark, saturnine man with a hooked nose and pockmarked skin. He too was crippled, with one leg ending at the knee in an ugly-looking mass of scar tissue. Beside him lay his wooden peg. He nodded his head in acknowledgment of Isabeau's greeting, though his stern expression did not lighten. Across his lap he held a slim wand of hazelwood, all carved with waving lines that had once been painted a soft violet blue.

Arkening the Dreamwalker sat at Meghan's right hand. Old and frail with a vague, anxious face, hands constantly in motion, Arkening fidgeted with the rings she wore on either hand. Before her was a silver chalice of water.

Beside her sat Riordan Bowlegs, beaming a welcome. Although he alone among the witches there had not won his sorcerer's ring, he was here today for Isabeau's Testing because of their long friendship and affection for each other. Isabeau grinned at him and took her place at the sixth point of the circle. Daillas reached out one thin trembling hand and closed the circle behind her with the point of his dagger.

"Isabeau the Apprentice Witch, ye come to the junction o' Earth, Air, Water and Fire, do ye bring the Spirit?" he asked.

"May my heart be kind, my mind fierce, my spirit brave," Isabeau answered.

"Isabeau the Apprentice Witch, ye come to the pentagram and circle with a request. What is your request?"

"That I be found worthy o' being admitted into the Coven o' Witches, that I may learn to wield the

One Power in wisdom and in strength, and serve the people o' the land with humility and compassion. May my heart be kind enough, my mind fierce enough, my spirit brave enough."

All five witches made a circle with the fingers of their left hand and crossed it with one finger of their right, and Isabeau repeated the gesture.

"Meghan, your guide and guardian, tells us that ye have passed the First and Second Tests o' Power, and that ye have studied hard during your years as an apprentice o' the Coven. However, it has been noted that the last Testing took place on your sixteenth birthday and at the height o' the red comet, a most auspicious date for any young witch to sit her Tests. There is no comet magic to draw upon tonight and it is no' your twenty-fourth birthday, contrary to the usual traditions. Do ye feel ye are ready to sit the Third Test o' Power, even though ye are two years short o' your coming o' age?"

"I hope so," Isabeau responded with utmost sincerity.

She saw the sorcerer's lips twitch but he repressed the smile, saying sternly, "As the Third Test o' Power decrees, ye must first pass the First and Second Tests again."

Isabeau nodded. Smoothly and competently she did all that they instructed, unable to help feeling a little glow of satisfaction even though she was careful to let no expression cross her face. Isabeau remembered clearly how she had been reprimanded for being too conceited and willful the last time she had sat these Tests. She knew the council of sorcerers had argued long and hard about permitting her to sit her Third Tests of Power so early and she wanted to do nothing to risk them losing their faith in her. Witches with the potential to achieve the High Magic were rare these days, and Isabeau knew Meghan was eager to see her young apprentice inducted as a sorceress before she died. Consequently she had persuaded the council to go against a thousand years of tradition and Isabeau was determined the old sorceress would not be disappointed in her.

At last Isabeau had finished all the trials of the First and Second Tests, having been careful to do no more than they asked. Without giving her a chance to rest, the witches immediately began the third round of Testing.

The Third Trial of Air involved a more complex manipulation of the forces of air than before, but Isabeau was easily able to move around several objects at once. She lifted the apples from the bowl and threw them up into a spinning circle as if she were a juggler like Dide, all without moving a finger. After a moment the bowl and knife flew up to join them, waltzing together through the air.

Meghan held up her hand. "Enough, Isabeau."

Isabeau gently lowered the apples back into the bowl and the bowl back to the floor.

"Isabeau the Red has shown us she has great skill for a mere apprentice, and has passed the Trial o' Air with flying colors," Gwilym said. "Breathe deeply o' the good air and guidwish the winds o' the world, for without air we should die."

Isabeau inclined her head to him in thanks for his praise and breathed deeply of the warm, summer scented air.

Arkening rose stiffly to her feet, lifting the chalice of water with both gnarled hands. Isabeau leaped to her feet so that the old woman would not have to bend down to place it on the ground. As she lifted the chalice from Arkening's unsteady grasp, the sorceress peered up at her, smiling wistfully, and reached up one hand to pat Isabeau's cheek. "Such a bright, bonny lassie," she said dreamily and made her painfully slow way back to her place. Isabeau put down the chalice of water and helped the old woman lower herself back to the ground, before returning to her own spot, careful not to step outside the lines drawn in the dirt.

Isabeau had always found the element of water the most difficult to manipulate, for it was by its very nature fluid, inchoate, impossible to grasp. It required the most subtle and controlled use of the One Power, something which her impetuous nature had always found difficult. Her time spent with Maya, a creature of the water, had taught her a great deal, however. Maya had taught her how the pull of the two moons moved the tides, immense masses of water dragged first one way then another. She had shown Isabeau how reefs and sandbanks could create rips of terrifying strength, and described to her how the wind could whip a calm sea into a frenzy of wayward waves or even suck it into a vortex of spinning water. Of all the elements, water was the most receptive to the force of the other elements and paradoxically, the most resistant to change.

Isabeau stared into the chalice of water, seeing her own shadowy face reflected back at her. She took a deep breath and pointed at the gleaming, shifting liquid, slowly rotating her finger in a clockwise direction. Slowly the water began to swirl, gaining speed until it was spinning in a whirlpool, following her finger. She reversed the direction of her finger and the water followed, spinning widdershins. Isabeau clenched her hand into a fist and the water slowly subsided into mirror stillness again.

"Ye have passed the Trial o' Water, my bairn," Arkening said in her rather tremulous voice. "Drink deeply o' the good water, lassie, and guidwish the rivers and seas o' the world, for without water we should die."

Obediently Isabeau drank deeply, the water cool and tasting of herbs. When she had put the chalice down she looked across the fire to Meghan with a rather impish grin on her face. "I ken, I ken, I shouldna be using my hands but indeed, Meghan, it is so much easier!"

The sorceress allowed her grimly compressed mouth to relax. "Aye, I ken, lassie, which is why ye shouldna be doing it. A sorceress should be able . . ."

". . . to use the One Power with both hands bound and a sack over her head. I ken, I ken!"

Meghan shook her head repressively. She said sternly, "Enough idle chatter, Beau. It is time now for the Trial o' Earth. Show us what ye can do."

Isabeau looked down at the little pot of soil before her. Earlier that morning she had chosen three seeds and planted them in this pot, watering them and fertilizing them with essential minerals. That had been the First Trial of Earth, the test of knowledge of the earth's properties.

Now she drew in her will and held her hands over the soil. She imagined the dry brown seeds unfolding, a little white rootlet creeping out, groping through the damp soil. She imagined the root spreading, dividing into delicate white lacework, imagined a frail green finger reaching up for the sun. The soil stirred and three green seedlings sprang up, unfurling leaves. Isabeau concentrated all her strength into the seedlings and was rewarded with a burst of growth that saw one spread out heart-shaped leaves and softly colored flowers, another spring up into a little hazel sapling and the third into a delicate oat stem with a full head of seeds.

Isabeau had often seen Meghan use her powers to help seeds grow and had developed the Skill herself during the long months of hunger after the Samhain rebellion. She remembered with a little smile how she had impressed all the witches at her Second Testing by showing off this Skill and wondered a little at her presumption. No wonder she had been scolded for vanity.

"Isabeau the Red has passed the Trial o' Earth— the challenge o' blossoming," Meghan said, deep pleasure in her voice. She brought Isabeau a plate of bread and cheese and the bowl of apples and poured her a goblet of goldensloe wine. "Eat deeply o' the good earth, my bairn, and guidwish the fruits and beasts o' the world, for without them we should die."

Isabeau ate again with pleasure, for it was now high noon and she was starving after her exertions of the morning. Even though she had not taken a step since sitting down at the fire in the dawn, she felt as if she had taken an arduous hike through the mountains.

Next she had to show she could handle the element of fire, something all the witches assembled knew Isabeau could do with ease. This time she did not juggle balls of fire, as she had done last time she had been asked to perform this Trial. She simply leaned forward and put her hand into the flames, cradling a burning coal as if it were an apple. There was a little sigh from the witches for this was a sign of great power indeed.

"Red has passed the Trial o' Fire—the challenge o' handling fire," Riordan Bowlegs said. "Draw close to the good fire, lassie, warm yourself and bask in its light. Guidwish the fire o' the world, for without warmth and light in the darkness we should die."

Although it was warm in the sunshine, Isabeau obeyed. She returned to her place, her skin slick with perspiration, and drank a little water to cool herself down. Then she looked about her with anticipation. It was time for the Third Trial of the Spirit, and as always Isabeau had been told very little about what they expected from her.

All of the five judges had their faces downturned, their eyes closed. There was no expression on their faces to indicate what they were thinking. Isabeau shut her eyes too, breathing deeply to refocus her mind and her will. As the clamor of her thoughts gradually subsided, she seemed to hear Arkening's dreamy voice. She listened to it. The old sorceress was rhapsodizing about the old days at the Tower of Dreamers, when she had been the High Sorceress and the tower had been a busy, happy place filled with witches who had worked and studied and worshipped together in idyllic peace. In Arkening's memories the tower was golden hued, filled with the chime of bells and the scent of flowers.

It must have been lovely, Isabeau said gently, keeping her own memory of the cold, ghost-haunted ruin firmly locked away.

Aye, but all is gone now, Arkening said with great melancholy.

Happen we shall build it anew one day, Isabeau answered.

The old sorceress responded with a wistful thought image of hope and drifted off again into a dream. Isabeau became aware of another presence in her mind. It was Gwilym. He was thinking of a mysterious landscape all shrouded in mist, black-skinned creatures with huge, lustrous eyes peering shyly out from the tall swaying rushes. Water gleamed dully as the mist was blown apart, and then Isabeau saw a dreamlike palace rising out of the mist, its towers and domes painted in all the delicate colors of a sunrise. She could smell the mist and feel its cold fingers on her flesh, and wondered at the yearning she sensed in Gwilyn for this land of marshes and lakes.

Ye wish to return to Arran? she asked.

The swamp has a way o' seeping into your soul, he answered wryly. *Once I swore I would never set foot there again—or wooden stump for that matter—but all I need is a misty autumn morning and I find myself dreaming o' the swans flying in from the sea, their wings crimson as the dawn sky.*

I have never been to Arran, Isabeau thought. *I always thought o' it as a scary place, but ye make it sound so bonny.*

Aye, bonny, but frightening too. Happen that is why it draws ye, life is somehow more vivid there.

In her mind's eye Isabeau saw an enormous lily-shaped flower, yellow as sunshine with a pathway of crimson spots leading deep into its secret heart. She smelt its rich, intoxicating scent, felt a wave of

delicious dizziness, and saw the flower head shift
and sway toward her as if seeking to devour her.

Aye, the golden goddess, Gwilym said, *always hungry
for warm blood.* There was an odd note of wistfulness
in his voice. For a moment Isabeau tasted a sweet
heady wine and experienced an impression of close
and sweaty intimacy. Then Gwilym, an intensely private man, withdrew his thought from her. She sent
him a soft thought of thanks and sympathy and left
herself wide open for the next contact.

It shocked her when it came, a nightmare of torture
and taunting and agony that sent her mind reeling
back, her own body tensing in remembered pain. She
could not help crying aloud. Immediately the flash
of memory was gone and she was caught in a close
mental embrace of apology and remorse.

*I be sorry, my bairn, I did no' mean . . . It is just the
memories are always so close, they come whenever I open
my mind . . . I never meant to inflict them upon ye . . .
but ye ken, ye understand . . .*

Aye, I understand, Isabeau replied softly, opening
and closing her maimed left hand, the tightness of
the scars a constant reminder of her own torture and
nightmares. She had a moment of closeness with the
old sorcerer, then Daillas the Lame withdrew his unhappy mind and she tried to gather back the rags
of her concentration. It was hard. That moment of
connection had brought that terrible hour with the
Awl's Grand-Questioner screaming back into her
mind. Like Daillas, she had trouble banishing the
memory. It was forever beating against the barriers
of her mind like a dark-winged bat, screeching and
mocking and haunting her. Her impulse was to let
her consciousness curl into a tight little ball, shiv-

ering and whimpering, but with ironclad determination she breathed in and out, in and out, until the walls were erected again and she was calm.

How are ye yourself, lassie? Riordan Bowlegs asked with deep concern.

Aye, I be fine, she answered coolly.

I did no' ken what it was like for ye, lassie. I be sorry . . .

What is done is done. Besides, Meghan always said only the maimed can mourn, only the lame can love. What are two fingers compared to the capacity to feel grief and joy? Despite all her best efforts, Isabeau was unable to inject any warmth into her voice.

Still, it be a hard road ye've traveled, my bairn. Riordan's voice was troubled.

Isabeau tried to communicate some kind of reassurance and he must have understood, for she felt the mental equivalent of a comforting pat on the shoulder.

In our different ways we are all hurt by life, Red, he said. *I am glad ye think the rewards are greater than the costs.*

Isabeau moved her shoulders uneasily, not sure that she truthfully did, at least not all the time. The old bow-legged groom was thinking of his own childhood, though, and Isabeau was drawn irresistibly into his chain of thought images. Isabeau saw a little dark room, smelling strongly of goat. The only light came from a fire glowing sullenly on the open hearth. A huge man with a mean face was beating a thin cowering woman. He smelled of whiskey and sweat. The shadow of his arm rose and fell over Isabeau's face. She was crouched beneath the table. He was a giant, towering over her. She could hear her own whimpers and feel her heart beating rapidly against her ribs. She was hungry, so hungry she was sick with it. The woman screamed and fell. China broke. Still that thick, burly giant's arm rose and fell. The woman scrabbled away and he bent and seized her hair, shouting. Suddenly Isabeau could bear it no longer. She dashed out, caught hold of that immense arm, tried to drag it away. She loved that thin, cowed, battered woman, loved her intensely. The tree trunk leg kicked her away. She was flung against the table, fell to the floor, crying. Then the giant loomed over her. His eyes were glaring. His face was purple with whiskey and rage. The huge hard fist lifted, then descended like a hammer, again and again. The woman was crying, begging, trying to hold him back. The floor was filthy. Isabeau tasted dirt and blood, heard pain rushing in her ears like a hurricane. Some sort of darkness descended.

Isabeau came back to herself only slowly. The scene in the tiny cottage had been so vivid that she had completely lost all sense of herself. She said, rather shakily, *Your father?*

Aye, Riordan answered shortly and she remembered her own glad childhood, free and content and smelling always of summer.

I am glad ye remember it thus, Meghan said. For a moment they shared an image of a flower-strewn glade where thousands of butterflies dipped and soared, a small, red-haired child spinning among them, arms stretched wide.

Then Meghan took her back to her own childhood, showing Isabeau some happy scenes—playing chase and hide with her sister Mairead, cuddling up to her father while he told them stories of the First Coven, pulling a sleepy dormouse out of her pocket and feeding it nuts.

Then, with a surge of excitement and pride that quickened Isabeau's pulse, the old sorceress remembered the day she had been given the Key of the Coven. Even now, so many years later, the memory was sword sharp in Meghan's mind—the cold snap of the air, the smell of woodsmoke and dying leaves, the tingle in her palm as her fingers closed over the talisman, the pride in her father's rheumy eyes.

Meghan had been only thirty-six, the youngest sorceress ever to inherit the Key. Normally the Keybearer carried the Key until death, but Meghan's father, Aedan Whitelock, had decided his work had been done with the creation of the Lodestar and the uniting of the land, and so had retired at the proud old age of sixty-nine. Giving the throne to one daughter and the Key to the other, Aedan Whitelock had gone to live with the Celestines until his death, thirty-three years later.

All this Isabeau knew in an instant as she shared the Keybearer's memory. She looked down through Meghan's eyes at the Key in her hand. Delicately wrought, it nestled within her palm, shaped in the sacred symbol of the Coven. The Key's flat surfaces were inscribed with magical runes and symbols, and it was warm, as if it were a living being. Tingles were running up Meghan's arm from where the metal touched her skin, and all her senses thrummed with its power, as if she held thunder and lightning captured within metal.

Slowly, in her memory, Meghan lifted the Key and hung it around her throat, so that the talisman hung between her breasts. The rhythm of her heart steadied until it seemed to thrum in tempo with the Key. Tears stung her eyes. Her breath caught. One hand came up and pressed the talisman hard against her body, at the place where her ribs sprang out, the center of her breathing. Gazing up at her beloved father, she made a silent vow to carry the Key with all the wisdom and strength and compassion she could find within her. She would prove worthy of following in the footsteps of all the great Keybearers who had preceded her, she swore it with all of her being. Aedan smiled at her, well pleased, but Meghan had been unable to smile back, overawed and humbled by the power thrumming beneath her hand.

The thought image faded and Isabeau slowly came back to a realization of herself, tired and stiff, her throat parched. She opened her eyes and stretched, hearing bones in her back crack. She could not help glancing at Meghan, and at the Key that hung between her withered breasts. The longing to hold it to her own heart almost overwhelmed her. Slowly she raised her eyes and met Meghan's, black as spilt ink and as inscrutable.

"Isabeau has passed the Third Trial o' Spirit, the challenge o' clear hearing," Daillas said, smiling at her wearily. "Feel the blood pumping through your veins, my bairn, feel the forces o' life animate ye. Give thanks to Eà, mother and father o' us all, for the eternal spark, and guidwish the forces o' Spirit which guide and teach us, and give us life."

Isabeau made the sign of Eà's blessing, joy welling up through her, and all the witches smiled at her and repeated the gesture.

"Now ye must show us once again how ye use all

o' the elemental powers," Daillas said. "At the end
o' your Second Tests ye made yourself a witch dagger. Ye must do so again and pour into it all ye have
learned in your years as an apprentice. With this dagger ye will cut your witch's staff, sign o' full admit-
tance into the Coven as a fully fledged witch, and ye
will use it to cast your circle o' power in the workings o' spells. Take the silver o' the earth's begetting,
forge it with fire and air, and cool it with water. Fit
your blade into a handle o' sacred hazel that ye have
smoothed with your own hands. Speak over it the
words of the Creed and pour your own energies into
it, in the name o' Eà o' the green blood."

Isabeau knew that a witch should always make her
own tools and instruments because something made
or used by another always held a residue of their
powers and purpose, and so may not be in harmony
with hers. Even more important, to forge her own
witch knife and whittle her own staff also meant that
she would be fully engaged with the work, having
poured much of herself into the making. So Isabeau
had spent many hours with the palace blacksmith,
watching him forge weapons for the soldiers and
tools for the palace gardeners and carpenters. She
had practiced with the bellows and smithy hammers
until her ears had rung and her hands had been
pockmarked with burns from the flying sparks. She
had observed the carpenters shaping wood and spent
many idle hours whittling discarded lumps of wood
until her hands had grown sure and strong. The apprentice's knife she had forged at her Second Tests
now looked childish and clumsy to her eyes and she
was eager to put her newly honed skills to the task.

So Isabeau made her witch dagger with great care,

taking her time to make sure the task was done as
well as possible. She forged the silver blade with two
sharp edges, and inscribed upon it many runes of
power. While it cooled in the chalice of water, she
drew out her battered apprentice's knife and cut the
third finger of her right hand so that blood welled
up, thick and dark. The witches believed a vein ran
from this finger directly to the heart and so it was
her own heart blood that darkened the little knife's
blade. She smeared both sides of the blade with her
blood, then carefully cut a branch from the hazel tree
now growing vigorously in the pot of soil before her.
As she lovingly stripped away its fresh new leaves,
blood continued to pump from the cut in her finger,
smearing the wood.

Carefully she whittled the branch into the stylized
shape of a dragon, its wings folded along its sides.
She set a tiny dragoneye jewel to shine in its crowned
head, and polished it all over with starwood oil so
the wood glowed.

Isabeau then picked up her little apprentice's knife,
its hilt plain and stained with the marks of her fingers, its blade poorly made. She gave it a little caress,
remembering the pride and excitement she had felt
as she made it. She had lost it soon after, Lachlan
stealing it from her the first time they had met. He
had given it back to her many months later, when
they had met again. It seemed to Isabeau the little
knife still carried some of his life essence. After a
moment she broke it in half and dropped the blade
into the crucible where she had melted the silver for
her witch knife. Ceremoniously she threw the hazelwood hilt into the fire and used her powers to bring
the flames leaping up around the crucible until it was

white-hot. Slowly the metal within softened until it was like putty and she used her tools and her witch powers to spin it into a long silver thread.

Her fingers trembling a little with weariness and nerves, she fitted the narrow silver blade to the dragon hilt, binding it into place with the silver thread, and softly murmuring incantations of power over it. At last, many hours after she had started, Isabeau was finished. Her skill was not as great as her intention, but the dagger hilt could clearly be recognized as a resting dragon, the long tail curled around its curving hindquarters, the bright blade gripped between all four claws.

Isabeau felt a deep thrill of pride run through her. She looked up to see the witches all smiling at her wearily. They had sat in complete stillness for all that time and she saw by their faces that they were as stiff and tired as she was. The shadows of the trees were long over the grass, the sun sinking down toward the western horizon.

"Ye have passed your third Test o' Powers, Isabeau the Apprentice Witch, with great skill," Daillas the Lame said. "We are glad indeed to welcome ye into the Coven o' Witches."

"By the Creed o' the Coven o' Witches, ye must swear to speak only what is true in your heart, for ye must have courage in your beliefs. Ye must swear no' to use the Power to ensorcel others, remembering all people must choose their own path. Ye must use the One Power in wisdom and thoughtfulness, with a kind heart, a fierce and canny mind, and steadfast courage. Do ye swear these things?" Meghan said.

"I swear. May my heart be kind, my mind fierce, my spirit brave." Isabeau spoke the ritual with a break in her voice, so tired and so happy she was close to tears.

"May Eà shine her bright face upon ye," Arkening said and the others added their blessings and congratulations.

"It is time for the Midsummer celebrations. Come and eat and be joyful. In the dawn ye must cut yourself a staff and say Eà's blessing over it, and then shall your new life as Isabeau the Witch begin," Meghan said. "Congratulations, my bairn, I am proud indeed o' ye."

Painfully they all got to their feet, rubbing their limbs to aid the return of their circulation. As the other witches packed up their paraphernalia and doused the fire, Meghan held up a long robe of white linen for Isabeau to put on. Cut from the one length of cloth, it was made without any buttons, buckles, hooks or knots. It was growing cool under the huge old trees and Isabeau received it gladly, for this was the first sign of her new standing within the Coven. Apprentice no longer, but a fully accredited witch, and at the age of only twenty-two and a half. Despite all her efforts to maintain a proper humility, Isabeau could not help glowing with pride.

Although Lachlan and Iseult had traveled with their court to Rhyssmadill for the Summer Fair, held in Dùn Gorm each year, the witches were still throwing the traditional feast to celebrate Midsummer's Eve. As Isabeau and her teachers walked slowly through the warm dusk, the gardens were beginning to fill with people dressed in their finest clothes. Nisses were busy garlanding the trees with flowers, and a little band of cluricauns were tuning their instruments on a stage erected before the rose garden.

In the square before the Tower of Two Moons a huge bonfire had been built which would be lit at sunset. Those who wished to be handfasted would leap the fire together, giving them a year to live together as man and wife before being married. Those who had been handfasted a year earlier and wished to build a life together would jump the fire a second time, sealing their marriage vows. Midsummer's Eve was considered a time for loving and many a child was conceived on the night of the summer solstice.

Isabeau was so tired that it was an effort to keep her balance, but she stood for a while watching the dancers and mummers, and sampling some of the delicious spiced cakes. Children from the Theurgia were running everywhere, shrieking with excitement, and the older apprentices and witches were sitting under the trees or dancing. In her flowing white gown, with the new dagger hanging in its sheath at her waist, it was clear Isabeau had passed her Tests and so many came to grasp her hand and congratulate her. She smiled tiredly and thanked them, but would not stay for long. The one glass of goldensloe wine she drank made her head spin and so she made her weary way back to the tower and so to bed, sleep swooping down upon her like an owl upon a mouse.

Hand in hand, Lachlan and Iseult made their way through the dark garden, their way lit only by the light of the sinking moons. The tall spires of Rhyssmadill soared high into the sky, etched blackly against the starry sky. In the distance they could hear the faint sound of chatter and laughter, and the strumming of a guitar. A couple was entwined together under a tree, the woman's bare leg gleaming white against the darkness of her clothes. With a smile at each other, Lachlan and Iseult passed by silently.

Through the branches they saw the flicker of flames. Only a few revelers still clustered around the bonfire, drinking and laughing and listening to the music. From the bushes they heard a little trill of laughter and smiled at each other again.

"It is almost dawn," Lachlan said. "Our guests must be wondering what has happened to us. I hope none suspect we have been having secret meetings at midnight . . ."

"It is Midsummer." Iseult smiled up at him. "No one will be wondering."

He caught her throat in his strong, brown hand and tilted her face up so he could kiss her. She felt the quickening of her pulse, and the same rise of urgent desire in him.

"It is our wedding anniversary tonight," he said when he at last released her.

Iseult leaned her head against his shoulder. "Aye, I ken."

"Have ye been happy these last five years, *leannan?*"

"Ye ken I have."

He shook his head, trying to read her face in the moonlight. "It is hard to ken what ye are thinking sometimes. All that Khan'cohban reserve o' yours, it is impossible to break through at times. Are ye sure ye do no' regret jumping the fire with me?"

"Aye," she answered. "I'm sure."

He cupped her face in his hands. "Ye do no' sound sure," he said, only half joking. "Ye have never

wished ye had chosen differently? Ye never long for
the snows?"

"I swore a sacred oath that I would never leave ye
and I shall no'," she answered, drawing a little away
from him.

"That is no' what I asked."

She drew even further away, looking up at him
seriously. "I miss the snows," she answered, "but ye
ken that. What is it that ye are asking?"

He was scowling and she put up one hand to
smooth his brow. He caught her hand and kissed it
passionately. "Do ye love me?" The words were spoken low and with difficulty.

She slid her arms about his neck and kissed him
on the mouth. "Ye ken that I do," she whispered into
his ear, kissing the soft flesh of his throat. As her
mouth moved lower, to the curve of his collarbone,
he gave a little sigh and cradled her in his arms, his
wings cupping around to enfold her.

"Do ye remember that first night we made love?"
he whispered, slowly backing her under the shadow
of a great tree. "In the forest, on the ground, among
all the tree roots?"

She nodded and smiled against his skin.

He pressed her up against the rough bark of the
tree trunk, his hands slowly undoing the laces of her
gown. "I've rather missed the forest," he said huskily, sliding his mouth down her bare shoulder.

"We have a nice soft bed up in the palace," she
whispered, drawing him down with her onto the
ground, "with pillows and blankets and curtains to
close against prying eyes."

"But it be Midsummer," he mocked, the words
coming slowly, in between kisses. "We canna make

love in a bed like an auld married couple when it's
Midsummer Eve."

Naked now, his warm, rough hands and silky-soft
feathers gently stroking the whole length of her
body, Iseult sighed and looked up at the dark fretwork of leaves against the silvery-blue moon.

"There's something to be said for Midsummer
madness," she said.

Isabeau woke, her body arcing upward instinctively.
For a moment she was disoriented, the pattern of
twigs and leaves against the moon etched sharply on
her mind's eye. The dark room with its smell of bees-
wax and old leather confused her, the slight weight
of her sheet. She had been in the garden, making
love under the Midsummer moons, silken feathers
caressing her . . .

Understanding came. She lay back against her pillows, her skin hot, her heart beating too fast. Deep
inside her she still felt the twisting coil of desire.
Though she tried to calm her breathing, the ache and
throb would not fade. At last she drank some water
from the mug by her bed and dampened her sheet
so she could dab it against her face, fever-hot, fever-
dry. Buba hooted anxiously, sensing Isabeau's distress, and crept close to comfort her. Isabeau could
not bear the brush of the owl's feathers against her
skin and pushed her away abruptly.

You-hooh angry-hooh?

"Nay, I . . . I just had a bad dream," Isabeau said.
She wondered if Iseult knew that she experienced
her twin sister's moments of passion as vividly as
she shared her moments of pain. Surely not. Surely

Iseult could not open herself up to sensation so freely
if she knew, if she realized. A flash of her dream
returned to Isabeau—the hard curve of Lachlan's
arm, the silken feel of his bare skin under her hands,
the hot insistence of his mouth . . .

Isabeau shuddered. She scrambled out of bed and
dragged her new white gown over her head, leaving
her hair hanging free in wild disorder. Wrapping her
plaid about her against the early morning chill, she
hurried down the stairs and into the garden. With
an anxious hoot, Buba flew after her.

A few revelers were still sitting on the front steps,
leaning against each other and smiling drunkenly.
Isabeau ignored their invitation to join them, plunging into the garden. Shadowy fronds closed over her
head. The air was cool and smelled green with new
growth. She pressed her body against a tree, the
rough scrape of the bark grazing her skin, its solid
strength supporting her. Tears stung her eyes but she
did not weep. Buba came to rest on Isabeau's shoulder, butting her head against Isabeau's neck. She
stroked the feathery head and took comfort from that
until the tumult of anger, desire and frustration at
last began to ease.

Birds were beginning to test their voices against
the dark. Isabeau raised her head and looked about
her. She could see now the fronds which had swallowed and enclosed her. Feeling tired and heavy with
the weight of her dream, she slowly made her way
through the lawns and shrubberies to the sacred circle where the witches had tested her yesterday.

She reached the glade in the center of the ring of
seven ancient trees. In the growing light she could
clearly see the black ashes of their fire. At one of the

points of the six-sided star a large clay pot still stood, with a tall straight hazel sapling springing out of it. Among its roots nestled a clump of heart's ease. On the other side was a tall spray of oats, heavy with seeds.

It was Isabeau's task this morning to make herself her witch's staff, symbol of full acceptance into the Coven. She had to meditate for long quiet minutes before she was able at last to put aside the effect of the dream. Even then it was not lost but only locked away somewhere where it would no longer disturb her so powerfully.

Feeling very calm and very distant, Isabeau knelt under the oak tree and drew her witch's knife and the crystal she had found in the mountains out of her satchel, washing them carefully in the pool. Alone in the dim garden, she carefully drew the knife along her finger, watching the dark blood well up. She smeared the blade with her blood, then dipped it in the ashes of the fire till it was thickly encrusted. She then knelt at the sixth point of the star, breathing deeply and slowly.

At the very moment that the sun rose above the horizon, flooding the garden with warmth and color, she cut down the leafy sapling with one swift movement. Slowly, ceremoniously, Isabeau stripped all the twigs and leaves from the sapling then scoured the branch with earth and ashes till it was smooth and white. She washed it clean in the pool and stained it a pale silvery-white with starwood oil. Kindling the fire again with twigs gathered from beneath all seven trees, she then forged a silver cap for the end of the staff, magnetizing it with a lodestone as she had been

taught. Finally Isabeau set the crystal at the head of
the staff in delicate claws of silver, with a spring
clasp that could be clicked open to allow the crystal
to be lifted out of its crown.

As Isabeau labored she chanted words of power
over the staff, pouring her energies into the wood
and the crystal, making them a part of her.

"I make ye, staff o' hazelwood, in the name o' Eà,
mother and father o' us all, and infuse ye with all
that is good in me, all that is wise and strong and
kind.

"I make ye, staff o' hazelwood, by the power o'
the stars and the moons and the unfathomable distance o' the universe, and infuse in ye all that is
bright and dark, all that is known and unknown.

"I make ye, staff o' hazelwood, by the power and
virtue o' the four elements, Earth and Fire, Wind and
Water; by the power and virtue o' all things, all
plants that grow and die, all animals that crawl and
fly and run, all rocks and mountains, all suns and
stars and planets.

"With these things I infuse ye, that ye may stand
as sure as the tree from which ye sprang, as full o'
ancient power and wisdom, that ye may support me
and shelter me as ye did the creatures that hid in
your branches. With these things, I infuse ye, staff o'
hazelwood, and make ye mine."

Then she blessed the staff, sprinkling it with water
from a bunch of leaves from each of the seven trees,
wound about with flowers plucked from the grass—
rosemary, thyme, gilly-flowers, and clover. She stood
up, lifting the staff toward the sun. "In the name o'
Eà," she cried, "I command ye, staff o' power, to

obey my will in all things. I command ye, staff o' power, to summon the powers I wish to call, and break and reduce to chaos all that I wish to destroy.''

The crystal caught the sun's brightness and refracted it into a white flame, blazing as bright as a tiny sun. Rainbow sparks shot out from the stone, dancing over the glade like multicolored fireflies. Isabeau felt a surge of power run down her fingers, shooting along her veins and nerve endings and up into her brain so that for a moment her whole body was seared with a white-hot energy. Then the clamor and pain receded, and the light sank down to a twisting flame of blue and gold and crimson, deep within the crystal's translucent heart.

Isabeau had consummated her bond with the staff of power, had poured all her sorrow and desire and impotent rage into its strong white body. She fell to her knees and kissed the crystal, incoherent thanks to Eà and the Gods of White and her own sorcerous powers mute and struggling in her heart.

I'll be a great sorceress, she thought. *No man's love can be worth as much!*

THE ISLE OF DIVINE DREAD

Fand crouched in the darkness, listening. Although the silence was undisturbed by even a shiver of air or a slow trickle of water, Fand knew that they were there, listening to her as intently as she listened to them.

Gingerly she risked moving, stretching out one foot and extending her toes, clenching and unclenching her fingers. It had become a horrible sort of game to her, the only sort of resistance she had to the constant torment of their regard. They wanted her to die, she knew it, they wanted her to give up and let her muscles lock, her lungs collapse, her blood freeze. Although Fand longed for the gentle release of death, to die would be to allow them to triumph. Some stubborn shred of resoluteness kept her alive within the ruins of her mind and spirit, kept her heart beating despite all they did to her.

Fand did not know how long she had been trapped here. Her life before the sisterhood was like a fragment of dream that lingered on long after one had woken, more an impression of emotion than a memory. She had been happy, she knew. There had been a shining sea and soft sand and warm kisses that had filled her body with light and life. There had been a face, dark skinned and proud, with silver-blue eyes intent with passion . . .

The darkness stirred. She froze.

"Who?" they whispered. "Who do you love? Who do you hate?"

Fand did not reply. Slowly the lurid green light grew up all around her. A circle of priestesses stood over her, their faces made grotesque by the shifting green phosphorescence.

"Why do you not die?" one asked.

"Are you not cold enough? Are you not hungry enough?"

"Why do you not die?"

"Do you hate us?"

"Do you wish we were dead?"

"Do you love us?" They bent over her. Doom-eels wriggled in their left hands, their squirming tails shining blue-white. Fand shrank back. "Who do you love?"

"I love you," she said, her voice hoarse. Her limbs twitched uncontrollably.

"Well, we do not love you, stupid spawn jelly," they said and lashed her with the electric tails of the doom-eels. She scrabbled away, but they were all around her, laughing. She curled up into a ball, her arms about her head, her knees drawn up to her chin. The doom-eels did not strike again. After a moment she looked up.

"Do you love Jor?" The hiss was soft, sibilant.

"Yes, yes, I love Jor," she gabbled.

"Jor is all. Jor is might. Jor is strength. Jor is power." The priestesses paced around her, their voices rising in passion. "Jor is all. Jor is might. Jor is strength. Jor is power."

"Jor is all," Fand agreed. "Jor is power."

For a long time the only sound was the swish of their furs on the stone, the hiss of the doom-eels' tails. Fand waited.

"Who?" they whispered. "Who do you love? Who do you hate?"

"I love Jor. Jor is all. Jor is might. Jor is strength. Jor is power."

"Jor is all. Jor is might. Jor is strength. Jor is power," the priestesses echoed.

"Jor is all. Jor is might. Jor is strength. Jor is power," Fand repeated desperately.

Again there was silence. Fand felt sweat springing up along her hairline, on her palms and the soles of her feet. Every muscle in her body was clenched tight in anticipation of pain. It did not come.

One of the priestesses bent and smoothed back the hair from her brow. Fand flinched, and she clucked her tongue in sympathy. "Hush, hush, little girl-human. You do well."

"You have not died," one of the others said.

"Why have you not died?" asked another.

"Are you not cold enough? Are you not hungry enough? Are you not weak enough?"

The hissing tails of the doom-eels writhed about her. Fand pressed herself against the icy stone.

"You do well," the first repeated, stroking Fand's hair tenderly. "Maybe you are not so weak as we had thought."

"Not so weak, not so weak," the others echoed softly.

Fand could not help looking up at the priestess's face, tears springing to her eyes.

"Do you love me?" the priestess said gently. Fand nodded, the tears beginning to spill down her face. The priestess unhooked her heavy sealskin fur and let it drop upon her. "Sleep, little one," she said.

Gratefully Fand clutched the warmth and softness to her and closed her eyes.

She was woken only a minute or two later by a freezing deluge of snow and water, the fur cloak wrested away from her. She could not help screaming in shock and pain. They lashed her with the doom-eels, shrieking at her, accusing her. Among the cacophony of voices, she heard them crying, "You must love none but Jor, none but Jor. Jor is your god, your master, your lover, your purpose for being. Jor is all. Jor is might. Jor is strength. Jor is power."

"Jor is all. Jor is might. Jor is strength. Jor is power," Fand repeated dully, but the attack did not abate. All she could see were blue-white arcs of hissing light as the doom-eels were raised and brought lashing down, and behind, the floating spheres of green-dark light. She closed her eyes and endured.

After that they left her alone for a very long time. She wept a little, then when the deep well of grief within her was all dried up, Fand lay there in a sort of stupor. Words and images ran through her mind, noisy, brightly colored, incoherent.

"Is it the prince Nila you weep for?" a gentle voice asked.

Fand did not respond. *Nila*, she thought.

"You must try to forget him," the voice in the darkness said, soft with sympathy. "He has forgotten you, that you may be sure of. He will have found himself some other concubine in which to spill his seed. Men are fickle, inconstant creatures. They do not love like women. Their love does not endure."

There was silence again for a very long time. Then softly, insistently, the voice spoke again. "Love will bring you only grief and pain, do you not know that? I loved once, a very long time ago. I am wiser now."

Fand felt a gentle hand on her hair, then a beaker of sea-squill wine was held to her lips. She drank thirstily, then accepted a few tidbits of raw fish held to her lips. The food and wine brought a rush of vigor to her body, so strong it made her feel nauseous. The hand stroked her damp forehead, and then the cloak was drawn up over her again. She sighed and turned her cheek into it.

"Do you love me?" the voice asked softly.

Fand shook her head. "No," she answered, so low her voice was almost inaudible. "I hate you."

"Do you love Prince Nila?"

"No," she answered, her voice a little stronger. "I love only Jor."

"That is good," the voice replied and then she heard the swish of the priestess's furs as she was left alone in the darkness, alone for the first time in months.

Dark silence was broken by oscillating green light and whispering voices. Pain was followed by dark silence. There was no other division of time. Darkness, green light and pain, darkness. Always they asked her the same questions, and Fand searched desperately to know the right answers. Gradually the pain came less often, though the questions changed.

"What is your name?"

"I have no name."

"Who are you?"

"I am nothing."

"Do you love me?"

"No, I hate you. I hate you all."

"Do you love Prince Nila?"

"No. I hate him. I love only Jor."

"Why do you hate Prince Nila?"

"Men are selfish, fickle. He abandoned me."

As the priestesses brought the doom-eels down upon her naked flesh, she cried out desperately, "I love only Jor! Jor is all. Jor is power. Nila is nothing. Nothing!"

The pain stopped. "Why are you not dead?"

"Because you wish me to live. Jor wishes me to live!"

"Why does Jor wish you to live?"

"So I may serve him."

They whipped her, ruthlessly, over and over again. "What worth are you, sea scum, spawn jelly? Weak, sickly, stupid, halfbreed human. What use are you? Nothing. What can you do? Nothing. Why would Jor want you? You might as well be dead, no one wants you. Why do you not die? We do not want you, useless pathetic bag of bones. Why would we? Can't even grow a tail. What use are you? Can't skin you to keep warm, no flesh on you to eat, no blood in you to drink, no fire in you to keep us warm . . ."

Something inside Fand snapped. There was a sudden incandescent flare that penetrated through the screen of her hands. Her flesh was red, the bones within dark. She heard a dreadful screaming. She uncovered her eyes, her heart hammering. The cave was lit up with golden warmth and light. All around her stood six pillars of fire, shrieking, beating themselves with flaming hands. On and on the screaming echoed. The priestesses rolled on the floor, threw themselves against the walls, while the hot, hungry flames devoured their flesh, their eyeballs boiling within their sockets of bone. Eventually they screamed no longer, writhed no longer. The flames sank down to smolder upon the shapeless, blackened forms. The cave stank of burned flesh.

"You wanted fire," Fand said. "Are you warm enough now?"

The tiny island of the Priestesses of Jor rose gray and forbidding from the seas, a tumult of white water raging around the feet of the sheer cliffs. The melancholy cry of thousands of seabirds filled the air, the loneliest sound Nila had ever heard. He floated in the icy water, staring at the steep rock with a heart frozen by foreboding. What would they do to him if they found him here?

I do not care, he thought. *What more can they do?*

It had been a bitter six months for Nila. All joy had gone out of his life without Fand, all hope and happiness. His failure to save her haunted him. But what could I do? he had asked himself a hundred thousand times, without ever finding relief.

Nila had been watched closely by his father's minions, unable to even seek the solace of solitude at the ruined witches' tower or in the dark depths of the Fathomless Caves. Every step he took there was someone behind him, spying on him, reporting his every move. He flaunted the black pearl upon his breast, allowed an undertone of mockery in his voice when he spoke to his brothers, and killed two of them in duels on the slightest of pretenses. He was filled with a reckless disregard for his own life, yet somehow this gave him an acute sensitivity toward anyone else's disregard. Nila survived three more attempts to murder him, killing another of his brothers and seven of his lackeys in the process. As the endless night of winter at last began to fade, Nila's tusks began to bud and he noticed a new favor in his father's voice. The Fairgean King approved of Nila's pride and insolence, his newfound aggression. Even his thirteen surviving brothers regarded him with a new wariness.

The ice that sealed shut the mouth of the Cave of a Thousand Kings melted away, and the warriors were able to go out in pursuit of the whales swimming past in their annual migration south. Nila at last had a chance to escape his father's scrutiny and he had swam at once in search of Fand.

The priestesses' island was not far from the Isle of the Gods. Nila had reached it in only a few hours, and he had spent the rest of the day trying to find some way in. He had circumnavigated the rock three times, tried to climb its cliffs, dived deep into the ocean to find an underwater cave. All to no avail. At last he had given up and swam back to rejoin his pod.

His absence had not gone unnoted, of course. He was humiliated in front of the whole court, his father frothing at the mouth with rage as he demoted Nila and sentenced him to six lashes by doom-eel. Nila endured the whipping in grim silence and smiled in private over his demotion. When most of the court left the Isle of the Gods to swim in the wake of the whales he would be left behind to guard the Cave of a Thousand Kings with the other second-grade warriors, considered too weak or old or unskilled to swim to the south. Although Nila would have been cut to the quick over such a demotion at any other time, now he could only be glad. He would have all summer to try and find his love.

Yet now the summer was almost gone and still Nila had not been able to find a way into the Isle of Divine Dread. And now a horrible fear lay upon him, choking him like an octopus's tentacle.

All through the months they had been apart Nila had been aware of Fand as clearly as if she called out to him through the darkness. He had felt pain and grief and anger and desolation, he had felt a slow dying within her. Then last night, the night of the summer solstice, he had been jolted from sleep, crying aloud her name. He had dreamed of fire, that terrible weapon of the humans, that all-destroying, profane, unnatural power that melted ice, evaporated water, and burned flesh to cinders. The horror of the dream lingered all day, and when at last he shook himself free of it, he realized that he could no longer feel Fand. It was as if she was dead.

Desperate with fear he had escaped the pod and swam for the Isle of Divine Dread, unable to admit that he might be too late. This was the sixth time he swam all around the towering rock and he had seen no other sign of life but the clouds of crying seabirds. Black despair filled Nila once more.

Suddenly the seabirds roosting on one side of the rock burst into flight, screeching and circling. Nila watched in bemusement, wondering what had startled them. Suddenly all his nerves tightened. He dived beneath the waves, swimming strongly toward the rock, his long black hair streaming behind him. Far ahead he saw the bubbling green phosphorescence of a drowned nightglobe. Abruptly he stopped, wrenching his tail sideways. He floated deep in the water, his nostrils clamped shut, his gills fluttering. The light grew stronger, then he saw six priestesses come swimming up out of the inky black depths, carrying their nightglobes close to their bodies. With their eyesight dazzled by the green brightness, they did not see him. They swam up toward the glowing surface and then their heads broke through, so that all Nila could see was their strong silver tails undulating powerfully as they swam away.

He waited until his lungs were burning and his gills were quivering with strain, then swam up to the surface to breathe. He was very close to the island, perilously close. Just ahead of him the waves rose in long green swells that smashed upon the rocks in a welter of white foam. He could feel their strength dragging at his tail. He filled his lungs with air and then dived.

Down into the blackness he swam, his eyes wide open and staring. His hand brushed the plunging roots of the island, smooth and slimy to the touch. He followed the rock down, one hundred feet, two hundred feet. He had never dived so deep. His heartbeat slowed, a deliberate muffled pounding in his ears. His lungs burned with pain. Three hundred feet. Nila felt sick and giddy. He no longer knew which way was up, which way down. Only the rock sliding past his fingers reassured him. He wondered how long he had been diving. Certainly longer than

he had ever dived before. Most Fairgean could only
stay submerged for five minutes or so. He had been
diving for three times as long. He had to fight the
desire to breathe through his nose, knowing he
would take in only water. Spots of color danced before his eyes. His heartbeat was so slow he panicked
in each long moment before its returning throb. Just
as he had decided he was about to die, his fingers
felt nothing but emptiness. He slowed his descent,
twisted his tail, and followed the curve of the rock.

His head broke through into air. Nila took great
whooping breaths, his starved lungs struggling to
swallow more oxygen. His head swam, his pulse
leaping erratically. He felt a ledge of rock below him
and crawled out of the water, too exhausted to even
attempt to change back into his land-shape. All was
dark.

Minutes passed. His pulse steadied, his breaths
grew more even. He transformed shape, crawled
higher out of the water, banging his head on a wall
of rock. The darkness was so complete it terrified
him. It was as dark as the octopus's pit, as dark as
any of the Fathomless Caves. The darkness reminded
him that he was committing sacrilege of the worst
kind. A man trying to penetrate the mysteries of the
Isle of Divine Dread?

Yet he had come too far to turn back. Nila crawled
along the ledge, feeling his way with his hands, his
head ducked down at an awkward angle to avoid
any more collisions with the wall. He felt a breath
of air on his cheek, turned that way, crept down a
passageway that scraped the skin from his knees and
palms. The wafting of air grew stronger. He received
the impression of space. Although there was no

sound, all the hairs on his head lifted, his scales shrank. He was being watched, being listened to. He froze into stillness, straining all his senses, trying to tell himself it was his terror that made him think so.

Suddenly light flared all around him, the queer distorted luminance of viperfish trapped within glass. He was surrounded on all sides by Priestesses of Jor, staring down at him malevolently. They did not speak, just stared at him, their pale eyes gleaming oddly in the greenish light. Nila stared back, a fatalistic calm settling over him.

"Prince Nila, fourteenth son of he that is Anointed by Jor. Why do you come creeping and sneaking into our home? Do you not know that we can have you gutted and skinned like a fish for your effrontery?"

"I have come for Fand," he said. His voice sounded odd to his ears.

"There is no one called Fand."

"Fand. My concubine. I have come for her."

"There is no one called Fand."

His head felt light, his pulse beat fast and erratic. "Fand," he said obstinately.

"The slave you knew as Fand is gone," the priestess said. Her voice was soft and sibilant, yet somehow terribly frightening. "She is now a Priestess of Jor. She has no name. She is nobody."

"Fand," he said desperately, searching all their faces, which were lit from below by their nightglobes, giving them all a look of demonic glee.

"Rise, Prince Nila, fourteenth son of he that is Anointed By Jor. You have dared to trespass upon the Isle of Divine Dread, and so you shall pay the price. But first, let us show you your one-time concubine."

The circle of priestesses parted. Somehow Nila found the strength to stand, though his bowels were weak and his knees trembled. He followed them through endless caves and passages, stumbling in the uncertain glow of their nightglobes. They came at last to a gallery and looked down upon a huge cavern that was filled with concentric rings of priestesses, all holding aloft glowing nightglobes. Fand stood in the very center, her eyes wide open and blank of all thought, her hands upon an enormous nightglobe set in a base of carved crystal. His eyes widened at the sight of it. The Nightglobe of Naia was the most secret and precious relic of the Priestesses of Jor. Many thousands had died to save it from the human attack, and it was sacrilege for any to look at it unbidden, let alone touch it. Fand must have very great powers indeed to be allowed to place her hands upon the Nightglobe of Naia.

"Only the most powerful may touch the Nightglobe of Naia," came the sibilant hiss of the priestess in his ear, as if reading his thoughts. "Your former concubine is blessed indeed."

Nila stared at Fand unhappily. She had the gauntness of all the other priestesses, the look of gloating fanaticism, the sickly paleness of a skin that sees no sunlight. He had meant to call to her but the words choked in his throat so that he could hardly breathe.

"You may listen if you wish," the priestess whispered in his ear. She made a little sign with her hand, and as one all the priestesses below suddenly spoke.

"What is your name?" they hissed.

"I have no name."

"Who are you?"

"I am nothing."

"Do you love us?"

"No. I hate you."

"Do you love Prince Nila?"

"No. I hate him. I love only Jor."

"Why do you hate Prince Nila?"

"I love only Jor."

"Why do you love Jor?"

"Jor is all. Jor is might. Jor is strength. Jor is power."

"Jor is all. Jor is might. Jor is strength. Jor is power. Jor is all," the priestesses chanted, and Fand chanted with them, her eyes staring straight ahead, unnaturally wide.

As the chanting swelled into a crescendo, the priestess made another almost imperceptible gesture and suddenly Nila found himself seized and dragged away, the sound of the chant ringing in his ears. He struggled against them but could not match their strength. As he was dragged back into the passageway he suddenly found his voice.

"Fand, I am so sorry . . . Forgive me! Forgive me, my darling, my love, forgive me . . ."

Fand stood with her hands pressed against the Nightglobe of Naia, staring into its luminous green heart. Within the great glass orb were two very ancient viperfish with enormous bulbous eyes. As they swam back and forth the light cast by their luminescent organs flowed over her face in wavering ripples. For a moment her staring eyes shone brilliantly green, then they sank back into cavernous shadows, then shone oddly green once more.

Around the sacred nightglobe stood an inner circle

of six high-priestesses, each with her own nightglobe held beside her in her left hand, their right hands resting on top of the nightglobe of the priestess beside them. Around them stood a circle of twelve more priestesses, who were in turn circled by a ring of eighteen, and so on until a last ring of thirty-six young priestesses, all connected by the touch upon their nightglobes.

"Jor is all. Jor is might. Jor is strength. Jor is power Jor is all. Jor is might. Jor is strength. Jor is power. Jor is all." The chanting of the priestesses swelled and surged like the sea, rhythmic and unrelenting. Fand chanted with them, her eyes stretched wide and unblinking, the rhythm of the words in perfect harmony with the beat of her pulse, the rippling of green luminance, and the deliberate to and fro movement of the immense fish trapped within the glass.

"Jor is all. Jor is might. Jor is strength. Jor is power. Jor is all. Jor is might. Jor is strength. Jor is power. Jor is all."

Suddenly Fand's voice faltered, her eyes blinked. She heard, from somewhere very far away, from another life altogether: *Fand, I am so sorry . . . Forgive me!*

Fand, she thought. *I am Fand.*

The ripples of light wavered, broke up. The two fish within the nightglobe stared at her with their huge white eyes, no longer drifting back and forth in their terrible unrelenting rhythm. Fand stared back at them, her heart beating so fast it almost suffocated her. I am *Fand.*

THE TAPESTRY
TAKES SHAPE

Hunting the Cuckoo

Isabeau smiled as she heard the sound of giggling from within the playroom. She opened the door and stepped inside, only to be soaked with a deluge of icy-cold water. She shrieked involuntarily as a basin balanced on the top of the door missed her head by inches, clattering on the floor.

"April Fool, April Fool!" Donncan chanted, hovering in the air above her, his golden wings beating strongly.

"Who's the great gowk now?" Neil cried, shouting with laughter. The twins clapped their hands with glee.

Isabeau sighed, laughed, and shook out her wet robe. "Och, ye wicked lads," she cried. "Could ye no' have given me some warning?"

"But it be All Fools' Day," Donncan grinned, landing lightly on the ground, his wings folding. "What be the point o' a trick if ye warn the sucker?"

Isabeau ran her hands down her dripping hair and it sprang up as vigorous and curly as if it had never been drenched. Then she ran her hands down her body until the linen steamed. She looked over at Elsie and grimaced. "Whoever thought o' All Fools' Day should be hung, drawn and quartered!"

"Ye've only just stepped in, my lady. I've been wi' these rapscallions all morn and no' a moment's peace I've had!" the blonde maid replied with a smile. She was sitting sewing by the fire, a white cap framing her pretty face. "First o' all I found an empty eggshell upside down in my eggcup, so when I broke the shell wi' my spoon all I found to eat was air. Then they told me I had a spider on my head and when I shrieked, they rolled on the ground and laughed fit to split their sides. I've been made the gowk o' four times already this morn, my lady, and I've only been here an hour or so."

"But what do ye do here, Elsie? Where be Sukey?"

"She had to step out to run an errand and asked me to mind the bairns for her," Elsie replied, "though she's been gone so long, I think she must be hunting the gowk."

Isabeau gave a sympathetic grimace. "Have ye sent poor Sukey off on a fool's errand?" she said sternly to the boys.

They shook their heads, though Donncan replied cheekily, "We would've if we could've!"

"I'll see if I can find her," Isabeau said frowning. "I want to talk to her about Cuckoo's birthday lunch."

Neil gave another shriek of excitement. The little boy was nicknamed "cuckoo" or "gowk" for he had been born on the first of April, Huntigowk Day. Gowk was another name for cuckoo, and although it was usually used to imply a fool or simpleton, in Neil's case it was used affectionately. Isabeau hugged him lovingly. "Have ye had a happy birthday so far?"

"Aye, indeed! Look! My da and mam had a whole pile o' presents sent for me from Tìrsoilleir! There be my very own sword!" Neil brandished a small wooden sword excitedly. "Donncan and me have been playing Bright Soldiers all morning and 'cause it's my birthday, I got to be the seanalair o' the Graycloaks for a change!"

"Well, that was very nice o' Donncan to let ye have a turn, Cuckoo," Isabeau said. Donncan grinned, perceiving the subtle irony of her words, but it went straight over Neil's head, the little boy agreeing happily.

The son of Iain MacFóghnan of Arran and Elfrida NicHilde of Tìrsoilleir, Neil had been sent to stay within the safety of Lucescere while his parents were busy winning back the Crown of the Forbidden Land. The NicHilde clan had been deposed as the rulers of Tìrsoilleir when Elfrida was just a little girl, the land being ruled by the cruel and corrupt Fealde of Bride. Elfrida had spent her childhood locked up in the infamous Black Tower, only being released as a young woman when the Fealde negotiated a marriage of convenience for her with the son of Margrit NicFóghnan of Arran. Although both Iain and Elfrida had been unwilling pawns in Margrit's machiavellian plots, the marriage of convenience had soon blossomed into a true, abiding love. The young couple had managed to break free of those who sought to manipulate them, fleeing Arran and giving their support to Lachlan. In return, the young Rìgh had helped to drive the treacherous Margrit out of Arran, giving the throne to her son. Now he endeavored to do the same for Elfrida.

Neil's face suddenly clouded and he looked down. "I wish Da and Mam could have been here for my birthday."

Isabeau knelt beside him and hugged him close. "Aye, I ken," she said softly. "But the last news we had from Tìrsoilleir was very good indeed and they do no' think it will be very long afore all o' Tìrsoilleir submits to your mother's rule. Once the country is at peace again ye can go and join your parents again, and get to see what the land beyond the Great Divide looks like. Will that no' be an adventure, my wee cuckoo?"

"I wish the war was over. They've been away such an awful long time."

Isabeau nodded. Nine months seemed like a long time to her too, and she was not six years old. She hugged him again and said, "Never mind, dearling. At least ye are here at Lucescere with us, no' in Arran all by yourself. And today is your birthday, and no time to be sad. Happen your parents will have sent a pigeon with a birthday message for ye?"

"That be what Sukey said," Neil replied, brightening. "Do ye think they would?"

"I'm *sure* they would," Isabeau replied.

"My da and mam sent me a birthday letter by pigeon post," Donncan said, floating up near the ceiling so he could examine the painted nisses' strange, triangular faces. "And even though it was snowy and stormy the pigeon made it safely, though it was three days late."

"Pigeons do no' ken much about days and times," Isabeau said, smiling, "but they always fly just as fast as they can so if there be no letter today, Neil, I'm sure there will be one soon."

He nodded and began to play again, Donncan flying down to join him. Isabeau smiled at Elsie rather ruefully. "I'll go and see if I can find Sukey. I do hope she has no' been made an April Fool. If she's been made to hunt the cuckoo, she could be anywhere!"

Elsie nodded. "No' that I mind, my lady," she said. "I be far more comfortable here by the fire than I would be down scrubbing pots in the kitchen. I be hoping that if I help Sukey out often enough she'll be putting in a good word for me to Her Highness and I'll be getting a job as assistant nurserymaid."

Isabeau nodded, hoping that Elsie was not dropping a hint in her direction as well. She had known Elsie since they had been scullery maids together at Rhyssmadill and had never really liked her. It may just have been that Elsie was altogether too pretty and knew it. Though Isabeau preferred to think she disliked the maid because Elsie was quick to tease others. Or at least she had been in the days when Isabeau had been nothing but a clumsy cook's apprentice with a crippled hand. Now Isabeau was sister-in-law to the Rìgh himself and a banprionnsa in her right, Elsie was all smiles and friendliness.

Isabeau bid the children farewell, promising to return soon, and went out into the corridor, smiling at the guards who stood poker-faced against the wall.

Although Isabeau did not have the precise searching and finding powers of the MacRuraich clan, she could still sense out the minds of those she knew well, if they were nearby. She was worried Sukey may have been sent "hunting the gowk" as a practical joke, sent perhaps to find a penny's worth of elbow-grease or a pot of striped paint as was common on All Fools' Day.

To her relief Isabeau felt Sukey close by, somewhere in the tangle of stables, kennels, pigpens, hencoops and fishponds behind the kitchen gardens. She made her way through the kitchen wing to the pigeon loft above the stables.

"Be Sukey Nurserymaid here?" Isabeau asked the pigeon-fancier who was busy cleaning out cages near the doorway.

"Och, aye, she be here," he answered, twinkling at her. "She is often here checking on her birds, making sure I be caring for them properly."

"Sukey has her own pigeons?"

"Och, aye. She be a right fancier herself. Lovely it is, to see a lassie taking such an interest in the bonny wee birds. It seems the puir lass be homesick, and she and her young brother send each other bits o' news about their doings. It make sense, rightly, for ye can never trust the jongleurs or the peddlers no' to take months in the taking o' a message, or no' to be forgetting it, while the pigeons'll never let ye down."

"Aye, but ye must be able to read," Isabeau reminded him. "Most o' the common folk canna read, remember, and so asking the peddlers to remember their news and pass it on is the only choice they have."

"Aye, that be true, unless o' course ye can be speaking wi' the birds, like ye and our blessed Rìgh."

"Aye, but then ye must rely on the pigeons remembering the message and ye must admit they be rather birdbrained."

The pigeon-fancier laughed heartily. "Och, it's a wit she is," he said. "And me never hearing that one before."

Isabeau smiled. "Where she be?"

"Her birds are kept right down the far end, on the right," he answered. "She loves her pretty doves, young Sukey."

Isabeau made her way down the long, dim, dusty room, the cooing of the pigeons masking the drum of her boot heels on the wooden floor. She came around the corner and found Sukey sitting on a barrel, reading a scrap of paper, her forehead creased in a frown.

"Dinna tell me ye were sent to find a pint o' pigeon's milk?" Isabeau asked cheerfully. "Surely ye're no' such a gowk!"

Sukey gave a little scream and leaped to her feet, the paper clutched to her heart. "Havers, ye scared me!"

"Sorry," Isabeau said. She poked a finger in through the slats of one of the cages to stroke the soft plumage of the pigeon inside. Softly she cooed to it and the pigeon cooed back.

"Can ye be speaking to pigeons then?" Sukey asked a little uneasily. "I only thought it was owls ye could talk to."

Isabeau cocked an eyebrow at her, a little surprised at the nursemaid's unease. "I can speak both the common language o' birds and most o' the dialects. Dinna ye ken?"

Sukey shook her head. Folding up the paper and thrusting it into her pocket she pushed past Isabeau, saying, "Let's get out o' here, the dust and straw gives me an itchy nose."

Isabeau followed her, saying, with some puzzlement, "Seems an odd hobby for ye to have then, if pigeons give ye hayfever."

Sukey glanced back at her, smiling. "Hobby? I

wouldna call it that. Nay, I was just up here to see
if there was a message for Cuckoo from his parents,
it being his birthday and all."

"Oh, was there?" Isabeau said eagerly as they
came out of the long rows of coops to the front part
of the loft where the pigeon-fancier was grinding
corn.

"Aye," Sukey answered, just as the pigeon-fancier
cried, "Has she given ye the happy news then?"

"I havena had a chance yet, ye auld tattlemonger,"
Sukey laughed. She grinned up at Isabeau. "The
news is only just in and yet I swear the smallest
chimneysweep will ken it all before the chancellor
has even opened the message tube!"

"News from Tìrsoilleir?" Isabeau cried.

"Aye. They've won through to Bride with barely
a man lost, and the Fealde and the General Assembly
have all fled or surrendered! The NicHilde is to be
crowned this week," the pigeon-fancier cried.
"Grand news indeed, aye?"

"Och, the wee Cuckoo will be so happy," Isabeau said.

Sukey's face clouded a little, but she nodded and
smiled, leading the way down the rickety ladder to
the stables.

"Is something wrong?" Isabeau asked, remembering the frown on Sukey's face as she had read her
note. "Have ye had bad news from home?"

"Och, no' at all," Sukey replied. "Although I shall
be sad to lose our wee cuckoo. He be such a sweet
laddiekin and such company for Donncan, who I
swear grows naughtier every day."

Isabeau told her about the basin of water above

the door and Sukey laughed. "Indeed, Huntigowk Day just gives them an excuse for even more mischief," she said. "I put my arm into my dress this morn only to find the sleeve sewn up, and then found an upside-down eggshell in my eggcup . . ."

"They repeated that trick for Elsie," Isabeau said with a smile. "And when we could no' find ye, we were afraid ye'd been sent off hunting the cuckoo."

"Nay, hunting the pigeon instead," Sukey said cheerfully. "What were ye wanting me for?"

"I just wanted to make sure all our plans for Cuckoo's birthday lunch were in place," Isabeau answered as they walked through the kitchen garden. She bent and crushed some rosemary leaves in her fingers, inhaling the sharp odor. "He misses his parents so much, the poor wee laddie, that I really want to do something special for him. Meghan has given me the key to the secret door in the back wall so we can take them out into the forest for a picnic as we planned."

"They'll love that! The hours they've spent trying to find that door. I swear they have pushed and pulled every knob and shield on that back wall a hundred times."

"If it was that easy to find, it wouldna be much use as a secret door, would it?"

"Nay, I suppose no'. I must admit I'm curious myself, having heard the story about how the rebels came in that way and took the palace guard by surprise more times than I can count."

"I've asked Fergus the Cook to prepare us all Cuckoo's favorite foods and I made his birthday cake myself for I swear I was afraid the Cook would cause it to fall flat with all his sour looks."

"Aye, he's a crosspatch," Sukey giggled. "If he were no' such a good cook, he'd have been thrown out years ago."

"Very well then, bring the bairns to the Tower around noon and we'll take them out the back then. I've got another surprise for the laddiekin, this time from Iseult and Lachlan. They've asked me to pick out a pony for him."

"Och, he'll love that!' Sukey cried. "He was so jealous o' Donncan when he was given his pony at Hogmanay."

"Aye, I ken. I'll make sure both ponies are waiting for them just beyond the secret door. They'll be able to go riding all through the forest, which ye must admit will be much more exciting than being taken around the home meadow on a leading rein."

"Will it be safe?" Sukey asked anxiously. "I do no' want them to have a fall and break a bone."

"Och, I'll have a chat to the ponies before I let either lad on their backs," Isabeau answered. "Dinna ye fear! The ponies willna let the boys fall if I threaten them with no carrots or sugar for a week."

Sukey gave Isabeau another odd little glance. "I keep forgetting ye can talk to horses and such," she said. "It must be wonderful to ken what they are saying all the time."

"Och, it's pretty much like talking to people," Isabeau said with a grin as they climbed up the grand sweeping staircase toward the royal suite on the top floor. "They're always talking about the weather or wondering what they're going to have for dinner. It's no' that interesting really."

As they crossed the landing, a passing squire gave the nursemaid a bold glance and smile. The color came up in Sukey's face but she dropped her eyes and ignored him.

Isabeau teased her, saying, "I think ye spend too much time *cooped up* with pigeons, Sukey. A bonny lass like ye should be out gathering may with some young man."

"When do I have time to go agathering may?" she retorted, blushing hotly. "I canna take my eyes off those lads for an instant without them getting into some kind o' trouble."

"Does no' Elsie mind them for ye at times?" Isabeau asked, remembering the days when she had been Bronwen's nursemaid and had been on call all night and all day, lucky to find time to drink a cup of tea in peace.

"Sometimes. Though I worry about leaving the bairns with her, she has no idea how quick they can be."

"Well, Sukey, ye can always ask me to mind them for ye a while. Particularly in the evening, for I do naught but study and I may as well do it here as in my own room."

Sukey shot her a look of gratitude and said diffidently, "Well then, happen ye wouldna mind staying wi' them tonight? It just so happens that Gerard, that lad ye saw just now, has been teasing me to go walking wi' him . . ."

"Glad to," Isabeau said.

"Och, thank ye, my lady!" Sukey cried, her round cheeks pinker than ever. "Though happen ye should be walking out wi' some young man yourself instead o' spending all your time wi' your head stuck in a book."

Isabeau spread the ring-laden fingers of her right

hand. "If I wasted my time flirting wi' lads I would no' have won three elemental rings in less than nine months," she answered. "See, that ruby is for the element o' fire, the jade is for the element o' earth, and that beautiful blue topaz is for the element o' air. I'm now studying hard for my ring o' water. I want to win them all!"

"That be a bonny big ruby," Sukey said.

Isabeau gave her a penetrating glance. She was finding the nursemaid rather hard to understand today. Again she wondered if Sukey had received bad news from home and was trying to conceal her distress. "Aye, it belonged to Faodhagan the Red, my ancestor, ye ken. I'm proud indeed to be wearing it, for he was a great sorcerer," she answered.

"Aye, I ken," Sukey replied.

They walked on in silence, Isabeau wondering at the sudden constraint that had grown up between them. She thought perhaps it had been the reminder of her royal ancestry and wondered if it had sounded as though she had been boasting when she had only meant to explain. She had no chance to clarify further for the guards were swinging open the door to the playroom for them and the children were all tumbling out, shouting questions and telling Sukey how they had made a gowk of Isabeau too.

Exhausted by their day in the forest behind the palace, the children were easy to settle into bed that night. Isabeau read them all a story in the twins' nursery, a lofty room with blue and gold paneled walls and a cloudy ceiling painted with the delicate shape of dancing nisses. A set of gilded doors led to

Sukey's bedroom on one side and the big, high-ceilinged room that Donncan shared with Neil on the other.

When the drowsy twins were securely tucked up with their favorite soft animal, Isabeau snuffed the candles with a snap of her fingers and ushered the two bigger boys into their own room. She sat with them for a while as they recounted their adventures of the day for the umpteenth time, then firmly tucked them up in their little beds.

"Go to sleep now, laddies," she whispered. "Sweet dreams."

"Night, Aunty Beau," Donncan whispered. "We had a simply marvelous day."

"That's good, dearling," Isabeau replied with a smile. "Sleep now."

She shut the door, sighed, stretched, then forced herself to sit down at the table where all her books sat in a pile. Buba settled down on the back of her chair, blinking her golden eyes sleepily. Isabeau would have quite liked to have curled up in the big chair by the fire and had a snooze herself, but she was eager indeed to win her ring of water and had given herself to mid-summer to do so. Once she had accomplished that, she would be able to sit for her sorceress ring and become the youngest witch to achieve the high magic since her own mother.

She poured herself a glass of wine and opened the book Gwilym the Ugly, her teacher in the powers of water, had given her before he rode off with the army to Tìrsoilleir. Gwilym had been appointed the court sorcerer and so accompanied Lachlan wherever he went, making it hard for Isabeau to continue her studies with him.

"Life is believed to have originated in the oceans of the worlds," she read. "Water is essential to all life, being present in virtually every process that takes place within all plants and animals, whether in the form of blood, sap, saliva, or digestive juices."

Isabeau yawned, drank another mouthful of her wine and read on. "Water is, paradoxically, made up of air and fire, which are its two greatest enemies. Without heat, water is transformed into ice, and with heat back into water and thence into steam and thence into nothing. The heat of fire can thus cause water to evaporate into nothingness, into air, but water can never be destroyed. It will always return."

Isabeau nodded, knowing this to be true. She read the passage over again, committing it to memory, then read on as the candle at her elbow shrunk lower and lower, her wine untouched as she became absorbed in her subject.

It had been a long and tiring day, however, and Isabeau's chair was very comfortable. She found it increasingly hard to concentrate on the words swimming about on the page and so at last she pushed away the textbook, letting her head sink back against the satin cushions.

She woke with a start. The fire had sunk low and the candles were guttering in their sconces. Feeling uneasy, Isabeau got to her feet and went toward the bedroom door. A slight sound within made her step quicken.

She swung open the door and felt shock like a hammer blow to her solar plexus. The light from the room behind her shone over the two little white beds within. Both were empty. The big window was wide open, the brocade curtains swaying. Isabeau ran to the window, hardly able to breathe with the terrible certainty that something was wrong indeed.

Soaring away from the window was a long sleigh pulled by a wedge of thirteen swans. Cracking a whip over the swans' shapely necks was a tall woman with dark hair and a dark slash of a mouth in a white face. In the bright light of the two moons Isabeau could clearly see two small boys struggling to be free of the grasp of a thickset man in a tricorne hat. As she watched, frozen in horror, the man raised one huge fist and slammed it into the side of the head of one of the boys. He fell, senseless. The swans curved away over the dark garden.

Isabeau launched herself into the shape of an elf-owl and flew desperately after the swan-sleigh, Buba close behind her, hooting in alarm. Her small wings could not match the strength and speed of the swans, however, and she soon fell far behind.

Wishing she had had the forethought to shapechange into a golden eagle instead of an elf-owl, Isabeau turned back. She had never tried to change shape from one animal to another and was unwilling to try midair in case her magic proved insufficient for the task. Instead she flew back to the palace as quickly as she could, desperate to call the alarm and get the search for the kidnapped boys underway.

Isabeau saw the windows of the nursery suite were blazing with light and thought with a little quickening of her pulse that Sukey must have returned and realized what had happened. *Sukey will have called the guards, thank Eà!* she thought. She flew in the window and changed back to her natural shape, falling to her knees with a thump.

Sukey stood in the center of the room, weeping,

with four guards standing on either side of her, their spears at the ready.

"There she is!" she cried. "That be Isabeau the Red, who I left to care for the young prionnsachan. What have ye done wi' them, Red? What have ye done wi' the laddies?"

As always Isabeau was sick and dazed from the effort of working such powerful magic and for an instant she did not comprehend what Sukey was saying. She shook her head and tried to get to her feet, only to have her legs wobble alarmingly. Realizing she was stark naked, she clutched one of the fallen bedcovers to her.

Only then did she realize the guards all had their spears pointed directly at her.

"What are ye doing?" Isabeau cried. "Do ye no' realize the lads have been kidnapped . . ."

"Aye, and who was it doing the kidnapping?" Sukey cried. Isabeau stared at her, flabbergasted. "This is no' the first time she has done this," the nursemaid said to the guards, wringing her hands in distress. "Remember how she stole away the Rìgh's wee niece? Naught has ever been seen o' her again, has there? Och, my poor wee laddies. I should never have let her persuade me to leave them."

"But I never . . ." Isabeau began indignantly. To her amazement, the guards threatened her with their spears. She drew herself up haughtily. "What is wrong with ye? I be the Banrìgh's own sister. Donncan is my nephew . . ."

"Do ye think we are fools?" the head guard snapped. "We have all been on guard out in the corridor and none have been in or out except ye yourself. We all saw ye fly in through that window in the shape o' an owl—who else could have spirited the boys away with none seeing or hearing?''

"She did the same when she stole away the young banprionnsa, do ye remember?'' one soldier said. "We searched for her everywhere but her horse's footprints just disappeared into thin air.''

"It be uncanny the way she does it,'' another said with a shiver.

"Aye, she must lay her plans deep,'' another said. "Tricking young Sukey Nurserymaid into leaving the bairns wi' her . . .''

"And all ken the Rìgh has long suspected her,'' another chimed in. "Why, ye were on guard wi' me that day, Herman, when we heard the MacCuinn say he thought she was the spy that had been betraying him.''

"Aye, that I was,'' Herman replied. "And he would no' let her stay in the palace, remember, even though she be the Banrìgh's own sister. She was put out in the auld tower.''

Isabeau had been turning from one to the other, hardly able to comprehend that they thought she was responsible for the boys' disappearance. Who would have thought she would find herself so accused, all because of a few hasty words Lachlan had spoken in anger months ago? If only there was someone to speak up on her behalf! Meghan was riding through the countryside blessing the spring crops, and all of Lachlan and Iseult's retinue were in Tìrsoilleir. There was no one left in Lucescere but the old chancellor and a few soldiers and servants, none of whom knew Isabeau well except for Sukey.

At the thought of the nurserymaid, Isabeau's eyes suddenly stung with tears. She had thought Sukey

was her friend. She could not understand how the
nurserymaid could have turned so suddenly and so
violently against her. Isabeau looked at her and saw
how calculatingly she listened to the guards and
added fuel to the fire of their suspicions.

Turning to Buba, Isabeau hooted desperately, *Go-
hooh! Pursue-hooh!*

Immediately the little elf-owl took flight from the
bedhead where she had perched, watching the
guards with inscrutable golden eyes. She soared out
the open window while Sukey screamed, "Stop it!
Stop the witch's familiar."

The guards were all shouting at her and menacing
her with their spears but Isabeau ignored them,,
watching until Buba was out of sight. Then she
turned back to them, clad only in the blue and silver
brocade of the bedspread.

"Ye are all fools," she said icily. "The heir to the
throne has been kidnapped and ye waste time accusing *me?* Do ye no' ken that I am the Banprionnsa
Isabeau NicFaghan, sister to the Banrìgh herself and
apprentice to the Keybearer Meghan NicCuinn?"

The guards all shifted uneasily, unable to meet
her eyes.

The head guard said stoutly, "We ken who ye are,
my lady. That makes no difference to us in the per-
formance o' our duty."

Isabeau looked at him sternly but nodded. "And
neither should it," she answered. "But ye are wasting
time standing around accusing me. We need to send
out a search party straightaway."

Sukey began to cry again. "I should've kent she
had some wicked plan up her sleeve when she in-
sisted I leave the prionnsachan in her care. His High-

ness has never trusted her, never! Ye ken that as well as I do, Herman, dinna ye?''

Herman sighed heavily. "It be true he did say she could be the spy, Sukey, but—"

Sukey sobbed. "I only hope that it is no' already too late! Wha' if she has murdered the wee prionnsachan like she did their wee cousin? She must need their bodies for some wicked spell she be brewing up."

"Sukey, why are ye saying such things?" Isabeau cried, caught between anger, distress and sheer disbelief. "Ye ken I could never do such things. I be no cursehag to use the organs o' murdered children in my work . . ."

Sukey's sobs became hysterical. "My poor laddiekins, my poor wee lads!"

"And ye must ken that I never harmed Bronwen, I'd never harm a hair on her precious wee head . . ."

"So what happened to her then?" one of the guards asked. Ye disappear into thin air wi' her one night, then return months later wi' never a word to anyone about wha' happened to her."

Isabeau stared from one to the other, explanations trembling on her lips. She wanted to cry out, *Her own mother has her, I gave her back to her mother!* But she could not speak. It was too hard to explain, and she knew Lachlan had not wanted anyone to know in case Bronwen once again became the focus of rebellious factions. She closed her lips firmly, looking at the guards with angry, defiant eyes.

"These be questions for her trial," the head guard said. "Happen we had best take her into custody and see what we can do to track down the prionnsachan. If only Himself was here! It be hard to ken what to

do. We had best send a message to Tìrsoilleir and let
them ken the lads have been taken. It will be a month
or more before they can return themselves, though,
and there be no one here to take command but
auld Cameron . . .''

Isabeau groaned. The Chancellor of the Exchequer
was a very old man who had served both Lachlan's
father and his brother faithfully. He should have retired years ago but Lachlan was too soft-hearted to
insist, knowing how much the position meant to the
kindly old man. Cameron would be greatly distressed by the news the boys had been kidnapped.
He would dither about, wringing his hands and giving contradictory orders until the whole palace was
running about like chickens with their heads cut off.
And by now the swan-carriage could be anywhere.

"If only Meghan was here!" Isabeau cried despairingly. "She could use the Scrying Pool to see where
the boys are. Oh, if only she were here!" She clutched
the bedspread closer about her naked form, then said
with the ring of command in her voice, "Send a message to the Tower at once! Tell Arkening the Dreamer
what has happened and ask her to scry for the boys
through the Pool. Tell her the boys were taken by—''

Sukey's sobs rose in a piercing scream. "How
could ye, how could ye?" she accused Isabeau. "Your
own nephew! And dear wee Cuckoo. Och, ye are an
evil-hearted witch.''

Isabeau's voice was drowned by hers as the nursemaid threw herself across the bed, sobbing hysterically. The guards hastened to calm her and Herman
gestured with his spear. "Happen ye had best come
with us, my lady.''

"Tell her the boys were stolen by a woman in a

swan-carriage!" Isabeau called. "Tell her I think it must be Margrit the Thistle! Tell her to tell Meghan . . ."

But no one listened.

Isabeau gave a shriek of frustration and soared up toward the ceiling, clothed in the golden magnificence of an eagle's feathers. Her keen eyes scanned the room once, noting the panicked confusion of the guards, the dismay in the eyes of the nursemaid peeking up through her fingers. Then she swooped down, seizing her jeweled rings, the owl talon on its leather thong and her staff of power in her strong eagle claws. The guards lunged at her with their spears but she shrieked in rage, slashing at them with her talons. As they scrambled back in instinctive fear, Isabeau launched herself into the air again, soaring out the window and into the night.

I must scry to Meghan and to Iseult and let them ken what has happened, she thought. *And then I must go and rescue the lads myself, for I can see no one here will do anything useful!*

The garden lay below in patterns of moon-silver and shadow-black. Isabeau soared away over the trees toward the Tower of Two Moons. She circled down, landed lightly on the terrace, and transformed back into her own shape, her rings and necklace clenched in one hand, her staff in the other. Although the usual wave of exhaustion swept over her, she did not wait for the dizziness to subside but ran inside the great doors and through the halls and corridors until she reached a small inner courtyard in the heart of the four spires.

In the very center of the courtyard was a round pool, enclosed within stone arches all fretted with entwining lines and knots, and covered over with a crystal dome that glittered in the light of the two moons.

Isabeau sank down on one of the stone benches and gazed into the pool. For a long time she tried to locate the boys but received nothing but an impression of rushing air, swan feathers, stars and the crack and whistle of a whip. So she turned her attention instead to her sister, desperately calling her name. *Iseult! Iseult!*

For a long time there was no response, then slowly the gleams of silver light on the water's surface shifted and changed, became her sister's face.

"Isabeau, what is it? It's the wee small hours. Ye woke me up . . ." Iseult's voice was sleepy. Suddenly her tone sharpened. "Isabeau, ye're naked. What's wrong?"

"Iseult, I'm so sorry! It all happened so quickly. I swear it was no' my fault!" Isabeau gulped back tears. "I'm sorry. It's the laddiekins. It's Donncan and Neil. They've been kidnapped."

"They've been *what?* Isabeau! Try and calm yourself. Tell me what has happened."

Isabeau did her best, though she was so torn between anger and tears that her explanations were rather garbled. When she explained that the guards had been quick to suspect her because they had overheard Lachlan's accusation all those months ago, she saw Iseult's mouth thin in sudden anger. Her twin said nothing, though, waiting till Isabeau had told all of her story.

"So ye think it was the Thistle who stole the boys?" Iseult said when Isabeau had finished. "Are ye sure?"

"Nay, how can I be?" Isabeau replied. "All I saw was the swan-carriage and a tall woman with dark hair. I just ken the story o' how Margrit escaped Arran. Besides, she is Neil's grandmother, is she no'? And she hates the MacCuinn clan, always has. She must hate Lachlan more than ever now she has been dethroned."

Iseult nodded. Her face was very white, but she was in perfect control. "I must wake Lachlan. We shall set sail for home with the next tide. It will be at least a month before we are back, though, Isabeau. Ye must do what ye can to rescue them. I hate to think o' Donncan and Neil in that cursehag's hands. By the White Gods, I dread to think what plans she has for them! She's like some swarthyweb spider, squatting in a dark corner and spinning her evil webs to choke and entangle us. We should have kent better than to imagine we were free o' her!"

"I sent Buba in pursuit," Isabeau said. "Let us pray to Eà she discovers where they have gone. I'll get the boys back, I promise ye, Iseult! I be so sorry. If only I had no' fallen asleep . . ."

"Your wine was probably drugged," Iseult said. "I do no' think they would've taken the chance o' having a trained witch awake in the next room, no matter how powerful the Thistle may be. This would have been carefully planned, no doubt o' that. Do no' blame yourself, Beau."

"Lachlan will, though," Isabeau said bitterly. "He always thinks the worst o' me."

Iseult's lips thinned. "Even Lachlan is no' such a fool as to think ye can be blamed for this, twin. Besides, I think ye are right when ye say Sukey must be the one who has been betraying us for so long. It makes my blood boil to think o' it! Why, she was never more than a few steps away from us at any time, living right within the royal suite. We never suspected her, never, with her sweet face and shy manner. Who would have guessed it?"

Isabeau's eyes stung with tears. "I thought she was my friend. I canna believe it even now."

"No sense in blaming yourself, Beau. It is Lachlan and I who have been made the fools o'."

Isabeau said, "I'd best be going. I swear I'll bring Donncan back for ye, twin, and the wee Cuckoo too."

"Have a care for yourself, I beg ye. Margrit Nic-Fóghnan is a powerful sorceress indeed. Do no' put yourself in danger trying to get the boys back. I be sure she does no' mean to harm them, just hold them to ransom for a return o' her power . . ."

Isabeau could tell her twin was lying but she nodded and agreed, saying, "Aye, she would no' hurt them, I'm sure. I'll get them back, though, Iseult, I promise ye."

"May the Spinners be with ye." Iseult's voice was suddenly choked with tears.

"And with ye," Isabeau replied, her own vision obscuring. She knew how desperate Iseult must feel, being so many hundreds of miles away and helpless to do anything at all.

Once her twin's face had dissolved away into ripples of moonlight once more, Isabeau concentrated on reaching Meghan. It took only a few seconds for the old sorceress's face to materialize in the pool.

"Isabeau, what has happened?" Meghan's voice was sharp with alarm. "I could feel your distress but all I have been able to see through my crystal ball are feathers and confusion. Have ye been changing shape?"

"Aye, but I had to!" Isabeau defended herself. Quickly she told the Keybearer what had happened. Meghan's reaction was characteristically one of anger—at the guards for their stupidity, at Lachlan for his foolish prejudice against Isabeau which had fed their suspicions, and at herself for ever believing Margrit would be content to remain in exile.

"I am the only one who can rescue the boys," Isabeau said when Meghan had finished expressing herself. "I can fly after them much faster than any search party could, even on the swiftest o' horses. And I can ask the birds o' the air and the creatures o' the field if they saw the swans fly by. I'll be able to sneak right up to her stronghold hidden in the shape o' some animal. But I must make haste. It is already some hours since she left the palace. If only I had thought to become a golden eagle straightaway, I could have avoided all this fuss and trouble."

"If only, if only!" the old sorceress snapped. "If wishes were pots and pans, then we'd have no need for tinkers."

When she had broken off the connection with her guardian, Isabeau became aware of the noise of shouting and running feet. Lights blazed all through the great building around her. Isabeau had no desire to explain herself any further that night, nor to risk a confrontation with the palace guards. However, there were things in her room that she would need if she was going to undertake such a perilous journey. After a moment's thought she hid her witch's staff, rings and owl talon under one of the benches, then transformed herself into a large black rat.

None of the many people milling about the corridors noticed her dark shape slipping through the shadows, they were too busy exchanging news and conjectures to look down. Isabeau had some of her hurt feelings salved at the indignation most of the witches and apprentices expressed at the idea she could have been in any way involved. The guards were too busy searching for her to listen, though, and so Isabeau stayed in her rat-shape until she had reached Meghan's room. With no time to search for a rat's way, she transformed herself back into a woman and opened the door as quietly as she could. She was shivering both with cold and the aftereffects of all her sorcerous work, but she ignored her physical straits, searching desperately through Meghan's chest until she found a small black pouch of nyx hair.

"Thank Eà!" she sighed. She unceremoniously dumped the little bag out on the bed, smiling just a little as a peculiar collection of miscellaneous objects poured out until they covered the Keybearer's huge canopied bed. Meghan kept many of her treasures in the bottomless bag, just in case she should ever need to make a quick exit. Isabeau could not afford to carry around such a load, though, particularly since one had to take things out in the order in which they were put in, which could make retrieving anything a long and rather boring task if the bottomless bag were too full. So Isabeau chose only what she needed from the pile, threw those objects back in the bag, and let herself out of Meghan's room.

She transformed herself back into the black rat, and put her head through the drawstring of the pouch.

Dragging it along with her, she crept down the crowded stairs. Her bedchamber door was wide open and Sukey was in there with two guards, riffling through Isabeau's belongings in search, they said, of evidence. Anger began to win over hurt disbelief in Isabeau's heart. She darted under the bed and used her clever rat paws to unlatch the chest hidden there. Her satchel of medicinal and spell-making herbs was inside and she drew it out with great difficulty, holding her breath as the buckles clinked against the floor. No one noticed it over the sound of Sukey's shrill orders, however, and so Isabeau was able to slowly maneuver it into the bag of nyx hair. She found her witch-knife and her old battered water bottle, her coin purse and a nest of three pewter bowls that fitted one inside the other. She was just pushing them into the bottomless bag when the bedspread was suddenly flung back and the chest dragged out into the light. Isabeau crouched down unnoticed as the guards began to go through her trunk.

With the black bag once more around her neck, Isabeau wriggled through a hole in the back of her cupboard to seize whatever clothes she could drag from their hooks. The sound of all her scrabbling must have alerted someone because there was a sudden hush and the cupboard door was thrown open. Isabeau peered out from under a pile of fallen clothes as a guard began to poke about inside. She saw Sukey standing by her desk, about to slide onto her finger a ring that flashed with golden fire. Rage ignited in Isabeau's breast. That was Isabeau's sorceress ring, the one made for her by the dragons! With a squeak of outrage, Isabeau leapt from the cupboard, straight for the nursemaid's face.

Sukey screamed and dropped the ring. Isabeau dived and caught it up in her mouth. She then dashed back under the bed, crouching against the wall as spears were swiped under the bed. One spearhead missed her by a rat's whisker and she bared her teeth and snarled. Blind rage fueled her as she wove through the stomping boots and thrusting spears, scurrying out the door and into the safety of the dark.

Running as fast as her nimble rat paws could carry her, Isabeau made her way back down to the Scrying Pool. Once there she thrust her rings and owl talon into the nyx hair bag, then struggled to draw the mouth of the pouch over her staff of power. At last she managed it, the staff simply disappearing within the little pouch, even though it was almost as tall as Isabeau herself. She then scurried out into the dark garden, scrambling down a drainpipe and along a gutter, leaping into a tree and then down its trunk, dragging the black pouch along with her.

Once in the shelter of the moonlit garden, Isabeau changed into the shape of a blizzard-owl, deciding that was the most suitable shape for flying at night. It was the first time she had changed from one animal shape to another, and for a moment, everything lurched about her, all her rat senses overwhelmed by owl-sight and owl-wit. It was a horrible sensation, like falling from a great height and then being flung upward agáin, her stomach left somewhere in between. Isabeau had to crouch in stillness for some minutes before she was able to spread her great white wings and take flight.

She had soon left the city far behind her, soaring silently above the forest, seeing every flicker of leaf, every scurry of mouse. It did not take her long to catch up with Buba, who was still flying valiantly in pursuit of the swan-carriage. The little elf-owl was trembling with exhaustion, for owls did not usually fly ·great distances. They required only occasional short bursts of speed to surprise their prey on the ground. Dwarfed by Isabeau's immense size, the elf-owl could only tell her that the swans were flying south. Isabeau rubbed her round white head against Buba and thankèd her with long, grateful hoots.

Owl pursue-hooh, she said. *You-hooh snooze-hooh, stay-hooh. Owl return-hooh.*

Owl go-hooh with you-hooh, Buba protested.

Too-hooh far-hooh. Owl return-hooh.

Buba nodded and hooted a mournful farewell. Isabeau spread her snowy wings and soared back up into the sky. All night she flew, only pausing to ask the owls of the forest if they had seen the swan-sleigh. They were able to direct her ever southward, their soft hoots the only sound in the vast, silent night.

Just before dawn she transformed into her own shape to sleep, even her strong blizzard-owl body unable to maintain the strenuous pace. When she woke it was midmorning. Tense with anxiety she ate hurriedly, then transformed into the shape of an eagle to fly onward. Her sharp eyes soon spotted the dark circle of a campfire and she flew down to investigate. It was immediately apparent that the swan-carriage had stopped here, and all her protective rage was aroused once again when she found the print of a very small bare foot in the dust.

Och, the laddies must be so frightened, she thought to herself and, galvanized with fresh energy, flew on.

Isabeau was aware of the dangers of staying within another shape for too long. She made sure to change back to her own shape to eat and rest, though it grew increasingly difficult remembering who she was and why she flew so recklessly. So it went on for four days until at last she reached the sea: owl, woman, eagle, owl, woman, eagle.

There was no way of tracking the swan-carriage over the water. Isabeau retreated into the comfort of her own shape and slept the sleep of utter exhaustion. When she awoke she was dizzy and nauseated, with a pounding headache. She had to dose herself with her own medicines before she felt well enough to even sit up and eat some food. She wanted desperately to go on but remembered all Meghan's warnings about sorcery sickness. She would only make matters worse if she fell into unconsciousness, or lost her wits, so Isabeau gave herself a full day in which to recover.

During the afternoon she felt well enough to walk a little way on the cliff face and look down at the sea, smashing white on the rocks. The strong salty wind blew away the last of her headache and she held up her hand to the seabirds swinging in the air. Isabeau had never learned their dialect, having always lived so far from the sea, but she spoke to them in the common language of birds and was able to make herself understood. They had seen the wedge of swans flying over the waves and were able to point that way, though they shrieked mockingly at her and tried to splash her with their sloppy guano.

Isabeau stared out at the wild sea, her heart sinking. The birds had pointed due south. Isabeau had been taught her geography well and she knew the

Fair Isles lay that way. A group of small, lush islands, the Fair Isles had once been governed by Eileanan's rìgh, but in the time of Jaspar the Ensorcelled they had been overrun by pirates. No attempt had been made to wrest control of the islands back from the pirates, thanks firstly to Jaspar's fading strength and resolve, and then to Lachlan's absorption in winning peace elsewhere in the land. The pirates had been able to rule the waves ever since, raiding coastal towns and plundering merchants' boats with none but the Fairgean to contend with. Given how few merchant ships had set sail in the past ten years, the pirates had not had rich pickings and so they had grown bold and greedy indeed in their forays against the mainland. Isabeau had heard many stories of how they had devastated fishing villages and seaside towns from Clachan to Rurach, stealing young men and women as well as grain, coin and livestock, and burning everything behind them. The flood of refugees inland from the coast was due as much to the pirates as it was to the Fairgean, who at least did not steal and burn as well as kill.

But had Margrit NicFóghnan, the deposed Banprionnsa of Arran, thrown in her lot with the pirates? They had become much better organized in recent years, Isabeau knew from her attendance at the Rìgh's councils. She remembered also how Lachlan had complained it seemed as if the pirates knew every time one of his ships left harbor, no matter how clandestinely. Indeed, Sukey had earned her spy's wages well!

Dreading the journey ahead of her, Isabeau gave herself another night to recuperate. She knew there was nothing but a few bare rocks between her and the Fair Isles, and that the islands were several days' sailing away at least. She did not know how long it would take to fly but she feared it would be as long, and that she would have difficulty finding anywhere to rest and change back into her own shape again. The swans must have rested somewhere, though, and Margrit too. She would just have to keep careful watch and stop whenever she found somewhere large enough.

In the bright dawn Isabeau undressed, stowed away all her belongings in the bottomless bag once more, and willed herself into the shape of a swan. She had only ever seen swans from a distance and so she chose this shape with some trepidation, it being that of a creature she was not fully familiar with. The native swan was one of the largest of all birds in Eileanan, however, and capable of flying great distances at high speeds. More important, a swan would surely be a suitable disguise for approaching and infiltrating Margrit's stronghold.

Isabeau visualized the long curving neck, the wide webbed feet, the strong crimson wings and deep feathered breast, making the image as perfect as she could, then willed herself into that shape. To her relief the transformation occurred without a hitch, and she looked herself over in a puddle with some pleasure at her graceful long neck and beautiful wings. However, when she turned to slide her head through the drawstring of the bag, she was rather taken aback by the awkwardness of her heavy body and out-turned feet. Swans always looked so graceful gliding on the palace loch or soaring through the air. She had no idea that they *waddled*.

With her long neck outstretched, she launched her-

self into the air and glided majestically over the
waves, her wings beating slowly and powerfully.
Higher and higher she climbed, until the sea was a
spread of wrinkled blue silk and the shore of Eileanan a hazy gray smudge behind her. Isabeau was
amazed at how swiftly she flew, faster by far than
the blizzard-owl, whose wings were better suited for
gliding. She rested that night on a bare, windswept
rock, wrapped in her plaid against the lash of the
spray, and in the morning flew on again.

Midafternoon she saw a blue hump of land rising
out of the ocean ahead. By early evening she was
flying down toward a crescent of six islands that
floated enchantingly upon a sea of translucent aquamarine. On the seaward sides most of the islands
rose straight up out of the water, with white-crested
waves crashing down upon sharp black rocks. On
the leeward side the islands faced each other across a
lagoon of a breathtaking blue, with the cliffs gentling
down to little crescents of white sand scattered with
pebbles. Moored in the bays were ships of every
shape and size, all flying a distinctive red flag with
a black hammerhead shark upon it.

Most of the boats were in a wide bay on the inner
shore of the largest island, moored in front of a
rough-looking town. Frowning down upon the town
was a very old fort built upon a high cliff. Isabeau
swooped around it, noting the many purple flags
with flowering thistles emblazoned in gold upon
them. She flew lower and saw a beautifully carved
sleigh with long, curved runners was parked on the
highest tower. Nearby was a row of rough wooden
cages. Crammed within were bundles of white feathers. Then Isabeau saw with a little shock that the

feathers were indeed swans, packed in so closely they could barely move.

She alighted on the top of the tower and waddled over toward the cage, wondering for the first time if she would be able to speak to the swans. Vaguely she remembered an old minstrel's song about how swans only sang as they were dying. She was met with a loud hissing and flapping of wings, however, and knew at once she would have no trouble communicating.

Seeeee the saucy cygnet, strutting about as if sheeee were queeen. Just beeeecause sheee beee freeeeee . . .

Isabeau folded her wings back and bent her long neck submissively. *Pleeease forgive meee, I mean no impertinence.*

The hissing died away and then the largest of the swans called imperiously, *What then do you do heeere, young pen? Your accent is coarse indeed but your curt-seeeey is courtly and your words courteoussss. Do you not know that thissss place is an ensnarement for swanssss? If you do not beeeware, you too may beeee trapped into slavery.*

Have you been so trapped? Isabeau asked. *Why are such reeeegal creaturesss kept in such squalid surround-ingssss?*

There was a hissing of displeasure. *We are slavesss to a cruel, evil-hearted queeeen who has forgotten the respect due a swan and keeps us penned as if weee were mere chickenssss or duckssss.*

But do you not pull along a carriage for her? Why do you not throw her out when you have a chance? Then you would beeee frreeee again.

We are under an eeeenchantment. She has chained usss

*with her magic and we cannot defy her. Many genera-
tionsssss have been enslaved by her and many have tried
to throw off the enchantment, all to no avail.*

*What issss the manner of the enchantment? Perhapssss
I can releease you from it.*

The swans laughed mockingly, lifting their wings.
*Indeed you are callow and naïve, young pen. Forty years
I have been in ssservice to the evil queeeen and · fifty
yearssss my forebearssss. If we have been unable to unlock
the chain of enchantment, what makessss you think you
could?*

*I am out here and you are in there, loath assss I am to
remind you,* Isabeau replied. *I alsssso have an advantage
that you cannot share. I have magic of my own. I can
change myself into the shape of a woman.* After looking
about her carefully, Isabeau demonstrated for them,
changing back into her natural shape. The drawstring
of the pouch almost choked her and she had to
loosen it quickly.

There was much soft hissing and sighing, and then
the largest of the swans said, *Ah, a swan maiden. We
have heard talesss of such thingssss. What a cruel enchantment to put upon you. We pity you, swan maiden, that
you are forced to take on such an uncouth, ugly, grace-
lesssss shape. We hope that you can be freeed of your curse
one day.*

Thank you, Isabeau said, unable to help a little
quiver of laughter in her voice. *Until that day, I hope
I can freeee you from yourssss.*

The swans sighed. *We have tried many times to break
the chainssss but all we do is strangle ourselvessss.*

Isabeau looked closer and saw each swan wore
about its neck a chain of diamonds and rubies. She

reached out a hand to touch one and withdrew it with a little hiss as the jewels stung her finger. *Those necklacessss, they are what bind you to her will?*

They raised their wings and bent their long necks, a few grunting mournfully.

If I break them for you, will you help meeee in return?

You will not beeee able to break them.

If I find a way, will you help meeee in return?

One good ssservice deservessss another, of courssse. What is it that you would wish usss to do?

I come in search of two young cobs, human cobs. They too have been enslaved by your evil queeeen and I must releeeease them and take them home to their mother. Have you seen two such creaturesss?

Two young human cobs. Indeed, yessss, swan maiden, two such creatures were carried here only a day or two ago. That was the last great journey weeee were forced to make and wearying it was.

Do you know where they are now?

The swans shrugged their slim white shoulders.

If I can break the chainssss that ensslave you, will you carry us to safety in the sleigh? Will you pull it one more time?

They muttered among themselves, wings rustling uneasily. *Sheee will not be able to follow us, weeee will be freeee*, they hissed. At last they agreed. Isabeau thanked the swans and promised to return when she had freed the two boys.

Isabeau dressed hurriedly in her brown knee-breeches and linen shirt, leaving her feet bare, then pushed open the door and ventured into the fort in search of the boys.

Room after room was empty of anything but filth,

broken furniture and cobwebs. Isabeau's step grew
more confident as she saw no living thing but beetles
and spiders. Then a little mouse scurried across the
hall, racing for a hole in the skirting board. Isabeau
knelt in the dust, put out her hand and squeaked to
it. It stopped, looked up at her with black dilated
eyes, and squeaked back.

After only a few moments of conversation, Isabeau
once again took off all her clothes and stowed them
in the black pouch. The world swelled and distended
alarmingly until the walls were like cliffs and the
hole in the skirting board yawned blackly. The
mouse led her into the cavern and through a bewil-
dering maze of dark, cramped passageways. Here a
row of rusty nails was a rank of cruel javelins to be
squeezed past, a spider was a many-eyed monster
with slavering jaws, a fall of old plaster a landslide
that had to be dug through. Isabeau's whiskers quivered and her ears twitched backward and forward as
she sought to make sense of this world full of terrors.
More than once she ran blindly, startled by some
sound or smell, the black pouch dragging and bouncing behind her.

At last they slid down a long drainpipe full of
leaves and dirty spiderwebs, landing helplessly in a
filthy gutter, then scrambled through a broken win-
dowpane, paws scrabbling. Isabeau and the mouse
fell together onto bare floorboards in a dark room
full of noise and the terrible stench of humans. Terrified, they scurried under the shelter of a large sideboard and crouched there in the darkness, while
voices boomed all about them. At last there was the
crash of a door closing and then silence, broken only

by a loud moaning like a winter storm in pine trees. It took a long moment for Isabeau to recognize the sound as a little boy sobbing.

She crept out from under the sideboard, her paws trembling, her whiskers twitching. She could see nothing but the great brown cliffs of furniture so, after a long moment trying to overcome her terror, Isabeau changed shape once more.

Sick and dizzy she lay in the dust for a long time, hoping she had not been mistaken that there was no one in the room apart from the two boys. At last her nausea passed and she was able to sit up and hug her bare legs and look about her.

Only one candle lit the room, its flame wavering in a draft. Isabeau brought light to life in her palm, cupping her hand about it so it did not shine too brightly. There was a tray on the table loaded with apple tarts, crumpets and jam, dried bellfruits, little sugared cakes and a jug of frothy goat's milk. It all smelled very delicious.

Chained to the bed were the two little boys. Donncan was lying on his stomach, asleep, one chain secured to his wrist, the other to his ankle. Neil was crying miserably, his face buried in the pillow, his bottom sticking up in the air. He too was securely chained. Both boys were still dressed in their nightshirts, their feet bare.

Isabeau scrambled into her clothes and came quietly up to the side of the bed. "Cuckoo?" she whispered, sitting beside him. "Ssh, sweetie. Dinna cry. It's all right, my wee cuckoo, I'm here now."

Neil sat up abruptly. His face was very dirty. He stared at her blankly, then flung himself into her arms, wailing. She soothed him, stroking his hair as if he were some small animal. At last his sobs quieted and she bent her head, whispering into his ear. "Are ye all right, Cuckoo? Are ye hurt?"

He shook his head, hiccuping a little. "Donncan was hit on the head, though, and he's been all funny since, sick and sleepy all the time."

Isabeau made him let her go so she could move around the other side of the bed. Quickly she examined Donncan, frowning as she saw an ugly bruise discoloring one side of his face. "What did they hit him with, a brick?" she asked angrily.

Neil shook his head. "Hammerhead the Pirate just punched him."

"He should be called Hammerhand," Isabeau said, disgusted. "Have ye tried to wake Donncan?"

"He's woken a few times but he's been really sick and funny. She yelled at Hammerhead and said he'd hit him too hard and told him to get a leech. What good would a leech do, Beau?"

"She means a kind o' healer," Isabeau explained. "Has the leech come yet?"

Neil shook his head. "She said he'd be here soon, though. Donncan told her to do something rude with her leech, and so she yelled at us and then left. She had Stumpy put all that food there so we could see it and smell it but no' eat it. I call that mean!"

"So do I," Isabeau said. "Are ye hungry? Let's wake Donncan up and we'll all have something to eat and then think how we can get out o' here."

She shook Donncan awake and though he protested sleepily, at last he opened his eyes blearily and tried to roll over. The chains prevented him, however, and the jerk on his wrist and ankle made him try and sit up.

"Where are we? What happened?" His voice was weak and he had some trouble focusing. Isabeau gave him some *mithuan* to drink and some color returned to his cheeks. He tugged on his chain and said, "That's right. The horrible woman with the whip. She kidnapped us. But what are ye doing here, Aunty Beau? Have ye come to rescue us?"

"O' course," Isabeau said. "I havena quite figured out how yet, but I will. Ye'd better no' let anyone ken I be here though, until I do figure it out."

They nodded and she brought the tray floating over to the bed so they could all eat, Isabeau as ravenously as the two boys. When there was nothing left but crumbs, Isabeau sent the tray whizzing back to the table. "If they ask ye, Donncan, the two o' ye brought the tray over by yourselves, all right?"

He nodded and said, "I bet ye we could've too!"

Isabeau knew both the boys had a great deal of natural Talent and nodded. "I bet ye could too. I wonder when the leech is coming. I dinna want him to walk in on us halfway through cutting those chains. Happen I'd best wait till he has gone."

Neil whimpered. "Dinna leave us, Aunty Beau! Please?"

Donncan clung to her, the bruise dark against his white face.

"She canna mean to hurt ye though, she would've already if she meant to," Isabeau argued. The boys would not listen, pleading with her to free them now and take them home. She sighed heavily, unable to resist their terror. She rose, went to the door, listened for a long while, then came black and drew her dagger.

Although the blade was diamond-sharp and

strengthened with her own magic, it made no impression on the chain at all. Indeed, it made her fingers sting so much that she dropped the blade with a little shriek. Like the swans' necklaces, these chains were obviously forged with magic.

She thought for a little while, nursing her hand, then thrust her fingers into the pouch and withdrew her staff of power. The boys showed no surprise at seeing the long stave with its large crystal knob pulled out of such a little bag, seeing much stranger things every day of their life. She planted it on the floor, cupped her hands under the crystal and concentrated with all her will and desire, drawing power from deep inside herself and from all around her.

From the heart of the crystal came a thin, almost invisible ray of hissing blue light. It sliced down through the chain effortlessly, scorching a black line through the pillow, mattress and bedsprings until Isabeau switched it off hurriedly.

She had just released the last chain when the door crashed open. Isabeau swung around. In the doorway stood a tall woman dressed in a flowing gown of violet-colored silk, a large silver brooch in the shape of a thistle on her breast.

"Who dares work witchcraft in my domain?" she cried. "Ye fool, to seek to break *my* chains! I shall flay the skin from your body and hang ye from the battlements for the crows to gorge upon. Seize her!"

HONEYED WINE

Isabeau's first impulse was to transform herself and flee, but she gripped her staff tightly and turned to face the sorceress.

"I am Isabeau NicFaghan, Donncan's aunt," she replied courteously. "And ye must be Margrit NicFóghnan."

The sorceress was taken aback. She stepped into the room with a luxurious rustle of silk. Behind her were three men, all considerably shorter than she. One was a fussy old man in a velvet cap with a tassel, carrying a jar of leeches and a battered leather bag. Another, carrying a lantern, was a fat pirate with a wooden leg, a bristling gray beard and a very red face. The last was young and very beautiful, dressed in silks and laces. They all kept well to the rear of the sorceress and it was clear from their nervous demeanor that all three held her in very high respect.

"Isabeau NicFaghan . . ." the sorceress repeated, eyeing Isabeau up and down. "So, ye a banprionnsa then, unlikely though it seems at the look o' ye. And a witch as well." Her eyes flickered to the bed where the boys crouched in terror. "A powerful one too if ye could cut through my chains. I must say I am impressed."

Isabeau inclined her head. "Thank ye."

Margrit tapped her damson-colored mouth with one extremely long, damson-colored fingernail. "Ye interest me, Isabeau NicFaghan." She swept forward and stood by a chair at the table. After a moment she turned her head and snapped, "Are ye deliberately trying to insult me or are ye merely slow-witted? Do ye expect me to pull out a chair for myself?"

The beautiful young pageboy rushed forward and pulled out a chair for her, and she caressed his cheek with her fingers. "Thank ye, sweet boy," she purred and sat down. With a graceful wave of her talons, the sorceress indicated Isabeau should also sit.

Isabeau said, "Thank ye, but I prefer to stand."

The sorceress smiled, her eyes glittering. "It is a mark o' high favor to allow ye to sit in my presence, Isabeau NicFaghan. Do ye dare insult me by refusing such a favor?"

"Actually, I am rather weary," Isabeau replied. "A seat would be most welcome." She smiled at the pageboy as he clumsily pulled out a chair for her, then she sat down, her staff held between her knees.

Margrit observed her through narrowed eyelids. "Almost I find myself amused, my fledgling witch. It is no' an emotion I have experienced in recent years. I may well let ye live."

"In that case, I shall endeavor to amuse ye some more," Isabeau replied. "What tickles your fancy, my lady?"

The sorceress smiled and Isabeau's hands gripped

the staff more tightly. Never had she seen such cold menace in a smile. "How do ye come here?" Margrit suddenly rapped out. "And do no' think to lie, witch, for I shall ken."

Isabeau's mind raced, though her face remained impassive. Coolly she replied, "I flew, my lady. Ye must remember my mother was Ishbel NicThanach, she that is called the Winged."

"How did ye ken where to find me?"

"I followed the swan-carriage," Isabeau replied. "I was minding the children the night ye came and stole the boys. I saw ye from the window."

"Aaah, I see. Ye were the scapegoat the young nursemaid wrote about. Ye were meant to be drugged."

"I did no' drink more than a mouthful o' my wine," Isabeau answered. "Inebriation and reading textbooks do no' mix well."

"So ye are still an apprentice," Margrit said with a small crease between her brows. "I thought ye were too young to carry a witch's staff and I see your hands are bare o' all rings. Have ye stolen someone's staff? It must be a staff o' some power to raise fire strong enough to break my chains."

Isabeau did not answer. Although her hands and body were very still, she was preternaturally alert, watching every flicker of the sorceress's hands and lashes, every nuance of her expression.

"So ye have come to rescue your wee nephew," the sorceress said, "and my grandson too, I suppose. How were ye intending to do that?"

"I do no' ken," Isabeau admitted. "It was difficult enough getting here, I did no' have time or energy for making plans."

Margrit frowned. "Ye are dressed like a farm lad, ye have a crippled hand, ye look little more than a child yourself, yet somehow I suspect there is more to ye than appears on the surface. Ye carry a stolen witch's staff and must have some power yourself for ye used it and used it well. And ye sit there as calmly as if we were at an afternoon tea party instead o' caught like a cat with her paw in the cream jug. Are ye no' frightened?"

"Aye, terrified," Isabeau admitted truthfully.

Margrit's frown deepened. "It is a shame I shall have to kill ye. Ye intrigue me, indeed ye do. I would quite like to find out more about ye, examine ye myself, see just what your powers are. It is a shame I canna take the risk."

Isabeau smiled. "Somehow all I feel is relief, even though I ken that means ye will kill me sooner rather than later."

The sorceress scowled with joy. "Ye are quick, quick as an elven cat."

"Thank ye," Isabeau replied modestly. She saw Margrit's fingers lift and said rather hastily, "Ye said before that a young nursemaid wrote to ye. Do ye mean Sukey, Donncan's nursemaid? She has been spying for ye?" As she spoke she slowly loosened the drawstring of the nyx hair pouch and surreptitiously began to ease it down over the crystal head of her staff.

Margrit frowned in pleasure. "Aye, for years now. And here is the joke. She does no' ken she does it!"

"What do ye mean?"

"Sukey was Maya's spy, Maya the Once-Was-Blessed, Maya the Fairge's daughter." There was contempt in the silken voice. "Maya came to me for help

once and in return we set up lines o' communication
for her spies. She was no' with me long and I have
no' seen her since, but faithfully the little fool nursemaid has been sending me all the information I need
and more, for years now! I sign my missives to her
with Maya's name and much effusion o' gratitude
and she addresses them to me, 'my beloved Banrìgh.'
If it did no' make me nauseous I'd find it amusing."

"I dinna believe it!" Donncan suddenly cried, his
voice trembling between tears and anger. "Sukey
would never betray my mam and dadda!"

"Oh, but she has, my lad," Margrit replied, her
voice as soft and cold as silk. "Many, many times.
And when I have thought fit I have passed on my
information to the Tìrsoilleirean, who have been my
allies in the past. They pay well for news on the
plans and strategies o' your father's armies. It has
given me much pleasure to see the MacCuinn
thwarted time and time again, all his clever tactics
made hollow and useless, his men cut down in ambushes, his ships plundered and sunk, his ability to
rule questioned over and over again. A few more
defeats like the ones he has suffered recently and
the people o' Eileanan will be looking around for a
new rìgh."

"They will no'!" Donncan shouted.

"Yes, they will, and ye, my hot-blooded young
fawn, shall be the one."

"Me?"

"Aye, are ye no' the heir to the throne? With a
wise and loving regent like me to guide ye, ye shall
be a rìgh that history shall never forget."

Isabeau forgot her need to listen to every nuance

of Margrit's voice. "Is that your plan?" she blazed. "Ye stole Donncan so ye can make him a puppet rìgh while ye rule!"

Margrit smiled at her. "Aye, that's the plan. Though, mind ye, initially I just wanted to have a look at my grandson in the hope he may have inherited something o' me, but nay, it is as I feared, Neil is as weak and foolish as his father. Indeed, he is well named the gowk."

"And just how do ye plan to make Donncan rìgh when his father is alive and well? Do ye think Lachlan will give up the throne to ye so easily, when he has fought so long to gain it?"

Margrit's smile deepened. "As we speak my fleet o' pirate ships are preparing to set forth to attack the MacCuinn's fleet. For I am sure once the winged *uilebheist* hears his son has been stolen he will hurry to Dùn Gorm to overlook the hunt for him. Am I wrong?"

Isabeau could not say a word.

Margrit's dimples flashed. "As I am sure ye ken, my pirates are renowned for their ruthlessness. They have been given orders to kill every man, woman and cabinboy on board the royal fleet, with all booty to be divided between them. For this one special occasion I shall no' demand my usual levy."

Donncan sobbed. "Nay, no' Mamma, no' Dadda!" He launched himself from the bed. Margrit threw up her hand and suddenly he dropped midflight, his face turning purple as he choked for breath. Vainly his hands pounded on his chest and throat, trying to clear his airways. Isabeau leapt up and ran to him, but as suddenly as it had begun, the choking fit was

over. Wheezing for breath, Donncan lay on the floor,
and Isabeau helped him sit up, soothing him as best
she could.

"Ye are a mean, nasty auld woman!" Neil said
clearly, sitting up and pointing at Margrit. "I dinna
believe ye're my granddam. I willna believe it!"

Margrit laughed. "Tie the brats to the bed," she
ordered the one-legged pirate, "and ye, ye might as
well make yourself useful and drain some o' the cho-
ler from their bodies with your dear wee pets."

The doctor nodded, his hands trembling as he
struggled to undo the top of the jar.

"And ye, carrot-top, ye have ceased to amuse me.
It is time for ye to depart this hallowed earth and
reunite with the universe." Margrit raised her hands,
her dimples flashing in her cheeks.

Suddenly there was a loud bang and a flash of fire
which left behind it a cloud of thick black smoke.
Margrit coughed and waved her hand to clear the
air. All that was left of Isabeau was a little pile of
discarded clothes on the floor. The sorceress cried
angrily, "Where has she gone? What is she, a firework magician to disappear in a puff o' smoke?
Find her!"

Isabeau crouched within the safety of the skirting
board, the precious bag of nyx hair clutched in her
trembling paws. All she could hear was the uneven
stamp of boot and wooden peg-leg as the pirate
searched all through the room, the low hiss of Margrit's voice, his blustering reply. After a very long
time she heard the swish of Margrit's skirts and the
rat-a-tat of the pirate as they left the room, followed
by the nervous tread of the pageboy. Then there was
only the nervous fussing of the doctor as he moaned

and muttered over his task. At last the door shut behind him as well, and there was silence, broken only by the occasional sob of one of the boys.

Isabeau looked out from behind the skirting board, her whiskers quivering. When she was sure there was no one left in the room beside herself and the boys, she crept out and transformed back into her own shape. Her clothes had been flung to one side and she threw them on hurriedly, grateful she had been wearing nothing but a loose shirt, a pair of cotton drawers and her knee-breeches.

The boys were tied to the bed, fat black leeches hanging all over their bare torsos, their striped tails wriggling happily. Swiftly Isabeau rummaged through the pouch until she found the bag of salt which all witches kept by them for use in ritual. She sprinkled salt on the leeches until they fell off, writhing, leaving the boys with many small Y-shaped wounds that streamed blood.

"Do no' worry, they'll stop bleeding soon," she whispered to the boys, who were white-faced both from loss of blood and a squirming horror. It took only a few swift cuts of her knife to free them, and then Isabeau was lifting them off the bed and cuddling them close. "We have to get out o' here fast so we can warn your parents!" she said. "Besides, I do no' ever want to see that blaygird cursehag again."

She put her ear to the door and could hear the tortured breathing of the one-legged pirate on the far side. Very, very slowly Isabeau manipulated the lock with her powers until it clicked free, then in a flash she opened the door. The pirate's chair, which had been leaning against the door, crashed to the floor. The old pirate gave a stentorian grunt and struggled to rise, only to find Isabeau's knife pressed against his windpipe so hard he could scarcely draw breath. His face grew even redder and he wheezed and whuffed a little, but did not shout the alarm.

She had him tied to the bed in minutes, the boys enthusiastically helping her gag him with a torn pillowcase, then she locked the door behind them, setting Stumpy's chair back where it had been.

"Come, my laddiekins, let us pretend to be mice and creep through the castle as quietly as can be," she whispered.

"Aunty Beau, ye really were a mouse, wasna ye?" Neil said.

"Aye, my cuckoo, I was."

"Canna ye show us how to become mice too and then we willna have to pretend?"

"I wish I could, Cuckoo, but I'm no' quite sure how I do it myself. Come now, ssshhhh! Tiptoe and do no' say a word. I be sure there are many people in this place we do no' want to meet."

They crept along the dark corridor, Isabeau casting out her witch senses in all directions, her pulse galloping. Now she had the boys freed, she wanted to escape this filthy old fort just as fast as she could.

She felt the minds of many people about them, some so cruel and loathsome she recoiled from the contact. Frighteningly, she also felt the mind of Margrit, searching for her. She did her best to shield herself, grateful that she had been taught this skill so well by Latifa the Cook, one of her first teachers.

Isabeau knelt down so she could face the boys. "What I want ye to do, my lads, if we get separated, is to head up as far as ye can go, right up to the very top o' the fort, on to its roof. No one shall look for ye there, they shall expect us to head down toward the sea, to try and steal a boat or stow away on a ship. Get into the cages with the swans, they will hide ye with their wings if anyone does come searching for ye. Do ye understand me?"

They nodded, looking very small and dirty in their crumpled, blood-stained nightclothes. "Ye will no' leave us though, will ye, Aunty Beau?"

"No' if I can help it, dearling. They search for me though, all through the fort they search, and soon they will realize ye are gone too. We must be very, very careful."

Hearts hammering, they crept through the dark corridors till they came to the stairs. Light flickered up the stairwell and Isabeau held the boys back, looking cautiously over the rail. Men carrying lanterns were climbing up from a lower floor, the flickering orange light illuminating their cruel faces and sharp cutlasses. Some wore eyepatches, others had hooks for hands, or leaned on crutches, or limped along on wooden legs like Stumpy. It was clear they had lived a rough, bloodthirsty life. Isabeau could not help a shiver of dread. She drew back, chewing her nail indecisively. Then she crept forward once more, beckoning to Neil.

"I'm going to create a diversion. When the men look away, ye must run up the stairs as fast and quiet as a wee mouse. Do no' look back, just run! Promise?"

He nodded and Isabeau hugged him close. "Be careful, Cuckoo."

She peered over the rail again and when the men reached the landing below them, used her powers to cause a clatter from down the corridor. All the men whipped around. As they shouted and pointed, Neil went running up the stairs, his bare feet making very little sound on the wooden steps. As he reached the top, one of the boards squeaked and a few of the men turned around, though too late to see him.

"Ye next, Donncan, my mousekin. Are ye ready? Be careful o' that step."

He nodded, and she repeated the clatter, so that more of the men went charging down the corridor, calling and waving their weapons. Donncan spread his wings and flew up the stairs. The breeze caused by his wings caused the lantern-flames to waver and one of the men glanced up, just in time to see the white flutter of the little boy's nightshirt. "Up there!" he cried, pointing.

The men began to charge up the stairs and Isabeau leaped back, spun on her heel, and ran down the corridor, trying to make as much noise as possible. As she had hoped, the men followed her instead of climbing up the stairs to investigate. She led them far away from the staircase, having to stop to fight once or twice as they caught up with her. None was expecting a lassie with a crippled hand to be able to fight, so the first few times she was able to escape them easily. As they grew warier it became more difficult, for they came at her from all sides with weapons drawn, but she somersaulted over their heads and ran on, searching for some way to escape them. If she could only have a few moments to herself she could transform into a mouse again, but they were too quick and too many and Isabeau was already dangerously overwrought by all the magic she had been using.

She ran on, her breath sharp in her side, then turned to look back over her shoulder. Suddenly she collided with someone very large. With all the breath knocked out of her, Isabeau could not react quickly enough to escape the hard hands that seized her. She had a brief impression of an ugly face all bristling with black hair under a tricorne hat, a grinning mouth of stained, broken teeth and an enormous crooked nose before a huge, hard fist slammed into her temple. She fell into a roaring darkness.

She woke to a crippling headache, lights scorching her eyes. She turned her face away, lifting her hand to cover her eyes.

"The sorceress-babe has woken," Margrit's silken voice emerged from the clamor in Isabeau's ears. "I'm glad o' that, I was afraid ye had killed her, Hammerhead."

"Ah," Isabeau said, not lifting her hand. "So at last I meet Hammerhand, the man who beats laddies black and blue. I wish I could say it was a pleasure."

There was an inarticulate growl and then Margrit said, "No, no, Hammerhead, do no' hit her again. I want to talk to her and she canna answer if she's unconscious."

Isabeau spread her fingers and looked through. "Can ye please move that light so it is no' shining right in my eyes?" Her voice was plaintive.

"Ye must admit she has impudence," Margrit said, grudging admiration in her voice. "We will soon break her o' that, however." The light was moved so it stabbed more cruelly into Isabeau's eyes. "So ye are a sorceress," she purred, and Isabeau saw a flash of golden fire as the dragoneye ring was turned in Margrit's long white fingers.

"I have no' yet sat my sorceress Test," Isabeau replied in a neutral tone. She sat up gingerly, trying not to flinch as her movement brought her rather too close to the black-bearded pirate. She rubbed her temple ruefully. "I do feel rather like I was hit by a hammer," she remarked to no one in particular. "I do no' suppose I could have some powdered willowbark?"

"But ye have a sorceress ring? Two, in fact, for as well as a dragoneye jewel ye also have a ruby. A very large, very beautiful ruby."

"The ruby belonged to my ancestor, Faodhagan the Red. As I already have a dragoneye for my sorceress ring, I wear his ruby for passing my Test o' Fire."

"And I see here ye have rings for all o' the elements except for water. Ye are very young to have passed so many o' the Tests o' Elements. In my day ye had to be twenty-four before ye were even admitted into the coven, let alone allowed to sit your Tests o' Elements."

"Times change. There are few enough with power these days to be quibbling over birthdays."

"Mmmmm, interesting. I should have been more careful, but the dirty face and rough clothes deceived me. I thought ye some foolish peasant bairn who did no' ken any better."

Suddenly the lantern was snuffed so it no longer blazed directly into Isabeau's face. She gave a little sigh of relief and rubbed her temples, looking about her. It was dim in the room without the lantern, but Isabeau could see she was in a grand room beauti-

ully decorated with heavy dark furniture and huge
apestries, an intricately woven carpet on the floor.
The only light came from candelabra on the sideboard behind Margrit, so the sorceress's face was cast
n shadow while Isabeau's was clearly illuminated.

The pirate with the crooked nose was standing
grinning at her nastily, his enormous red hands
thrust through a wide belt. He was dressed in a filthy
velvet doublet, breeches and long black boots, with
an enormous beard and greasy black hair sticking
out from under a tricorne hat. An emerald flashed in
one ear.

The young pageboy was kneeling at Margrit's feet,
a golden tray in his hands. His face was downturned
but Isabeau could see by the droop of his shoulders
that he was desperately unhappy. She looked away,
embarrassed, and saw with some surprise a fat toad
squatting on a purple velvet cushion. Sudden recog-
nition made her mouth quirk upward but she said
nothing, and the little smile died as she saw the nyx
hair pouch lying on the table before them, all her
belongings strewn about carelessly. She tried hard
not to let her consternation show but Margrit was
watching her closely and frowned with pleasure at
the little quiver of Isabeau's lip.

"So where are the lads?" Margrit asked suavely.
'That was clever o' ye to release them again so
quickly. I wonder how ye managed to hide there in
the room without us finding ye."

Isabeau said nothing.

Margrit tapped her teeth with one purple fingernail, as long as a knife. "I have decided no' to kill
ye, at least no' yet," she said pleasantly. "It is clear
ye have power, exceptional power, to so trick and

deceive me. I have decided that such power will be
o' use to me. Ye will stay here and work as my
apprentice."

Isabeau was watching her closely. "I thank ye for
the honor ye show me," she answered with a little
inflection of irony. She saw the dimples in Margrit's
cheek deepen and her fear intensified.

The sorceress sat with a graceful spread of her
silken skirts. "Ye may pour us some wine, my sweet
boy, and then ye may go."

"Aye, my lady," the pageboy answered, pouring
wine from an ornate gold jug into two crystal glasses.
The wine shone with the same golden fire as Isabeau's sorceress ring. Isabeau's eyes widened a little,
for crystal glasses were rare and expensive indeed.

"I can see there will be some advantages to being
your apprentice, my lady," she said sweetly. "I have
heard wine drunk from crystal tastes finer than any
other wine."

"Aye, it does indeed," Margrit agreed. "And this
wine, my wee sorceress, has been sweetened with the
honey o' the golden goddess flower. I promise ye it
will awaken in ye a lust that is no' easily satiated."
She laughed and caressed the pageboy's cheek, before sliding her hand down his body and inside his
breeches to fondle him lewdly. Isabeau's color rose
and so did the pageboy's, who cast her a quick, fur-
tive glance.

"If ye please me, Isabeau NicFaghan, I may send
ye my sweet boy as your reward. I can promise ye
he shall please *ye*."

Isabeau said nothing, averting her eyes, wishing
her color would not rise so readily and betray her.

Margrit laughed. "Have I embarrassed ye?" She

laughed again and pushed the pageboy away with a little pat to his silk-clad posterior. "Go, go! I shall call ye when I want ye."

"Aye, my lady," he replied, putting the tray on the little side table and bowing as he left.

"Ye can go too, Hammerhead. I expect the fleet to be ready to sail with the dawn tide."

"But my lady—"

"Go, go! Do ye think I can no' manage this wee lassie who blushes at the thought o' coupling with a lad?"

"Very well then, my lady, as ye please." The pirate gave the sorceress a perfunctory bow and strode from the room.

"So, Isabeau NicFaghan, if ye are to be my apprentice, happen we should begin our relationship with a toast?" Margrit pushed the glass of wine across the table to Isabeau, who smiled and bowed and took the finely cut crystal glass in her hand.

"To the future?"

"Aye, to the future," Isabeau agreed and lifted the glass to her mouth. She drank a little, the honeyed wine warming her skin and quickening her blood. She put the glass back down on the table and faced the sorceress, who was smiling at her with the same self-satisfaction of a cat toying with a mouse. Isabeau breathed deeply and calmly, her eyes fixed on Margrit's face, her body deceptively relaxed.

"So tell me, my dear apprentice, how it is ye escaped me before, in a puff o' smoke like a firework magician? What is your Talent, for it is clear to me that ye do indeed have a Talent o' a sorcerous strength." As she spoke, Margrit played with the many rings on her fingers, twisting them with her long, curved nails. She smiled sweetly. "Come, my dear. Drink up, enjoy. Be frank with me. I am sure ye do no' wish to make me angry."

"No, indeed," Isabeau agreed, pretending to sip her wine again. Her sharp eyesight had not missed the surreptitious twisting aside of one of Margrit's rings, nor the subtle change of the sorceress's expression. All her senses warned her of danger and she dared not drink the wine the sorceress pressed upon her so assiduously. "It is no great Talent though, I am afraid. I merely brought fire and smoke, and then crawled away under the bed while ye were coughing and choking. I do hope ye are no' disappointed."

Margrit's dimples deepened. She reached out and topped up Isabeau's glass, smiling into her eyes. "Nay, o' course I am no' disappointed, my dear. Please, ye are no' drinking."

Isabeau did not pick up the glass, gesturing across the table to the toad, who sat impassively on his velvet cushion, watching them with black lustrous eyes. "Do please forgive my curiosity, my lady, but can that by any chance be the Scarred Warrior who once served ye?"

Margrit looked at her swiftly, unable to contain her surprise. Then her brows lowered in a little frown of mingled satisfaction and amusement, and she bent and stroked the toad's ugly, warty head. "Aye, indeed he is. Maya transformed him into a toad and sent him back to me with a most impudent message. I have no' forgotten. If the Spinners ever bring our threads to cross again, I shall make her regret her words." She glanced back up at Isabeau, who was regarding her impassively, her hand cupped around her glass. "But now I ken who ye are. Ye are Isabeau the Red, the witchling that stole the NicCuinn brat. It was your braid that Maya brought to me and ye I saw through my Scrying Pool, up on the Spine o' the World. That is how ye come to fight so cannily. And that is the explanation o' the scars on your face. I should've guessed."

Isabeau nodded. "Aye, I be the one."

"And so ye are the one who stole the wee Fairge babe and threw us all into such confusion?"

"Aye, I be the one," she answered again. All her pulses were hammering so hard it was a wonder Margrit did not hear.

Margrit laughed and sipped her wine. "Indeed I was right to fear ye," she said. "Ye are the wild card in our game o' poque. It is because o' ye and your sister that so many o' my schemes have failed. Ah, well, as Eà wills so will it be. Let us drink to forgetting our differences." She raised her glass high.

Isabeau smiled, clinked her glass to Margrit's and drained it dry, though her head spun from the heady brew and her loins warmed. Margrit also drained her goblet, then flung it on the ground with a shattering of glass. "It is a shame I could no' let ye live, wild card," she purred. "But indeed ye were too dangerous to me, and besides, revenge is sweet, sweeter even than honeyed wine."

Isabeau looked at her rather sadly. "Is it?"

Margrit's smile suddenly twisted awry. She put her hand up to her throat, glaring at Isabeau wildly. "No!" she screamed. "Noooooooooo!"

The scream gargled away to nothing as the sorceress's face grew infused with choleric color. She choked, her hands frantically clutching her throat, then suddenly she toppled from her chair. For a time she thrashed about on the ground, her face a mottled purple, gray spittle frothing from her stiff lips. Isabeau looked away, shocked and sickened. So Margrit had dropped poison of some kind into Isabeau's glass. She had not been sure until now, distracting Margrit's attention and swapping the wine on little more than a hunch.

At last the drumming of the sorceress's heels died away and she lay still, engorged eyes staring. Isabeau hurriedly gathered up her belongings and thrust them back into her nyx hair pouch, her heart slamming in her breast. If it had not been for her unnaturally keen eyesight, it would have been Isabeau lying on the ground, her back arched with the agony of her death. It would have been Isabeau who had drunk the poisoned wine.

She gave a little shudder of horror and, without looking at Margrit's purple, foam-flecked face, bent and examined the dead sorceress's hands, frozen into claws. She soon found what she was looking for— one of the rings had a secret compartment that could be unlatched with a slight push of a finger. Within the compartment there was still a residue of white powder. Isabeau worked the carved turquoise ring off the stiff finger and tucked it into the pouch with her own rings. She then covered up Margrit's horrid staring eyes with a cloth and left the room as silently as she could.

Her luck ran out on the stairs. She was creeping along as fast as she could when suddenly a group of pirates emerged from the gloom of the landing, talking and laughing together. They shouted at the sight of her, and Isabeau seized the railing and somer-

aulted over their heads, landing on the stairs
bove them.

She leapt up the steps, ignoring the stitch in her
ide, slammed open the door onto the battlements,
wung it shut and heaved a pile of old crates against
t. Already she could hear the pounding of fists
gainst the wood and knew the pirates were close
ehind her.

Hands trembling, she unbarred the cages of the
wans, who flapped their wings and hissed at each
ther as they struggled to get out. The two boys were
iding inside and she pulled them out, saying urgently, "Throw the cages up against the door, lad-
lies, as fast as ye can!"

As they obeyed she hustled the swans to the sleigh,
hissing at them to get into position. Once they were
ll in harness she gathered together her powers and
egan to cut through the enchanted chains that
ound them. It was difficult to keep her mind fo-
used with such precision when she could hear the
plintering of wood as the pirates bashed through
he door. Every nerve in her body was screaming at
er to hurry but she forced herself to remain calm.
ven the slightest wavering of her concentration
ould see the razor-sharp ray of witch-fire slicing
hrough one of the swans' necks instead of their
ecklace.

Isabeau heard Neil scream just as she released the
ast of the swans. She spun around, thrusting her
taff into the nyx hair pouch. The first of the pirates
ad broken through and had seized the little boy by
he arm. She called to the swans to take flight, then
an to grapple with the pirate. Bugling loudly in tri-

umph, the swans soared into the air, dragging the sleigh behind them.

"Donncan, seize the reins!" she screamed. The little prionnsa flew up to the sleigh, grabbed the trailing reins, and turned the swans around, just as Isabeau kicked the pirate in the head. He fell, taking Neil down with him. Isabeau dragged the little boy free, then turned and flung him up into the air with all her strength, both natural and magical. He shot straight up, as swift as an arrow, and landed in the sleigh with a resounding bump.

"Go, go!" Isabeau cried. "I'll catch up." She had no time to say any more for all the pirates were bearing down upon her, waving wickedly curved cutlasses and shouting.

For a time Isabeau had no time to think, dodging, weaving, punching, kicking, feinting first one way and then the other. She saw a gap in the melee, somersaulted high into the air, and transformed herself into the shape of a swan.

Crimson-tipped wings beating strongly, Isabeau soared away from the battlements, her clothes falling down upon the pirates' heads. They fought free of the garments, letting loose a volley of foul expletives. Isabeau turned and swept north, following close behind the swan-sleigh which she could see clearly in the brilliant light of the morning.

Suddenly an agonizing pain seized her in the breast, paralyzing her wing. Isabeau began to tumble down, down, an arrow shaft protruding from the hollow below her left wing. Down, down, she plunged, her long black eyes closed against the pain and the dizzying fall of space, one wing hanging useless.

She hit something hard with a bang, and lay, half stunned. Then she heard Neil's voice in her ear and felt small hands cradling her head. "Oh, Aunty Beau, Aunty Beau, are ye dead?"

"I dinna think so," Isabeau replied faintly. She opened her eyes and saw Neil's grimy anxious face bent over hers. Donncan still clung to the reins, though his head was craned back so he could see her, his golden eyes shining with tears. "Ye caught me," she said.

He nodded. "I dinna think we would reach ye in time."

"I'm back in my own shape."

"Ye changed back when ye hit the sleigh."

"I must have blacked out for a couple o' seconds. Interesting to ken I change back to my own self when unconscious. I wonder if I change back when I'm asleep." Isabeau struggled to sit up and almost fainted again as the arrowhead bit more deeply into her flesh. "Eà curse and confound them! They would have an archer among them, the filthy maggots!" She managed to sit up and seized the arrow shaft with both hands, breathing harshly.

"Ye're bleeding badly," Neil whispered.

Isabeau looked down and saw crimson ribbons of blood winding down her bare skin. All around the wound the flesh was torn and black with blood. She nodded. "Aye, the arrow's gone deep. I can feel it grating against bone. We have to get it out. Ye'll have to help me, Cuckoo."

He looked sick. "I canna."

"Hold the reins, ye gowk!" Donncan commanded. "I'll help ye, Aunty Beau."

"That's my soldier!" Isabeau said, trying to smile,

though she felt so sick and dizzy it was all she could do to retain consciousness. She reached up with her good arm and grasped the bag of nyx hair which was still hanging around her neck. "Undo this for me, and get out my medicine-satchel."

Donncan found the little bottle of poppy syrup which all healers carried with them, and gave it to her to drink. She gulped down a few mouthfuls, then went on unsteadily. "Now I need ye to tear your nightshirt up for me, dearling, and wad it all around the arrow shaft."

"My nightshirt is filthy," Donncan said.

"Find something clean in the bag then. Just hurry!" He dragged out her only other shirt and tore it up hastily, making a thick pad to press against the wound.

"Press as hard as ye can, we have to stop the bleeding." She winced as he obeyed, white-hot streaks of pain shooting through her. "That's good. Now break the shaft. Gently, Donncan, gently!" She screamed as the shaft snapped, jerking the arrow-head inside her. The world receded into fuzziness.

"Aunty Beau, Aunty Beau!"

"I'm fine," she answered, her voice sounding very odd and far away. She shifted her weight, drinking more of the poppy syrup, trying not to breathe too deeply. "Now, Donncan, I need ye to do something hard for me. I ken ye have moved things with your mind before, havena ye?"

He nodded, tears making new white tracks down his dirty face. "No' very well, though," he whispered. "I broke the window by mistake."

"I need ye to concentrate on the arrow. Breathe in very deeply, very slowly, breathe out, breathe in.

Concentrate on the arrow. Now imagine ye are holding it in your hand. Jerk it out through my back."

The young prionnsa hesitated and she snapped,
"Jerk it out, Donncan!"

He obeyed with a catch of his breath. The arrow
flew out through Isabeau's back and embedded itself
in the high carved stern of the sleigh. Isabeau
screamed in agony. Tears burned her eyes and she
sobbed a little, gulping down another mouthful of
the syrup. The pain receded to a hot throbbing, and
she pressed the bloody wad in closer.

"Wash the wound for me with that lotion," she
instructed, "then pad it well with some clean cloth.
Then bandage me up as tightly as ye can, Donncan.
It needs stitching but I canna do it myself and I do
no' suppose sewing is something anyone ever
taught ye."

He shook his head, unable to speak, and bandaged
her up as instructed. Isabeau closed her eyes and
almost succumbed to the temptation to drift away
into blackness again. The poppy syrup was working
its magic, however, numbing the pain to a strange
hot glow that made her fingers and toes tingle.

"Help me up," she whispered. "Where are we?"

She looked over the gilded side of the sleigh and
saw they were flying over the sea, the Fair Isles re-
ceding behind them. Far below, the water glimmered
brightly. With white sails proudly spread, a great
fleet of ships glided through the waves, all flying the
red and black flags of the pirates.

"The pirate fleet!" Isabeau whispered. "Oh, we
must stop them!"

For a moment it was all too hard. She wanted to
curl up and sleep, to let the swans take them where

they willed. She gritted her teeth, however, and said, "Neil, take the swans down. Donncan, get me my staff. We canna let the pirates reach your parents."

The winged prionnsa passed Isabeau her staff of power and she cupped the crystal within her palms, breathed deeply in through her nose and out through her mouth, calming her frantic pulse, drawing upon the coh, drawing upon the One Power. She felt her heart and her lungs and her veins fill with power until she was brimming over with it. Then she let the boys raise her up so she could see the ships racing along below her, their sails billowing out with the breeze.

Isabeau raised her staff, her hands clenched so tight upon it the knuckles were white, and then let the power go in a great whizzing fireball that smashed down upon the lead ship. They were so close now they could hear the screams of pain and terror, smell the stench of burning wood and canvas, see the panic in the sun-browned faces turned up toward them. The swan-sleigh wheeled and passed over the fleet again, and Isabeau once more flung down a great ball of flame. Seven more times she bombarded the fleet and then suddenly she had no strength left and the spinning darkness reared up and overwhelmed her once again.

A long time passed. Occasionally Isabeau was aware of her voice babbling, of laughing hysterically or sobbing. Most of the time she drifted in a hot sort of darkness, unable even to think.

The blessed quietness of sleep claimed her, and for a long time she passed in and out of dreams.

Occasionally she was conscious of a cool hand on her brow, a beaker of water at her lips, a spoonful of food on her tongue. She swallowed as instructed, though all she could see were dark shapes and bright streaks of light. Sleep came again, longer and darker this time, healing her fevered mind.

At last Isabeau opened her eyes and was able to make some sort of sense of what she saw. Sunlight was striking down through the plaited weave of some narrow-leafed plant. It was very warm and Isabeau's throat was dry and swollen. She moved cautiously, her skin feeling hot and tight. Below her sand slithered away and she put out one hand and felt it between her fingers. She wondered where she was.

Children's laughter rang out and she glanced that way, her head aching too badly for her to lift it. There was the glare of blue water and the dazzle of sun, and she shut her eyes against the pain. Someone lifted her head and once more Isabeau tasted cool water against her lips. She drank gratefully, opening her eyes again.

Leaning over her was a woman with a straight fall of silky dark hair and eyes of a most unusual color, so pale a blue as to be almost silver. Her face was strong and square, with high cheekbones. One side of her face was marred by a fine cobweb of scars. She was dressed in the tattered remains of what had once been a long gown of red velvet.

"Maya," Isabeau said blankly.

"Red," she answered with a wry lift of her thin lip.

"What do ye do here?"

"I live here," Maya answered.

Isabeau looked about her. All she could see was blue water and sand. "Where are we?"

"On an island in the Muir Finn," Maya answered. "I do no' think it has a name. If it does, I do no' ken it. Ye could call it the last refuge o' the dispossessed."

"How do I come to be here?"

"The Thistle's swans brought ye here. Apparently the MacCuinn lad told them to bring ye to the nearest person who could help. I must have been the nearest."

Isabeau lay back, puzzled. "How long have I been unconscious?"

Maya shrugged. "Close on two weeks. I thought ye would die."

Isabeau put up one hand and felt her shoulder, which was still tender to the touch. "I'm glad I did no'," she answered awkwardly. "Thank ye."

Maya shrugged. "Ye tended me once and saved me from dying. I had to return the favor."

The two women regarded each other, many unspoken tensions in the silence that stretched between them. "I thought at first, when I saw the swans pulling along the sleigh, that ye were Margrit," Maya said rather diffidently. "I thought she had discovered where Bronwen and I were hidden. It was a bad moment, I promise ye. I was glad indeed to find it was only ye, and gladder still when the boys told me Margrit was dead."

Isabeau gave a little wince, and tried to smile, though the memory of Margrit's purple, engorged face flashed before her. Then she heard the shriek of children's laughter again.

"And the laddiekins?" Despite herself Isabeau's voice was anxious. She knew Maya, like Margrit, regarded the MacCuinn clan with absolute hatred. She could not help fearing the Fairge may have decided to do Donncan some harm.

Maya smiled rather sadly, guessing Isabeau's thoughts. "Apart from being a wee bit sunburned, they are fine. Bronwen has enjoyed having playmates her own age very much indeed."

"Och, it will be lovely to see Bronny again!" Isabeau cried. "It is hard to believe she be six and a half already! I canna believe it is three years since I last saw her." She sensed rather than saw Maya stiffen and looked at her quickly. The Fairge's face was impassive, however. Isabeau said rather stiltedly, "She probably does no' even remember me."

"Och, she remembers ye," Maya replied. "I will call the bairns and tell them ye are awake. They have all been anxious indeed about ye." She rose and went to the edge of the little hut, calling out the children's names.

Isabeau lifted herself up on one elbow so she could see them running across the sand. Leading the trio was a young girl with a long fall of silky-straight hair, blue-black as a raven's wing, with the distinctive white lock of the MacCuinns at her brow. Her eyes were as translucent blue as water over white sand, and her skin had the same iridescent shimmer as her mother's. Her beauty was striking, even more so than Maya's, for her mouth was beautifully curved and warm with color like any human's, and although her face was square with high cheekbones, it did not have the flatness of the Fairge's. She was naked, her skin tanned to a golden hue by the sun.

The two little boys running along behind her were also naked, their skin red with sunburn, their faces alight with laughter. All three were wet and sandy, and it was clear they had been playing at the water's edge.

"Your Aunty Isabeau has woken," Maya said neutrally.

Bronwen's headlong pace slowed so that the two boys were able to run past her, shouting with excitement. They threw themselves on Isabeau, babbling so fast she had trouble understanding them.

"How are ye yourself, Aunty Beau? Do ye feel better? Is this island no' just grand? Cuckoo and I have been fishing but we couldna catch anything, Bronny caught it all. How is your shoulder? Eà's ears, ye slept a long time. We were afraid ye were going to die!"

"That be enough, laddies, ye'll hurt her shoulder," Maya said and hauled them off, rather to Isabeau's gratitude.

The patient smiled at them wanly and said, "I be just grand, my lads. I'm glad to see ye looking so stout. Have ye been having fun then?"

"Aye, indeed," Donncan answered and cast a shy look of admiration at the little girl, who was hanging back, one leg hooked around the other. "Bronny has been teaching us to swim."

"Well, ye canna have a better teacher than a Fairge," Isabeau said. "Bronny swims like a fish." She smiled at the little girl and held out her hand. "Och, Bronny, it is lovely indeed to see ye! How are ye yourself? Gracious alive, ye've grown."

Bronwen muttered something in reply, twisting her leg about, her face downturned. She gave a little peek up at Isabeau, then dropped her eyes again.

"Och, she's gone all shy," Maya mocked. "And

she's spent all week hanging over ye, wondering
when ye'd wake, and muttering little spells to make
ye better."

"Och, has she?" Isabeau cried. "Well, her spells
have worked, I feel amazingly better."

Bronwen looked up, her face lighting up, then
blushed again and dropped her gaze.

"Ye'll have to forgive her," Maya said. "She is no'
used to other people. We've been here alone for three
years now, wi' no other company but each other."
Her voice was bitter.

"Ye must have been lonely," Isabeau said, more to
the little girl than to Maya. Bronwen returned her
gaze more fully, smiling shyly, but it was Maya
who answered.

"Och, no! Why should I be lonely when I have
been used to being the first lady o' the land, the toast
o' all the minstrels and troubadours, wi' a horde o'
servants to answer my every whim and a feast in my
honor every night?"

Isabeau said nothing, troubled and a little embarrassed. Maya got to her feet, saying, "That's enough
now, bairns, Red is looking very pale. Go and see if
ye can find any ripe ruby-fruit and let her rest
awhile. Ye can talk with her again tonight."

Reluctantly the boys got to their feet and followed
Bronwen out into the sunshine again, the little girl
staring back at Isabeau with a look of yearning. Isabeau closed her eyes and listened to the lapping of
the waves, the rustle of the dry leaves overhead, the
shrill sound of the children's voices.

The next day Isabeau felt strong enough to sit up
in the shade of a tree and watch the children play.
Under the warmth of her gentle approaches, Bron-

wen gradually thawed until she was as loving as she had ever been, curling up by Isabeau's side to listen to her stories and bringing her shells and curious stones and clusters of the little red fruit that grew all over the trees in the jungle.

The island was very small and completely encircled by coral reefs which protected it from the raging sea. There was only one sandy beach which faced onto a wide shallow lagoon. It was here that Maya had built herself a small hut from driftwood and woven leaves. A flimsy structure, it provided shelter from the blazing sun but afforded little protection from the fierce tropical storms that often swept over the island. When the winds and rain came, Bronwen told Isabeau, they fled into the jungle and clung to the sturdiest trees they could find. When at last the storm blew over they would come back and rebuild the hut, dry their tattered clothes on the rocks and search the shoreline for anything the storm might have thrown up that they could use. So they had lived for three years, growing adept at catching fish with their hands, climbing the tall milknut trees to shake down their hairy hard-shelled nuts to crack open on the ground below, and prying open oyster shells on the rocks for the soft salty flesh inside.

Maya had clearly worked hard to make the island livable, digging out the one small spring so they had constant fresh water, collecting the debris of the sea to make their hut more secure and comfortable, planting a little garden of roots and wild herbs behind the hut to make their food gathering easier. Remembering Maya from the days when they had first met, Isabeau was barely able to connect this hard-faced, self-reliant woman with the sweet-voiced, soft-skinned, velvet-clad banrìgh she had been. It was clear Maya had not accepted her exile easily, but she had not only survived but had made a fairly comfortable life for herself and her daughter on this lonely coral island. Isabeau could not help feeling admiration for her.

To Isabeau's dismay, she and the boys were as marooned on this island as Maya and Bronwen, for the swans had only stopped long enough to have their carriage unhitched before flying on. Isabeau could have kicked herself for not making the swans promise to fly them back to the mainland of Eileanan before seeking their freedom, but all she had asked was that they take them to safety. That the swans had done, she had to admit, though of all the islands in all the Muir Finn, why the one that Maya the Ensorcellor had hidden herself on?

"Ye must admit the threads o' our lives are somehow twisted together," Isabeau said to Maya one night as the children slept curled on their woven mats under the shelter. She and Maya were sitting out on the sand together, gazing at the stars which hung huge and brilliant in the sky. "For some reason the Spinners have a design for us, that I am sure o'."

"And what would that be, Red?" Maya asked cynically.

Isabeau shrugged. "I do no' ken. All I am sure o' is that the Spinners are spinning their wheel and weaving the cloth o' our lives, and one day the pattern will be clear to us. It surely can be no coincidence that the swans brought us to the very island that ye had taken refuge on, do ye no' agree? There are many other populated islands in the Muir Finn, yet the swans brought us here."

"Happen we were the closest," Maya said. "This island was too small and rocky for the pirates to pay much attention to. Many a time we've hidden in the jungle and watched their ships sail by. Any o' the bigger islands nearby have been ransacked time and time again by the pirates and are naught but ruins now."

"Happen that be true," Isabeau said, "but something tells me there is a deeper, more complex reason. The Coven believes that coincidences are often the workings o' the Spinners, and I feel by the twitching o' my thumbs that this is such a case."

"So why were ye brought here, then?" Maya's skepticism was unabated.

"I do no' ken," Isabeau said again. "Happen it is time for your thread to be brought back into the Spinners' tapestry."

Maya made an impatient gesture. "I do no' understand all your talk o' threads and tapestries. The Fairgean do no' believe in your Spinners. Indeed, how could we? We do no' make cloth so it is a metaphor empty o' meaning for us."

Isabeau hesitated. "Ye could say the Spinners are a metaphor for the workings o' fate, the great motion o' events that work unseen upon our lives. Ye could think o' fate as being like a tide at the full, that sweeps ye onward. Ye were the one who taught me that it is the moons that cause the tides to rise and fall. It seemed incredible to me, that the swing of those two small moons through our skies should have the power to drag the seas to and fro, to make them rise so high and fall so low.

"So it is with our lives. There is a power that works upon us, carrying us forward to who kens where. We can fight against the tide and be dragged down by it, or we can allow ourselves to be carried along by it. Even better, we can use our own will as a rudder to steer a course upon it, navigating by what we have learned upon the journey and so avoiding rocks and sandbanks and sea-serpents. To believe in the tide o' destiny is no' to surrender belief in one's own will. We always have a choice. Even deciding to swim with the tide and no' against it is a decision.''

Isabeau came to a halt, conscious that her voice had risen in pitch and intensity as she had sought to make Maya understand. She continued more softly: "Unfortunately most o' us do no' learn enough upon our journey to steer the best course for our lives. We run aground or are swamped by waves or are wrecked upon the rocks, sometimes many, many times before we learn to recognize the danger signs. And the choices we have made in the past determine the course we are sailing, for how we choose to act and react to the workings o' fate is what makes us who we are.''

Maya was staring at her, leaning forward, her lips parted.

Isabeau continued: "I think, though, that the metaphor we o' the Coven use is a better one in some ways, for to think o' our lives as a ship is to imagine ourselves as solitary, our choices only affecting our own course. And that is simply no' true. Our lives, our fates, are like a thread woven into the fabric o' the whole world. It is quite unique, quite separate, yet totally interlaced with the destinies o' others. Pull out just one thread and the whole cloth unravels.''

Maya was silent. Isabeau could see her hands were

clenched tightly in her lap. "How can any o' ye ever act, if that is what ye believe?" she said at last, her voice husky. "Everything ye do would have such repercussions . . ."

"Aye, it does," Isabeau agreed. "Sometimes far beyond what we could ever have imagined. I once turned over a pair o' dice in a gambling game so that a friend o' mine should not go hungry that night. I am still being astonished by some o' the consequences o' that choice. Ye being here on this coral island is one o' its long-reaching effects. No' only o' the choices I made, o' course. Many o' the forces that drove ye here were unleashed by your own choices and by other people's—your father's, the Priestesses o' Jor, your husband's, Lachlan's . . ."

"Aye, I can see that," Maya said, a little tremor in her voice. "It is odd, thinking o' that. I wonder . . ."

"If ye would have done things differently had ye kenned? Maybe your present would be different if your past had been, but then again, maybe no'. Ye have told me yourself that ye were driven by forces beyond your control, the ambitions o' the priestesses and your father, the hatred against humans instilled in ye from birth. Happen it is true and ye could no' have made different choices along the way."

There was a long companionable silence, both women lost in their thoughts. Then Isabeau stirred. "Until now."

"I beg your pardon?"

"Happen it is time for ye to be making different choices now."

She felt Maya stiffen, withdraw. Isabeau said quickly, "I have been wondering . . ." She hesitated.

"I think it is time for ye and Bronwen to return to Eileanan."

Maya sat up straight, shooting her a furious glance. "Are ye mad?"

"The boys and I are stuck here," Isabeau said. "We canna return to the mainland without your help. I have no way o' reaching my sister to tell her where we are, for I canna scry over the sea. It is too far for us to swim. We canna hail down a passing ship for if one did happen to sail past, it would be a pirate ship and they would kill us." And though she did not say this to Maya, Isabeau knew she could not transform into a bird to fly the distance for she had barely survived the last bout of sorcery sickness. It would be too dangerous for her to use her witchcraft for some time yet.

"And what would your loving brother-in-law do to us if we returned to Eileanan?" Maya said icily. "I would be lucky if I were hanged, for at least then I would escape being burned to fire, which is what he threatened to do to me if he ever caught me! And what about Bronwen? Ye were the one who took her and fled Lucescere in fear o' what he might do to her, his own niece."

"Aye, but Lachlan is aulder now and no' so afraid o' losing his throne," Isabeau argued. "And if ye were the one to help restore his son and heir to him, he would no' be so quick to condemn ye. Besides, the Fairgean threat has grown worse every year. Ye would be able to advise him on how best to overcome them . . ."

Maya laughed harshly. "Och, ye are a simpleton! Once the *uile-bheist* had me in his clutches and his wee son safe in his mother's arms, do ye think he would care that I had aided in returning him there? I think I must ken him better than ye! He hates me, I tell ye, hates me with a passion."

"Ye should no' call him *uile-bheist*," Isabeau protested. "Lachlan is no monster! Indeed, he has ruled wisely and kindly since he won the throne, and though he has his black moods, ye canna blame him when ye think what he went through as a lad, his father and all three o' his brothers being murdered and he himself being turned into a blackbird! It canna have been easy to have adjusted to life as a man again, and as a hunted outlaw instead o' a beloved prionnsa."

Maya opened her mouth to say something scathing but Isabeau went on impetuously, "Besides, all that was your doing, Maya. Ye transformed him and his brothers into blackbirds and set your blaygird priestess hawk to hunt them down, and ye ensorcelled his eldest brother and sucked him dry o' all his power and vitality until he was dead, and ye were the one who ordered all those witches to be burned to death. Lachlan is justified in hating ye! And ye are bitter and resentful because ye have lost your power and wealth and the adoration o' your people and are now exiled on this wee island. Well, ye are here because o' all that ye chose to do. It is time for ye to accept the consequences. Ye canna hide for the rest o' your life—"

Maya stood up abruptly. "And who says I intend to?" she sneered. "Was no' Bronwen declared the rightful heir by my husband the rìgh on his deathbed and proclaimed banrìgh? There are still those who mutter against the rule o' the Winged Pretender."

"Who?" Isabeau cried. "I canna see any on this wee island."

But Maya had turned and strode off into the night, leaving Isabeau alone and much troubled in heart and mind. *And still I make the same mistakes, too quick to speak and too quick to argue*, she thought ruefully. *When will I learn?*

The companionship which had grown up between Isabeau and Maya was replaced by a silence that seemed to reverberate with hostility and suspicion. Although they remained polite to each other, both were preoccupied with their own thoughts and worries.

The days passed and gradually Isabeau's strength returned. She began to think her only recourse was to leave the boys on the island while she resumed the shape of a swan and flew in search of help. Not only was she eager to let everyone know they were safe, she was anxious indeed about the pirate ships sailing in search of the royal fleet, for despite all her efforts, Isabeau had been able to cripple only a few of the pirate vessels. However, she did not dare risk changing shape, not only because of the sickness, but because she was loath to leave the boys in Maya's care while she was gone. What would the Fairge do if she knew Isabeau would be returning to the island with Lachlan and his men?

It would be terribly dangerous for Maya to try and flee to another island. As the days grew warmer the seas would fill with the migrating Fairgean. Isabeau knew the peculiar topography of this small rocky island was all that had kept Maya and Bronwen safe from the sea-fairies in the past three years. Surrounded on all sides by sharp-edged reefs, it was not worth the struggle to reach its one small beach when there were so many other islands nearby with long stretches of sand where the sea-fairies could rest and bear their young. As she could not leave, Maya might decide to use the boys as hostages. Lachlan's volatile temper and Maya's ruthlessness were like lightning and a forest dry from too little rain. Bringing them together could cause wildfire.

And it was not just the little prionnsachan that concerned Isabeau. The weeks she had spent on the coral island had rekindled all her love for Bronwen. With her sweet, winning ways, her striking beauty, her obvious intelligence and Talent, Bronwen had them all enchanted. Yet Isabeau was troubled to find Bronwen was very quick to use her beauty and the force of her nature to keep Donncan and Neil dancing in attendance upon her. She was even prone to use compulsion upon them, a trick of bending others to your will which was forbidden under the Creed of the Coven, since all people had the right to choose their own path.

So charming was Bronwen in her requests, so prettily grateful when they were acceded to, that it would have been easy to think it was just a natural desire to please her that drove the boys to compete with each other for her favors. But before long the friendship between Neil and Donncan became so strained that they came to fisticuffs, and then Isabeau's disquiet deepened into real distress. Not only did she feel it important to break Bronwen's dominance over the boys, Isabeau also knew that the young Fairge needed to be taught the rules and responsibilities of power. It was time Bronwen went to the Theurgia.

One morning Isabeau sat upon the headland, staring out at the great expanse of blue sea that stretched before her, crisscrossed with the curling break of water over reefs and great dark beds of swaying kelp. Desperation filled her. She had to find some way to escape the island! Her attention was suddenly caught by a splashing movement below her. She looked down and smiled in sudden delight, for a playful family of sea otters were romping about below her. There was a tall rock with a steep incline down into the sea and the baby otters were using it as a slippery slide, shooting down the wet slope on their backs to splash into the sea. One or two of the baby sea otters were chasing each other through the waves, while their mother watched tolerantly from a rock, rolling over occasionally to bake her other side in the sun.

Isabeau had known otters all her life and had counted them among her greatest friends. She had never seen a sea otter before and was struck by how much larger they were than the ones she had known, with strong webbed feet and a thick reddish-brown fur. Their antics were as playful, however, and their dark eyes as intelligent. As Isabeau watched, entranced, the father of the family floated on his back with a large stone resting on his belly, smashing mollusks with his powerful paws. He tossed the mollusks to his children and they leaped and dived for them, making sharp little cries of delight.

An idea suddenly came to Isabeau and she leaned forward eagerly, noting the strength and power of the sea otters' legs, the speed with which they swam through the waves. If swans could pull a sleigh through the air, why not sea otters through the water?

She would need more than this one family, however. The wooden sleigh was heavy and it was a long way to the mainland. She glanced around, wondering if there were many other colonies of sea otters on the island.

Out beyond the reef were a number of dark sleek heads bobbing up and down in the waves. Isabeau's heart leaped in delight, for she could easily get together enough sea otters to pull the sleigh with that great number. Then her heart was suddenly squeezed in the viselike grip of fear. She stared at the bobbing heads. She could see pale ovals of faces, and sharp upcurving tusks. Then a great scaled tail with a frilled fin broke the water's surface. They were not sea otters surfing along the break of water but Fairgean!

TIDES OF DESTINY

Lachlan strode up and down the forecastle deck, his wings all ruffled up, his black curls in disarray. His dark face was haggard.

"Canna ye whistle up any more wind?" he called down to a tall, fair-haired girl who clung to the bowsprit below him, just above the *Royal Stag*'s antlered figurehead.

"Nay, Your Highness," Brangaine NicSian called back breathlessly. "Any more wind and the sails shall tear free! We sail at full speed already. Besides, I can barely control the wind as it is. It is taking all my strength to keep it blowing fair."

Lachlan gave a groan of frustration and swung around, his kilt swirling up. Back and forth he paced, his hands clenched around the Lodestar. "If only there was something I could do!" he burst out.

"Ye could come and play cards with me," Dide said, looking up from the guitar he was lazily strumming with long brown fingers. "I thought long sea journeys were meant to be restful, but watching ye pace up and down like a caged saber leopard is about as restful as a march to war. Will ye no' sit down, master, and set yourself to amuse me? For, indeed, all this display o' energy is most wearisome for the rest o' us."

Lachlan cast the handsome young jongleur a look of exasperated affection. "As if I could sit and play cards while that cursehag has my son," he burst out, despair in his voïce. "Och, surely we can sail more swiftly than this?"

Duncan Ironfist, the captain of the Yeomen of the Guard, said calmly, "We are doing all that we can, Your Highness. Wearing out the fo'c'sle deck with all this to-ing and fro-ing shall no' make the ship sail any faster. Why do ye no' rest and let the captain do his job? Ye have been driving yourself for months now, securing the peace in Tìrsoilleir and keeping the lairds happy. Ye canna keep on this way. Rest, my liege, and let—"

There was a shriek of anger. Lachlan's gyrfalcon suddenly plunged out of the sky, talons clenched. Duncan took an involuntary step back. As solidly built as an ancient oak tree, with arms the width of most men's waists, even Duncan Ironfist could be dismayed by the sheer power and speed of the great white bird, which dropped as fast as a boulder and with almost as much weight. At the last moment Stormwing flung out his great white wings and landed on the Rìgh's shoulder, golden eyes blazing.

"No point in getting angry with me, Your Highness," Duncan said stolidly.

Lachlan stared out at the sea, his fists clenched. It was clear he was trying to control his temper but the young rìgh had hardly slept since hearing the news of his son's kidnapping. His shock and horror had come close on the relief and joy of their victory in

Tìrsoilleir, the contrast of emotion making it all that much more terrible.

Duncan looked at the rigidly set shoulders of his rìgh and said gently, "We are making record time down the coast, thanks to the NicSian's wind-whistling. Another week and we shall be sailing into the Berhtfane."

"Another week!" Lachlan cried. "And to think my poor wee laddie is in the hands o' that cursehag Thistle. It twists up all my insides even thinking about it."

Iseult had been standing against the rail, staring unseeingly at the waves billowing and surging against the ship's sides. She turned now and said, with a little quaver in her voice, "Isabeau went in search o' them. Isabeau will save them."

Lachlan turned on her with a falcon's screech, his wings outstretched, his head thrust forward. "Isabeau!" he cried. "Isabeau should've kept a closer eye on them. This would never have happened if she—"

Iseult went white, her blue eyes as hot with anger as his own. "Do no' dare blame Isabeau for this! It is Sukey who betrayed us, Margrit who stole the laddies. Isabeau is the only one who has a chance o' saving our son."

For a moment they stared at each other, then slowly Lachlan's wings lowered, the hostility dying out of his eyes. He stepped forward, his hand held out, his mouth twisting in contrition. "Och, I'm sorry—" he began.

Iseult was red with anger. "I've had enough!" she cried. "Why must ye be always so unfair? Isabeau saved ye from the Awl, she was tortured in your place and crippled horribly; she was the one that helped ye most to save the Lodestar and win your throne, she has been loyal and faithful every step o' the way! Yet right from the very beginning ye have been against her, ye have misread all her motives, ye have been cold and hostile to her. Why? Why?"

Lachlan did not answer, his wings hunched. Iseult drew away from him. "Isabeau is my sister, my womb-sister!" she cried. "She is as like me as my reflection in a mirror. How can ye love me and hate her?"

The black wings stirred. Lachlan looked away, color running up under his swarthy skin. "Happen that be why," he muttered.

She fell back a step. "What?"

He turned on her, every muscle in his strong body tense with anger and frustration. "I met Isabeau first, remember!" he cried. "When I met ye later, I thought ye were her. Apart from the cropped hair, ye were exactly the same, exactly! The same bonny face, the same fiery curls and summer sky eyes. I thought ye the most beautiful, bright thing I had ever seen. I thought *her* the most beautiful, bright thing I'd ever seen. She was naught but a child though. She had no idea what she was getting into. Ye say she saved me from the Awl and was tortured in my place. Ye are right! And aye, it was my fault, all my fault. But how was I to ken? I thought I had to get away from her to keep her safe. But all I did was throw her to the wolves. And when we met again, all that sweet innocence, that shining beauty, was ruined. Ruined."

Iseult stared at him, tense as a bowstring. He turned away, his golden eyes brooding, his wings hunched close about him. The gyrfalcon gave a hoarse, melancholy cry, and Lachlan smoothed his white feathers. "How can I love ye and hate her?" he said with a dark, mocking edge to his voice. "What else can I do? She has your face, your body, your fearless gaze. Or she *had*. Now she has a crippled hand and the knowledge o' terror in her eyes. And I gave her both. If I am no' to hate her, what am I to do? Love her?"

He laughed harshly and went away downstairs, leaving Iseult standing alone on the forecastle deck, the wind blowing her red-gold curls about.

Dide stepped forward, his face troubled. "He does no' mean it," he said gently. "Ye ken what he is like when his black mood be upon him. He does no' mean—"

Iseult turned her cold, autocratic gaze upon him. "Does he no'?" she said with a chill in her voice. "I think he does."

"Iseult—"

"Do no' look so troubled, Dide," she said. "Lachlan always suffers from feeling things too much, too intensely. He fears for Donncan very much. He will feel better when he is no' so confined by the ship. Once we are on land and he can stride about and shout orders and feel like he is doing something, then he will feel better." There was the slightest edge in her voice.

"Iseult . . ."

She turned away from Dide, drawing her plaid up about her shoulders, her profile set as cold and white as marble. "Oh, I ken," she said impatiently. "He will be sorry he spoke when his temper dies. I ken what he's like, better than ye. It does no' mean he did no' speak the truth." She gave a little shiver and looked out again at the blue undulating horizon. "Another week . . ." she murmured. "Oh, Isabeau, please, save them, save my wee laddie."

Isabeau scrambled down the rocks and ran along the sand, terror driving her steps. She burst into the hut, crying, "There be Fairgean in the water! They look as though they're swimming for shore."

Maya leaped to her feet, alarm on her face. She threw open the lid of a large, battered wooden chest and dragged out a clàrsach. "Bronny, where is your flute?"

The little girl was white with terror, but she scrambled to her feet and grabbed her flute, which she always kept by her. It was her favorite possession, along with a ragged doll. Isabeau had given both to her back in the days when Bronwen had lived with her at the Cursed Towers. With the flute clutched in her small hand, Bronwen followed her mother out on to the beach.

"What are ye doing?" Isabeau cried. "Should we no' hide? I tell ye, they were swimming in past the reefs."

Maya did not answer her, striding down to the edge of the lagoon where she sat down on a rock with the clàrsach on her lap. Bronwen stood beside her, the flute raised to her lips.

"What do ye do?" Isabeau cried again. "This is no time for a musical concert! Had we no' better find something to use as a weapon?"

Maya indicated her clàrsach with a contemptuous gesture. "This be a far better weapon than any stick ye'll find on the beach."

With the frightened boys behind her, Isabeau stared out to the edge of the lagoon. She could see the dark heads of the Fairgean as they swam in past the last ridge of coral. "I thought ye said the Fairgean never bothered to negotiate the reefs!"

"They come sometimes," Maya said abruptly. "They harvest the kelp. Stop talking! Go and hide if ye wish. Bronwen and I shall defend ye." The last was spoken scornfully as Maya swept her hands over the strings of the clàrsach. Beautiful music spilled out. Bronwen's fingers moved along the flute, silver notes trilling, catching the melody of Maya's little lap-harp, blending into delicate harmonies.

The intensity of Isabeau's fear and anxiety was dulled, wrapped about in music. Her mind was clouded, her senses benumbed. Her eyes began to shut and she felt her body swaying in response to the melody. Although all her witch senses prickled at the thrum of power in the air, the smell of enchantment, she was unable to fight against the fog which sank over her. It was like a dream in which she fought to stay awake, knowing there was something important she had to do. But the need to sleep was too powerful, too imperative. It dragged her down, a dark, heavy, oily wave that closed over her head and drowned her.

She woke much later, feeling as if her head was stuffed with wool. There was sand in her mouth and she spat it out, sitting up and looking about her.

It was just before dawn. The lagoon shifted and murmured before her, silvery in the growing light. Behind her the two boys slept where they had fallen, their naked bodies curled against the night chill. Bronwen sat beside Isabeau, the flute grasped in both her hands. There was enough light for Isabeau to see that her face was puffy with tears.

"What happened?" Isabeau asked groggily. She sat up and rubbed her face, trying to shake off her sluggishness. "Where are the Fairgean?"

Bronwen pointed down to the lagoon. There Isabeau saw, with a sudden little jolt of her pulses, the dark shapes of bodies strewn along the shoreline, half in, half out of the water.

"What?" she asked, uncomprehending.

"We sang them to sleep," Maya said from behind her. "They drowned."

"Can Fairgean drown?" Isabeau said, still bemused, not believing what she saw. "Do they no' have gills?"

"Aye, we have gills," Maya said. Her voice was without expression. "But we are no' fish. Our gills do no' provide us with enough oxygen to stay submerged for more than five or ten minutes. Fairgean sleep on the land. Do ye think we would have fought so fiercely for the coastlands if we did no' need them to survive?"

Isabeau was aware of a growing distaste, a sickness in her heart and belly. "So ye sang them to death," she said harshly.

"What do ye think they would have done to us if they had come on shore and found us?" Maya asked. "Ye and your precious lads would have been killed at once, and probably Bronwen and I too, for we are human enough for them to hate us. If they had realized we were halfbreeds they might have taken us for slaves, and if any recognized me, the King's halfbreed daughter, well, I would have been taken back to face his justice." She spat out the last word. "This is no' the first time I have used the Talents I inherited from my mother to stay alive. She was a Yedda, did ye ken that? She could no' teach me her Skills herself, for my father tore out her tongue to make sure she could no' sing. Besides, she died when I was no' much aulder than Bronny is now. No, I learned the Yedda Skills from the few sea witches the priestesses allowed to live, ones too young or too weak to use their talents to save themselves. And I have taught them all to Bronny."

Isabeau looked from Maya's hard, closed face to Bronwen's, tear-streaked and swollen. "She is only six years auld and ye have taught her to murder?" she whispered, sickened.

"I have taught her the skills she will need to keep herself alive," Maya said harshly. "And why do ye look at me as if I were the monster? For centuries the Yedda sang the Fairgean to death. Why else were they honored and celebrated all over the land? They sang thousands to their death, babes among them."

"But ye are a Fairge yourself . . ." Isabeau was confused and dismayed, unable to express the repugnance she felt.

"My father was a Fairge and my mother was a Yedda. I am neither, hated and hunted by both. If the humans catch me I shall die, if the Fairgean catch me I shall die. What am I to do but save myself and teach my daughter to do the same?"

Isabeau could think of nothing to say. She stared at the dead bodies floating in the water, their long black hair streaming out like seaweed. The Fairgean were her natural enemy, they had inflicted great suf-

fering on her own kind for centuries. She should feel
relief and pleasure that they were dead. Yet she felt
only revulsion and horror.

"We have to leave here," she said abruptly. "This
is a horrible place."

"And how do ye propose to leave?" Maya said
roughly. "Fly?" She bent and put her arm around
Bronwen, who shrugged her away.

Maya straightened, her jaw set grimly. "It is so
easy for ye to judge me, ye with all your talk o'
choosing one's own course! Ye think this is the destiny I would have chosen for myself? What would
ye have done if ye were me? Ye do no' understand
what it is like to be chosen by the Priestesses o' Jor.
Ye think me cruel and ruthless. Do ye think I feel
nothing when I sing a man to his death? Yet if it be
a choice between my life and his, I will choose my
life every time. Every time! And I will kill to save
Bronwen's too, and yes, even yours, Isabeau the Red,
although ye despise me for it."

She raised both hands and rubbed contemptuously
at her eyes, which were glittering with tears, then
turned and strode away down the beach.

Nila sat very still, his furs arranged around him so
the black pearl hanging on his smooth chest could
be clearly seen by all. It was the only way he could
express how he felt, to his father and brothers, to the
Priestesses of Jor, and to Fand.

Those Anointed by Jor sat all around him, Nila's
thirteen brothers and his father, the King. The eerie
green light of the priestesses' nightglobes wavered
all over the cavern, giving all of their eyes and tusks

a peculiar luminance, deepening the hollows of their eye sockets.

Fear was knotted and cold in the pit of Nila's stomach. He had not been so close to the Priestesses of Jor since they had discovered him trying to sneak into the Isle of Divine Dread.

He did not know why the priestesses had not killed him. Perhaps they feared the anger of his father. Perhaps they had feared the wrath of Jor. One of the priestesses had lifted the black pearl in her hand, examining it closely in the weird green light. He had told the priestesses that Jor himself had led him to it, mocking them, flaunting the god's favor. He had seen the quick exchange of looks, heard the quick drawing-in of breath.

They had thrown him into a tiny dark pit then, and though Nila had spent all the long measureless hours waiting for their punishment, none had come. There was only the darkness and the cold and the malevolent sound of their breathing, the sense that they were hanging over him, listening, waiting. In the morning they had dragged him out and cast him into the sea. Weak from hunger and exhaustion, his limbs cramped from being so closely confined, Nila had barely been able to move. Somehow he had struggled through the waves back to the Isle of the Gods and his own bed-cave. It had been days before he had been able to stop starting at shadows, and the wavering reflection of light from a nightglobe was enough to make his heart slam and his throat muscles clench tight. Nila thought the priestesses had tried to break his spirit, but all they had done was teach him a bitter hatred of them and their cruel god.

The rings of priestesses holding high their globes

brought it all back to him, as painful as if it had all happened yesterday. The sight of Fand, gaunt and pale and expressionless, all the vivid life of her wiped away, was inexpressibly painful to him. He could not look at her, nor at the priestesses, standing so still and expectant in their formal rings, nor at his brothers, who all watched him gloatingly. He fixed his eyes upon the sullen red glow before him, and felt all his being shrink with a fear far more primal and superstitious than the memory of loss or pain.

They were all gathered at the lip of the Fiery Womb, the most sacred of all the caverns of the Fathomless Caves. Jor himself, the God of the Shoreless Seas, had been born in the Fiery Womb, and all the lesser gods too, the god of thunder, the god of ice, the god of whales and seals, the god of the wind, the messenger god of dreams and visions, the god of the dead and drowned. Here, in the Fiery Womb of the Isle of the Gods, the indomitable all-powerful men of the Fairgean royal family were abject before the Mother of the Gods, the ever rapacious Kani, goddess of fire and earth, volcanoes, earthquakes, phosphorescence and lightning. It was her caustic breath that stung Nila's nostrils and rasped his lungs, her spirit that heaved and muttered in the red slit below them.

On and on, monotonous as the rise and fall of waves, the priestesses' singsong chant built up toward a crescendo, a joyous shout of invocation. "Kani, hear us, hear us, Kani, Kani, hear us, hear us, Kani, Kani, hear us, hear us, Kani!"

Then there was stillness. Fand raised her hands and laid them on the enormous nightglobe set in place before her. Nila swallowed, his webbed hands clenching. The dark writhing shapes of the viperfish

nside stilled at her touch. Nila watched with horror
s the two huge fish inside rose and rubbed their
caled backs against Fand's hands, the light cast by
heir luminescent organs shining through her flesh
o he could clearly see the fragile shape of her bones
vithin. Her eyes rolled back in her head and she
quivered visibly. Softly, the chanting began again.

"Come to our call, Kani, goddess of fire, goddess
f dust, rise to our bidding, Kani, goddess of volcanoes, goddess of earthquakes, come to our call, Kani,
Kani, rise to our bidding, Kani, Kani, come to our
all, Kani, Kani, goddess of fire, goddess of dust, rise
o our bidding, Kani, Kani, goddess of volcanoes,
goddess of earthquakes, come to our call, Kani,
Kani, Kani . . ."

Suddenly a great arc of golden fire leaped out of
he glowing chasm, scattering drops of molten fire.
There was a hiss and the priestesses gabbled faster
and faster, "Kani, Kani, Kani . . ."

Suddenly Fand began to speak. Her voice was
hoarse and grating, much deeper than was natural.
"Why have you awoken me, cold children of the
sea?"

The High Priestess intoned, in counterpoint to the
chanting of the other priestesses, "Great Kani, powerful Kani, Mother of All the Gods, we have found the
one who can raise fire and move earth, as you fore-
old. We have brought her here to you, so that you
may speak through her and give us your oracle. Tell
us now how we may raise the tidal wave of Jor's
wrath and drown the land beneath the raging seas.
When last we asked, you told us we must find one
who can raise fire and move earth. Although we did
not understand, we did as you commanded. Here

she is, born of those that walk the land and those that swim the sea, here she is, the one who can raise fire and move earth, here she is, Kani, the one you foretold. Tell us now how we may raise the tidal wave of Jor's wrath and drown the land beneath the raging seas?"

There was a long charged silence, and then Fand replied, in the same deep hoarse voice, "To raise the tidal wave one needs to move the earth. To move the earth one needs to heave up its fiery heart. To heave up its fiery heart one needs to harness the fire magic of the red comet. To harness the red comet one needs great strength and courage. Does the one you found have such strength and courage?"

"We will make sure that she does," the high priestess answered with a cruel grin. "We have harnessed the comet magic before and we know the time of its coming. We shall make sure she is ready."

"Then you shall raise the tidal wave and drown the land," the hoarse voice answered indifferently. There was another brilliant arc of white-gold fire, another hiss of molten sparks, then the red slit darkened as the molten lava within sank back. Fand swayed and fell to the ground, a crumpled heap of white fur and dark hair.

Despite all his best intentions, Nila leaped to his feet, trying to reach her, but his brothers held him back, laughing. He watched helplessly as the priestesses bent and picked up Fand's slight body and carried her away, six more bearing the great weight of the Nightglobe of Naia. He shook off the restraining hands and straightened his furs, cloaking the anger and despair in his heart beneath a charade of indifference. They would kill Fand in their cold lust for revenge, or break her mind, and many, many thousands would die, not just humans but all the creatures that lived on the land and breathed the air. The thought filled him with black horror and he was helpless to do a thing. Helpless.

"The tidal waves of Jor's wrath roll slow," the King said with great satisfaction, "but to sand the rocks shall always be ground."

It was with heavy steps and heart that Isabeau walked back along the beach after having spoken with the sea otters and cajoled their help. Even though the sea otters had been quick to agree, being friendly, inquisitive creatures with a love of adventure, Isabeau was still deeply troubled by their impending departure. She had decided she must take Bronwen back with her, but somehow the decision had not lightened her heart or her conscience.

It seemed that no matter how hard she tried to hate and condemn Maya, she always found herself pitying her and empathizing with her. Would Isabeau have acted differently if she had been born in Maya's place? Would she have had the strength or wisdom to make different choices? Whenever she assured herself that of course she would have, Isabeau found herself remembering her torture at the hands of the Awl. She would have betrayed Meghan then, if she had been able to. She would have told the Awl everything in order to stop the agony of the rack and the pilliwinkes. And she had killed her torturer, murdered him to save her own life. As she had killed others, Margrit among them. It did not really matter that Margrit had died by drinking poison she had meant for Isabeau. Isabeau had still switched the wine and by her action had caused the Thistle to die. In what way was she better than Maya?

Maya had ordered the deaths of thousands, Isabeau reminded herself, and they had died in agony. She might say she did only as she was ordered by her Fairgean father and she was too frightened of the Priestesses of Jor to do otherwise. But the fact remained, she had ordered the deaths while she had been safe on land, married to the most powerful man in the world, rich, pampered and adored.

Her resolve thus bolstered, Isabeau thrust down her own ulterior motives for taking Bronwen back and hurried back to the hut. Tersely she ordered the boys to gather together as many of the milknuts, ruby-fruits, and vegetables as they could, while she oversaw the filling of the waterskins herself.

To Bronwen she said gently, "Dearling, it is time for us to return to the mainland. The sea otters have agreed to pull the sleigh for us, and as they are strong swimmers it should only take a few days. Will ye get together your flute and your wee dolly and anything else ye want?"

"I'm to go with ye?" Bronwen exclaimed, flushing with excitement. Isabeau nodded and she gave a little dance, hugging herself. Suddenly her steps faltered. "What about Mam? Is she coming too?"

"I hope so," Isabeau replied, not entirely truthful.

"But . . . they will kill her!"

"I dinna think so," Isabeau said soothingly, again conscious that she was breaking her oath of truthspeaking. "At least, I hope they will no'. I am sure if I can just explain—"

"I never thought ye were stupid," Maya said

coldly from the doorway. Isabeau swung around, her heart pounding.

The Fairge was standing with her arms crossed over her breast, her mouth set angrily. "What gives ye the right to steal my daughter away from me? I saved your life and the life o' your wee laddiekins and this is how ye plan to repay me?"

"I've saved your life before myself," Isabeau pointed out coolly. "Several times. And Bronny's, for she would've died at birth if it had no' been for me. And it was me that gave Bronny back to ye in the first place. I dinna givê her back to ye so ye could be teaching her how to do evil."

She raised her voice to drown out Maya's protests. "Only six years auld and compelling those around her to do her will, and singing people to death! It's wrong! She has so much Talent, she must be taught how to use it properly and taught the responsibilities o' power." Again she had to raise her voice over Maya's. "Do ye wish her to end up like ye?" she shouted. "I shallna let ye!"

Maya was shouting back at her, her pale face flushed. Isabeau took a deep breath and calmed her agitation. "Think, Maya, think!" she said. Although her voice was low this time, it was fervent and cut through Maya's anger. The Fairge stared at her.

"If ye let Bronwen go, it will be seen as a sign o' good faith," Isabeau said. "I promise ye that I will never let anyone harm her. Surely ye can see that? I will stand up for ye, tell everyone your story, explain that ye have had a change o' heart, that ye no longer wish to be their enemy. I will tell them how ye saved my life, and Donncan's and Cuckoo's too. I will tell them that ye will help in the fight against the Fairgean, if they offer ye an amnesty o' some sort. They offered pardon to all the Red Guards, why should they no' offer it to ye? Ye canna go on like this, on the run from human and Fairgean alike. Lachlan is no' a lad anymore, he's a rìgh! He seeks peace in the land, I ken he does. Why, he sent a messenger to your father seeking to make terms and he was bitterly disappointed when your father refused so horribly. Does that no' show it is a true peace he wants, no' some childish thirst for revenge? He will listen to reason, I am sure o' it. Ye told me once that all ye ever wanted was peace for ye and Bronwen. Well, this may be your chance."

For a moment she thought her words had won Maya over. There was a sorrowful longing on the Fairge's face, a bittersweet regret. Then Maya said sadly, "Och, such a lamb-brained lassie."

She gave a little gesture of one hand. Isabeau felt a sudden lurch. She staggered as the world reeled about her, growing huge and looming with gray shadows. All around her, from above and below, everything stank. She shied away, her hooves sinking into the sand. For a moment there was the familiar confusion of all her senses. She tried to cry out and heard herself bleating. In horror she looked down at herself and saw only woolly legs and little sharp hooves. It took her a moment to realize what had happened, for unfortunately a sheep's thinking processes are rather slow. Once she realized Maya had turned her into a lamb, however, she gave a little shiver of anger and turned herself back.

Bronwen and the boys were crying and shouting, and Maya was saying, "Och, what was I to do? I couldna let her take Bronny away."

Bronwen sobbed. "It's true, ye are an evil-hearted

witch! I do no' want to stay wi' ye. Turn her back, turn Beau back!"

"It's all right, Bronny, I turned myself back," Isabeau said with as much equanimity as she could muster. Her head was spinning so that she could hardly see and her ears were ringing, but she steadied herself with one hand on the wall and smiled coolly at Maya.

Maya was completely flabbergasted. "How . . . ? what . . . ?"

"Did I no' tell ye? I be a sorceress now," Isabeau said sweetly.

"But . . . But how could ye? No one . . . I turned Tabithas herself into a wolf and she was no' strong enough to reverse the spell. How could ye?" Maya demanded. She was white and frightened.

Isabeau smiled confidently. "Happen she did no' ken the way o' it," she answered. "Meghan always did say that anyone could learn a Skill if they watched and listened hard enough. I've seen ye transform before, remember."

Maya backed away a few paces. It was clear she was afraid Isabeau might decide to turn her into some other creature in retaliation.

Isabeau flexed her fingers and saw the Fairge turn ashen. "I am taking Bronwen and the boys and going home. Do no' try and stop me," she said menacingly. "I am sorry it had to be this way. I really hoped I could help ye somehow. Yet once again ye chose to go your own way."

She gathered up her nyx hair pouch and drew Bronwen and the boys close beside her. Compunction touched her and she said, "I'm sorry, really I am. I wish it dinna have to be like this."

Maya said nothing. Her face was deathly white, her pupils greatly dilated. It was clear she did not know what to do. She made an involuntary gesture toward her chest, as if seeking her clàrsach. Isabeau picked up the chest with her mind and hurled it through the grass-woven side of the hut. "I said do no' try and stop me!"

Bronwen followed her and the boys outside, her steps faltering. With her ragdoll and the flute clutched close to her chest, she suddenly stopped and looked back. "Mam?"

"Bronny!" Maya cried, tears suddenly flooding down her face. "Oh, Bronny, Bronny."

Bronwen ran back and embraced her mother fiercely. "Beau will make everything grand," she gabbled. "She'll fix it all up so ye can come home too, and we can be happy together and never be afraid again. Willna ye, Beau?"

"I'll try," Isabeau said, tears springing up in her own eyes. "Though I am afraid your mam will have to stand trial for what she has done."

"Nay, nay, ye'll make it all grand, I ken ye will," Bronwen cried, pressing her face against her mother's shoulder.

Isabeau once again felt all her doubts rise to engulf her. "Bronwen, the tide is on the turn," she said gently. "We must go."

Maya straightened, holding Bronwen away from her. "Do no' greet, my wee lassie," she said unsteadily. "Ye must go. The tide is indeed on the turn."

Maya and Isabeau's eyes met. There was a long moment of silent communion, acceptance, understanding, forgiveness. Isabeau helped the children into the sleigh, the sea otters already leaping and barking excitedly in their harness. She picked up the reins. "Maya, how will I let ye ken?"

Maya shrugged. "I will find out. Ye do no' think I would let my daughter into the care o' my greatest enemy without keeping an eye on her, do ye, Red? I am no' totally without power."

Seeing Maya's twisted smile Isabeau suddenly realized, with a triumphant and joyful leap of her heart, that she had succeeded in withstanding the most powerful and dangerous sorceress in the land. Tabithas had been defeated by Maya. Even Meghan had been sorely tested. Isabeau the Shapechanger had, however, defeated her and outwitted her and perhaps even converted her. Isabeau could not help smiling in pure satisfaction.

"If it is the moons that move the tides of the sea, who is it, or what is it, that moves the tides o' destiny?" Maya suddenly asked.

"It is Eà," Isabeau replied, smiling still. "Eà, the World-Soul, the stuff o' the universe, the source o' all life, all magic. Eà."

Maya stepped back, her brows creasing. Isabeau leaned forward and tapped her on the breastbone. "We all carry a wee bit o' Eà around with us everywhere we go," she said simply. "Your soul is part o' the stuff o' the universe, dinna ye realize that? That part o' ye that aches sometimes with the beauty and terror o' it all, that part o' ye that made ye weep just now, that part that wishes ye could live your life over again, be like one o' these wee bairns, all shining with love and trust and promise. Ye think I do no' feel that too?"

Maya was weeping again. "How will I ken? How will I ken?"

"Trust in the Spinners," Isabeau replied serenely and found her own faith renewed, when she had not even known it had been shaken. She reached forward and grasped Maya's hand, and the Fairge's tears fell upon her wrist.

"Have a care for my daughter?"

"I will indeed," Isabeau replied and squeezed Maya's hand one more time before letting it fall.

"Sails ahoy! Two points on the port side, sails ahoy!"

At the shout of the lookout, Iseult looked up. She had been staring blankly at the ornate carvings of lions, angels, devils and gargoyles that decorated the high poop of the ship, her expression very somber.

All around the deck, her companions looked up also. The crippled jongleur Enit Silverthroat craned around in her chair, her grandson Dide leaping to his feet in sudden concern. Elfrida NicHilde, her face blotched red from days of weeping, let her sodden handkerchief fall, while her husband Iain of Arran looked up from the navigational chart, his thin face creasing in anxiety. Dillon and Jay had been playing trictrac. The young squire dropped the dice at the shout, leaping to his feet with his hand on his sword hilt.

Even Lachlan came out of his cabin for the first time in three days. He was haggard and disheveled, his shirt hanging untied, his eyes bloodshot. "Sails?" he asked with a slight slur.

"Aye, sails!" the lookout boy called down. "Lots o' them. They're coming fast."

"Pirates?" the ship's captain frowned.

"Pirates?" Lachlan repeated. This time the slur was more pronounced. He endeavored to climb up onto the railing, but his foot slipped. Dide put his hand under his elbow and unobtrusively helped him up. Lachlan stared out at the horizon. He squinted first one eye, then the other. "Where?"

"Two points on the port side, Your Highness," Captain Tobias boomed. He was a tall, stern-looking man with close-cropped gray hair under a tricorne hat, and a clean-shaven face, tanned and creased with the sun like a piece of old leather.

"Speak Eilean, for Eà's sake, man," Lachlan replied irritably.

"Off to the left, master," Dide said softly, keeping his hand under Lachlan's elbow.

Lachlan shaded his eyes with his hand and stared where the young jongleur pointed. There on the horizon, like a billowing of soft cloud, were many curved white sails. The Rìgh's scowl darkened. "Och, there be a fair few o' them."

"Aye," Dide answered. "We canna be fighting off such a fleet! The odds are impossible. What are we to do, master? Try and outrun them?"

Lachlan nodded wearily. "Though they are bearing down upon us, no' attacking from the rear. Unless we turn about, they must meet up with us at some point, if that is their intention. Which it seems to be." He rubbed his temples.

"So should we change course, Your Highness?" Captain Tobias asked, his voice strained.

"Nay!" Lachlan burst out. "We could spend weeks dodging that bloody fleet! We have wasted too much time as it is. My son is in terrible danger, we canna let a bunch o' mangy pirates make us turn tail and run. What are we, chicken-hearted curs? We'll fight them and we'll defeat them!"

"That be the whiskey talking," Captain Tobias said coldly. "We have only six ships, remember, Your Highness, or are ye seeing double?"

Lachlan swung around on the captain, who took an involuntary step back at the look on his face. "Do no' ever talk to me like that again, do ye understand?" the Rìgh said softly. "Ye have sworn fealty to me, and by Eà's green blood, ye shall treat me with respect!"

"Aye, Your Highness," the captain replied with a little bow. "I beg your pardon."

"Pardon granted," Lachlan said crisply. "I am no' a fool, captain. I ken we have only six ships and they have thirty or more. I do no' need to understand much about sailing to ken we are in for a battle o' grand proportions. We have right on our side, though, and firepower. Have ye forgot that we have witches on board? No' to mention the Lodestar." He lifted the scepter from its sheath on his belt and a white radiance leaped to life in the milky sphere. "We must prevail and so we shall."

"Aye, Your Highness," Captain Tobias replied with a new respect in his voice. He made a gesture to the bosun who blew shrilly upon his whistle and called in a stentorian voice, "All hands on deck! All hands, I say!"

Though the six ships in the royal fleet strained all their sails and rigging to breaking point, sailing so close to the cliffs at times that all feared they must be swept upon the rocks, still the sails on the horizon grew closer and closer. Soon the fleet of ships were near enough for them to see the dreaded black and red hammerhead flag. There were thirty-seven ships in the attacking fleet, and Lachlan was enraged to see many of them were his own ships, lost to the pirates over the previous few years.

"They look as if they have already been under attack," Captain Tobias observed. "See how their sails are torn and charred? And look, there are holes in the hulls that have been patched with tar. Look at the size o' the hole in that one! That must have been some cannon."

"Isabeau," Iseult said with certainty, unable to help shooting a meaningful look at her husband. "Those holes be caused by witch-fire, no doubt at all."

Lachlan's scowl only grew deeper. He did not look at Iseult, lifting his fingers to surreptitiously massage his temples once more.

The captain snapped out his orders and the sailors leaped to obey. Weapons were handed out from the armory; the cannons were all lifted into position and secured, heavy cannonballs heaved down their throats and gunpowder carefully poured in. Buckets of water were hauled up the side in case of fire, and the sails were all trimmed and secured.

"Master," Dide said diffidently.

"Aye?"

"Have ye learned to use the Lodestar then? I thought . . ."

Lachlan flushed. He cast Dide an angry look, opened his mouth to snap at him, then closed it again. His wings fidgeted uneasily. "The Lodestar is no' an easy thing to master," he replied in a low voice. "And ye ken as well as I that I have had little time for lessons in witchcraft and witchcunning these past few years. We've been at war every day since I won the throne! But Iseult and I have been studying with Gwilym every spare moment we've had, and with Meghan when we're with her."

"But can ye sweep away a fleet o' forty ships?"

Lachlan gripped the Lodestar in both hands, his face set like stone. "Let us hope so."

The pirate fleet bore down upon them. They were close enough now to see the jeering faces of the pirates, who all hung over the railing, waving their pistols and cutlasses. Iain and the court sorcerer, Gwilym the Ugly, watched them with narrowed eyes as they discussed the best way to combat the pirates with sorcery. There was a sudden blast of smoke and fire as the pirates began to fire their cannons, and the royal fleet was quick to retaliate. Soon the air was thick with clouds of acrid smoke, the booming of the cannons, the shouts and screams of men, the dull bang of the harquebuses and pistols, the whine of arrows and then, ominously, the clash of arms as pirates leaped on to the deck of the *Royal Stag*. The crew fought to keep them away from the forecastle deck where Lachlan and his comrades gathered, awaiting their instructions.

"We had best m-m-make a circle o' power," Iain said calmly, taking up a lump of charcoal from the brazier. "Come, Elfrida, I ken ye are no witch but ye have s-s-strong powers, and ye too, Dide and Enit. J-J-J-oin us."

"If we could just manage to make a full circle o' thirteen, we might be able to summon some real power!" Gwilym said and began counting the heads of those in the Rìgh's party. His saturnine face suddenly lit up with a smile of rare charm. "By Eà's green bluid, do ye ken, I think we might just make it!"

As the others drew together at Gwilym's command, the Rìgh strode up and down the deck, the Lodestar clasped close to his breast. He was muttering under his breath, every now and again groaning and sighing and hitting his head. A soft white glow twisted in the heart of the Lodestar and Iseult could faintly hear the rise and fall of its song as it responded to Lachlan's closeness.

Iain drew a twelve-pointed star within a large circle, leaving a small gap on one side. One by one they filed inside. Lachlan sat cross-legged at the center of the circle, his wings folded behind him, the Lodestar held before him. He faced due east, the direction of the element of air, for that was the element whose power they needed the most.

Of the twelve people who took up their positions at the different points of the star, only Iain, Gwilym and Nellwyn, a Yedda who had been rescued in Tìrsoilleir, were fully trained sorcerers. Iseult had been studying hard though, and had already shown she had the power to conjure storms.

Elfrida was the descendant of Berhtilde the Bright Warrior-Maid and had shown some power, too, although she had received only a little training in the use of it. The jongleurs Enit and Dide were gifted indeed, even though they had always preferred to remain independent of the Coven. Enit's young apprentice Jay had already proved his strong natural Talent, while Brangaine was the direct descendant of Sian the Storm-Rider and had inherited the power to call up the wind at will. Similarly her cousin Finn was descended from Rùraich the Searcher and although her Talents did not involve the powers of the weather, her strength would lend much potency to the magic circle.

Lachlan's squire Dillon was also chosen for he wielded a magical sword with immense strength and ferocity, a sign that he had strong powers of his own. They had trouble convincing him that he must not draw his sword and join the fighting, for the nature of the sword *Joyeuse* was that it could not be sheathed until the battle was won.

"If the circle o' power fails," Iseult told him, "well, then we shall all be fighting for our lives and *Joyeuse* shall be needed indeed. But for now, Dillon, give us the strength o' your spirit and no' your arm."

The last to enter the circle of power was only thirteen years old. Although he was a thin, frail-looking boy, he had the potential to be the most potent of all. Tòmas the Healer had the miraculous power to heal with a touch of his hands and so always rode with Lachlan's army, saving many thousands of lives. All thirteen hoped to use the circle of power to support and strengthen Lachlan as he sought to raise the Lodestar, for the magical orb's powers were not easily evoked and the young rìgh had never before attempted to draw upon it.

"If only Meghan were here," Lachlan said despairingly.

"The Spinners are with us," Iain said reassuringly. "A full thirteen, and m-m-m-most with their greatest strength in the p-p-p-powers o' air and water. Do no' fear. We shall prevail."

Gwilym took up his position at the apex of the star, his staff set upright behind him. "Take each other's hands," he instructed. "Close your eyes. Draw in all your will. Focus it upon the Lodestar. Imagine it in your mind, imagine it flaming with power. Imagine feeding all your own power into Lachlan. Imagine he and the Lodestar are a sword that ye wield in your hand. Imagine he and the Lodestar are a flute into which ye pour all your breath. Imagine that he and Lodestar are a torch that ye carry in your hand, that ye light with all your energy. Feel yourself grow light and empty, feel how heavy and strong Lachlan grows . . ."

All seated within the circle of power were conscious of feeling light and giddy. A great wind of power rushed around them, dizzying them with its speed and brightness. They heard none of the crash and bang of the battle raging around them, did not smell the smoke or feel the shudders of the wooden deck beneath them. All their attention was focused on Lachlan, who seemed to loom huge and dark within the spinning spiral of power, his winged form flung in shadowed relief by the blazing Lodestar.

Then Gwilym began to chant and all felt a surge of excitement, for they recognized the words and were able to join in. Louder and louder they chanted, Enit's silvery voice rising in beautiful descant. Then Lachlan's deep, strong voice joined in and all felt the quickening of their pulse, the prickling of their skin, the smell of thunder in the air that meant great magic was being worked.

"In the name of Eà, our mother and our father, who is Spinner and Weaver and Cutter o' the Thread, who sows the seed, nurtures the crop, and reaps the harvest; by the virtue o' the four elements, wind, stone, flame and rain; by virtue o' clear skies and storm, rainbows and hailstones, flowers and falling leaves, flames and ashes; in the name o' Eà we call upon the winds o' the world, in the name o' Eà we call upon the waters, in the name o' Eà we call upon the winds o' the world, in the name o' Eà we call upon the waters . . ."

Then at a counterpoint to the other witches' voices, Gwilym began to chant:

"Come hither, spirits o' the east, bringing wind,
"Come hither, spirits o' the east, bringing storm,
"Come hither, spirits o' the east, bringing gale,
"Come hither, spirits o' the east, bringing whirl-
wind."

Suddenly the Rìgh rose and lifted the Lodestar high, shouting, "I command thee, sea and wind and storm, obey me! Destroy these black-hearted pirates and keep us all safe! Destroy these black-hearted pirates and keep us all safe! Hailstones and rain, gale and wind, sea waves and seafoam, lightning bolt and thunder, obey this, my will! Obey me! By the powers o' air and fire and earth and water, I command thee! Obey me!"

There was a sudden roar. The spinning cone of light whirled even faster about them. All they could see was the white incandescence of the blazing sphere and the black shape of Lachlan, his magnificent wings spread wide. All around was black motion, whirling faster and faster.

Iseult gave a sudden gasp. She had just seen a ship flying through the air, its masts broken, sails torn asunder like enormous white ghosts. A quiver ran around the circle as everyone tightened their grasp, many crying aloud in amazement and fear. Suddenly lightning blasted all around them. Everyone flinched. Again and again the lightning flared, the masts black against all that brilliant white. In each flash they saw scenes of incredible devastation. Waves tossed wildly, ships foundered, ships flew, men screamed in terror.

All their hair and clothes were whipped about crazily. They had trouble retaining their grip on each other's hands. The heavens were torn apart by thunder. It boomed through their heads, threatening to explode their eardrums, resonating through every chamber of their bodies. The deck of the ship pitched so wildly they had to cling tightly to each other's hands to avoid breaking the circle. Still Lachlan stood, a figure carved of black marble and silver, his face exultant in the blazing radiance of the Lodestar.

Then suddenly silence fell, an immense stillness. They released their aching fingers, flexed them, breathed for what seemed like the first time in minutes, looked about with wide amazed eyes, feeling as drained and empty as if they had been without sleep for days.

The *Royal Stag* was pitching wildly in a riotous sea, all its sails flapping. The sky overhead was low and heavy with clouds. Rain thundered down upon the tossing waves, thick as fog. The *Royal Stag* was bathed in sunlight, however, all its masts and sails lit up with golden light. On either side the other five ships of the royal fleet sailed, illuminated with the same warm burnished light.

Spinning off toward the west was a great black vortex of cloud and water, many thousands of feet high. Scattered behind it was the whole fleet of pirate ships, broken and smashed. Some had been thrown onto the rocks where they rested, their masts and spars split and fallen. Others had overturned and were half sunk in the water, or floating in a tangle of sails and ropes. Others had completely disappeared.

None of the circle spoke. They were too drained, too exhausted, too overwhelmed by the sight of the spinning whirlwind, the destroyed fleet. The crew of the *Royal Stag* were leaping about, throwing their caps in the air, beating each other on the back, shouting in amazement and triumph. They could hear the wild hoorays from the other ships as well, and see the same joyous capers.

Captain Tobias stumbled forward, his stern face transfigured. He fell to his knees before Lachlan, seizing his hand. "My liege!" he cried. "Ye did it! I be sorry I doubted."

One by one all the sailors fell to their knees too. "The Rìgh!" they shouted. "Eà bless our Rìgh!"

The faraway look on Lachlan's face faded. He stirred, looked down at the captain, smiling rather oddly. "Do ye think we can recover the ships?" he asked. "Indeed, I hate to see my Ship Tax being wrecked upon the rocks like that."

A few days later the royal fleet was tacking to and fro among the islands of the Bay of Deception when the lookout suddenly cried out, "Craft ahoy! On the starboard side, sir!"

"What kind o' craft, porridge-head?" Arvin the Just, the first mate, shouted back.

There was a short silence then the lookout said with rather an odd note in his voice, "I couldna say, sir."

Curious as ever, Finn shimmied up the ropes and into the topcastle, her familiar, a tiny black elven cat, bounding along behind her. She seized the far-seeing glass and held it to her eye for a long moment. Very faintly she heard Lachlan cry, "Well, what is it, Cat?"

She leaned over, putting both hands to her mouth and shouting, "The oddest thing I've ever seen, Your Highness. Best come and see for yourself."

Lachlan spread his wings and flew up to join her, making Finn groan with envy. What she would not give to be able to soar up like a bird, instead of having to climb up all that great height of rope and mast!

Lachlan stared through the eyeglass for a very long time.

"It looked like a sleigh o' some sort," Finn said at last. "Pulled by enormous otters."

"It be Isabeau," Lachlan replied shortly and passed the far-seeing glass back to the lookout boy, who took it with a shy bob of his head and a reverent, "Thank ye, sir, I mean, Your Highness."

Lachlan spread his wings and flew back down to the deck, leaving Finn and the elven cat to make their own slow way down. By the time Finn reached the deck again, all were leaning over the side staring at the strange craft gliding toward them.

It was a long sleigh with high curved sides, all painted with delicate colors and brushed with gilt. Drawing it at great speed through the water was a team of sea otters, barking with excitement, their great dark eyes alive with intelligence. Holding the reins was a very thin, gaunt Isabeau, her skin badly sunburned and peeling in places. She was dressed only in a ragged shirt and breeches, one arm bound up in bloodstained bandages. Clustering around her were three young children, the two boys dressed in filthy, torn nightshirts, the little girl in what could only be described as rags.

"Cuckoo!" Elfrida cried, bursting into tears. "It's my wee Cuckoo!"

"Donncan!" Iseult called and took flight off the ship deck, soaring over the waves with her arms held out. "My babe!"

Donncan spread his golden wings and flew to meet her, mother and son embracing joyfully midair, the waves tossing about just below them. Lachlan flew with strong beats of his great black wings to join them, catching his son up and hugging him close. "Och, my wee lad! We have been so afraid . . ."

"Aunty Beau saved us," Donncan replied cheerfully.

Iseult shot her husband a fierce look. "I kenned she would," she answered and hugged Donncan to her again, almost causing them all to fall into the sea below. Lachlan turned and flew to the sleigh, his weight almost causing it to capsize as he landed with a thump. He bent and raised Isabeau up, embracing her fiercely.

"Thank ye!" he cried. "With all o' my heart I thank ye!"

THE RING OF WATER

Meghan stood in the cool gray hush of dawn, her lined face very serious. Isabeau stood beside her, wearing a wreath of flowers on her head and carrying a bouquet of herbs and sacred twigs in her hand.

Close beside her stood the little cluricaun Brun, dressed in a brown velvet doublet and brocade breeches tied with velvet ribbons. Around his neck hung a fine chain hung with keys, rings, buttons and a silver christening spoon. As he danced about with excited anticipation, he chimed like sleigh bells.

Gathered all around Rhyssmadill's great square were a crowd of men and women, all dressed in their finest clothes. There was much jesting and laughing, particularly from the group clustered around Dide.

The young jongleur was dressed all in green, from the long feather stuck in his cap down to his knee-high boots. A crowd of laughing girls were tying leafy branches on to his arms and legs. Isabeau could not help smiling at Dide's antics and, noticing her, the jongleur swept off his hat, bowed and blew her a kiss.

Meghan held up her hand and silence fell over the

crowd. They all turned to the east, watching as light began to spill over the violet curve of the horizon. Bells rang out joyously, and Brun raised his silver flute to his mouth and played a haunting tune. Meghan flung out her arms dramatically. The bonfire in the center of the palace square burst into flame and everyone clapped and cheered riotously.

Isabeau passed Meghan the bouquet and she flung it into the fire. Then Dide ran forward and thrust the torches he held in either hand into the bonfire. They kindled quickly and he spun them and threw them up into the air, catching them with great dexterity. The laughing men and women crowded forward, thrusting the brands they carried into the fire, then formed a procession behind Dide as he danced down the tree-lined avenue toward the city, singing joyously:

"Rise up, bonny lassies, in your gowns o' green,
"For summer is a-coming in today,
"Ye're as fair a lady as any I've seen,
"In the merry morn o' May."

At his heels, Brun the cluricaun leaped and frolicked madly, the bells on his toes ringing. Isabeau smiled at Meghan. "Dide makes a good Green Man."

"Aye, that he does, with his bonny face and merry heart." The old sorceress looked at her closely. "Ye do no' wish to join the procession?"

"Och, time enough for dancing," Isabeau replied. "Is it no' a Fair Day all day and evening? Besides, I have no' seen ye in months. I ken ye wish to climb the tower and watch the bonfires being kindled. I thought I'd climb with ye."

"That would be nice," Meghan said, smiling at her. 'How is your wee owl?"

Isabeau smiled and put her hand up to stroke Buba, who was huddled upon her shoulder, her sleepy head nestled in to Isabeau's neck. "She will no' leave me for an instant, no' even to *snooze-hooh*. She is afraid I will fly away and leave her again."

The two witches walked back into the palace and began the long climb up to the tower heights. Isabeau was content to climb slowly, for she had not yet recovered her vitality after the past arduous few weeks. Once again she was forbidden from working sorcery or from studying too hard, and for once she was happy to accept her teachers' restrictions. It had been a week since the *Royal Stag* had berthed in the shelter of the Berhtfane and in that time she had done little but sleep, cuddle her elf-owl, walk in Rhyssmadill's beautiful gardens and play with the children.

In contrast, Lachlan had been very busy, arranging for the retrieval of the pirate ships, sending his instructions to his army still holding martial rule in Tirsoilleir, and reading out in court a public proclamation charging Sukey Nursemaid with treason, sedition and kidnapping. She had been arrested in Lucescere a week after Isabeau's desperate flight away from the Shining City and was now held there awaiting her trial. If found guilty, as she surely would be, the pretty young nursemaid would be executed. Although the hurt of Sukey's betrayal ran deep, Isabeau could feel only misery that the life of her first friend at Rhyssmadill was to be so tragically wasted.

Meghan had only arrived back in Rhyssmadill the

night before and so this was the first chance she and Isabeau had had to talk since the kidnapping of the little prionnsachan. The old sorceress was very eager to hear Isabeau's story and was full of questions and exclamations that greatly slowed their progress. They had only reached the sixth floor by the time Isabeau was describing the last confrontation with Margrit, and she stopped to show her guardian the carved turquoise ring she now wore on the thumb of her right hand. A large square ring of vivid blue, it was set in an ornate silver casing and had been carved with *lagu*, the rune for water.

"See, if ye press just here, the ring swings sideways, allowing ye to tip out the poison. Is it no' ingenious?"

Meghan gave a little shudder. "Just the sort o' thing the Thistle would do too, poison one's enemies instead o' facing them cleanly and boldly. But tell me, how in Eà's green blood did ye ever manage to switch the glasses without her noticing? Margrit would no' easily be hoodwinked."

"Nay," Isabeau replied, "and she was watching my every move, as I was watching hers, all the while being as sweet to each other as ye could imagine. So I had no time to swap the glasses. Instead, I swapped the wine in the glasses. I had to evaporate both liquids, move them through the air without mingling them, and then transform them back into liquid, all in the blink o' an eyelash. It was a tricky maneuver indeed and Gwilym says a sign o' true Skill in the element o' Water. He says I deserve to wear the ring, even though I have no' actually sat the Test o' Water yet."

"I'm no' surprised," Meghan said, visibly im-

pressed. "To move wine from two glasses simultane-
ously is sorceress level! I am no' sure I could do it
myself without mingling the wine together."

"But if I'd mingled them, both o' us would've
died," Isabeau pointed out. "Needs must when the
devil drives, as Elfrida would say."

"Well, look at ye with a ring on every right finger,"
Meghan said. "And ye no' yet twenty-four."

Isabeau looked at her bare left hand. "I just want
to wear my dragoneye ring," she said. "Now that I
have won all my elemental rings, when can I sit my
sorceress test?"

"Patience, Mistress Impatience," Meghan said
shortly, stopping once more to catch her breath. Isabeau grinned and winked at Gitâ, hanging to the
Keybearer's long white plait. *She never changes,* she
chittered to the little donbeag who chittered back,
would you want her to?

"I may be getting auld but I'm no' deaf," Meghan
said austerely. "Must ye talk about me in front o' me
as if I were some doddering auld fool?"

Maybe she's getting crankier, Isabeau chittered.

Gitâ replied, *No, she was always as disagreeable as a
bear with a sore head.*

Meghan scowled. Isabeau smiled at her, slid her
hand under her arm and helped her up the last few
steps. For once Meghan accepted her help and they
came into the tower room together.

The sun was just raising its bright face above the
dark ocean, a ruffled skirt of crimson and gold
spreading out across the water. The land behind
them was still sunk in shadows, so both Meghan and
Isabeau could clearly see the bright spots of bonfires
leaping on every hilltop, as far as the eye could see.

Down in the city the procession of torches wound its way through the streets and plazas, and Isabeau could see similar ribbons of flame winding through the villages on the other side of the river. She pointed them out to Meghan, saying, "Is it no' grand to think the Beltane fires are being lit on every hill in the whole country, for the first time in my entire lifetime."

Meghan said gruffly, "Everywhere but in Carraig."

Isabeau sobered. "Aye, everywhere but in Carraig. They'll have to do something about that now, willna they?"

Meghan nodded. "Aye. We lop off the head o' one enemy and there's a host o' others needing our attention. In truth, I am growing tired o' the harlequin-hydra o' this war."

"We all are, I think," Isabeau answered, troubled by the note of fatigue in the Keybearer's voice. "Lachlan and Iseult both seem weary and preoccupied, do ye no' think? Still, we are at peace with Tìrsoilleir now, and the pirates have been vanquished and the Thistle is dead. Gradually all our enemies have been dealt with."

"All but the Fairgean," Meghan said.

Isabeau nodded, her face very grave. Every night Isabeau dreamed of webbed hands reaching up out of a dark pit to drag her down, dreamed of wet black hair streaming out like seaweed. The nightmares darkened all Isabeau's days with a shadow of foreboding that no feasting fire could drive away.

Meghan saw how somber Isabeau's face had grown and laid her hand on her arm, saying, with a return of her usual briskness, "Come, it is May Day and time to be celebrating! We shall worry about the Fairgean another day."

Yes, Isabeau thought. *At least for this day we can be at peace and rejoice. We shall worry about the Fairgean tomorrow.*

Far below, in the briny darkness of the sea caves that riddled the rock upon which Rhyssmadill was built, the Fairgean warriors floated. They could see nothing, for no light penetrated the sea caves, but the Fairgean warriors did not mind. They were used to darkness. They were used to waiting. They had crawled through the cramped subterranean passages under the cover of the night and there, deep in the sea caves, they drifted, grasping their tridents, waiting for the dark again. When the tide once again began to rise at the setting of the sun, they would swim silently through the darkness to the well from which the humans drew their water. Up the ladder they would climb and out into the very heart of the fortress, a thousand Fairgean warriors driven by a thirst for revenge that a thousand defeats had not quenched. For months the king and the priestesses had been plotting and preparing, eavesdropping and spying, waiting for a time when as many humans as possible would be gathered in this one place, unprepared and unsuspecting.

"The waves of Jor's wrath roll slow," the king said with a predatory smile, "but to sand the rocks are always ground."

GLOSSARY

dan MacCuinn: the first Rìgh, High King of Eilea-
n. Called Aedan Whitelock, he was directly de-
:nded from Cuinn Lionheart (see *First Coven*). In
) he united the warring lands of Eileanan into one
untry, all except for Tìrsoilleir and Arran, which
nained independent.

dan's Pact: Aedan MacCuinn, first Rìgh of Eileanan,
:w up a Pact Of Peace between all inhabitants of
: island, agreeing to live in peace and not to inter-
·e in each other's culture, but to work together for
ity and prosperity. The Fairgean refused to sign
d so were cast out, causing the Second Fairgean
ars.

layeh: the art of fighting.

earn Horse-laird: One of the First Coven of Witches.

slinna the Dreamer: One of the First Coven of
tches.

sdair MacFaghan: baby son of Khan'gharad
agonlaird and Ishbel the Winged, twin brother of
·loïse and younger brother of Iseult and Isabeau.

kening the Dreamwalker: sorceress who was rescued

367

from the death-fire in the Sgàilean Mountains and became one of the new Council of Witches.

Arran: south-east land of Eileanan, consisting mainly of salt lakes and marshes. Ruled by MacFóghnans, descendants of Fóghnan, one of the First Coven of Witches.

Aslinn: deeply forested land ruled by the MacAislins, descendants of Aislinna, one of the First Coven of Witches.

autumn equinox: when the night reaches the same length as the day.

Awl: Anti-Witchcraft League, set up by Maya the Ensorcellor following the Day of Reckoning.

banprionnsa: princess or duchess.

banrìgh: queen.

Bay of Deception: large gulf of water to the south of Eileanan, so called because of its deceptive peace and beauty which covers many reefs and sandbanks.

Beltane: May Day; the first day of summer.

Berhtfane: sea loch in Clachan.

Berhtilde the Bright Warrior-Maid: one of the First Coven of Witches.

berhtildes: the female warriors of Tìrsoilleir, named after the country's founder (see *First Coven*). Cut off left breast to make wielding a bow easier.

blaygird: evil, awful.

Blèssem: The Blessed Fields. Rich farmland lying south of Rionnagan, ruled by the MacThanach clan.

blizzard owls: giant white owls that inhabit the snowy mountain regions. Sorcha the Murderess had a blizzard owl as her familiar.

ue Guards: The Yeomen of the Guard, the Rìgh's vn elite company of soldiers. They act as his per- nal bodyguard, both on the battlefield and in eacetime.

ve Book of Shadows: an ancient magical book which ntains all the history and lore of the Coven.

angaine NicSian: the daughter of Gwyneth NicSian's unger sister. She is named banprionnsa of Siantan the Second Pact of Peace.

ight Soldiers: name for members of the Tìrsoil- irean army.

onwen NicCuin: young daughter of Jaspar Mac- uinn, former Rìgh of Eileanan, and Maya the Ensor- llor. Was Banrìgh of Eileanan for one day.

un: a cluricaun.

ba: an elf-owl; Isabeau's familiar.

andlemas: the end of winter and beginning of spring.

rraig: Land of the Sea Witches, the most northern unty of Eileanan. Ruled by MacSeinn clan, descen- nts of Seinneadair, one of the First Coven of 'itches. Clan has been driven out by Fairgean, tak- g refuge in Rionnagan.

ve of A Thousand Kings: the sacred cavern of the irgean royal family.

lestines: race of fairy creatures, renowned for em- thic abilities and knowledge of stars and prophecy.

rcle of Seven: ruling council of dragons made up of e oldest and wisest female dragons.

achan: southernmost land of Eileanan, ruled by the acCuinn clan.

aymore: a heavy, two-edged sword, often as tall as man.

cluricaun: small woodland fairy.

coh: Khan'cohban word for the universal life-death energy.

craft: applications of the One Power through spells, incantations and magical objects.

Cuinn Lionheart: leader of the First Coven of Witches. Descendants called MacCuinn.

cunning: applications of the One Power through will and desire.

cunning man: village wise man or warlock.

Cursed Peaks: what the Khan'cohbans call Dragonclaw.

cursehags: wicked fairy race, prone to curses and evil spells. Known for their filthy personal habits.

dai-dein: father.

Daillas the Lame: sorcerer and headmaster at the Theurgia.

Dide the Juggler: a jongleur.

donbeag: small, brown shrew-like creature that can fly short distances due to the sails of skin between its legs.

Donncan MacCuinn: eldest son of Iseult and Lachlan. Has wings like a bird and can fly.

doom-eels: sea-dwelling eels with phosphorescent tails that deliver an electric shock if touched.

dragon: large, fire-breathing flying creature with smooth, scaly skin and claws. Named by the First Coven for a mythical creature from the Other World. Since they are unable to adjust their own body temperature, they live in the volcanic mountains, near hot springs or other sources of heat. They have a highly developed language and culture, and can see both ways along the thread of time.

Dragonclaw: a tall, sharply pointed mountain in the northwestern range of the Sithiche Mountains. Isabeau and Meghan lived by a small loch at its foot, in a secret valley. Called the Cursed Peaks by the Khan'cohbans.

dram: measure of drink.

Duncan Ironfist: the captain of the Yeomen of the Guards.

Dùn Gorm: the city surrounding Rhyssmadill.

Eà: the Great Life Spirit, mother and father of all.

Eileanan: largest island in the archipelago called the Far Islands.

Elemental Powers: the forces of Air, Earth, Fire, Water and Spirit which together make up the One Power.

Elfrida NicHilde: exiled banprionnsa of Tìrsoilleir.

elf-owl: the smallest of all the owls, about the size of a sparrow, with a round head and big yellow eyes.

Elsie: a scullery maid at Lucescere Palace.

elven cat: small, fierce wild cat that lives in caves and hollow logs.

Enit Silverthroat: a jongleur; grandmother of Dide and Nina.

equinox: when the sun crosses the celestial equator; a time when day and night are of equal length, occurring twice a year.

The Fair Isles: a group of lush tropical islands to the south of Eileanan.

Fairge; Fairgean: fairy creatures who need both sea and land to live. The Fairgean were finally cast out of Eileanan in 710 by Aedan Whitelock when they refused to accept his authority. For the next four hundred and twenty years they lived on rafts, rocks jutting up out of the icy seas, and what small islands were still uninhabited. The Fairgean king swore revenge and the winning back of Eileanan's coast.

Fand: slave in the Fairgean king's court.

The Fang: the highest mountain in Eileanan, an extinct volcano called the Skull of the World by the Khan'cohbans.

Faodhagan the Red: One of the twin sorcerers from the First Coven of Witches. Particularly noted for working in stone; designed and built many of the Witch Towers, as well as the dragons' palace and the Great Stairway.

The Fathomless Caves: the sacred system of caves and grottos that riddle the Isle of the Gods.

The Fiery Womb: cave deep within the Isle of the Gods where the Fairgean believe the gods were born.

Finn the Cat: nickname of Fionnghal NicRuraich.

Fionnghal NicRuraich: eldest daughter and heir of Anghus MacRuraich of Rurach; was once a beggar-girl in Lucescere and lieutenant of the League of the Healing Hand. Has strong searching and finding powers.

The Firemaker: honorary term given to the descendants of Faodhagan (see *First Coven*) and a woman of the Khan'cohbans.

First Coven of Witches: thirteen witches who fled persecution in their own land, invoking an ancient spell that folded the fabric of the universe and brought them and all their followers to Eileanan. The eleven great clans of Eileanan are all descended from the First Coven, with the MacCuinn clan being the greatest of the eleven. The thirteen witches were Cuinn Lionheart, his son Owein of the Longbow, Ahearn

Horse-laird, Aislinna the Dreamer, Berhtilde the Bright Warrior-Maid, Fóghnan the Thistle, Rùraich the Searcher, Seinneadair the Singer, Sian the Storm-Rider, Tuathanach the Farmer, Brann the Raven, Faodhagan the Red and his twin sister Sorcha the Bright (now called the Murderess).

frost giant: lives on Spine of the World.

geal'teas: long-horned, snow-dwelling creatures which provide Khan'cohbans with food, milk and clothing. Their very thick white wool is much prized all over Eileanan.

geas: an obligation due to a debt of honor.

Gitâ: a donbeag; Meghan's familiar.

The Great Crossing: when Cuinn led the First Coven to Eileanan.

The Great Stairway: the road which climbs Dragon-claw, leading to the palace of the dragons and then down the other side of the mountain to Tìrlethan.

Gwilym the Ugly: one-legged sorcerer who spent the years of Maya the Ensorcellor's rule in Arran but who escaped the autocratic rule of Margrit NicFóghnan to help Lachlan win the throne. Was rewarded with the position of court sorcerer.

harlequin-hydra: a rainbow-colored sea serpent with many heads that lives in the shallow waters near the coast of Arran. If one head is cut off, another two grow in its place and its spit is deadly poisonous.

Haven: large cave where the Pride of the Red Dragon spend their winter.

Heloïse MacFaghan: baby daughter of Khan'gharad Dragon-laird and Ishbel the Winged, twin sister of Alasdair and younger sister of Iseult and Isabeau.

Iain MacFóghnan: prionnsa of Arran.

ika: a potent Khan'cohban drink brewed from berries.

Isabeau the Foundling: apprentice to Meghan of the Beasts, twin sister of Iseult. Also called Khan'tinka.

Iseult of the Snows: twin sister of Isabeau, banrìgh of Eileanan by marriage to Lachlan the Winged. Also named Khan'derin.

Ishbel the Winged: windwitch who can fly. Mother of Iseult and Isabeau.

Isle of Divine Dread: island in the far north of Eileanan; traditional stronghold of the Priestesses of Jor.

Isle of the Gods: island in the far north of Eileanan; traditional home of the Fairgean royalty. It was invaded and occupied by the MacSeinn clan in the early history of the Coven and not regained by the Fairgean until after the Day of Betrayal.

Jaspar MacCuinn: eldest son of Parteta the Brave, former Rìgh of Eileanan, often called Jaspar the Ensorcelled. Was married to Maya the Ensorcellor.

Jay the Fiddler: a minstrel and apprentice to Enit Silverthroat. Was once a beggar-lad in Lucescere and lieutenant of the League of the Healing Hand.

jongleur: a traveling minstrel, juggler, conjurer.

Jor: the God of the Shoreless Seas, a major Fairgean deity.

Kani: the Mother of the Gods in the Fairgean cosmology, the goddess of fire and earth, volcanoes, earthquakes, phosphorescence and lightning.

The Key: the sacred symbol of the Coven of Witches, a powerful talisman carried by the Keybearer, leader of the Coven.

Khan: Khan'cohban word meaning "child." All young, uninitiated Khan'cohbans are called "child" until after they have successfully won their name and totem in a dangerous journey of initiation.

Khan'bornet: Scarred Warrior of the Fire Dragon Pride and Isabeau's teacher in *ahdayeh*.

Khan'cohbans: Children of the Gods of White. A fairy race of snow-skimming nomads who live on the Spine of the World. Closely related to the Celestines, but very warlike. Khan'cohbans live in family groups called prides, which range from fifteen to fifty in number.

Khan'deric: Soul-Sage of the Fire Dragon Pride.

Khan'derin: twin sister of Isabeau. Also named Iseult.

Khan'derna: First of the Scarred Warriors of the Fire Dragon Pride.

Khan'fella: twin sister to Khan'lysa, the Firemaker.

Khan'gharad the Dragon-Laird: Scarred Warrior of the Fire Dragon Pride, lover of Ishbel the Winged, father of Isabeau and Iseult.

Khan'katrin: Isabeau and Iseult's cousin, and heir to the Firemaker's position.

Khan'lysa the Firemaker: Isabeau and Iseult's great-grandmother.

Khan'merle: Isabeau and Iseult's aunt, and heir to the Firemaker's position.

Lachlan the Winged: Rìgh of Eileanan.

Lament of the Gods: river in Tìrlethan.

leannan: sweetheart.

Linley MacSeinn: the prionnsa of Carraig.

loch; lochan (pl): lake.

Lodestar: the heritage of all the MacCuinns, the Inheritance of Aedan. When they are born their hands are placed upon it and a connection made. Whoever the stone recognizes is the Rìgh or Banrìgh of Eileanan.

Lucescere: ancient city built on an island above the Shining Waters. The traditional home of the Mac-Cuinns and the Tower of Two Moons.

Mac: son of.

MacAhern: one of the eleven great clans; descendants of Ahearn the Horse-laird.

MacAislin: one of the eleven great clans; descendants of Aislinna the Dreamer.

MacBrann: one of the eleven great clans; descendants of Brann the Raven.

MacCuinn: one of the eleven great clans, descendants of Cuinn Braveheart.

MacFaghan: descendants of Faodhagan, one of the eleven great clans, newly discovered.

MacFóghnan: one of the eleven great clans; descendants of Fóghnan the Thistle.

MacHamell clan: lairds of Caeryla.

MacHilde: one of the eleven great clans; descended from Berhtilde the Bright Warrior-Maid.

MacRuraich: one of the eleven great clans; descendants of Rùraich the Searcher.

MacSeinn: one of the eleven great clans; descendants of Seinneadair the Singer.

MacSian: one of the eleven great clans; descendants of Sian the Storm-rider.

MacThanach: one of the eleven great clans; descendants of Tuathanach the Farmer.

Mairead the Fair: younger daughter of Aedan Mac-Cuinn, first Banrìgh of Eileanan and the second to wield the Lodestar. Meghan's younger sister.

Margrit NicFóghnan: deposed Banprionnsa of Arran.

Maya the Ensorcellor: former Banrìgh of Eileanan, wife of Jaspar.

Meghan of the Beasts: wood-witch and sorceress of seven rings. She can speak to animals. Keybearer of the Coven of Witches before and after banishment of Tabithas.

Melisse NicThanach: Banprionnsa of Blèssem.

Mesmerd; Mesmerdean (pl): a winged ghost or Gray One; fairy creature from Arran that hypnotizes its prey with its glance and then kisses away its life.

Midsummer's Eve: summer solstice; time of high magic.

moonbane: a hallucinogenic drug distilled from the moonflower plant. Grows only in the Montrose Islands, to the southwest of the Fair Isles.

Neil MacFóghnan: only son and heir of Iain MacFóghnan of Arran and Elfrida NicHilda of Tìrsoilleir.

Nellwyn: a Yedda who had been rescued from the Black Tower in Tìrsoilleir.

Nic: daughter of.

Nightglobe of Naia: the most secret and precious relic of the Priestesses of Jor; a globe of immense power.

nisse: small woodland fairy.

nyx: night spirit. Dark and mysterious, with powers of illusion and concealment.

Nila: Fairgean prince, youngest son of the Fairgean king.

old mother: a Khan'cohban term for the wise woman of the pride.

Olwynne NicCuinn: baby daughter of Lachlan MacCuinn and Iseult NicFaghan; twin sister of Owein.

One Power: the life-energy that is contained in all things. Witches draw upon the One Power to perform their acts of magic. The One Power contains all the elemental forces of Air, Earth, Water, Fire and Spirit, and witches are usually more powerful in one force than others.

Owein MacCuinn: second son of Lachlan MacCuinn and Iseult NicFaghan; twin brother of Olwynne. Has wings like a bird.

Parteta the Brave: former Rìgh of Eileanan; the father of Jaspar, Feargus, Donncan and Lachlan MacCuinn. He was killed by the Fairgean at the Battle of the Strand in 1106.

pilliwinkes: instrument of torture similar to thumb-screws.

prides: The social unit of the Khan'cohbans, who live in nomadic family groups. Seven Prides in all, called the Pride of the Fire Dragon, the Pride of the Snow Lion, the Pride of the Saber Leopard, the Pride of the Frost Giant, the Pride of the Gray Wolf, the Pride of the Fighting Cat, the Pride of the Woolly Bear.

prionnsa; prionnsachan (pl): prince, duke.

Ravenshaw: deeply forested land west of Rionnagan, owned by the MacBrann Clan, descendants of Brann, one of the First Coven of Witches.

reil: eight-pointed, star-shaped weapon carried by Scarred Warriors.

Rhyllster: the main river in Rionnagan.

Rhyssmadill: the Rìgh's castle by the sea.

rìgh; rìghrean (pl): king.

Rionnagan: together with Clachan and Bléssem, the richest lands in Eileanan. Ruled by MacCuinns, descendants of Cuinn Lionheart, leader of the First Coven of Witches.

Riordan Bowlegs: witch with the ability to whisper horses. Was once head groom at Rhyssmadill.

Rurach: wild mountainous land, lying between Tìreich and Siantan. Ruled by MacRuraich clan, descendants of Rùraich, one of the First Coven of Witches.

Rùraich the Searcher: one of the First Coven of Witches. Known for searching and finding Talent. Located the world of Eileanan on the star-map, allowing Cuinn to set a course for the Great Crossing.

saber-leopard: savage feline with curved fangs that lives in the remote mountain areas.

sacred woods: ash, hazel, oak, blackthorn, fir, hawthorn and yew.

Samhain: first day of winter; festival for the souls of the dead. Best time of year to see the future. Celebrated with fire festivals, masks and fireworks.

Scarred Warrior: Khan'cohban warriors who are scarred as a mark of achievement. A warrior who receives all seven scars has received the highest degree of skill.

seanalair: general of the army.

Seinneadair the Singer: one of the First Coven of Witches, known for her ability to enchant with song.

Sian the Storm-rider: one of the First Coven of Witches. A famous weather witch, renowned for whistling up hurricanes.

Siantan: northwest land of Eileanan, between Rurach and Carraig. Famous for its weather witches. Ruled by MacSian clan, descendants of Sian the Storm-rider.

Sithiche Mountains: northernmost mountains of Rionnagan, peaking at Dragonclaw. Name means "Fairy Mountains."

skeelie: a village witch or wise woman.

Skill: a common application of magic, such as lighting a candle or dowsing for water.

Skull of the World: the highest mountain in Eileanan, an extinct volcano which plays an important role in the Khan'cohbans' mythology and culture.

solstice: either of the times when the sun is the farthest distance from the earth.

The Spine of the World: a Khan'cohban term for range of mountains that runs down the center of Eileanan, in Tìrlethan.

Spinners: goddesses of fate. Include the spinner Sniomhar, the goddess of birth; the weaver Breabadair, goddess of life; and she who cuts the thread, Gearradh, goddess of death.

spring equinox: when the day reaches the same length as the night.

Stormwing: Lachlan's gyrfalcon.

summer solstice: the time when the sun is farthest north from the equator; Midsummer's Eve.

syne: since.

Tabithas the Wolf-runner: Keybearer of the Coven of Witches before disappearing from Eileanan after the Day of Betrayal.

Talent: witches often combine their strengths in the different forces to one powerful Talent; e.g. the ability to charm animals like Meghan.

Tears of the Gods: a waterfall at the Skull of the World.

Test of Elements: once a witch is fully accepted into the coven at the age of twenty-four, they learn Skills in the element in which they are strongest; i.e. air, earth, fire, water, or spirit. The First Test of any element wins them a ring which is worn on the right hand. If they pass the Third Test in any one element, the witch is called a sorcerer or sorceress, and wears a ring on their left hand. It is very rare for any witch to win a sorceress ring in more than one element.

Test of Powers: a witch is first tested on his or her eighth birthday, and if any magical powers are detected, he or she becomes an acolyte. On their sixteenth birthday, witches are tested again and, if they pass, permitted to become an apprentice. The Third Tests take place on their twenty-fourth birthday, and if successfully completed, the apprentice is admitted into the Coven of Witches.

Theurgia: a school for acolytes and apprentices.

Tìreich: land of the horse-lairds—most westerly country of Eileanan, populated by nomadic tribes famous for their horses and ruled by the MacAhern clan.

Tìrlethan: Land of the Twins; once ruled by Faodhagan and Sorcha, twin sorcerers. Called the Spine of the World by Khan'cohbans.

Tìrsoilleir: The Bright Land. Northeast land of Eileanan, populated by a race of fierce warriors. Was once ruled by the MacHilde clan, descended from Berhtilde, one of the First Coven of Witches. However, the Tìrsoilleirean have rejected witchcraft and the ruling family in favor of militant religion. Have dreams of controlling Eileanan.

Tòmas the Healer: boy with healing powers; formerly apprentice to Jorge the Seer.

The Towers of the Witches: Thirteen towers built as centers of learning and witchcraft in the twelve lands of Eileanan. The Towers are:

 Tùr de Aisling in Aslinn (Tower of Dreamers)

Tùr na cheud Ruigsinn in Clachan (Tower of First Landing; Cuinn's Tower)

Tùr de Ceò in Arran (Tower of Mists)

Tùr na Fitheach in Ravenshaw (Tower of Ravens)

Tùr na Gealaich dhà in Rionnagan (Tower of Two Moons)

Tùr na Raoin Beannachadh in Bléssem (Tower of the Blessed Fields)

Tùr na Rùraich in Rurach (Tower of Searchers)

Tùr de Ròsan is Snathad in Tìrlethan (Towers of Roses and Thorns)

Tùr na Sabaidean in Tìrsoilleir (Tower of the Warriors)

Tùr na Seinnadairean Mhuir in Carraig (Tower of the Sea-singers)

Tùr de Stoirmean in Siantan (Tower of Storm)

Tùr na Thigearnean in Tìreich (Tower of the Horse-lairds)

trictrac: a form of backgammon.
Tuathanach the Farmer: One of the First Coven of Witches. (See *Bléssem*)
two moons: Magnysson and Gladrielle.

uile-bheist; uile-bheistean (pl): monster.
uka: Khan'cohban word for "demon" or "monster."
ulez: a woolly coated horned creature of the Spine of the World.
unza: Khan'cohban word meaning all that is dark and unknown.

The White Gods: nameless, shapeless gods of the Khan'cohbans, and greatly feared and revered by them.